Crossing Clayborn

Crossing Clayborn

A Novel

ROBERT WILLIS

authorHOUSE®

AuthorHouse™
1663 Liberty Drive
Bloomington, IN 47403
www.authorhouse.com
Phone: 1-800-839-8640

Published by AuthorHouse   01/15/2013

ISBN: 978-1-4817-0332-1 (sc)
ISBN: 978-1-4817-0331-4 (hc)
ISBN: 978-1-4817-0330-7 (e)

Library of Congress Control Number: 2012924285

Any people depicted in stock imagery provided by Thinkstock are models, and such images are being used for illustrative purposes only.
Certain stock imagery © *Thinkstock.*

This book is printed on acid-free paper.

1

South Florida offers wonderful opportunities to retirees and still more wonderful opportunities to those who prey upon retirees—and would-be retirees, as in Clayborn Redmond's case. To borrow an outlook from the strict constructionists, an ordinary guy might go so far as to say that these opportunities are limited only by one's small-time vision, one's private attitude as opposed to public acts. To go a step farther and amend this vista to fit Ewen Leetboer's view of the matter puts one on the fast track to wealth with *no* limitations. His formula for success was simple, too. That old "tough lover," Ewen, saw opportunity in boundless quantities wherever and whenever a serious asset accumulator such as himself could look his fellow real estate partners in the eye, even as they stared adversity in the face, and simply declare that "business is business," with never an impulse stirring under his skin to grant a single exception to the rules of foreclosure.

Clayborn Redmond, a real estate broker, didn't know he had been cheated out of a budding retirement nest egg until some time after the egg disappeared. Redmond was not exactly an old guy either. Only forty-one, the perfect age for youthful indiscretions, but he had his heart set on an early retreat from the work-a-day world. His book of plans required enough life left in his aging carcass to enjoy ocean cruises, trips to Europe, tours of all the great museums and historical landmarks from Madrid to Moscow, annual rides on the Orient Express and brief residences in exotic places scattered around the planet which weren't poverty-stricken or hostile but had some respectable amenities to offer. Pretty women for instance.

It was just another time-worn case of trust betrayed. Redmond was dumbstruck. His own partner of all people. Redmond believed this long-time business associate, Ewen Leetboer, was not the kind of guy to take advantage of a fellow partner, especially one who considered him a personal friend. For one thing, Leetboer had grown too rich to engage any longer in petty theft. For another, the aging tycoon was preoccupied with a beautiful young bride whom he had acquired shortly after his last wife died and who would divorce him in a Silicon Valley nanosecond if he damaged her assets in any way. Or so the story went.

It happened so smoothly, so businesslike, and tied together in such a neat legal package that not even the lawyer handling the Chapter Eleven case stopped to blush when he first began to turn his knowledge of the law against innocent, trusting, undercapitalized souls of a simple joint venture. In short, in his jurisprudent wisdom, this handpicked lawyer of Ewen Leetboer's had taken all the necessary steps toward becoming just another dirty little partner in crime himself.

His name, for the record, was Stanley B. Conover. Stanley's dress, style and professional bearing reflected well in the legal community. His paperwork projected cleanness, authority, precision. Each page befitted a man with impeccable habits. Every paragraph of the document satisfied all parties in the "protection" suit, even Clayborn Redmond, at least until the wheels of justice started to roll and then rolled right over him and his dream of early retirement.

Clay, as Mr. Redmond was called by his friends, grew up in the country and knew how to bend with the wind and dodge falling limbs, even how to extract revenge from aggressive bloodsuckers hanging out in the wilds, not to mention theme parks, beaches and other civilized habitats requiring a healthy respect for eternal vigilance. As soon as his partner's outrageous deed dawned on him and after he had recovered from the hurt and shock of being swindled by a trusted colleague, Clay Redmond set about the matter of figuring out a plan that would not only recover his losses but would leave his partner a little bit crippled himself for all his trouble. With luck, perhaps a broken leg or two . . . or worse. Definitely worse off than the sneaky old marauder had intended to leave his guileless prey, which, with all due respect to the man's efficiency and lack of conscience, meant "wiped out."

It was the judge who pissed Clay Redmond off the most, excluding the chiseler Ewen Leetboer, of course. Clay's opinion quickly formed around the notion that Judge "Cotton" Brussard fitted Webster's definition of an old-fashioned shitass, the kind of shitass who would have added depth and range to the definition had Webster's wordsmiths known the man at the time they were struggling with the term. *What a shitass*, the plaintiff thought—often aloud in mixed company, the reason being that the bastard threw the case out without giving Clay his day in court. Brussard said something like, "Mr. Clayborn should of known better . . . ." The Judge wasn't good at names either, further proof to Clay Redmond of his rotten mind. The broker's opinion of the Judge never softened. "As they used to say in the old days," Clay replied to Mason Riley when the attorney disclosed Judge Brussard's final ruling, "that judge doesn't know his ass from a hole under the outhouse."

In a nutshell, Clay Redmond's mistake was *expecting* better, if not from a friend then certainly from the scales of Themis, that sexy, blindfolded goddess holding truth in a balance. Foolish expectations constituted a defect in his social nature that he hadn't yet learned to live with, a flaw he finally acknowledged during the throes of several critical reassessments following Leetboer's grubby little stunt. But there was also a greater flaw—a "flaw in the law," as Clay sometimes recited in a vicious chant. This flaw allowed Ewen Leetboer to manipulate his fellow joint venturers, allowed him to turn the poor gullible dupes upside down and shake every penny out of their pockets while they were busy dreaming about their growing wealth and all those wonderfully carefree retirement years ahead.

After the dismissal of his lawsuit, Clay slumped into a cynical posture. He thought the judge had cut a deal with Ewen Leetboer's lawyer, maybe took a few "thou" under the bench to make the case go away. For some ungodly reason Leetboer seemed to prefer this method of parting with his money to more straightforward ways such as making payments directly to creditors when it was time to honor a debt.

"He made his money screwing his partners," was the most prevalent comment to emerge from the lips of informed sources. During the early years of their association, Clay Redmond tried not to let such gossip influence his opinion of Ewen Leetboer. If the screwing comments had a basis in fact, Clay decided, Ewen, to his credit, had screwed his way into one hell of a fortune, one in pursuit of which he must have started to screw around the age of five and, over the next fifty years, seldom if ever allowed himself to be handicapped by *coitus interruptus* in the wake of an astonishing string of fiscal conquests.

Clay Redmond retained Mason Riley to represent him. The attorney was well known among trial lawyers, had even won a few cases lately, albeit his notoriety stemmed as much from his prowess with a guitar as from his courtroom heroics. At any rate, Clay approved of the legal strategy advanced by the attorney, who sounded perfect for the job: vicious, resolute, uncompromising.

In a hurried conference, and without further delay, Clay Redmond paid the retainer, directed Mason Riley to file suit, and thereupon became a formal plaintiff of the court for the first time in his forty-one years of litigation-free existence.

After a lengthy period of case construction, together with its attendant but critically obligatory reams of motions and counter-motions, and thence after a few rounds of legal sparring via memoranda and frightful verbiage, old "Cotton" Brussard suddenly dismissed the case in a short flurry of words that sent even Clay Redmond's banjo dueler, Mason Riley, into a ridiculous flounder when he tried to explain their meaning to his foolishly expectant client.

This is what pissed Clay off about the judge. The old poot didn't wait for Clay to come before him and explain his side. He just passed his ruling down to Mason Riley and left Clay hanging out in the country without a clue to the conversation.

It was a legal slam-dunk for Ewen Leetboer. It was also an occasion for Clay Redmond to indulge in further suspicions, deeper cynicism. His attorney seemed too complacent about the judge's action. Mason Riley's tongue had, ipso facto, gone limp, impotent, bereft of muscle and sadly divested of its usual free-swinging gusto. Moreover, Mason remained increasingly unable—or stubbornly reluctant—to offer a plausible explanation for the dismissal. It appeared to Clay Redmond that his highly acclaimed attorney had joined hands with Judge Brussard and they were both enjoying a good rock in Leetboer's cradle of cash. Whether the two men had joined hands literally or only symbolically in private and mutual unawareness of a common pursuit didn't seem to Clay a distinction worthy of quibbling over. The bastards, he said, were both guilty of obstruction of justice and deserved to be deprived of one, if not both, testicles in full public view on the courthouse square.

Clay Redmond was not a man to rush into action. He preferred to sit and ponder awhile, to mull over the facts and circumstances for a few days or weeks, even months sometimes, before jumping headlong into a scene that might suddenly mushroom into a full-blown situation—one bristling with a much-too-hardy growth of angles and sharp edges. The longer he pondered, though, the quicker his sense of outrage dovetailed into a serious battle plan; and as he mulled along, week after week, the less concern he had for the straight and narrow.

His plan was simple: Forget castration. *Kill* Ewen Leetboer. Deny him his ill-gotten gains. The law had failed Clay but ancient instincts had arisen from the primordial pool inside his brain to fill the void. Clay Redmond didn't want a messy affair either. He wanted an air-tight alibi for himself even as he pulled the trigger. In short, he wanted a perfect crime, except in his mind the killing of Ewen Leetboer would hardly constitute a crime. The skunk was bound to stop somebody's bullet sooner or later. Clay's frontier solution would give taxpayers a break, substitute for the more costly judgment a jury of peers would surely have rendered had Mason Riley insisted on a jury trial and had Judge "Cotton" Brussard done his duty and allowed the case to go forward and be heard by honest citizens. They would have handed down a verdict probably worse than death in Ewen Leetboer's eyes. That is to say, a jury would have awarded *just compensation* to the plaintiff, including heavy punitive damages. Twelve citizens honest and true simply would not have allowed the defendant's rip-off of a sacred retirement trove to stand.

Also, Clay Redmond mused, Ewen must realize during his last few minutes on earth who had brought him to his end, and why. The greedy fucker must be granted a stay of execution long enough to ponder a bit himself in the presence of his executioner, to beg for mercy and promise millions only to wind up reflecting on his massive store of wealth and what little value it held for him in the final hour of his personal doomsday.

2

In the old days of the Wild West aggrieved men called each other to the street and "shot it out." A fast draw and steady aim usually settled the score between them. The victor could then walk away in broad daylight, sufficiently avenged and unmolested by legal structures of the time, although family and friends of the vanquished soul might carry on the grudge awhile longer out of respect for the departed or from a rush of pride that compelled at least an appearance of honor, if not a stout defense of the family name.

Clay Redmond fancied himself spiritually linked to these old westerners. Their practice of frontier justice was particularly appealing in its simplicity, its directness and inviolable certainty. Modern guardians of due process had long since abandoned, or watered down, those nobler means of settling disputes which they couldn't otherwise corrupt absolutely, and Clay's options, now that the law had failed to deliver even a smidgen of justice, would thrust him into the same category as a purveyor of Jack Daniel's beloved spirits enjoyed during Prohibition: i.e., a *lawbreaker*. Clay would have to operate outside the law, something that did not square with his regard for even keels, the straight and narrow, and so on, yet he was faced with a moral dilemma which a rebellious conscience directed him to ignore for the sake of another freedom, namely *movement*.

Ancestral genes formed out of the union of Miocene creatures urged Clay to "go for it," to follow his nose, his passion, his bliss—whatever—and use his god-given talents to correct a territorial infringement that had gotten out of hand, if not out of mind, but still managed to bring too much of its weight to rest in his gut. The dispatch of Ewen Leetboer would stand throughout the ages as a fitting acknowledgment of Clay Redmond's ancestry.

By coincidence one of Clay's favorite aunts had recently left to him in her will, among other good and valuable items, a Remington pocket automatic pistol, Model 51, .380 caliber. Apparently she, too, had been endowed with strains of the same ancient genes as Clay, for the location of the gun and her celebrated readiness to use it no doubt had a disquieting effect upon burglars. At least the record shows that criminal activities in and around the vicinity of her small bungalow, a tree-shrouded den of openness where she had passed a long and happy life, amounted to approximately zero.

The Model 51 was by no means one of those cheap little "Saturday night specials" but rather a classic piece of armory worthy of a will and a gentleman's choice. The timely, solemn transfer of the Remington property, therefore, seemed mysteriously prearranged and, as Clay Redmond perceived the event, divinely bequeathed to aid and abet his purpose.

Ewen Leetboer maintained on Miami Beach an ocean-side "hideaway," as he smugly called the place. In truth it met the local property appraiser's guidelines for a mansion of above-average grandeur. The old Dutchman also owned and managed a thriving empire of businesses in Canada where he lived most of the time in filthy opulence. After World War II he abandoned his native Holland, being then still a young buck on the make and having determined that postwar Europe had already been picked over by the Germans. Each of his businesses had prospered in direct proportion to the somewhat routine, somewhat manipulated "collapse" of Ewen's various joint ventures in and around Miami and in certain parts of the West Indies, notably Curaçao in the Netherlands Antilles. Cuba was even taking on a certain appeal now that Fidel Castro had opened the island to foreign investors. Sugar, rum, cigars, hotels—these businesses all needed partners. Shortly before that unfortunate lawsuit he'd pumped Clay Redmond about it. Clay had connections down there. Clay knew what was happening and how to get in on it. Leetboer would wait for his favorite broker to cool off, bide time, maybe do a deal or two with him to rebuild confidence then move onto that exciting new stage as soon as Clay could line something up.

Clay Redmond had different plans, although Ewen Leetboer's ability to write large checks would fit right in. The man from Amsterdam had deep pockets indeed, and deeper pockets when it came to resuscitating a collapsed partnership but not even a fob for a partner caught in his trap. "Business is business," he would confide gravely to the partner as Attorney Stanley B. Conover presided over the transfer of the distraught chap's beneficial interest. Stanley knew how to bait Leetboer's verbiage traps better perhaps than anyone in the Western Hemisphere. According to rumors, the tricky prick was paid handsomely for it, too. While awaiting default provisions to kick in and snare an unsuspecting partner, Stanley and Ewen made good use of their time by seizing the assets of still other woebegone partners whom Stanley's default provisions had most recently seduced into a mistake. So much did the process resemble the movements of a fine Swiss watch, and since default was a function of time anyway, Leetboer allowed Stanley B. Conover to register his shell corporation in the name of "Clockwork Investments, Inc."

The so-called "Gold Coast" of South Florida, though, held the edge insofar as Ewen's choice of partnership hunting grounds went. For several years he and Clay Redmond managed to work together without incident other than minor disagreements over contract structure, brokerage fees, attorney "meddling," and so on. Friction began to build and had reached a critical point about the time Ewen Leetboer got married again. It was here, at the Bella Mar condominium complex in Coral Gables, where Clay Redmond first made his new wife's acquaintance. After two years he still remembered the day well. Clay was holding an open house for another valued client and in walks his partner one rainy afternoon wearing a toupee of such quality that the old devil must have thought that a "little snot" of a real estate agent wouldn't notice or remember that *all* his hair was fake. Equally obvious, Ewen Leetboer was looking for one of those Sunday bargains plucked from the classified pages to give to his lovely new wife in exchange for bedroom favors. She was a lovely lady all right. With a grace and presence light-years beyond Ewen Leetboer's ability to match, she accompanied him through the richly appointed penthouse but was forced to slap his hands on several occasions when his subtleties of reach intruded upon her notions of respectability, or otherwise proved embarrassing.

The wife's long, bushy, free-hanging mass of Irish red hair, so explosively enriched by a pair of emerald green eyes peering through, struck Clayborn Redmond with the sudden force of a truck bomb when she smiled a greeting at him and offered her hand. It was warm and soft and squeezed with just enough mind-boggling gentleness to remind him that here stood one of those super beauties whose exquisite charm epitomized the marvelous but often under-appreciated benefits of good eyesight. *How'd Ewen catch her?* Clay grumped to himself. *He's an old geezer. What grace she has, what youth, what smiles, what shape!* No wonder the peachy color in her cheeks—further enlivened by a vivacious fluidity of body—evoked more attention than surprise when the lady was fondled in Clay Redmond's presence after the "old geezer" lured her upon a magnificent ocean view full of the kind of storm and fury that must have been raging in his own passion centers right about then.

From the lofty heights of Penthouse #9, the condo's *nom social*, the lady almost swooned over the scene she beheld through the plate glass. Here was what she wanted—romantic outlooks and quiet elegance within, which discovery became the memorable turning point of the tour. Also, the instant deal clincher.

As for Ewen Leetboer's perspective, his view was greatly humbled by a king-size sofa near the window. Its cozy playpen characteristics offered the very touch of welcome convenience needed to further the ambitions of his lower extremities should he buy the place. Nor did its cover lack in beguiling sensual designs, another feature not lost upon the lady's observant spouse. Even Clay Redmond later admitted that his aging partner, Ewen Leetboer, didn't fit the "old geezer" mold in all respects.

Ewen merely introduced her as "the new Mrs. Leetboer," but Clay now and then heard him call her Vanessa, sometimes wedged between a flow of saccharine terms that seemed to annoy the little woman more than please her. The "lecherous old goat," as Clay began to think, was a mold the Dutchman *did* appear to fit, at least in one glaring respect. The two names—*Vanessa* and *Leetboer*—sounded no less out of place when joined together than she looked beside him. This gorgeous creature, who had to be at least twenty-five years younger than Leetboer if a day, seemed as ill-matched to her deadpan, colorless wig of a spouse as any woman Clay Redmond ever had the pleasure of meeting.

It was a day the re-energized broker could not forget. There were good reasons *never* to forget. Vengeance for one. Meeting Vanessa Leetboer ran a close second. To his credit, though, Ewen Leetboer had brought more than two people together. By some strange, ironic quirk that often defies the theory of an orderly universe, the old Dutchman brought love back into his ill-tempered partner's life, and he did it without a clue that he was doing it, with no sense that he was committing his life-time "good deed" when he twisted the knob on Clay Redmond's open house that day and ushered her inside. As so often happens when a door opens, something good comes in. Leetboer opened a door and in walked a whole body of goodness, straight into Clay Redmond's heart. And what a body it was!

If Ewen Leetboer hadn't screwed him later, Clay Redmond might never have allowed himself to go past a little innocent coveting. It was such a wonderful thing his partner had done—*opening a door*! Clay Redmond's newfound enemy had brought in sweetness and light, making (but not realizing he had made) his broker's insides feel alive again. Now, after the ripoff of his retirement nest egg, Clay's outlook changed. Yet he still felt *some* gratitude, a little, enough to make him utter a silent promise to return the favor by seeing that Ewen Leetboer got a Christian burial. Clay would also take something beautiful away, not from the deceased, but from another kind of death even more horrible: the living death that must arise out of those close encounters, those nightly beddy-byes and early morning tussles with her reptilian Lord of Clockwork.

Vanessa deserved a better fate than being married to a morally bankrupt crumb of a man like Ewen Leetboer, even if he was as rich as Croesus. With his estate in her control, she might feel grateful enough to see that Clay Redmond's retirement account was restored to good health, particularly if he could convince her that he'd also been fucked by her husband. Perhaps, if she became implicated in some small way in the scoundrel's abrupt demise, she would feel still more gratitude.

Like any complicated or dangerous venture, plans must first be drawn. Clay spent many anxious hours going over in his mind the critical steps he must take. Would he do the job in Miami or Montreal? Should he forget about a Christian burial and just toss the body in a remote Everglades sinkhole? Or perhaps leave it exposed on some lonely back street in, say, Philadelphia for the drug pushers and homeless to find and wonder over?

Clay mulled for a while, then concluded that such questions dealt with events too far beyond the climax and tended to deaden an otherwise lively interest in the process. His anger was still so immense that it was hard for him to focus on preliminary issues such as those involved in a project of this magnitude. Above all, he wanted to enjoy—step by step—the slow, methodical assault and subsequent annihilation of a monster hiding under a beastly store of hairpieces and trying to pass itself off as a person.

Why didn't I see him for what he was—a scoundrel, a chiseler? Why did it take years to learn this? Clay would ask himself these kinds of questions over and over again. Then he'd curse loudest about that last year, the year of frustration and disappointment in court. But the long ordeal was not altogether without its bright side, since there had been no cessation in wet dreams about the asshole's wife, Vanessa. Clay didn't keep score, although it was impossible to forget the first one. It woke him up in the middle of the night following that rainy afternoon when she first turned her beautiful emerald eyes on him at Penthouse #9 and squeezed his hand. That's the way she always looked at him in his dreams—glowing, full of passion, squeezing, embracing his nakedness with her own.

The broker began to wonder if he shouldn't soften his approach a bit, perhaps negotiate a temporary truce with Ewen Leetboer now that the lawsuit was behind him, maybe resume at least the appearance of their old friendship and try to catch the blackguard a few clicks off guard. At least he would enjoy seeing Vanessa up close again, for real, take home some fresh imagery for dreamland use, if nothing else. He remembered that Leetboer always encouraged his partners to see him as a fair and forgiving individual, as a man who placed business at the epicenter of all considerations, including transactions even with bitter enemies.

"A good deal is a good deal," the old Dutchman liked to say. "Business is business."

Clay pictured Ewen Leetboer's dead pan as those sentient words tumbled out of his mouth amidst a carefully preserved Dutch accent. During such moments of contemplation he could almost smell Ewen's halitosis, which rarely failed to tweak his nose in close quarters. With Vanessa also in the picture, though, with the retirement rustler's pretty wife sitting by the pool in a skimpy outfit or strolling along the beach in a Swedish bikini while the two men followed and talked turkey behind her, Clay concluded that a visit or two at Leetboer's Miami mansion perhaps wouldn't turn his stomach as quickly as first imagined. Clay only needed an "excuse to call," a nifty concept that dripped with Machiavellian charm among real estate professionals, and with matters perking in his favor for a change, Clay just happened to have one.

Reports of new investment opportunities were beginning to circulate around Coral Gables, the very kind of reports that Ewen Leetboer loved to hear about and who always had room in his forward-bending ears for further accommodation along these lines. A contingent of Cuban businessmen—former refugees who had brought their brains and their riches to Miami back in the 1960's to escape *socialismo o muerte*—maintained a very active grapevine and were whispering among themselves and dropping hints of phenomenal deals in the heart of historic Havana. Legal descriptions and inventories of chosen properties along Havana's oceanfront boulevard, the Malecón, were being gathered by a well-known but nameless cabal. Some of the ingredients needed to draft preliminary partnership agreements, assemble investment packages, establish prices, etc., had already been smuggled off the island to Miami. Portfolios would be made available to a select group of investors—*insiders*, as the talk went—immediately following Castro's flight, which was said to be imminent. Money and partners were being lined up for lightning action once conditions were right.

Such news would quickly sweep away any animosities that Ewen Leetboer might still be harboring in spite of the cash he must have shelled out to the twin doublethinkers, Judge "Cotton" Brussard and Clay's guitar whiz and sometimes attorney, Mason Riley. Fortunately, the cost of Leetboer's court defense against Clay didn't seem to bother him. The man never objected to legal fees. By Leetboer's own confession, they formed the keystone in each of his partnerships and therefore represented a legitimate and necessary cost of his thievery. Actually Leetboer never confessed to thievery as such. Neither did he withhold "inducements" nor question more than once the bills of loyal members of the Bar who looked after his interests.

While some of his interests were believed to be better than others, his team of legal Foo Dogs worked with the same even hands and neutral passions as their beloved goddess of the scales always did. Efforts were equal in all cases, whether one interest involved a simple default action against a partner who might be a few days late in mailing in his pro rata share of a mortgage payment or whether another interest involved more challenging litigation against their client—charges of fraud, embezzlement, perjury, racketeering, and so on. No one worried about Leetboer's credit rating. Unlike many of his partners caught in a temporary bind, his payments were prompt, his bribes generous.

Sooner or later Ewen Leetboer amazed everyone. But as Clay Redmond theorized, time was running out for the sly, prickly pirate from Amsterdam.

3

Ewen Leetboer greeted Clay Redmond at the door of his Miami estate without a trace of resentment showing. The old Dutchman's customary dead pan had risen to full mast. It was eleven o'clock in the morning and he was still wearing his gray satin robe.

"Hello, Clay," he intoned, extending his hand.

"Hi, Ewen. Good to see you again."

"Thanks for coming over."

"Thanks for inviting me over."

Clay shook Ewen's claw-like appendage, thinking, *God, what lies we tell in the name of courtesy!*

On the telephone the previous day when Clay called to make arrangements to meet, Ewen had seemed more excited about getting an overview of the current Miami market than discussing a possible Cuban venture. The news from Havana was yet too murky for his taste. Clay knew better. He figured the devious old rascal was posturing, setting the stage for a cheap buy-out of some ailing business around Miami while he waited for details of the Cuban venture to materialize.

Ewen's patronizing, big-daddy manner as they walked through the mansion toward the patio struck Clay as amusingly hypocritical. Although no great surprise in itself, it left the clear impression that Ewen Leetboer had already decided that this irreverent associate of his was once again ready to help himself to an easy commission to offset legal expenses suffered in their recent lawsuit. Leetboer might have looked pleased for other reasons, but Clay was satisfied to think that his former friend and client, who had suddenly become the biggest asshole in North America, needed to feel that he had made an upstart broker-partner "pay for his mistakes."

Clay accepted for the moment Ewen's attempt at woodshed discipline, imagining sweet revenge close by. He took a seat at a glass-top table next to the pool. Several newspapers were spread around on it. Clumps of lush, tropical plants dotted the patio, which was covered by a huge, three-story-high screen enclosure.

The smell of smoked snapper drifted out of a barbecue grill across the patio. Vanessa was lying on a plastic float in the pool, reading a thick paperback and sipping on an iced drink as red as her hair. When Clay caught her eye, she smiled and wiggled a finger from around the glass at him. His heart raced. Even at thirty paces the details of her physiognomy were still delightfully evident. Clay stood and stretched for a moment, then moved closer to Vanessa's float when Ewen stepped over to the grill to inspect the snapper filets.

"You look, uh, relaxed," he said to her, straining for something to say but sounding intimate, as if they talked to each other every day. "Too relaxed. Didn't you hear the news this morning about the explosion in Ireland?"

"Hi, Clay! It's so nice to see you again! I've missed our little tête-à-têtes. Ewen doesn't like to discuss academic topics, you know." She scanned the broker for a bit, causing him to swallow and mention Ireland again. "Oh, yes—Ireland—it's so terrible!" she exclaimed, wrenching an unfamiliar sadness upon her normally cheerful face. "The bombers—absolutely no regard for human life! Irish against Irish. Honestly, I don't know my own people any more."

"Not an easy thing sometimes," Clay responded. "Knowing people, I mean." His voice reflected her sadness but the underlying thought traveled on a different wave. "Not easy to know anybody these days."

Vanessa winked smartly at Clay, sensing his dig at her husband. She glanced over at Ewen. "How does it look, dear?" she asked.

"Ten more minutes," the old dear answered into the hood. His back remained turned. Ewen continued to wield his oversized spatula and poke around the grill in the pompous style of one of those leisure-class husbands who wanted all hands to know he could cook. But it was evident to Clay from previous experience that his host was listening to every word. "You'd better come now, Vanessa," her spouse added in broken but spicy Hollandese, "or I chase you to the bedroom again."

Clay Redmond watched as Vanessa paddled to the shallow end of the pool and eased off the float. With startling grace she ascended the steps and onto the patio beside him, then rose to her full height and took a brief stretch, revealing a stunning posture that Clay had not hitherto observed. Ewen Leetboer apparently hadn't observed it either, or enough, for he'd turned around and was ogling from the grill. For longer than the usual instant, his dead pan gave way to earthy, off-color expressions. A different order of muscles seemed to take hold of his face and set it into a variety of human-like, emotional waffles, with alternate swings ranging somewhere between a glare of shock and a glaze of above-fifty euphoria that stemmed like crabs' eyes out of an equally horny head.

The rest of the day went well. Clay resisted a show of "broker excitement" when his host pressed him to continue their previous talks about Cuban opportunities. After the subject arose, and with visible reluctance, he fumbled through his brief-case before finally pulling out a large manila envelope stamped *confidential* in bold red letters in several places. It contained Clay's "hip-pocket collection"; i.e., his private real estate assessments plus a few choice listings which, as Ewen Leetboer knew, the broker kept in reserve for special clients.

Documents pertaining to Cuba were among the packet. These he had brought along to test the Dutchman's appetite for further dealings with a courtroom adversary. Then, if he—Leetboer—passed the test, Clay would follow up with a detailed pro forma as soon as he could put something together with the help of Silvio Alvarez, one of his Cuban friends and a valued confidant.

To satisfy Leetboer's insatiable appetite for inside information, Clay went over his hip-pocket papers in succinct fashion but cleverly introduced alternate investments for consideration and avoided any show of bias or urgency one way or the other.

With regard to his own appetite, Clay enjoyed a light lunch of delicious fish, smoked by the master smoker of Clockwork fame. Salads and elegant side dishes prepared jointly by Vanessa and a live-in *bon vivant* added grace and drama to the meal as well—not to mention a few "Goombay Smashes" which Clay mixed for himself. It all combined to suspend temporarily the offended broker's methodical search for an acceptable crime scene within the confines of the Leetboer mansion. Clay would not want Vanessa in the home when the axe fell, if it fell in the home at all. It had to fall somewhere, though, and soon.

At one point Ewen questioned Clay about the taste of the snapper, noticing that his guest had looked a bit edgy during the course of the luncheon.

"What's wrong!" Leetboer yelled, sounding more indignant than curious. Clay gaped at him for a moment, then smiled uneasily at Vanessa. She was also gaping at her husband but with more disgust in her gape than surprise. Clay turned back to Leetboer.

"Why do you ask?" he said.

"You were squirming. Don't you like the snapper?"

Clay laughed, realizing that his metaphorical reflections were showing. It was the image created by a falling axe that made him squirm, not the taste of smoked snapper. But those were details he would explain to Ewen at a later date, at his last supper perhaps.

"Great fish," Clay answered with a savvy nod, chewing connoisseur-like on a hunk to register his approval. "May I have your recipe, Ewen?"

While the idea of a good chop across Leetboer's neck with a sharp axe held some appeal—mainly because the instrument seemed better matched with the job of slaughtering a beast than did his small pocket automatic—Clay nevertheless rejected the notion as too bloody messy. A neat round hole in the son of a bitch's head, he thought, or perhaps his heart, or both, offered a much cleaner, more dignified solution.

After a final squeeze of Vanessa's hand at the door, Clayborn Redmond left the Dutchman's mansion that afternoon wondering, not about Leetboer's fate but about Vanessa's. His fascination seemed more and more impossible to hide. Coincidentally, almost from the first encounter in the romantic Coral Gables penthouse, the lovely lady had been nurturing her own fascination as well over this very Irish, very macho fellow, and she appeared increasingly willing to use every trick in the book to make him aware of it.

Vanessa hardly cared whether Ewen noticed when her hand touched Clay's shoulder or leg while the two of them were engaged in a passionate discussion of art, literature, history, politics, and any of the other subjects that equally bored her husband. Business was Ewen Leetboer's business. His preoccupation with partnerships sometimes kept him from noticing the obvious. Besides, Vanessa frequently confused him with deceptive chatter, with nuances in the English language he found difficult to follow. For some reason which he could not fathom, she liked to joke about Clay Redmond's big nose. At least *his* woman, the Dutchman concluded, could run fast, could escape Clay's big nose if it became too intrusive. Then, of course, she was "still a child" in many respects and liked to play jokes on other people and gesture tenderly with her hands, her fingers, even with her bare feet under the table.

Another motive had suddenly emerged which Clay imagined would not go unnoticed by the police. Those guys would surely prefer to sink their teeth into a nice juicy scandal-oriented murder rather than dust for fingerprints in the Miami International Airport or poke through the trunks of vehicles and pick over sexless clues to a dull revenge hit.

Many people knew that Ewen Leetboer had enemies. Most of them *were* enemies, for Leetboer's fortune did not come without a price. He paid the price, and from all accounts, he paid gladly. Informed sources kept spreading the word about how the Lord of Clockwork made his money. "By screwing his partners!" continued to be the overwhelming refrain. Clayborn Redmond would join the list as just another suspect among the many, a more comfortable position he felt than, say, explaining a rendezvous with Vanessa Leetboer on the missing tycoon's luxury yacht. Burial at sea was definitely not an option.

4

Over the next several weeks Clayborn Redmond worked the areas around Miami that he knew best. Coral Gables was one of his favorites. It challenged him in personal ways, starting with the arrival of the Cubans, then later the redhead from Ireland. Plenty of international action there. The broker wanted to line up one final partnership for Ewen Leetboer. A "fare-thee-well" venture seemed devilishly appropriate. It would also give Clay Redmond more time to refine his plan for ridding the world of a world-class chiseler.

The restaurants and food joints in Little Havana were always good places to visit, to chat with friends and make note of the rumors and hot tips of the day. The Versailles on *Calle Ocho* topped Clay's list. This restaurant offered a fine menu of Cuban fare and was a favorite mecca among Cubans who enjoyed its island ambiance. They also met to chew on things other than food, to palaver in Spanish and plot strategies for getting rid of Fidel Castro and restoring the island nation to the glory days of Máximo Gomez, its nineteenth-century liberator from Spanish colonial rule and a colossus among the all-time greatest champions of Cuban freedom.

The subject of Castro consistently held first place among topics of interest along *Calle Ocho*, where the bearded one had endured as an all-seasons issue year after year for more than forty years. In many parts of Coral Gables talk centering on the dictator and what to do about his olive-green presence in their country surpassed in spirit and intensity the levels associated with international pastimes of the caliber of Brazilian soccer, Chinese ping pong and Russian roulette, to name just three.

Patriotism reigned supreme in Little Havana. *Calle Ocho*, perhaps its most recognized thoroughfare, meant more than just a street name. The very term quivered on the tongues of the Versailles crowd and sharpened a hearty sense of common foe. Nor was the Republican Party excluded from occasional outbreaks of nationalistic fervor within Coral Gables' proud Cuban community. Cubans loved *Estados Unidos*, too. Not many were new arrivals but quite a few came in the Mariel boatlift back in 1980, and on makeshift rafts before and since. The ones with big money had fled the island in 1958, some as late in the year as the ill-fated New Year's Eve when choruses and crowds of *Auld Lang Syne* singers made a lot of these *Calle Ocho* compatriots cry, not for a dying year but for a lost homeland. A dwindling few of them still make the rounds among these establishments, the older ones who had arrived in Miami even before revolutionary zeal turned the country over to a new Sugar Daddy, and ultimately to the flies.

As it happened, the flies never surrendered but the new Sugar Daddy did. The flies ignored the revolution as well as the new Sugar Daddy. Promises of caviar, nuclear rockets and other noisy toys made not a whit of difference to those fearless insects. In spite of the new Sugar Daddy's long arms, his reach was simply too short, so the flies prevailed. Underground sources claim that these little gaum-footed masters of biological warfare remain about the only free creatures alive and well in Cuba, except tourists to some extent and the gringos at Guantánamo, of course, whom Castro hated more than the flies. Whatever the bearded one's animosities might be, though, or whoever were his choice of allies, the flies continued to hold an unhealthy advantage over him.

Clay Redmond waited in the restaurant for Silvio Alvarez to come with the latest rumors concerning investment opportunities in Havana. Ewen Leetboer had finally confessed he'd like to hear details. Silvio, a devout hustler and holy freedom fighter, came on Tuesdays late in the afternoon. According to the ancient Greeks, Tuesday was a good day to engage in martial activity. If the day infused the atmosphere with a warlike quality, it was hardly noticed by Clay Redmond. Of late his face reflected a warrior's mood day in and day out. Thoughts of Ewen Leetboer continued to gore his insides as furiously as a simple Castro poster turned the stomachs of Miami's Cuban community.

As he sat in the restaurant and watched eyes flash and chins and lips move in heated exchanges, he felt their pain, the kind of pain that words and politics can only mock. Clay was wearing blue jeans, cowboy boots and a richly tailored white *guayabera* shirt. Without trying to be inconspicuous and with no ulterior motive other than maybe disposing of Ewen Leetboer in one of the Dumpsters out behind the restaurant, the youthful broker blended in quite well with the Versailles crowd.

Several patrons and most of the staff recognized him and appreciated his interest in them as refugees, as immigrants, as naturalized citizens of the United States. Most of them knew he supported the Cuban cause—with hard cash and action, not just lip service. They supported his cause as well, at least those who bought property. As a dealer in real estate, Clay had helped many of them find homes and start businesses after they landed in Miami. They trusted him. This gringo spoke their language. One of the things they didn't understand about Clay Redmond, though, was how much he enjoyed Versailles' *sopa de pollo*.

Silvio Alvarez came rushing to Clay's table a few minutes after four o'clock. His thick black hair was in disarray, perspiration showed through his shirt, and his deeply set eyes stayed busy for the first few minutes as he took inventory on the customers in the restaurant. Silvio's hand waved out to someone off and on as he and Clay talked over a local version of the famous *mojito* cocktail that Hemingway favored so much and loved to drink with his friends at the *Bodeguita del Medio* in Havana.

Silvio and Clay worked together during the Mariel boatlift. Before that, Clay made a few trips to Cuba with him using phony passports. There he met Silvio's kid sister, Graciela, an adorable young woman still in her teens then, who almost changed the direction of Clay Redmond's life forever. Having no family of his own, Clay became part of Silvio's family. Their friendship grew stronger through the years.

"A boat is coming in tonight," Silvio whispered, abruptly getting down to business. "My brother Ramón will be on it with news and more papers. He says the buy will be a fantastic one for your client—a steal of the century!"

"What about Castro?" Clay asked, looking a bit leery even though his friend and confidant had always been on top of things, and usually right in his assessments. "I can't wait for a miracle, Silvio. When do you suppose *El Jefe* will fly out to Timbuktu or Hezbollahville or some hellhole compatible with tyrants?"

"They say soon but who knows? The beast needs dollars, though, even if he doesn't leave. A rich investor will get special treatment."

"A state-sponsored partnership, huh?"

"Something like that. With guarantees."

Clay's eyes rolled. He stroked his nose briefly then sighed and ordered another round of *mojitos*.

"Guarantees you say? Fidel's guarantees? Yeah, sounds good. Ho ho ho. Listen, Silvio, I love you like a brother but I can't afford a mistake on this one. Talk with Ramón. Find out if he's in a position to give my client the usual tour."

"Who is the client?"

"A former partner, Ewen Leetboer."

"*Jesús*! The Bella Mar man you sued?"

"The same, yes—and got my ass kicked in the courtroom, you'll recall."

"Can you trust him?"

"If I don't make any mistakes, yes. He's a heavy hitter, Silvio. I'd like to make him partner again before he gets too old, falls and breaks a hip or something vital." Clay paused to let his comment soak in. He wanted to sound reconciled toward the S.O.B. yet technically truthful, in case Silvio wondered later on when he read the obituary.

Clay didn't relish the idea of his friend being hauled before a grand jury and indicted for covering up a crime. "Maybe . . ." he resumed, hanging on to the word for a moment, "maybe I can talk Leetboer into a quick flight. Or a yacht trip."

"To Havana, to the Malecón?"

"Yeah," Clay answered.

"No problem. Your client has a Canadian passport, right?"

"I think so. Could be Holland. Definitely not American."

"No problem. Not many from Holland but Canadians come and go like clockwork in Cuba."

Clay chuckled into his *mojito*. "I get the picture," he mumbled.

"Did I say something funny? Why do you laugh?"

"Nothing, Silvio. Just a coincidence. Sometimes in a spasm of adulation I call Ewen Leetboer the Lord of Clockwork. He's one shifty client. He's also a robber of retirements and my former partner. His corporation goes by the name of Clockwork Investments, Inc. He'll fit right in over there with Fidel. But let's be sure to remind your brother Ramón to count his fingers before Leetboer leaves Cuba. The man is very clever. He prefers confiscation over purchase. Sound like anybody you know?"

"Sure. You said it already—the beast himself!"

"I would love for them to meet."

Silvio nodded at Clay, his dark, busy eyes working in thought. "If you are serious, perhaps it can be arranged. Fidel will bite off his mother's tits for dollars."

Clay rocked back in his chair, laughing but trying not to attract attention. "Damn, Silvio, I know you're good but that's a big rabbit to pull out of the hat!"

"No problem. You want me to set it up?"

"Wait—you're making me choke!"

Clay was joking about a meeting between Leetboer and Castro, two of the biggest desperados he could imagine—right up there with Capone and Blackbeard and truly worthy of each other. When Silvio picked up on the comment and sounded so casual and yet positive, Clay began to mull.

"Let me sleep on it," he said.

Silvio smiled. Clay smiled back, noting that his confidant appeared to savor the second *mojito* more than the first. "*Muy sabroso,*" he declared several times.

Clay slid one of his business envelopes across the table to Silvio. "This is for Graciela," he said.

"Bless you," Silvio replied, rushing the glass back to his lips to keep from having to say anything further. He looked at the envelope for a moment or two, then poked it inside his shirt.

The crisp hundred-dollar bills, ten of them, would be converted into smaller bills later on and travel by way of Nassau in the custody of a trusted courier who would then deliver the bills to the Alvarez family in Cuba. Silvio never asked for money. He knew that Clay would insist on paying him in his own special way for whatever information and help he might give. Clay Redmond was like a brother, too, and most of the time they didn't mention money when they helped each other. Clay called it "ad valorem" to the family. Silvio called it "life support in a desperate land."

The Cuban declined to "qualify" his friend's client. He had helped Clay celebrate one of his big sales not long before and remembered the talk about how rich this old Dutchman must be. Silvio thought the story was funny as well as strange—the story about Ewen Leetboer buying a luxury penthouse condominium at Bella Mar merely because his wife asked for it. *Yes*, the Cuban reflected, *she made him buy it. Clay's partner he was. They owned a valuable tract of land on the Dixie Highway. The guy knew Clay was holding an open house. He wanted to impress Clay with his new, young wife and they came in out of the rain and he showed it to them and wrote up the sales contract that very same day*. Silvio remembered Clay's puzzled face and the curious way his gringo friend told the story about how pretty she was and how she asked for it with no more thought than she might ask for a mango at the fruit market, even though her husband already owned a mansion on South Beach, and many properties elsewhere.

Most all of Clay's friends toasted his good luck but many of them joked for months about the Canadian's extravagance. The ease and rapidity with which a three-million-dollar transaction closed prompted a wider audience to view it as a gauge of the man's means as much as his judgment.

Silvio also remembered that the Canadian had later cheated his friend, along with others, out of a partnership interest in that expensive tract of land on the Dixie Highway. Ewen Leetboer's wealth and reputation for dirty dealing had become legend in Coral Gables. As far as Silvio was concerned, the "crook had more money than sense" and didn't need to be qualified to buy anything in Cuba. Besides, Clayborn Redmond's word was good with him, just as it was always good on *Calle Ocho*.

Turning antsy again, the enterprising Cuban lapped up an appetizing bowl of *sopa de pollo* at Clay's invitation and rushed out of the restaurant on another of his missions, waving at people as he went and pausing to chat when some of them grabbed his arm as he passed. Silvio was a popular man at Versailles.

5

When Clay got in bed that night following his meeting with Silvio, he flicked on the late news to check out local events of interest. In the back of his mind lurked a nagging fear that someone else may have beaten him in the race to exterminate Ewen Leetboer. He least of all did not want to be the last to hear of this late-breaking, heart-shattering particular.

The black screen opened up to the usual marathon of loud, frenetic, silly commercials, then turned red with a bloody spectacle infinitely more tragic than Leetboer catching a bullet in the old pump. A brave CNN camera crew had filmed Israelis screaming and shouting and dashing about the streets of Jerusalem following another bomb attack set in motion by Palestinian terrorists. Fifteen people had been killed, scores injured. The scene was gruesome, yet sadly familiar.

The network gave a demonstration to show how a terrorist could pull off such an act. A man came before the camera strapped and wired to the hilt with explosives, or what appeared to be explosives. He was wearing a vest-like garment lined all around with cigar-shaped pockets, each one stuffed with a stick of dynamite. In the real world the vest would be hidden by a coat worn over it. No doubt the vest was an "exclusive" design of the terrorist group.

The commentator called the wearer a "suicide bomber," meaning to others less charitable a member of the "lunatic fringe," usually one too young and too burdened with state-sponsored ignorance to appreciate his own personal worth and potential, one who seemed eager to blow himself away for the witless pleasure of blowing along with him a few Hebrews in a shopping center. The more the merrier.

Clay watched the report with a sense of disgust but also a curious fascination. What depths of hatred existed, he wondered, to make a person sacrifice his life in order to kill another—someone the sacrificial lamb didn't even know, a stranger? Clay's feelings toward his adversary—about getting rid of Ewen Leetboer—*never never never, not once,* ran this deep. If a suicide-bomb episode offered the sole means of seeking reprisal, and if Clayborn Redmond happened to be the last "volunteer" available to wear the vest, then Ewen Leetboer could safely enjoy a life-time romp through his garden of corrupt business practices, subject only to the Lord taking control of vengeance again.

"What a way to do it, though," Clay mumbled to himself.

He turned the volume down and lay back on his pillow, thinking. How easy it would be to walk right up in front of Leetboer, maybe catch the turd in Stanley B. Conover's office after the secretaries had left, and set off the charge while Stanley and Ewen were plotting another default action against some hapless partner. Or maybe wait until they'd had at least one good piss in their pants and were on their knees in the conference room praying through the glass of Stanley's big silicon table for a second chance to review the issues. "*Missing documents . . . found this morning in Stanley's mini storage!*" they'd scream in unison. The two shitheads would promise the moon along with double—*hey man . . . let's make it quadruple!*—indemnity if the facts so warranted, which they were both "absolutely certain" would be the case now that the mini storage doors had been unlocked.

Thinking about Leetboer going up in smoke, with the added bonus of Stanley B. Conover having a seat on the same flight, soothed Clay into a deep and restful sleep for the rest of the evening. Being true to himself above all, sleep was aided by a General Sherman-type refusal to see his body parts going up in smoke with them. In the pit of his stomach Clayborn Redmond knew that he was not suicide-bomber material. The Remington Model 51 looked better and better to him as a sensible option. The questions yet to be answered were *where* and *when*.

Later in the week a story appeared in the *Miami Herald* which an uninformed reader might consider damaging to the image of an upscale shopping mall in the Kendall area just south of Coral Gables. Ewen Leetboer phoned Clay to ask about it. The story had the ring of a disaster unfolding, he suspected. Leetboer also suspected that Clay would have the answers. In spite of their differences, the old Dutchman hadn't lost his confidence in Clay Redmond's integrity nor, more to the point, in the man's knowledge of corporate enterprises and investment groups in the Miami area. Clay had read the story in his early-morning scan of the business section and knew the principals on a first-name basis.

"Are the owners in financial trouble?" Leetboer asked in his most innocent, philanthropic tone.

"You still have a good nose for crisis," Clay answered. "Let me check it out. Something's not right. The story failed to cover certain aspects of the mall's problems. I'll call you this afternoon."

A brief silence ensued. Moments later Clay heard voices in the background. Leetboer apparently was in the middle of a conference somewhere and had turned away from the phone to engage in another conversation. Men's voices were loud, profane, which suggested that Vanessa was not among the group.

The Dutchman finally came back on the phone, sounding stiffly apologetic for the delay. "Clay," he said, purring a little, "perhaps you could stop by the hideaway and we can discuss this matter over a drink. Will you be finished with your research by, say, four o'clock?"

"If the right people happen to be in town," Clay answered. "Call my mobile number if you have a change of plans. You still have it?"

"Of course." Leetboer squeaked a laugh into the mouthpiece, talking over it. "You are the best man for the job. As they say in America, 'top dog' among the agents. Around here you hold strong cards in your hand and—what is even more important—many trade secrets in your head. Do you think I would lose your number or let a minor dispute come between us and good business?"

"That's nice of you to say, Ewen," Clay replied, trying to sound sincere but not too cozy. "Perhaps I did blow things out of proportion. If luck is with me, though, I'll blow them back together again." The word made him think of the bloody TV report he had watched the night before. "I've been in a blowing mood lately," Clay added with a cryptic chuckle.

"Now you talk sense! Very smart, very smart! Now, young man, we can make good business together again. See you at four."

"Wait, Ewen—one more thing. For reasons which should be obvious to you—"

"Nothing is obvious to me, Mister Redmond," Ewen shouted into the phone, interrupting with another squeaky laugh. "One must analyze!"

Clay tweaked his nose for a moment, waiting for the Dutchman's airy laughter to subside. "Touché," he said, his standard reply when he didn't want to argue. "You're quite right. You win again, doggone it. Anyhow, for good-will reasons let's say, I'm drinking Havana Club nowadays. Do you have any?"

"Uh-h . . . I don't think so. Is it available here in Miami?"

"If you know the right people. I'll bring along a bottle of Ron Matusalem. It sounds of old New England, something from a witch's pot perhaps, but you'll like the Antilles taste. You'll also like my news on the Cuban deal."

Clay hung up before Leetboer could respond. The pig's need for a "greed fix" was beginning to sicken him all over again. Memories of the Chapter Eleven fiasco and how Stanley B. Conover shaped the restructure document still made Clay's colon go spastic when he thought about it longer than five minutes. His retirement nest egg cracked under the pressure of bottom-line arithmetic, digital overkill. The bank, too, played its customary roll of Komodo dragon, caring naught whose tail got swallowed in its gluttonous rush to satisfy a crave for negotiables, especially those juiceless "nonperforming assets" resurrected from their vaults and marinated overnight in freshly laundered cash.

At times Clay tried to be objective. He'd look in the mirror and holler out loud, "Why should bankers give a lizard chip who got squeezed out of a Miami partnership as long as their Chicago columns balanced?" Then he'd cluck from the ticklish sensation of his scalp being overrun with little elves and tooth fairies bringing answers. *Bankers didn't need to say why. They let the fine print in their finely tuned instruments do the talking.*

The sprites were right. Clay's retirement hope had been pinned together with trust, good faith. Big mistake. It came unpinned. Devious hands and voracious onslaughts took trust and good faith to task, took hope apart. Clayborn Redmond heard all the pins collide with the floor, heard the shrill kibosh—and felt it's excruciating exactness—when the other lead shoe dropped on his sandy-haired brain box.

But Leetboer's addiction to squeeze plays, while obvious and sickening, began to take on an air of excitement. Retaliation could be a pleasant process regardless of the outcome. "Enjoy the moment," Clay reminded himself, "but don't forget to kill the bastard after you seduce his wife."

Business, to be sure, was beginning to pop. The Xanadu Shopping Mall in Kendall and a joint venture with Fidel Castro in Cuba both met Clay's specifications for deals he filed under the heading "Leetboer Yellowcake." They were leveraged partnerships in trouble for one reason or another: poor management, weak cash flow, heavy debt, and so on. Usually one of the partners, unexpectedly hit with a bomb from another financial front, just couldn't liquefy fast enough to step up to the plate in time to meet the mortgage payment. This sad circumstance would invariably create a default situation with the creditor unless other partners came to the rescue, which Leetboer gladly did. "To protect the partnership," he'd say. On first blush the gesture sounded decent. A "family" thing, brother helping brother. On second blush Stanley B. Conover's verbiage traps went on active duty. They kicked in and kicked ass on Leetboer's behalf until the "pot got right," as they say in cannibal country.

Underlying securities—base collateral and other guarantees—were the plum-babies to be picked when a take-over raid occurred, the irresistible glamour pussies that Ewen Leetboer loved to chase. Ripping off the beneficial interest of an investor bore a certain similarity to the ravishing features of carnal rape. Both were cold-hearted pursuits. In Leetboer's case, a rip in a fellow partner's financial robe *aroused* him, excited something deep within the man's lymphatic channels. Or possibly his heels—the ultimate stompers. Whatever turned him on surely must have sent signals to some part other than his genitalia. Perhaps to ductless glands, to mental lobes. Wherever the ebb and flow took place, scents of default unleashed a lust for conquest far beyond the power of sex, in any of its orientations, to rival.

"What a bastard, what a skunk!" Clay muttered, driving along I-95. Thoughts ran fast and furious. He usually drove his big Jeep on interstate highways. That tough mass of metal, which the broker referred to warmly as *El Toro*, gave one a safety edge over imports, compacts and shoddy passenger models. Clay was heading south toward the Xanadu Shopping Mall. If he caught Ewen Leetboer on the road in his little red Russian Lada, perhaps a high-speed collision wouldn't be a bad idea. *El Toro* would total that pint-sized toy of a car in a heartbeat. He'd mull on it awhile, ignoring suicide-bomber characteristics for the time being.

Clay turned on the radio and began to sing along with Gloria Estefan, who was then in the middle of a lovely number entitled *Tus Ojos*. He wanted to do more than mimic the lyrical imperatives palpitating in her pleas: *¡Mírame!* . . . *¡Mírame!* . . . His lips curved upward as he kept the rhythm. Each refrain reminded him of the enchanting green eyes of Vanessa. If things went well at Xanadu, he might catch a glimpse of the Irish lady's *ojos verdes* later that afternoon.

The Xanadu Shopping Mall happened to be the brainchild of Marcus Cunningham, from Youngstown, whose idol was fellow townsman and enormously successful shopping-mall magnate, Edward J. DeBartolo. Clay Redmond had put together an eighty-acre assemblage of land five years earlier, a difficult, time-consuming but profitable feat which earned him, among other good and valuable considerations, a solid friendship with Marcus Cunningham.

Xanadu opened with great fanfare in the previous fall just in time to greet the rush of winter tourists and stem the mall's negative cash-flow hemorrhage. Hurricane Andrew didn't help the situation either, coming one year after the first spade went in the ground. Concrete slabs were about the only thing left in place. Andrew blew the construction trailer and all of the blueprints away—far away. Pieces of it and its packed contents were later found twenty miles into the Everglades, headed for Louisiana. Marcus Cunningham had to start over. The area was hit hard: tourism fell off, year-round residents were having second thoughts about paradise, jobs went begging, many homes had not been rebuilt. A few doomsdayers thought some homes were down for good.

Marcus Cunningham lived day and night with the project—getting it out of the ground. After the doors opened he spent about the same amount of time on the job but didn't get soaked as much, by rain at least. Even under normal circumstances his face exuded a briar patch of worry lines, but the sight of a dependable, trouble-free visitor like Clay Redmond smothered the business-bred wrinkles instantly, overriding them with a livelier set of creases remindful of someone who'd just been asked by a photographer to say something corny.

"Clay Redmond! Son of a bitch—!"

"Don't hit me. Not guilty, Your Honor."

"Where the hell have you been all year?"

"In court mostly," Clay answered without much puff. Actually Clay's absence hadn't covered more than twelve weeks. To him it seemed closer to three years than three months, not to mention Marcus's estimate. He was glad Marcus noticed though. After the trial Clay needed to drop out of sight for a while, take some vacation, lick the wounds inflicted by the old poot, Judge "Cotton" Brussard, and get over his anger. "Speaking of Your Honor," Clay continued, "I wish to high heaven you'd been *His* Honor last month. Could have used a good blocker on my blind side."

"What the hell are you talking about?"

"Nothing important. What's happening, big guy?"

Clay had caught Marcus in the pedestrian area near his suite. They both paused to chat nonsense and slap shoulders to commemorate an overdue encounter. Shorter by a couple of inches than Clay, Marcus Cunningham was a solid specimen, his body thick and powerful. A graying shock of hair hung just over his eyes. His stare was intense.

Marcus Cunningham glanced in all directions at once. As his head was swiveling, he said, "Glad you dropped by. Listen—"

"Yeah, I read the article in the *Herald* this morning," Clay said to Marcus before the latter could ask.

"Figured you would have." Marcus shook Clay's hand again, the vigor undiminished. For a white-collar type he had a strong grip. "What do you think, pal?"

"I think an enemy resides in your camp."

"Any ideas?"

"Someone who'd like to take your place," Clay answered behind a stoic smile. "I'll put money on Frank Creuthop."

"Any *new* ideas?"

"One's good enough. Another thing, either the S.O.B. is using the press or the press has a gangster on the payroll. Are you ready to get rid of a snake in the group, take on a working partner?"

Marcus Cunningham motioned for Clay to come inside his private office. As they walked past his girl Friday, she looked up, smiled and bulged her eyes when she saw Clay.

"Hi, stranger," she said, extending her hand in mock high-fashion and waiting demurely until Clay bent over and kissed it.

"Hello, Heather," Clay responded. "You're looking delicious, as usual, like a juicy apple that needs to be nibbled on."

"You big flirt," she said. Marcus gave her a no-disturb sign and waved Clay toward the door ahead of him. She returned a faint nod, unnoticed by Clay but apparently well understood by Marcus.

Girl Friday was a woman named Heather Ambrose, a mature, capable personal assistant to Marcus Cunningham. No one who knew her doubted that she had earned the status of loyal fixture and well deserved her reputation for all-round efficiency.

Clay met Heather in Marcus's Youngstown office during one of his business trips North to make a presentation to the Xanadu partners regarding progress on land acquisition. She came down to Miami with Marcus and set up the office. Now Heather Ambrose ran the place. Chic looking, too, but no wispy piece of cheese cake. Clay figured that Marcus was banging her on the side. Or she, him. Clay wasn't sure and didn't care. "It's their fucking business," he'd chide himself when the question arose in his mind. A little private speculation was fun, though. In truth, he suspected Marcus and Heather had been in the banging game for quite some time. Years. Being a single, career-minded lady—a smartly sensuous one at that—exempted her from the usual censures of office girls, gave her the right to take risks, to choose and reject. Nor had Heather's credentials hurt her chances for promotion within the Cunningham firm. Marcus kept an eye out for such talent. He lay foursquare between marriages, and Heather Ambrose, after a short apprenticeship, learned how to take care of him as well as the books. But for her, the project might have folded long ago.

"The partners are upset," Marcus related after he and Clay finished with trivialities. "Three want out. Unfortunately Frank is not one of them."

"Too bad. Frank needs a rest. As usual, his brain is out of the loop when it comes to thinking. Bet he's the asshole feeding these wild stories to the press."

"Could be. But in a way I still need him. Next to me, Frank Creuthop holds the biggest interest in the partnership."

"Uh-huh. And he'd love to hold more except he can't afford it. Frank reminds me of another guy in Miami. Both are ruthless. Big difference in style though."

Marcus chuckled. "Maybe we should put them together in Xanadu. Couldn't get much worse."

"For Christ's sake, Marcus, this is a new center! New centers, big ones like Xanadu, always have growing pains. You're not fully leased yet. What do you have now?"

"Seventy percent. Need another major anchor. Heather's after Saks at the moment."

"Not bad, considering. Things are slow, been slow ever since Andrew. Give it another year. Xanadu will have a waiting list by then."

Marcus stiffened and began to pace around the office. "That's not it, Clay. Leases—no problem."

"Okay, what's the problem?"

"You know what the problem is—Frank Creuthop."

Clay forced a smile. "Yeah. Just wanted to hear you say it. Frank's fat, itchy rump must be encroaching on his short hairs."

"No disagreement there. By the way, that newspaper article was bullshit. If Frank had anything to do with it, he's bullshit, too. Xanadu is far from broke. I'm being selective, qualifying the tenants with some pretty high hurdles. Can't allow a bunch of loser shops in here right off the bat pulling down the image. I want Xanadu to be the envy of every mall in Miami."

"Relax. It will be."

Clay was sitting in a leather recliner with his feet up, sipping on a cup of coffee, listening with the laid-back but singular focus of someone watching a stage play, a performance. Marcus held his attention. It was gratifying to hear his friend talk through the maze of problems inherent in the ownership of a major shopping mall. Not only major in itself but a mall sitting in the middle of a high-growth area in one of the preeminent cities of the country, Miami, a city sometimes called "the capital of Latin America."

Clay waited, with minor interruptions, for Marcus to talk himself out. At one point he broke into a grin that caused the Exanadu executive to stop and inquire.

"What the fuck you laughing about?"

"Sorry. I can't resist the notion of a certain guy becoming a part of Xanadu and having to deal with a troublemaker like Frank Creuthop. The guy's got this dickhead attorney, a crafty, backstabbing, four-star S.O.B. who worships his client and has never lost a case defending him. The prick has cut more notches on courtroom sidebars than Wild Bill Hickok ever cut on his six-shooter, but I bet even he couldn't save his client's ass from that sick old man."

"Who the hell could? The screwball would worry that poor schmuck and his attorney to death—calling ad hoc meetings every fifteen minutes, nitpicking, bitching, driving up maintenance costs, refusing to lease at fair market price, annoying tenants, smothering profits and pissing off if not scaring off every qualified buyer in South Florida!"

When Marcus Cunningham finally lapsed into silence and sat down, Clay eased forward in the recliner.

"Marcus," he said, "the three partners who want to sell—how much interest do they hold?"

"They're three percenters."

"Perfect. Why doesn't Frank buy them out?"

"Like you said, he can't afford it. I can but don't need it. Fuck no! I'd rather have somebody around to run interference against Frank. He's like one humongous dose of Black Draught."

"How bad do they want to get out?"

"Real bad. Bad enough to kill, I'd say."

"Hey," Clay blurted, "those fellows have my heartfelt sympathy! You won't believe this—right now I can hardly believe it myself—but—"

Marcus Cunningham crouched over his desk and waited for Clay to stop grinning and finish his story. "Come on, Redmond, what's sticking in your craw for Christ's sake!"

Clay dropped the recliner back and rested his head on the soft cushion. His eyes focused on the ceiling while he chuckled to himself, ignoring Marcus Cunningham. In a sudden shift of tone, accented by a low unsteady voice, he said, "Yeah, I may have just the replacement Xanadu needs at this juncture . . ."

As Marcus watched Clay's excitement build, his own heavy body began to shake, and with even more force than Clay's. A sense of bewildered amusement rose between them, then for a time the two men lost themselves in each other's laughter.

Marcus Cunningham spoke up first. "Save yourself some trouble, pal. Forget it. Frank has spoiled every fucking chance the other partners have had to sell their interest. When outside buyers come into the conference room for their interview, which Frank insists on according to the by-laws, when they listen five minutes to Frank's big mouth, his idiotic schemes and exhortations, they're up on their feet and out the door. No deal. Frank scares them all off, every fucking one!"

"Maybe not this one. Ever hear of Ewen Leetboer?"

"The guy you mentioned earlier—Frank's soul mate?"

"Uh-huh."

"I've heard of him. Bought the old Ferguson mansion over on South Beach, right?"

"Uh-huh. His 'hideaway' he calls it."

"*Hideaway*! Now that's a good one. They say he's plenty wealthy all right. They also say he made his money screwing his partners. That true?"

"True, unfortunately. I'm one of the screwed."

Marcus Cunningham stared at Clay with jarring, intense eyes. "You're kidding! What'd you lose?"

"Nothing big. Just an interest in a prime piece of commercial real estate I was saving for retirement."

"And you want to dump him on me? Shit, man, I got enough problems with City Hall, for Christ's sake!"

"Hold it. Leetboer only screws the little fish like me—and the big sick ones like Creuthop. He's afraid to try balling certified moguls like Marcus Cunningham. Listen, ol' buddy, Heather looks out for you. Always has, always will. She's not gonna let Leetboer pull any crap. Just watch out for that razor-lipped attorney I mentioned earlier. His name is Stanley B. Conover."

"The "B" stands for Bastard, right?"

"And then some. Don't let that crook get too cozy with the partnership agreement. He'll try to rewrite it. Aside from that, the old Dutchman is a natural choice to deal with Frank. You remember the story about the gingham dog and the calico cat?"

"What's your point, smart guy?"

"They ate each other up. Leetboer and Creuthop will eat each other up, too, and both our problems will disappear."

Marcus Cunningham shrugged and wiggled his hand in the air. After a few moments of reflection, his thick body started to shake again with laughter. "Why not?" he howled. "By damn let's do it! Otherwise, the police will be throwing me in the clinker in a matter of days—not weeks, not months, not years. *Days, man!* I'm a candidate for a first-degree murder rap right now. Clay, my friend, if you can get Frank Creuthop off my back, I'll put you in my fucking will!"

7

E wen Leetboer didn't ponder long when Clayborn Redmond laid out a smorgasbord of opportunities he'd uncovered at the Xanadu Shopping Mall. The situation sounded tailor-made for Ewen's purposes. A nine percent interest in the enterprise, even at fair market, was about right. It would put him inside at threshold cost and when further deterioration occurred, as he foresaw through his infallible clockwork prisms, he'd increase his holdings at ten cents on the dollar.

"Why do these three partners want to sell?" Ewen kept asking. "Tell me again . . ."

He and Clay were walking on the beach near his mansion. It was close to sunset, which meant that Vanessa would soon join them to engage in her nightly peek for the illusory green flash said to be sometimes visible just above the arc of the setting sun as it sank below the sea.

"They need the money," Clay replied, kicking at a conch shell in the sand and spying around for Vanessa.

He didn't consider his answer a lie, not a lie of fraudulent proportions at any rate. Everybody needs money, he reasoned. Not everybody needs a Frank Creuthop to micromanage an asset valued at over a hundred million dollars, especially a jewel like Xanadu.

To the broker's relief Ewen Leetboer didn't ask about Frank. Besides, even if it were a lie, Clay Redmond meant to kill the chiseler anyway, so what did a little fib matter? Failure to disclose pursuant to statutory law? Disclose what? Who but a fool would blame him for failing to disclose murderous intent? Fibs were irrelevant. Murder always took precedence over those fine ethical lines drawn by racketeers, legislators and real estate bureaucracies.

"I see," Ewen said.

"Make the offer attractive, Ewen," Clay advised. "The major partner hates bottom fishers. He can veto third parties. If you want in this partnership, don't fool around. Pay the price. No loop-hole contingencies, no refundable deposits after a three-day look at the books. Present yourself as a serious buyer and all will go well."

"I see," Ewen said. He raised his eyes to the sky and squeezed gently around his Adam's apple, pondering, careful to avoid an anxious run of fingers through his toupee. "Good," he resumed moments later with quiet dignity. "I will have Stanley draw up a contract."

Clay gritted his teeth. His eyes squinched together like Reverend Pat Robertson's in prayer mode while his head rocked side to side in a steady, protracted movement. "*Shit!*" he mumbled.

"Is something wrong? What did you say?"

"Shorthand. I was thinking in shorthand."

"And what were you thinking?"

"I was thinking: Forget about Stanley if you want to own a piece of Xanadu," Clay Redmond snapped without altering his facial expression. "That frigging attorney can screw up a two-car funeral faster than Frank Creuthop!"

"Creuthop?" the Dutchman said, feigning a smear of serious interest. "Who is Creuthop? A partner?"

"What is Creuthop you mean. You'll find out soon enough." Leetboer shrugged. He appeared to enjoy Clay's snippy burst of emotion. It made him feel in charge. The broker's apparent slip of tongue about Creuthop also had the ring of useful discovery.

"But . . . the documents . . . ?"

"Xanadu will provide its own paperwork," Clay answered. "Later you can ask Stanley to review the package if you like. Just be sure you instruct him to lay off his usual cute crap. First you must submit to an interview. One of the partners will want to know how long your bottom line is, probably your dick as well, so be prepared for aggressive interrogation."

Leetboer's face smeared over again, this time with unfeigned surprise. "You must be kidding!" he snorted. "Who is this partner? Does he hold controlling interest?"

"No, but close. The bastard has a way of controlling things nevertheless. Thinks like Rush Limbaugh—that he's on loan from God, a modern-day Jesus Christ. His name is Frank Creuthop, the guy we were just talking about. Be careful with Frank, Ewen. He's a real stinker. He'll try his damndest to scare you off. Frank Creuthop wants the interest of these three selling partners for himself, which would give him absolute control, but the old blowhard can't afford it right now."

"I see," Leetboer said, smiling behind tight lips. He slapped his knees and stared with walleyed candor at Clay. "Well, then, let's get on with business. Bring me the package!"

"I saw it, I saw it!" Vanessa shouted in a delightful effusion, appearing suddenly in front of them and pointing toward the sunset. *"The green flash—I saw it! I really did—oh wowee!"*

The frantic woman ran between the two men and grabbed each one's arm while she bounced out her excitement. Clay felt a rosiness in her touch. Some of the curls of her long, bushy red hair left an intoxicating fragrance on his shoulder when her head swung wildly or leaned fleetingly against him. A special warmth, flushed and ardent, oozed out of the Venusian structure of her body, through the Swedish bikini, across the nearness. He wondered if Ewen felt the same heat.

"Welcome to the club," Clay said to Vanessa. "Not many can willingly suspend disbelief like the poet—"

"What do you disbelieve?" Vanessa interrupted, her face bubbling with playful expectancy.

"Not you!" Clay answered. He waved his hand toward a marvelous afterglow which had taken shape on the western horizon. "I'm sure he would advise as much under these rather awesome, tropical circumstances. The poor souls who fail to heed such advice will continue to miss out on wonder after wonder, not merely the wonder you just observed. They say the green flash favors Irish ladies, that it's a shamrock of sorts which, if you're lucky enough to see it and make a wish at that very moment, will bring about a major

change in your life . . . something good . . . something you might already have wished for . . ."

Vanessa's emerald eyes locked on Clay, gleaming with curiosity. Her lips, full and moist and packed to the paint line with deadly temptation, seemed to be wishing for him right then. It didn't matter that Clay was only chattering, blowing off some of his melodious small talk, even making up stories about the green flash. Simply put, his voice sounded the sort of deep masculine tones that pleased her ears. His words resonated with romantic distinction; his presence—strong, knowledgeable, virile—unleashed feelings inside her body complementary to vibrant womanhood.

Ewen Leetboer knitted his brows. "Rubbish," he said, unaware of the dynamic but silent interactions pulsing around him. "Bring me the Xanadu package, Mr. Redmond, and I will flash some green for you that always works, always makes wishes come true."

"Touché," Clay responded behind a faint, cynical grin.

Leetboer eyed him for a moment then smiled. "Very wise," he retorted. "Too bad you didn't say touché before suing me. Think of the money we both would have saved."

Had the automatic been in Clay Redmond's pocket where, by Remington's own definition, it belonged, he might have had a difficult time resisting the impulse to dispense a few slugs in Leetboer's direction instead of that lame, insipid, acquiescent gesture of surrender. *Touché my ass*, Clay thought. To make matters worse, he'd humored the crafty old fox in front of Vanessa, who had no reason to catch the subtle differences between a gibe and a kowtow and might later tease him and try to decorate his big nose with chocolate icing. The gibe of choice, though, was not even apparent to Leetboer, who hardly flinched when Clay recited the tycoon's own pet phrase.

"Business is business. Right, Ewen?"

"Exactly right, yes. Now what news have you from Havana?"

Silvio brought his brother Ramón to the Versailles for another meeting with Clay Redmond. Ramón was a few years older, deeply tanned, taller and quite a bit thinner than Silvio, perhaps from spending so much time in Cuba, where the Horn of Plenty did not often toot these days. His face bore the sharp, solemn cast of a man of dedication and honor but also one besieged by too many frustrations, one too laden with stress.

New information had surfaced since Ramón's last trip over from Havana and the two brothers wanted to discuss an exciting development at Varadero which might interest Clay even more than a package of investments along the Malecón. Varadero was a resort city east of Havana, a kind of showcase "reservation" where foreign tourists were herded together and entertained lavishly to avoid an embarrassment of poverty elsewhere. It was Castro's way of sweeping the pitiful condition of the rest of the country under his national rug. To stretch the point, the resort initiative was born out of the Party's hope that tourists would bring needed dollars to the island and, in the spirit of *double play*, take away from Varadero favorable impressions of the communist regime. Such planning might be described as wonderfully bureaucratic in concept, although not all foreign tourists were content to remain on the regime's reservation during the entirety of their stay in Cuba.

The three men sat in the back dining room at a private table away from the noisy crowd and the pawing throng of Silvio's many greeters. Clay ordered *mojitos* and while they were waiting for the drinks, they chatted idly but nervously about the "old days" and about the risks they had taken going in and out of Cuba with phony passports and in small, overcrowded boats. An assortment of Cuban decor in the dining room prompted a few comments and appeared to soften Ramón's otherwise somber mood. To add his own touch, Silvio managed a sigh of gratitude when the waitress returned with doubles and a basket of fried green bananas. Clay surmised that Ramón's latest clandestine voyage across the Florida Straits had not been a pleasant one. The brothers both seemed eager for rum. They looked hungry, too.

"It will not be possible for your client to deal directly with Castro," Silvio said. The skin around his eyes crinkled as he glanced at Clay Redmond. He turned to his brother for confirmation. Ramón's head wagged in agreement.

"Not at first, no," Ramón said, his voice chocked with dreary undertones. "Maybe later . . . maybe . . . if the reports about your client's wealth are good."

"Not to worry," Clay answered with a shrug. "He's so rich he stinks. As for a meeting with Castro, or *no* meeting as you put it, I'm not surprised. Relax, fellows. I never believed for a minute you could pull *that* caper off. Heads of state surely must have bigger fish to fry."

"Yes," Silvio responded, "but Fidel may assign subordinates to work with us."

"Who? Carlos?"

"Perhaps not the vice president."

"Ricardo? Raúl?"

"Perhaps not the leader of Parliament either, or Castro's brother, but someone in authority for sure."

Clay rubbed his forehead. He hemmed and squinted in thought, but his eyes remained focused on Silvio. "Maybe we don't need anyone in authority," Clay said. "The *appearance* of authority will do. The Miami group has put together some nice investment packages. I can deal with them eyeball to eyeball but the packages are predicated on a free Cuba. That means no Castro, no communism. Those prerequisites could take years. I know it hurts your feelings for me to admit such a thing, but the dictator's name lends immediate authority to my project. Dammit, guys, I want Fidel Castro involved in my deal—and *now*, not twenty years from now after he's carried out of the Revolutionary Palace on a stretcher."

Silvio and Ramón glanced at each other, exchanging nervous, fretful smiles. "Not possible," Silvio repeated. "No way, José. Forget it."

"Listen to me, *hermanos*! Castro will sanction a wealthy investor, right?"

Silvio hesitated for a moment, scratching his head and crinkling his lips. "Yes, true. Castro approves every investor. Also each partnership with Cuba."

"Good. That's all we need. Let subordinates take care of the early work. Castro will invite himself into the picture later. I'll bet the plantation on it."

Ramón began to fidget. He glanced around the dining room, his eyes settling on three patrons, men, who had taken a table in the opposite corner nearest to them. "We could all be shot!" he whispered in shrill and spirited animation. "Including you, Clay Redmond, if you come with us!" The frail man swigged the last of the *mojito* then slammed the glass down on the table. "Sudden death—*pronto* and period! *Comprendes?*"

"Ramón—*por favor!*" Silvio said, patting his brother's arm. He turned to Clay. "You must forgive Ramón," he continued. "Last night—"

"Silvio—not now—" Ramón interrupted sharply.

"*Yes, now!*" Silvio replied.

The two brothers stared at each other before Silvio resumed. "Yes, now," he repeated, softer in tone, then turned back to Clay. "Ramón's boat was chased by the Cuban Coast Guard and fired upon. One of the crew—Manolito, a close friend—was hit. He fell into the sea. Ramón could not get back to him in time, could not . . . the Cuban boat was there—"

"Manolito is dead!" Ramón interrupted again, and more sharply. "My friend swam with blood gushing from his leg until the sharks took him. The searchlight kept missing us in the fog but I saw it in the reflection . . . saw Manolito's arms in one quick moment go high in the air, grasping at the sky, saw him pulled under without a sound. Manolito would not call out for help and risk our safety. He was not afraid of the sharks but he was always afraid—if the Cuban police caught him—that they would torture every inch of his body until he revealed whatever they asked, whatever he knew. His beautiful conscience would not allow him to endanger the rest of us, though. On this last trip he told me he would rather die than suffer in Castro's cruel prisons. It was a sign."

"I'm sorry," Clay said. "You should have spoken up sooner."

"Why bother you. You would worry and try to come back with me. These are the risks we take."

"*Damn*! What a night you must have had! Is there anything I can do?"

Ramón shook his head wearily. "Nothing," he said, then added, "unless you can spare a million dollars." Ramón tried to laugh at himself, at the spontaneous afterthought, but his dark face covered over right away with the same stressful look he had brought to the Versailles. "The underground needs money," he went on. "If my boat . . . if even a better engine, a faster one, Manolito would still be alive today."

Clay kept thinking about the sharks, but it was Leetboer he saw swimming among them, not Ramón's loyal friend Manolito. The old Dutchman had a .50 caliber hole in his chest and he was still swimming, still yelling his head off for Stanley B. Conover to come and negotiate with the sharks! For some reason Clay Redmond's imagination would not let those terribly awesome, predatory jaws pull Leetboer under, even though he could not quit thinking about Manolito and the water closing over him. Maybe it was because Manolito's act was a brave, unselfish one deserving more respect, more honored remembrance. To corrupt this heroic image by injecting Ewen Leetboer's ugly, chiseling mug into the scene would be a sacrilege, an affront to Manolito's memory, an insult to the Free-Cuba movement.

"Gentleman," Clay Redmond said, "If you don't mind, I'm going to order another round of *mojitos* and three big bowls of *sopa de pollo*. You're my guests. It would please me very much if we all ate steak and potatoes as well . . . and a Caesar salad, some dessert. Maybe a big meal will help us get past that terrible scene, at least for the moment."

He called the waitress and placed the order while the two brothers studied faces in the dining room and conferred with each other regarding the three men sitting at the corner table.

"Tourists from Italy," Silvio whispered to Ramón. "They must be, they're speaking Italian."

"Yes, I hear them now," Ramón said, relaxing.

Silvio and Ramón turned back to Clay after the waitress left with his sizeable order. It was enough to make them both stammer and gaze and nod at their friend. Silvio whipped out a hundred-dollar bill and laid it on the table but Clay shoved it back at him.

"Graciela," he said. "Let Ramón give it to the family when he returns."

Ramón grabbed the bill as if it might be a wild card in a friendly game of poker. "I will put it in the hands of our mother next week," he said, glaring at them with stern, determined eyes.

Clay seemed relieved. He knew that time was the scarce commodity, time and survival equipment, not petty cash for dinner, at least not in Miami. On the island, yes. Sometimes the Cuban brothers kept too busy to sit long at a table. Sometimes their appetites were lost in sadness for one reason or another, as now. But Clay insisted that they stop running long enough to eat, and if possible, stop feeling sad for an hour.

"I have an idea," Clay said as they settled into their meals. "Silvio, you and Ramón say you need a million dollars. Okay, I need something, too. Not money though. Maybe we can help each other."

"Only tell us what you need," Silvio said. His dark eyes blinked with a kind of pleasurable impatience, full of wonder and readiness. "*¿Qué quieres, amigo?* What? You are always helping us but you never ask for anything but a few names and numbers. Nothing big and solid, nothing we can do with our hands, our hearts, our minds. Tell us, Clay Redmond! In the name of Graciela, tell us! Her voice cries out from the grave. 'Find him a good woman, he mustn't be alone' she says. We are simple men but let us try to help."

Clay remembered times when one or the other of the two brothers had made this same speech. He rallied a smile and appeared grateful for the gesture Silvio had now made once again, and a little embarrassed by the attention.

"Graciela is not an easy woman to replace," Clay Redmond said, trying not to sound sentimental. "I've met someone, though. Really, guys, I'm working on it."

The two brothers nodded. At first they seemed doubtful but something resembling a faint spread of relief then crept over their faces. "Our mother will be pleased to hear this," Silvio remarked.

"True," Ramón added. "It has been fourteen years. Too often I still hear her say that you must not continue to live your life knowing only loose women."

"Give mama my love," Clay responded, then turned the conversation back to the mission. Now it was time to put his planning skills to the test. He released his spoon into the bowl, folded his arms and stared back and forth at the two bothers. They hovered over their plates, staring back, waiting for the words that seemed to be caught in Clay's throat.

After a lengthy silence Clay said, "Ramón, tell me about this Varadero project you mentioned earlier with such gusto."

"*Mara Paradiso* . . . ! Yes, of course," Ramón replied sadly. "Another Taj Mahal it was going to be in honor of a woman, a beautiful palace for tourists. Such a pity!"

"What happened to the developer?"

"Ah—the Spaniard!—Señor Valdez. 'El Cojonudo' they call him. He went broke. Castro seized the project."

"Then it's not dead?"

"No, but Castro is broke, too. He has no dollars to finish it. They say he's looking for another developer to take over but the word is out everywhere. Nobody will touch it—afraid of the Spaniard. Castro had to deport him back to Madrid to convince interested parties he would protect them from the danger they feared, but El Cojonudo casts a long shadow. Everybody is still afraid to take on the Señor's project because it is named in honor of his woman . . . his beautiful *Mara*, who now lives in Paradise. Sooner or later her awesome defender will carve the heart out of anyone who does. They all know it's true."

Clay soaked up every word, tweaking his big nose while Ramón described Mara Paradiso. Aside from a grand mausoleum, plans included an elaborate network of condominiums, shops, night clubs, theaters, restaurants, even chapels. Over two thousand units, some high rise, some ocean front, some golf front, some tucked privately into lush tropical jungle settings complete with howler monkeys to serenade tourists during dusk and pre-dawn hours.

"It will cost a half billion, maybe a billion dollars," Silvio explained.

He too was showing much interest in Mara Paradiso. Even his fellow exiles followed the stories as news filtered in from Cuba, mostly out of curiosity about the man called El Cojonudo but also to keep track of foreign investors and lay plans to take revenge against collaborators later on.

"The Spaniard has put enormous sums in the project already," Ramón said. "Rumors speak of Mafia money behind him. The drug cartel also. No one can understand it—or the Mafia, the cartel—why there is no more money to continue, only debts and workers and suppliers yet to be paid. It is in big turmoil. One day when Cuba is again free, maybe *Mara Paradiso* will become a reality, not just for tourists but Cubans as well. Ah, such a beautiful concept, such a magnificent dream!"

Clay dipped into his *sopa de pollo* again. His mind was racing. What a superb prospect—Leetboer and El Cojonudo in a face-off at this budding Shangri-La called Mara Paradiso!

"My good brothers," Clay Redmond said, his face beginning to ripple with devilish smiles, "after all our collaborations in the past, it would be an insult to you both if I asked for your confidence now. We've been through one hell of a lot together, you've always protected me."

The two men returned quizzical looks. "Now, Clay," Silvio chided, "What is this bullshit you are trying to feed us with the *sopa de pollo*?"

Clay's head rolled back from the force of his laughter. "Okay, guys, I didn't mean to shovel it on you so thick. What I'm trying to say is not easy for me. Look, I know that you know how to keep a secret, so let's not waste time with turd talk. Here's the plan: my client, Ewen Leetboer, may hold the solution to both our problems. You need a million dollars, I need to know how long Ewen Leetboer can stay afloat in deep doo-doo. This Spaniard—El Cojonudo—sounds like a man with answers."

The two brothers stopped eating. They glanced at each other, then back at Clay Redmond, whose face was beginning to erupt again with the old vengeful, wrinkly smiles.

"We don't understand," Ramón said. "You wish something *bad* to happen to your client?"

"Why not? He's a bad man—a rich bad man who cheats his partners. Let's say I want to save him from more sin."

"Oh," Ramón uttered. "Another beast!" He paused and studied Clay's face. "What is your plan, brother?"

"Leetboer craves a sweetheart deal in Cuba. Ramón, you still have contacts over there. You know professionals from one end of the island to the other. Can you set up a fake office in Havana, staff it with a couple of those gorgeous Tropicana dancers and someone who knows legal lingo, who can pass as an authority on Cuban real estate? Someone like you, for instance."

Ramón grunted. "For a million dollars? Sure, sure, no problem!"

"You don't believe me?"

Ramón scratched his head and mumbled across the table, but after a bit he beckoned to Silvio for the right words.

Silvio answered for him. "We believe you but—"

"But you need more details," Clay said, interrupting and chuckling in loud blasts, not because of the strained looks on the faces of Silvio and Ramón but over the visions of Leetboer strangling in an Olympic-size pool of diarrheal discharge. "Sure you do," he continued. "Forgive me. If I can round up a million dollars for each of you, will you help me pull off a sting operation? You know—like in the movie with Paul Newman and Robert Redford?"

Ramón's sad face began to brighten. "*Two* million dollars?" he said with hesitation, stammering and mumbling at Silvio in Spanish.

"Two million dollars—one apiece. Will you help me?"

The brothers both seemed stricken, tongue-tied. Silvio recovered his voice first. "Does a barracuda eat fish?" he said, easing into his former poise. "Of course we will help you! What is this . . . this *sting*, brother?"

9

Silvio and Ramón left Clay standing beside *El Toro* in the parking lot of the Versailles. They came on foot and soon disappeared down *Calle Ocho*, heading west. The two Cubans had parked somewhere else, for safety reasons. Most everybody in Miami's Little Havana assumed that Castro sent spies to the city to infiltrate the various organizations suspected of plotting against him, to eavesdrop, to keep tabs on the "gusano" movements, and certainly to search out and kidnap his designated "traitors." Refugees and *exiliados* who fled their homeland but who continued to parade patriotic personas through the streets of Miami—at times even inside Cuba itself while claiming to be on family mercy missions—were anointed with this odious term, were called *gusanos* by the dictator, and *worms* by his generals who could speak English.

Particularly obnoxious to Castro were those *gusanos* who never fled, who still lived in the country and enjoyed credibility as Cuban citizens but whose real purpose was to engage in sabotage, espionage and other counterrevolutionary activities on behalf of the Cuban-American front based in South Florida. Ramón was one of these.

Unlike his brother, Silvio could not operate openly in Cuba. He had been granted citizenship in the United States and traveled with a U.S. passport. On special occasions Silvio slipped inside Cuba to participate with Ramón in some bit of underground work but after the assignment was completed, Silvio would leave on the first pick-up boat available. The sight of Old Havana—the decay, the rot, the faded opulence, the broken windows, the chipped and pitted walls of those magnificent structures of history—sickened him to the core. The sad, vacuous faces of the occupants sickened him also, those voiceless, befuddled "people's people" who had no idea how to maintain the rich properties into which they had been thrust by no claim of their own. Money was not even an issue, although they possessed none of that either. The people's people whom Silvio observed didn't really live but *languished* within extraordinary interiors still graced with traces of splendor, languished and presided over deterioration at an accelerating rate. Cigar hustlers overran the streets, approaching all who looked foreign with their trays and pricey assortments. The people's people lolled out into the streets with them, through huge doors—beautifully crafted doors that should not have to endure their loathsome scars or sag on loose, rusty hinges. Old and young alike went about their daily commerce with the air of monkeys in a zoo, caught up in the high drama of sounds and movements as they scratched themselves in aimless distraction and waited on corners for nothing and no one or sat in a slump on their haunches and gazed through the invisible bars around them, watching anything and everything with myopic eyes full of pathetic wonder.

It all sickened Silvio too much to remain longer than necessary. More than any other assignment, he wanted from his fellow exiles a role in the city's restoration when democracy returned to the island nation. Beauty was still evident to those who loved Cuba and remembered her better days. Even those who didn't remember could still catch glimpses of bygone grandeur, could "feel" the centuries of elegance lying buried beneath the dirt and squalor swept in by a ruthless tenancy.

It was one of the world's grandest cities Silvio had said in the parking lot minutes earlier. Havana now suffered like an abused woman, starved for warm hands again, caring hands that would clean its horrible wounds, dress its scarred and unsightly façades, lift it out of the death throes brought about by forty years of malpractice and shameful violation. In Silvio's restored city, lights would come back on at night, glow in every corner, and people would dance in the streets once again.

Clay drove out of the parking lot feeling in high spirits over his meeting with Silvio and Ramón. Those two Cubans were already his good friends. Now they were going beyond the call of friendship, beyond the limits of polite association into the deeper waves of human design where casual friends didn't usually swim together. But the brothers never doubted that they would profit according to the risk. Clay Redmond was a man of his word, as generous in rewarding merit as Ewen Leetboer was in punishing mistakes. The money would come from somewhere but, unlike their gringo friend, they didn't expect it to come from a "Dutch treat," as Clay joked about. No acquaintance in his right mind would believe Ewen Leetboer fool enough to finance the cost of all these intrigues against him, these gathering premeditations.

That evening Clay flicked on the late news to relax his mind before turning in for the night, to free it of the usual worries that fate might have placed someone else's designs on Ewen Leetboer's scalp ahead of his own. The Israelis and Palestinians were back in the spotlight again. Somehow they managed to make headline news even without bombing each other. This time they had merely agreed to resume peace talks. As Clay watched the two sides posture for the cameras, watched them step forward and shake hands like bosom buddies, he wondered if he too shouldn't put the old Dutchman behind him, take his losses and pray to the Forces he never made the same mistake in character judgment again. If Arabs and Jews could kiss and make up, then why not Clayborn Redmond and Ewen Leetboer? But the wonder was short-lived, no less brief, Clay Redmond figured, than the time it took for the spirit of Oslo and Camp David to pass through the hearts of those two bitter enemies he was watching on TV.

Besides, there was Vanessa to think about. And Silvio and Ramón and Marcus Cunningham. They each had a stake in Clay Redmond's plans now. Vanessa just didn't know it yet. In time he would bring her into his confidence. At the moment he simply didn't know how to tell the woman that he intended to relieve her of her husband by violent means. Should he forewarn her, seek her help, or stick to post-mortems? How in the world could he talk of such brutality in the presence of that luscious leprechaun, that sprite from the sylvan glens of Erin whose visions danced through his head at night and frolicked in his dreams wearing gossamer gowns that seduced his subconscious with brief, loin-jarring exposés of lady fair. The very telling to her of his intended deed posed a challenge equally as difficult as the deed itself.

Yet common decency—if the term might be applied to his uncommon case—compelled him to find a way. An affair, he thought, seemed worth the try. It was not human frailty at work in his head but visions of her humanity rescuing his human condition. He'd long fantasized about it, had *serialized* each move, had sequenced it in his mind to yield the most delightful outcome, if not the greatest promise of success. In his reverie Clay Redmond imagined that Mrs. Leetboer was not fully absorbed in her marriage. At times he supposed he *did* detect cross words between her and her husband, did notice icy stares. Something to do with the prenuptial agreement Clay gathered after hearing the words bantered about on one of his recent visits, and so he resolved to pay more attention to spousal exchanges in the future.

Yes, he supposed, the seams were fraying, if not already in tatters. Something was out of whack in that relationship. Clay figured Leetboer had probably cheated her some way, an inference easily drawn from having been cheated by the same S.O.B. As he saw it, Leetboer deserved to have his wife seduced. In today's loose world where respect for the Seven Deadly Sins had grown like topsy over the past fifty years, an affair offered yet another way for both lovers to sweeten the pot, to add to their respective balance sheets in their quest for equity. But this scheme was only a prelude, not a replacement of Clay's more lethal plan for reckoning with Ewen Leetboer. Perhaps a tryst or two in Vanessa's Coral Gables penthouse would shed some light on her personal views, her private gripes. A wedge was all he needed to open the dialogue. The pretty woman had already invited him to drop by and help her clear up some of the mysteries at Bella Mar, explain the by-laws, walk her through the clubhouse, label the switch-box breakers, show her how to work the burglar alarm, the intercom, and so on. Clay decided to start there and, if Vanessa were as receptive to his advances as her eyes suggested, he'd refine his plan as they went along.

"Next Friday will be okay," Marcus Cunningham said, grunting and breathing noisily into the phone. "That is, if you need a week to bring your 'darling' to the table."

Clay grunted back. He was still in his apartment pulling facts and figures off the Internet and making long-distance calls before the eight o'clock premium hour kicked in for the day. "Ewen's no darling," he quipped, "only married to one. But the guy's a perfect match for Creuthop. Are you sure Frank will remember? He's prematurely senile, you know."

"Now, Clay, you know Frank's not senile. Definitely penile, though, as in prick."

Clay uttered agreement. "Okay, good distinction," he said. "Look, I'd appreciate it if you'd support me in my analysis first, before you let the gospel truth out of the bag in front of Leetboer. Senility was just a tidbit of *mis*-information I dropped on him to whet his appetite for another steal. Made him smile big. Yeah.

Damned if he doesn't seem more interested in Creuthop now than he is in the three selling partners. By the way, where are you as we speak?"

"In the fucking office, where else?"

"I thought so," Clay said, smirking to himself over the possibilities behind Marcus Cunningham's answer.

"You dialed me, didn't you? Look what time it is! For Christ's sake, Redmond—!"

"Hold it, buddy! I know you go to work early. Did I interrupt something? Sorry. Say hello to Heather."

"Knock it off! She's out."

"Out?"

"Making a postoffice run! What kind of question is that anyway? What the hell's going on, fellow?"

Clay leaned back in his swivel chair, swinging side to side while he listened to Marcus Cunningham. It amused as well as impressed him that Marcus was breathing so heavily, like he'd been jogging or just coming out of an orgasm. They're banging again, Clay thought. My burley friend is in his fucking office all right. Yeah, and maybe Heather had to run home for a quick shower on her way to the post office at seven thirty in the morning. What a life.

"Relax, Marcus," he said, sliding into a laugh. "This deal with Leetboer and the three selling partners is between you and me right now. Okay? I wouldn't trust my mother to keep it a secret for a whole week. Besides, Heather's too charming, too efficient. She'd have Frank lined up to kiss Leetboer's ass the minute he walked in your conference room. I'd like that screwball to stay in character, act natural. You know—piss Leetboer off ahead of schedule. It'll speed things up."

For a fleeting moment Marcus Cunningham's voice rolled with the spontaneous gush of solid, body-healing laughter. He liked to hear Clay use profanity with him. It added cement to their friendship. Gave him that birds-of-a-feather feeling, especially when they swapped expletives that modified Frank Creuthop's image in uncomplimentary but true-to-life ways.

"Okay, pal," he said. "Let's get it on. You'll not have a speck of trouble with me. I want that fat-ass Creuthop out of my hair at any cost. You know Frank. Are you sure your man Leetboer will be able to stomach the crotchety old bastard long enough to close this deal?"

"Hell yes, Marcus!" Clay exclaimed. "Ewen Leetboer enjoys showing off his immunity to insults. He came in the world sideways, not head first like a respectable fetus, not even feet first. *Sideways*, man! And the sidewinding son of a bitch has been shoving and gouging ever since, even laughing at his adversaries and bragging about his granite head, his steel-plated rib cage, his galvanized stomach. The only thing that turns it, by the way, that gives him a granite headache and melts those steel plates guarding his heart is a bad investment, which is to say one that won't quadruple his money in less than a year."

Marcus laughed again, stretching and expanding the rhythm of high-pitched staccato chuckles as grotesque caricatures of Clayborn Redmond's client flitted through his mind.

"Man, I can't wait," he shouted over the phone, "to meet this asshole client of yours. But, Clay, in all honesty I'm afraid this mall won't appreciate fast enough to suit Leetboer's aggressive style, not if he pays fair market."

"I told him fair market but what if he doesn't agree to pay fair market?"

"Then no deal."

"Told him that, too."

"Yeah. Frank will coldcock it with his usual shenanigans. He'll tie up negotiations, drag out the first-right provision in our partnership agreement. The old grouch will finger-wave paragraphs all morning. He'll stall and pussyfoot around with stupid questions until your man either empties the contents of his galvanized stomach on Frank's silver-threaded pompadour or just shakes his dick at all of us and walks away—maybe smiling, as you say, but with his granite head swinging sideways right along with his dick."

"Uh-huh," Clay muttered. "A fair appraisal, yeah. But don't worry about Leetboer. He's bastard enough himself to survive Frank. Can't say how much longer he'll survive after the closing, though."

"Who? Frank or Leetboer?"

Clay chewed on his lower lip for a moment. "Maybe both," he replied, "if we're lucky."

Marcus Cunningham lapsed into another intense chuckle, which was already in progress before Clay spoke. The sound of his breathing blew unpleasantly through Clay's earpiece. Then, following a weary sigh, Marcus continued with his previous comments.

"The selling partners are less firm on the fair market issue, of course. Those guys simply want out. They'll take an offer, you damn right they will, even a lowball, but our resident shithead is the mother of all deal killers, don't forget, and he'll kill this one, too. Sorry you have to spin your wheels, pal."

"You may be overlooking a critical point," Clay said, his voice faltering. He rose from his swivel chair and gazed up through an overhead skylight, then strode with phone in hand toward a shoe-box balcony adjacent to the living room of his tidy bachelor's apartment. Clay's mind began to wander. Leetboer flew to Canada this morning, he mused. Took Stanley B. Conover with him in the Clockwork, Inc. jet but no one else. Clay studied the sky. It seemed the kind of dismal, overcast day to spend with Vanessa over at her Coral Gables condo where he might bathe his spirits in her radiance, cheer himself under the aura of feminine mystique, enliven his illusions about romantic seduction. All the talk concerning Ewen Leetboer had begun to fan the old coals of anger smoldering inside of him. He knew he had to control it, had to put the skids on his temper and, either by coincidence or by the luck of the Irish, Vanessa possessed underneath her gossamer gown the ideal throttle valve.

"Hello? Clay? *Clay?*" Marcus Cunningham boomed over the phone. "What's this 'critical point' shit? Are you still there for Christ's sake or is my fucking phone dead?"

"I'm here," Clay shouted back, recovering his former train of thought. "Just thinking," he went on. "Leetboer won't quibble over the cost of a small beneficial interest in Xanadu. That's just seed money to set him up with voting privileges. Hell, Marcus, he flew out of Miami this morning in his corporate jet, heading for Canada to arrange a money transfer. Nine percent is peanuts to him, below or above market. He'll buy in spite of the Creuthop shuffle. You'll see. Old Frank might as well go ahead and have his heart attack now. Don't you forget either—Ewen Leetboer makes his money by screwing his partners. Appreciation is too slow."

"Screw him!" Marcus responded with a snort. "Listen, Clay, Leetboer will have the screwing privilege with one partner and one partner only—Frank Creuthop. Let him screw that bastard all he wants!"

"I have a better idea," Clay answered, gazing again at the dismal, overcast sky outside. His thoughts had returned to the gorgeous Irish lady, Vanessa, who seemed to be taunting him again via telepathic transmission, inviting him to drop by for a noon sandwich or something. "See you next week," he added, then cradled the phone before Cunningham could ask what.

10

S oon after the purchase Vanessa Leetboer developed a curious fascination for her penthouse condominium at the Bella Mar complex, the only real estate she owned with title solely in her name. In a word, it was the *only* material asset she could truly call hers other than bits and pieces of jewelry, remnants of a trousseau, a small but well chosen collection of books and CDs, and a few household objects which she had brought into the marriage. Even the Jaguar she drove belonged to some obscure entity named in a blind trust by Stanley B. Conover for legal reasons, to protect Leetboer from "frivolous lawsuits" in case Vanessa precipitated a liability "situation," perhaps ran over some kid with fatal consequences.

To be sure, Vanessa was viewed as a wealthy woman, being married to Ewen Leetboer. Other women, some of them complete strangers, envied the young lady almost to the point of collapse once they established her connection to Ewen Leetboer, whom they did know. "Such a catch," they would say behind thin naughty smiles, for Vanessa looked more the age of a feisty daughter than the buxom, heavyweight wife they expected to see. She'd read their faces and smiled back, but the smiles grew increasingly phony, even deliberately phony. Her envious circle of status seekers, however, didn't seem alert to the similarities between modesty and Irish "put on." From Vanessa's perspective, whatever wealth they assumed she'd acquired by virtue of marriage belonged to a man who chose to mete out small sums to her in strict allowance format. For the purchase of such things as clothing and cosmetics—i.e., whatever dressed her up, made her look good in public—his budget restrictions were waived, charge accounts opened at exclusive shops and blank checks issued bearing the unique Ewen Leetboer pen swirl. Anything dealing with bodily enhancement automatically met Leetboer's criteria, which landed quite a number of fashion boutiques, "skin" parlors, aerobic centers and beauty salons on his approved list of accounts. To further pacify Vanessa, he made all the arrangements without question or argument.

The condo fell into a different category. Vanessa had lived under his roof for almost two years, so the old Dutchman concluded one day that his pretty wife had earned a promotion, could now be trusted to manage an asset, at least on a trial basis, provided it was wrapped up in some of Stanley B. Conover's "gift paper" and duly inscribed with one of his tricky reversion clauses in the event the experiment didn't pan out. Penthouse #9 was Leetboer's first attempt at such in-house philanthropy and the gesture straightaway proved to be a disappointment to him of substantial magnitude, enough so to prompt Stanley to comfort his client by reminding him of the reversion clause in Vanessa's deed, that it could be exercised any time after one "lunation" *or* upon dissolution of the marriage.

The cost of the condo hardly ruffled the digits in Ewen Leetboer's offshore checking account, certainly none of the trailing zeros. What disappointed him most of all was Vanessa's preoccupation with the "unit," as he put it, her exacerbating excuses that kept them from taking advantage of its erotic ambiance, from holding rendezvous there, from enjoying its exciting hotel atmosphere and engaging in kinky conduct like the manuals recommended for adventurous partners.

Excluding the day of purchase, and particularly that stormy afternoon when she and Ewen Leetboer first inspected the condo, she never went there with him again. He was such a goat about sex, such an ill-mannered glutton. His presence would spoil the magic of privacy, the illusion of innocence, and destroy a sense of sanctuary locked within the walls of her "darling penthouse," as she put it, which she put often in chit-chat with Clay Redmond to annoy her husband if he happened to be within earshot.

Underneath the façade of virtue Vanessa still harbored friendly suspicions about this engaging fellow with the big, fleshy somewhat phallic "proboscis," as she sometimes referred to his nose in jest, who was standing inside the place when they first met. There was an unmistakable charm in his eyes. Large, open and well set over his wide mouth and strong chin, their twinkling blueness executed all the smiles required by the rest of a pleasing face. They spoke mutely but explosively in a universal language, and right away she felt a man's gaze when he looked at her, a *real* man's, not a lecher's. The lip-smacks, mauls, hugs and amorous pinches of a horny husband that day didn't carry enough spousal weight to persuade her *not* to notice Clay Redmond back, notice how he just stood there in the living room with those engaging but roguish eyes blazing up in his head every time some inner impulse compelled her to glance past him.

Because she believed that Clay might have ordered an extra key after she'd asked to have the locks changed, it was an easy stretch to picture him again in there whenever she opened the door to her sanctuary. Vanessa secretly hoped that he had kept one but she hesitated to accuse him or ask point blank. A sudden, chance encounter inside the apartment struck her as a more exciting way to find out. Sometimes she would come rushing in to catch the sly rascal by surprise, then spy around behind the sofas, pull the drapes, peek into the shower stalls, check the closets, merrily expecting him to spring out and overpower her with his long hairy arms and engulf her with the sort of roguish gusto that she'd observed in his rough man's face the moment their eyes began to take each other's measure.

In spite of Ewen's constant reminders that the "unit" was meant to be an investment, not a sacred memorial, she objected to his rationale each time, choosing to call her "darling penthouse" bartered merchandise instead. Sometimes he invoked the argument of *gift*, which was not altogether sincere and promptly offended Vanessa. "The unit was intended as a *trinkgeld*," he'd say, then follow up with some cryptic Dutch chatter about an "unspoken proviso" and plunge into a monologue explaining his "standing conditions" whenever he gave presents to ladies.

Vanessa and Ewen Leetboer were alone at the South Beach mansion on the evening before his flight to Canada to make business arrangements for closing Xanadu. The subject of her condo was broached several times during dinner by her husband, then a trail of unanswered questions growing out of the subject followed them both with the persistence of a leash-drawn poodle after they left the table. Vanessa's red hair, piled in a bulky, disheveled mass on top of her head, imparted a devil-may-care attitude which was reinforced by a lack of make-up and a loose, paint-smeared, unflattering T-shirt she had donned in lieu of something more provocative. But she didn't wish to appear provocative. To him she looked rather sloven, grubby. Any one of her many outfits would have satisfied his mood that evening far better than that grungy, shapeless T-shirt she insisted on calling a dress. Ewen thought, *Does my lady not feel well?* Vanessa paid no attention to his queries. She buried herself in the netting of a hammock and commenced to swing back and forth and thumb noisily through a magazine while her frustrated husband kept trying to initiate a conversation.

Strong European accents sometimes induced her to listen, to *seem* interested, a discovery he'd made early on and employed here and there in different Germanic inflections, although that night his attempts appeared to be having no effect whatsoever. Leetboer continued to speak formally, father-like, but without signs of rancor. The more he tried to bring her about, the more convinced he became that her sloppy appearance did not please him, nor her aloof manner on the eve of his departure.

"It is your duty, Vanessa, my dear," Ewen remarked after he had pulled a patio lounge within speaking range, "your *duty . . .*"

For a moment she thought he was leading up to another proposition. "My duty *what*?" she said, droning irritably over his stammer without looking up from the magazine.

Leetboer adjusted his accent and pressed on, " . . . to accept the added obligation of course."

Vanessa turned her head away from the magazine and stared at Leetboer across the open space between them. "What obligation?" she asked in a crisp, impatient tone.

"Look it—what else? To manage my gifts with prudence, not profligacy."

Vanessa threw the magazine on the floor and intensified her chilly stare. "Don't be an ass, Ewen. Let me remind you of the price I've already paid for your so-called gift."

"Listen, my dear, we are losing income! It may be a small amount but business is business. Money can be made by renting the unit, at least through the winter season."

"Don't *we* have enough money for Heaven's sake?"

He laughed in a stiff, patronizing manner and wiggled his finger at her. "There's never *too much* money, my dear. We must be prepared for emergencies, must defend my wealth. Someone is always trying to take it away, making up reasons, suing me for big settlements. What if the world goes into another collapse like 1929? The banks will foreclose mortgages, some people will lose everything—"

"Let them jump out of a window."

"Some will but some will kill others, too, their bankers maybe, over big losses. Many poor souls—men, women, children—get in the way and become targets of enraged losers—"

"So what. Innocent people get killed every day."

"Maybe we lose everything for not saving more—"

"I don't care," Vanessa replied, turning away. "I refuse to allow strangers to sleep in my bedroom, to put their greasy heads on my pillows, slobber all over my Denby and stick my precious sterling in their mouths. God knows what kind of disease they may be carrying! Now leave me alone. Bella Mar is mine, remember." When Leetboer turned his dead pan toward her but said nothing, she glanced up and added, "You do remember, don't you?"

"Yes," he answered with a faint, ambivalent sigh.

"Can I do with it as I please?"

He thought for a moment, choosing his words. "The deed is in your name, yes."

"Good! Then it's settled. Please don't talk about it any more."

"Wait—this question," he said. "What do you plan to do with the unit? Sell it and give the money away to charities?"

Vanessa smirked but soon noticed the displeasure in Ewen Leetboer's eyes. "No," she replied, "I simply want a little Camp David of my own. Besides, it's not scary over there at night like it is here in this monster place. When you leave for Canada tomorrow, I'm going to stay there for the whole week you're gone! Maybe longer if you don't shut up."

Leetboer squinted at the floor. One of the tiles looked set in too deep. Such sloppy work annoyed him. He rubbed his temples and without looking at Vanessa said,

"Shall we move to the bedroom? It's getting late."

"No, not yet. I'd like to watch A & E for a while in the den. Go on to bed. You have a long day ahead tomorrow."

Leetboer sought to make eye contact but Vanessa had resumed turning the pages in another magazine and seemed deeply engrossed. "Yes," he said a minute or so later, "I think I will go upstairs now. Must pack a few things for the flight in the morning. We leave at seven-thirty. Are you sure you won't change your mind and come with us?"

"No," she said, almost whispering, but in a still frosty voice. "You know I can't stand that man."

"Stanley looks after my interests," he replied, perking up and seeming grateful for any response from Vanessa.

"Stanley looks after Stanley. You're just a big fat payday to him. He's a leech."

"Maybe. But a loyal leech. I don't trust the other lawyers. They're all friends of Clay Redmond."

Vanessa stared at her husband. "What's wrong with that?" she asked, fluttering her voice.

"Stanley keeps my business confidential."

"Fine. You and Stanley go have lots of private fun in Montreal or Toronto or wherever you're heading."

"It's a business trip, Vanessa! My goodness, do you think I go to see other women up there?"

Vanessa shrieked. Her eyes rolled and flattened into a blank stare as she gazed into the high screened structure enclosing the patio. "Honestly, Ewen, you amaze me! But at least the thought of another woman does seem possible, considering how you love to expose yourself in my presence. Yes, now that you mention it, maybe you should expand your ports. Just leave me here out of your way. I have some things to do at the apartment."

Vanessa's arm folded again over her eyes. She laid the magazine aside and pulled on a cord that made the hammock swing back and forth, fast at first then as it slowed to a soothing rhythm, she mumbled to herself and slipped into another silence. For a time Ewen Leetboer ran his shoe sole around the exposed edges of the four tiles joining the one set in too deep. A blankness as deeply set covered his face while he tarried longer, waiting for any further words from Vanessa. Hearing none, he soon stood erect and strode in rigid silence toward the living room, then up the stairway spiraling in the direction of their sleeping quarters.

The guard at the gate recognized Clay Redmond and waved him on through with a friendly smile. Clay drove around the spacious park-like setting of Bella Mar before pulling *El Toro* into a visitor space near the condo's luxuriant entrance. His eyes blazed up when he spotted Vanessa's white Jaguar parked under the auto shelter assigned to Penthouse #9. He had checked the South Beach mansion following his phone call to Marcus Cunningham earlier that morning, concluding that she must have come over shortly after her husband drove off for the airport. She's up there, he thought.

The sky was full of dark clouds but only a light drizzle had fallen. Nothing torrential like on the day Vanessa first came to see the penthouse. He wondered if she would still radiate with the same incredible beauty and amiable nature he remembered from that fateful afternoon.

Now it was one-thirty again in another afternoon. The gnawing passion for her during those long months had not mellowed into an attitude more gentlemanly and restrained. To the contrary, desire proved infectious, had grown stronger and spread, had overwhelmed nobler considerations.

Clay sat for a time, sliding his hands along the smooth leather-covered steering wheel and gazing out toward Biscayne Bay. Bella Mar featured a style of architecture and landscape reminiscent of Vizcaya, the beautiful old palace up South Miami Avenue that gave the city one of its grandest Mediterranean flavors. A true art museum even without the paintings and sculptures, Vizcaya had become a kind of muckety-muck mecca and watering hole for politicians from all corners of the world. Bella Mar evoked a sense of resplendence, too, a high-flying pride born of the same stuff as Vizcaya, and it shared a similar modern indulgence of the rich and famous, not to mention free-spirited visitors like Clay Redmond.

He acted curiously reluctant to move until the door handle responded to his touch. What are you waiting for? it asked. Clay had arisen at six to confirm the flight and watch the plane take off, saw Leetboer and Stanley B. Conover climb into the corporate jet, then he waited in the terminal until it rose high in the sky over Miami and disappeared in a northerly direction. If business is business according to the schedule, Leetboer would be out of town for a week.

Not just the door but the world seemed to open to Clay Redmond with one sudden bold twist on *El Toro's* handle. Without further pause he stepped out of the Jeep. The locks slammed down with the press of a button on his key ring. He gave the fender an affectionate pat, arranged the buttons on a new guayabera shirt and ambled toward Vanessa's condominium tower humming *Tus Ojos*.

11

Over the past few weeks signs of a man's presence had begun to crop up inside the condo. Large shoe impressions, or tracks, with pointed toes like the cowboy boots Clay wore, showed on the bedroom carpet. On more than one occasion sofa pillows had been moved around, placed in a different sequence than Vanessa preferred, and strange little objects kept appearing from time to time in catch-all bowls which she didn't recognize but which sparked certain comical images of pack-rat collectibles. Or, as she viewed it, a roguish man's little game of "guess who."

Vanessa wasn't at all frightened. The signs and evidence looked too benignly arranged to suggest a dangerous intruder, signs no doubt planted for easy discovery, like a virgin's clues to a mystery played out in the family room by teenagers who really craved more intimacy in their pastimes.

Clay did not knock. He used *his* key, the one he had sneaked, the one Vanessa suspected he carried in his pocket illegally. His timing was perfect, although more from luck than plan. She had just taken a long bubble bath, shampooed her hair and restored herself to the glamorous woman that Ewen Leetboer wanted so eagerly to see the night before but never saw because he could never see past her "grungy T-shirt" and defensive, don't-touch-me behavior.

Vanessa was sitting at the breakfast bar snacking on an early lunch. Her shoulders were swaying to the faint tropical beat of island music in the background. Then something less faint but no less musical began to rattle and clink in her ears, tell-tale sounds she'd been waiting to hear for much too long. Like a shot Vanessa was on her feet and approaching the foyer in a jubilant, frenzied bustle when the heavy entrance door swung open and then quickly shut, leaving Clay Redmond at last inside—alone with Mrs. Ewen Leetboer!

They both stopped a short distance from each other, their tongues frozen in silence, their bodies suspended in motionless but palpitating awareness not aesthetically different from two statues fixed in place yet with life bursting through blank, stony orbs and energized by flashes of anticipation so breath-taking that the only escape was to plummet into deeper arousal and follow the fiery trail set off by mutually lustful stares.

Clay moved first. He stepped—*oozed*—up in front of Vanessa, who seemed nailed to the floor. He stopped again, inches away. His hand reached out and moved over her face, pressing both cheeks as if to test reality. Her bushy red hair hung menacingly beautiful over her shoulders and looked like something straight out of a Disney animation. *As pretty as the picture she is*, Clay thought. His mind raced in every direction. He pushed some of the bushiness aside, around her left ear and felt the soft white lobe, rubbed it between his thumb and finger and squeezed it with gallant gentleness while peering down into eyes as emerald green and gaping as his were blazing blue and wide open at that ethereal moment when neither seemed able to speak what both knew already.

His boots lifted him forward, or appeared to, nudging him ahead in a mighty effort to close the gap between them. The tips of their noses jousted briefly, then waved and circled around and met and brushed and then circled back again for another joust before the slow, inexorable facial drift ended. Their movements resembled a digitized performance. Two heads looked to be engaged in a synchronized slow-motion tango. Each head appeared somehow independent of its body, while both bodies floated like wispy jetsam lost among the stars. In another sense, perhaps by means of some time-warp technology, the pair, having been caught in a director's net and thrust into an old silent screen drama, were performing a love scene in a state of deep-space weightlessness. All of a sudden red-hot lips coalesced over glowing embers of desire and set off an explosion of magical sweetness so powerful and compelling that neither Clay nor Vanessa could seem to kiss enough of it away from the other's face.

Without relinquishing their embrace, the mesmerized couple began to sway to their own inner rhythm, unmindful of the music playing in the distance. They danced slowly into the living room, slowly winding in serpentine coils around the apartment, bumping into furniture and walls here and there but never altering the easy, metrical tempo undulating in their bodies, which by then were pressed so tight against each other from head to foot as to appear inseparable.

Not even that magnificent ocean view from the enclosed balcony or the convenient sofa with the beguiling sensual designs enticed the couple to break apart and look at each other again, not until the rising heat of passion finally awoke them.

During the dance they were not conscious of the world. To her later surprise, Vanessa had somehow loosened every button on Clay's guayabera shirt, had unbuckled his belt and pulled his zipper down to find that he was not wearing a stitch under his trousers. Clay came out of his trance when her hand went past the zipper, into further explorations, went with the urgent vigor of someone trying to keep a dream in place. Vanessa, on coming out of her own trance, was astonished at the sight of what she was holding in her hand, holding it like a club and with a grip not usually associated with surrender.

Rocked again by her touch Clay was doubly bedazzled, for he'd also loosened buttons—on her blouse—had stripped it away and unsnapped her bra while in a foment of blind rapture, and he was showing as much excitement over his discoveries as she was over hers when their eyes opened and they found themselves standing half naked in front of the panoramic view of bay and ocean merging, which excited them even more and sent them crashing upon the sexy sofa that had, ironically, inspired Ewen Leetboer to buy the penthouse.

In seconds Clay and Vanessa were out of the remainder of their clothes and locked together again, tighter than before. For quite some time they pitched and rolled over each other, taking turns on top, gasping more passion than either could believe, and sounding fierce, ecstatic shrieks that rose higher and louder until at last their bodies collapsed under a spasm of violent orgasmic trembles and came to rest against each other.

"You are unreal," Clay said later, repeating himself between kisses. "Totally unreal—and then again totally real, as real as a piece of gold—but right now you're the most unreal woman I've ever known." At times he would draw back from Vanessa and gaze over her smooth, unblemished Irish skin, her gorgeous face, her body, and swing his head in the incredulous motions of someone who couldn't believe what a mind-zapping creation lay beside him, bare of every human design and everything but her own wild, naked beauty.

"*Damn*—!" Clay shouted. He sat up on his buttocks in a sudden lunge and stared into space for a time before gazing back at Vanessa. "Look, lady, I didn't come here to fall in love with a married woman for Christ's sake! *Holy fuckamoley!*"

Vanessa's smile was packed with mischief. She pulled him back down beside her. "You big rogue," she said, exploring again and keeping her hand gently in motion while she talked. "I love you too. At least I must. There's no love for anybody else. You're the only man I think about, the only one who *lives* in my mind—hangs out there like a thief, stealing my heart in bits and pieces. *Oh God*! You've taken it all now, you rascal, you rogue, you stud, you and your wonderful wonderful . . . *everything*!" Vanessa gave Clay a spirited kiss then pounced on top of him, straddling with the agility and poise of a seasoned equestrian. "And I've *wanted* you in my thoughts, Clay Redmond, wanted you *inside* me, wanted you just like I've got you right now . . . wanted it *all* since the day we first met here in this darling apartment!"

For the rest of the week Clay and Vanessa rarely allowed themselves to separate for longer than an hour at the time. He showed her around the parts of Miami that she hadn't seen, took her to dinner at the Hard Rock Café, strolled through Bayfront Park together, visited the Metro Zoo and Seaquarium, even went as far as Islamorada's Holiday Isles to catch a rare appearance of Jimmy Buffett and hear him sing his Margaritaville songs while they fondled each other under the table and sipped rumrunners to cool their passion.

Penthouse #9, though, held them in virtual captivity for the intervening hours. They made love every morning, sometimes twice, then again during the evening—and even in the middle of the night if Vanessa woke up in a frisky mood and couldn't keep her hands off Clay while he slept. Sometimes her "rogue lover," as she began to call him, would play possum and let her maintain his erections with warm, tantalizing kisses until he couldn't pretend to be asleep any longer.

"What am I going to do with you?" Clay said louder and louder as the week progressed. He asked her again while they were engaged in a serious evening of foreplay on another balcony, this one open, where the heavens were as exposed as their bottoms.

"Make love to me for starters," Vanessa answered in a coaxing tone, refusing to be drawn into emotionally charged intercourse not involving the subject she was then stroking with such enthusiasm.

Later in the evening Clay poured Grand Marniers and they sat again out under the stars in their robes.

"Penthouses are like desert islands," he said. "Plenty of privacy, no peeping Toms to worry about."

"I love you, Clay! Without you I would never have gotten it. You sold me with your roguish eyes and that big sexy nose. Ewen thought he was responsible."

Clay took a deep breath. Life had just thrown him a classic curve, placed him on the horns of one of its most enduring dilemmas. Fate had set him up at last with a woman he could care about. Not a random pick off the street either but a real earth-born goddess so beautiful, so refreshing, it already hurt to think of losing her. Then there was the other horn: she was a *married* woman who appeared to be crazy about him, who saw strength and beauty even in his warts. With simple words and adoring glances she transformed him into a giant of a man, even made him feel good about love again. None of his other girl friends ever came close. Well, Graciela did but she was gone now. Like Graciela, this woman didn't mince words either or hold back out of fear she might be taken for granted. Direct and generous, she exhibited a candid eagerness in matters of affection. Vanessa opened her heart to him without reservations or restraint, with total spontaneity, with a sweet child's innocence. It was unbelievable, unreal. Clay hadn't yet decided how to deal with this woman; the attraction was powerful. To complicate matters further, she happened to be not only one of the most beautiful and stimulating women he'd ever met but she was also bound to the ugliest of his mortal enemies. This woman was sleeping with a dildo prick!

"Wish you'd never married that bastard," Clay groused. "Ewen cheats, you know, robs his partners."

"He doesn't discuss business with me," she replied. "Is that why you sued—he cheated you?"

"Yes, but I got exactly nowhere. The judicial system doesn't seem to exist for little guys like me. It's there for people like

Ewen Leetboer, fat cats who have the resources to buy their way out of difficult situations." Clay paused in thought, then, with the Xanadu Shopping Mall in mind, he added, "Or 'buy into' situations, depending on which way they wish to go."

Vanessa pressed her head against his chest. "I'm so sorry, darling," she said with earnest compassion. "And, yes, I agree—Ewen is awful! He uses people like paper towels, including you. Including me even!"

"You can't possibly love him. Is the money worth it?"

"*His* money is," she answered with a charming giggle. "Who I love is my business. Isn't it obvious, though, who's *who* in my heart?"

On their last day together, the day before Leetboer was due to arrive back from Canada, they dressed themselves in bright tourist colors and checked out sailing schedules at the Port of Miami, exhibiting the hauteur of world travelers.

"You must take me on a Caribbean cruise," Vanessa said. Her face was aglow as she examined brochures at the Carnival Cruise Line office. "Take me the very next time Ewen goes out of town, goes to Amsterdam or somewhere so remote he won't come back for ages!"

"Be careful what you wish for around me," Clay responded. "I've appointed myself your personal genie in a bottle."

He discovered a wall of posters at the visitor's center, showing destinations and stops along the various tour routes. Each island's publicity crew, not to be outdone by the next, emblazoned their colorful displays with similar romantic scenes of tropical cascades, calypso-hatted natives, palms swaying against brilliant waters and bare-chested gringos erupting with happiness as they chased young maidens even more bare but equally enthralled down pristine, empty beaches.

Clay stood for a moment in front of a huge mural map of the West Indies, pointing out to Vanessa some of the highlights of islands he had visited. Cuba dominated the mural but looked more like "no man's land," judging by the way the cruise routes bypassed every port on that island. Romantic thoughts at times co-mingled with his plans for getting Leetboer to invest over there. He wondered how Silvio and Ramón were coming along with their assignments and whether the intriguing fellow called El Cojonudo would really carve the heart out of Ewen Leetboer, as Ramón predicted, if the old Dutchman tried to take over his project, his sacred Mara Paradiso.

"Did you say Havana?" Vanessa asked, hearing Clay mention some familiar names under his breath. He didn't answer, seeming distracted by his own mumbled thoughts. While standing before the mural, he began to rehash in his mind what next steps to take, with whom and where. "You were describing some place, darling," Vanessa persisted, shaking Clay's arm to get his attention, "some place near Havana I think you said."

He refocused on her. "Did I?"

"Yes, but you were mumbling. Tell me about Cuba."

Clay turned back to the mural and studied it carefully before answering. "Fascinating country," he said. "I thought your spouse might have told you all about it already, even taken you for a weekend in Havana. It's only ninety miles away. With your Irish passport you can travel there but U. S. citizens cannot."

"The embargo, right?"

"Yeah."

"Ewen did mention a Cuba trip recently."

"Uh-huh. Figured he would. Canadians are as plentiful in Cuba as coconuts. They're taking over. The embargo has become a great program for them and the Mexicans."

Vanessa rolled her eyes and locked her arms behind Clay's as he studied the mural. She snuggled close to him, hugging with open affection and sneaking naughty squeezes here and there. Moments later she scratched her nose by rubbing it against his shoulder, then twisted around in front of him and dabbed at a few spots on his face with her fingers to remove traces of lipstick she had left there earlier.

"My, my, aren't we restless today!" Clay kidded, noticing her antsy behavior. "What's the matter, sweetheart?"

"Let's go," she replied.

"Go?"

"I *want* you—!"

Clay's eyes blazed up. As they started back outside, both paused near the door and stared at each other again. Their eyes conveyed the sadness their hearts felt. This would be their last day together until some unknown event at some unknown time created another opportunity.

Clay took the wheel of the Jaguar at Vanessa's insistence. Leetboer had already lived too long, he kept thinking as they drove through Miami on the way to Coral Gables. After spending a week in utopian bliss, Clay Redmond decided the old schemer's destiny had just taken a shortcut. The unknown event and the unknown time were fast coming into view. The opportunity lay only ninety miles off shore, if not closer.

Clay pulled into Penthouse #9's parking space at Bella Mar, laughing with Vanessa over the key episode and exchanging glib talk about everything but what weighed most on his mind. Before they got out, he leaned over and kissed her gluttonously.

"I hate the thought of you going anywhere with anyone else," he said. His eyes turned sad.

Vanessa smiled with delightful eagerness. She liked to hear him sound possessive. It added a sweet touch to their balance. Without a second thought she scrambled into his arms and kissed him back.

"Then don't let me go, darling!"

"But you may have to go with him to Cuba soon."

"Not this girl," she blurted. "I won't go with anyone but you. Let him and his Canadian friends, as you say, 'take over' Cuba—the whole country for all I care! *You*, Clay Redmond, can take *me* over!"

"Yes," he said. Clay thought for a moment. "Do you mean that?"

"Every word! I'm your woman now, am I not? My personal genie's personal mistress?"

"Let's go up," he said.

12

Marcus Cunningham's conference room at Xanadu was furnished with heavy leather chairs that moved with the ominous crawl of giant spiders. Twelve could sit comfortably at the long oval-shaped walnut table, not counting the ends where no one sat and not counting Frank Creuthop, who required two spaces and a special chair. Heather Ambrose had come to the office early, which was not unusual for her, as Clay Redmond observed the week before, but it was unusual for her to come to *work* at seven. She and Marcus preferred the stimulation of early morning hours for their private pursuits. To indulge then in off-duty activities while within the confines of Xanadu's closed administrative suite and its adjoining exercise room, or "gynaeceum," a term Marcus Cunningham thought cut closer to the chase, as it were—i.e., indulged together, enjoying their favorite contact sport—set their minds into an aggressive business mood for the rest of the day.

With respect to Ewen Leetboer's visit, a top-priority occasion from all appearances, Heather possessed the sort of get-up-and-go spirit that enabled her to slip into overdrive at a moment's notice. Private pursuits notwithstanding, she'd "spiff up the joint," as Cunningham put it, with remarkable attention to details when prospective investors—even tenants—came to execute a contract. The present day was no exception. Three coffee urns provided multiple choices. Along with hot beverages, a smorgasbord of Danish and other pastries, an assortment of juices, fresh fruit, potted plants, and several bouquets of flowers—including a center arrangement of tulips in honor of Leetboer's homeland—took up a sizeable portion of the room. These amenities were not just dumped there either. Heather laid them out on top of crispy white linen and Grecian pot stands with more artistic soul than one might find at Bloomingdale's or Tiffany's.

Legal pads and pencils honed to fine points lay in front of each participant's chair, along with copies of the partnership agreement and the latest annual financial report covering operations at Xanadu. Current trial balance sheets, run the night before on Heather's MacIntosh, also lay in the stack.

Marcus Cunningham's sense of humor was evident in at least one of the features of his conference room. To appease Frank and keep the three percenters in their places, he ordered framed studio pictures of the partners and hung them in a collage on the west wall, sized according to the beneficial interest each held. From time to time thereafter, Frank Creuthop would wander into the conference room just to admire the collage. His picture was second largest, exceeded in area of wall space taken only by Marcus Cunningham's, and conspicuously greater than any of the other partners, whom he despised for "meddling" in partnership business, in view of their low percentage of ownership.

The east wall contained a huge map of the greater Miami area, with a prominent arrow highlighting the Xanadu site. In addition, aerials and a series of poster-size photographs were arrayed in chronological order, showing the different stages of development at the shopping center. Audio-visual devices, closed-circuit TVs, a jumbo clock with artful signs of the zodiac in lieu of numbers, and a spacious chalkboard shared the south wall with a double-door entryway. The north wall was almost completely of glass, veiled from floor to ceiling with a sensuous line of dainty cambric sheers.

The entire conference room, structured and equipped as it was, tended to smack a little of a Pentagon command center, and as Clay Redmond viewed the agenda, the resemblance seemed appropriate.

It was almost ten in the morning, the appointed hour of business between Ewen Leetboer and Marcus Cunningham. Clay stood near the south end of the room eating a glazed pastry with a blueberry center while he talked with Marcus.

"Count on Leetboer to arrive late, at least an hour late," Clay said. "He's back in town, though. I, uh, spoke with his wife this morning."

Marcus shrugged, not sensing the intimate images aroused by Clay's disclosure. "Great. Frank will love that," he said. "The guy's liver gets spotty if he has to sit around on his big fat ass and wait for people he already hates. And, man oh man, does he hate Leetboer's guts, especially today!"

"Delighted to hear it," Clay said, grinning and rubbing glaze off his lips after a big bite. "Makes for a promising start. Where is Frank, by the way?"

"Probably in the john. These sales meetings give him diarrhea, you know. Don't worry. Frank wants to have the biggest picture on the wall far too much to miss out on this little ceremony. He's been measuring and calculating ever since your client agreed to buy out the three percenters. In a way I appreciate Frank's dedication to Xanadu. He's one *hell* of a watchdog."

"Yeah," Clay grunted, then broke into a chuckle. "You're almost right. Give the Devil his due: Frank Creuthop is a hell of a watchdog *from* Hell. With Ewen Leetboer in the partnership, though, he'll need to pay more attention to his own backside—of which there's plenty, I must say—and forget about all the petty shit he keeps smearing on everybody's face, pissing people off, killing deals . . ."

"Maybe the asshole won't kill this one," Marcus said, sounding more hopeful. "Let's pray not. But any way you slice it, pal, some*thing* or some*body* is gonna come out of this deal deader than Hector. If Frank kills it, I'll kill Frank. Simple as that."

At 11:15 a.m. Ewen Leetboer walked casually through the double door dressed in tennis garb and wearing a pair of shower shoes over bare feet. Stanley B. Conover followed on his heels, loaded with a briefcase as large as a Gladstone bag. Some blueprint rolls and a few manila packets were tucked under his arms. Stanley was dressed along more conservative lines, except for a smart new-style tie and a bright orange blazer.

Seeing Clay Redmond across the room, Leetboer acknowledged him with a single quick tilt of his head, the way stealthy, cautious bidders might give high signs at a Sotheby's auction. Then, concluding that he was in the right place, the Dutchman paused to gaze around the room at the other faces turned toward him and exuding mildly shocked expressions over his casual appearance. Leetboer's own face, if not his attire, reflected his trademark cast—businesslike, dead pan, wily but non-threatening. His attorney's face, though, reflected nothing that might be described as inscrutable. Stanley B. Conover, who always arrived at a closing lined and wrinkled from chin to scalp, produced a brilliantly troubled, testy visage and rudely avoided eye contact with anyone until he had set his briefcase down and straightened his shoulders.

Whether it was the weight of the briefcase or Stanley's penchant for adversarial drama, he nevertheless appeared blocked of free will and at the mercy of some inner stimulus that was forcing the strange little man to go through an odd act of neck-twists, head-rolls, knuckle-cracks and a few other bodily adjustments before permitting him to get down to business or even take notice of his surroundings. Neither Heather's magnetic smile nor her attractive room decor induced a single exceptional reaction from the dapper attorney. He even seemed smugly oblivious to Marcus Cunningham and Clay Redmond, who were only an elbow's length away, offering to help with the luggage and other paraphernalia Stanley had brought in. Leetboer's lawyer pushed on a step farther. He dropped his load beside one of the chairs, scowled without making eye contact and commenced to roll his shoulders and proceed further into his "command performance," as Clay Redmond called it. Whatever the stimulus, it prompted Heather to remark later that Mr. Conover looked very much like the lone man in the room who'd eaten too many prunes at breakfast, or too few.

Clay winked at Marcus then introduced the two men with a short line of superlatives, taking care not to allow his comments to slip below the threshold of good taste or sound insincere enough in tone to cause any discomfort or incite a backlash. To Clay's relief, Leetboer and Conover shook hands with Marcus Cunningham, each making a show of cordiality, at least as much as strained smiles and wary eyes could convey.

"Where are the principals?" Stanley B. Conover asked, glancing around and seeing no one but Clay, Marcus and Heather in the conference room.

"They signed yesterday over at our legal firm's office," Cunningham replied out of the corner of his mouth. "A major partner will join us in a few minutes."

The Xanadu executive remained intensely focused on Leetboer, who struck him as appearing quite ordinary in his tennis outfit. A laid-back fellow, by damn, easy going, a breath of fresh air compared to Creuthop and not the cold-hearted beast Clay Redmond's description had led him to expect.

Conover's eyes suddenly made contact. "Who's the partner?" he asked.

"Frank Creuthop," Cunningham replied with amusing nonchalance.

On hearing the name, Leetboer stroked his Adam's apple and continued to size up as much of the shopping center as showed from his vantage point. He worked his way along the refreshment tables, poured a cup of coffee, then stopped to chat with Heather Ambrose. In one brief conversation Leetboer came to several useful conclusions concerning the shopping center, even concerning the young lady whom he complimented with surprising aplomb after raising questions about the price of tulips in Miami.

While the closing party waited for Frank Creuthop to return, Clay studied Ewen Leetboer's every move, every gesture and remark. Already he felt a lightness of spirit when he looked at the slippery old Dutchman. Clay could now stare him in the eyes and feel the soothing effects of revenge working in his gut, not just a constant churn of bitterness and anger.

Even though Clay had initially embarked upon a guerrilla-style combat mission aimed at seducing Leetboer's wife, his outlook had changed now that the mission lay behind him. To his immense personal satisfaction, it was a roaring success. He refused to think of his week with Vanessa as anything other than a grand moment of life. No seduction involved, just the beginning of a beautiful love affair. This time Leetboer—the great clockworker—came out a major loser in a skirmish with one of his lesser victims.

The proud tycoon, of course, showed no awareness of his defeat. He carried on in the high style of one blissfully ignorant of the fact that betrayal had now bitten *him* in the ass and left big teeth marks for his wife and her lover to laugh over during their next rendezvous at Bella Mar. And later on, of course, but without remorse if they forgot to laugh while on a cruise through the Caribbean.

At some point in the future Clay wanted Leetboer to know the truth, the whole truth, and hear it from the mouths of both horses, perhaps a minute or two before El Cojonudo carved his heart out for fucking up the Mara Paradiso project.

For the present, however, Clay was content to enjoy feeling no longer alone, feeling no longer "had" without recourse, feeling no longer just another casualty in Leetboer's high-stakes screwing game. Leetboer himself now belonged to the club. Clay even felt a tinge of pity for the cagey old bastard when he looked at him, at his pompous air so lately stripped of dignity, at the conceit and deception still coiled like a snake beneath his French-Canadian postiche, at the slight prophetic crook in his knotty legs and hollow tennis-court frame that seemed to bend even more while he was talking with the ever-upright, chest-out, burly Marcus Cunningham.

Clay approached Leetboer when Marcus broke away to go look for Frank Creuthop. "As soon as we finish here," he said, whispering so that Stanley B. Conover would tune in, "I have stunning news about a project in Cuba that sounds tailor-made for you and your Canadian partners. Much more exciting than Havana's Malecón. A major developer from Spain . . . with Mafia connections . . . went broke in the middle of huge project . . . in an upscale resort area . . . Castro now searching for new investor to take over . . . forced Spanish developer out of Cuba . . . poor bastard left tons of equity on the table . . ."

Leetboer's eyes began to light up as Clay described Mara Paradiso. He stepped closer, leaning into Clay and exposing an obvious mood to hear more right then, but as Clay was about to proceed, Marcus came back in the conference room with Frank Creuthop waddling along with him.

Leetboer's mouth dropped when he saw Creuthop. The mass of Xanadu's weightiest partner, his height and particularly his girth at waistline, triggered a flashier spark than usual in Leetboer's eyes. The reaction was instant; the old Dutchman looked shocked, amazed. A smile followed, both predacious and obscene. He and Conover exchanged signs on seeing that Creuthop's size had to be off the scale at most clothing manufacturers. A partner so big and clumsy, and gray-headed to boot, fit certain profiles in their minds, which each transmitted to the other via nods and eyebrow squiggles.

"Mr. Redmond tells me you run this shopping center," Leetboer said, finally able to speak and to look at Frank Creuthop without cracking up.

Frank's face turned peach red and puffed into an even more blubbery texture. Remindful of an aging sumo wrestler in some respects, Creuthop moved in waves toward Leetboer and, with much heavy breathing, stood over him and gazed down in menacing form. After a deafening pause his voice broke in a torrent. "So you're the hotshot who wants to buy into my shopping center, eh? I had you pictured as a bigger man, a better dressed one for sure."

"I see. Look it, Mr. Creuthop, I'm not in your league," Leetboer answered, his Dutch accent thickening a bit. "Yes, that much is for sure. Sorry to disappoint you so soon into our partnership."

"Not so fast!" Creuthop roared. "We're not there yet!" He turned to Marcus and muffled his voice into a growl, "Where the hell are the by-laws, the list of restrictions? See here, Marcus, I never waived my first right to match this clown's contract. Look at the getup he's got on for God's sake! I have ten days—"

Stanley B. Conover spoke up. "According to my reading of the partnership agreement, Mr. Creuthop, your time to exercise rights in regard to this contract expired yesterday. If, however, you wish to match my client's offer, I'm sure he will be gracious enough to step aside. Are you prepared to deposit fifteen million dollars in escrow this morning via certified check?"

"Who the hell are you to tell me anything?" Creuthop shouted, his face turning as orange as Conover's blazer. He glared back at Marcus Cunningham. "Marcus, call our lawyer. Have him draw up a contract. I can't allow this yahoo in our partnership. Who the hell is he anyway?"

"I'm sorry, Frank," Marcus replied. "Our law firm is holding fifteen million in escrow. They're ready to close. Mr. Conover is right. You let the deadline slip by. Are you going to match the offer—*now*?"

Creuthop spun his huge body around, shaking all over in a rage of frustration. "Give him his frigging deposit back!" he shouted, twisting and stomping in front of Leetboer, who had been standing by passively, out of the fray, like an impartial observer. "Fellow, do me a favor and get the bejesus out of this mall! You wouldn't fit in here."

Leetboer shuffled around in his flip-flops, feigning a smile. He glanced over at Conover. They swapped nods and eyebrow squiggles in quick exchanges, then Conover pulled his shoulders up, exhaled a long, loud blow and commenced to search through his briefcase.

"You should control your temper, Mr. Creuthop," Stanley said. He extracted a legal folder and waved it in the air. "You would also be well advised to seek counsel. Having anticipated such a scenario as we are now engaged in, I took the liberty last week of putting together a formal complaint which I am ready to file with the circuit court today, suing this fine partnership for specific performance. You have no legal right to block this sale and I'm sure your partners will not look with favor upon your actions once they're served with a liability judgment. What say you now? Shall we go forward or must we proceed to court?"

Clay Redmond, like Ewen Leetboer, remained silent during the heated exchanges between Frank Creuthop and Stanley B.

Conover. The slick sound of the attorney and the blustery, befuddled reaction of Creuthop provoked painful memories, yet on this occasion, they were warmly tolerated. Creuthop was no match for Conover. The matter ended quite abruptly when the big guy faced the reality of a costly lawsuit, either that or deal with the harsher reality of having to write a check that morning for fifteen million dollars.

True to form, Leetboer placed himself on solid legal ground and then overpowered his opponents with a generosity they couldn't afford to accept. As decisions go based on money, Marcus Cunningham welcomed Xanadu's new partner aboard. Leetboer, though, had already lost interest in his little nine-percent purchase. Frank Creuthop's forty-two percent stake in the mall offered more appeal and, with his crafty attorney already busy at work on a new trap design, Leetboer shifted his focus back to Clay Redmond's latest discovery: the Mara Paradiso project at Varadero. He sat with Clay at the conference table and talked for an hour after Heather and Marcus departed with Frank Creuthop. Frank, it seemed, was beginning to show signs of life again, vowing in loud bursts as they moved down the hall to "sit on Leetboer's head" at the next partnership meeting.

Leetboer paid no attention to the fading threats of Creuthop. He turned his dead pan back to Clay and resumed their private talk about a more exciting subject. It sounded too good to be true, the Dutchman concluded, but, then, most of his investments were too good to be true. He decided to investigate this fabulous project, perhaps teach his agent another lesson, shut him out of the deal at some point, since he was foolish enough to hand over the facts without a signed agreement. People have to pay for their mistakes,

Leetboer mused. U.S. citizens weren't allowed to travel to Cuba anyway. What could Clay Redmond do for him over there other than pass along a name or two? Maybe he'd send the brash but not-so-smart agent a case of Cuban rum for introducing him to his Havana contacts. Ten percent of the deal was out of the question, even one percent.

Clay was happy to see Leetboer showing such strong interest in Cuba. So happy he almost forgot that, as agent of record, he'd just earned a sizeable commission for brokering the Xanadu sale. Plans were falling into place. Now he could put Xanadu on the back burner and move on to Mara Paradiso, where the "real deal," as Evander Holyfield would say, looked to be more enduring.

This was Vanessa's day at Penthouse #9 too. She had dialed his apartment number that morning while her trip-weary husband was still asleep. Sadly, and in a most sorrowful Irish brogue, she reported that the corporate jet did indeed land as scheduled the night before. On impulse Vanessa then threw out a challenge to test her genie's desire to please by giving him a time to appear "at her feet," as she phrased it, a time when they could spend a few hours together without arousing suspicion.

Leetboer and Conover left Clay Redmond in Cunningham's office following a near-altercation over the amount and timely delivery of Clay's brokerage fee. Marcus sided with Clay in the dispute to prevent a full-scale ruckus plus more distress to his furniture. After settlement in Clay's favor, the two men went off in a huff—to play tennis, Leetboer admitted without being asked. The Dutchman did seem unusually anxious to get to the court, it being such a hot day for vigorous outdoor activity, yet he had no reason to act shy about the sport. If, Clay thought, matters followed the typical script after a close of escrow, the two crooks would serve each other a few balls, then go hobnob with the fellows at the yacht club until late, celebrating a victory of the moment and hatching new take-over strategies to launch against Frank Creuthop.

Clay Redmond gave them a few minutes head start before taking his leave, since a fist fight in the parking lot with Conover and Leetboer might prove embarrassing or, worse, screw up plans for a more terminal victory later on. Besides, Marcus Cunningham wanted to swap a few jokes and chat about his new Xanadu partner, so the delay seemed natural enough.

Afterwards, and with no one the wiser, Clay left to make good on an earlier promise that morning—to have lunch with Vanessa, drink a glass or two of rum punch, bow at her feet like a dutiful genie, kiss her all over and enjoy the clear Miami sky that afternoon while they toned up their tans on Bella Mar's highest and most secluded sun deck.

13

The phone rang a few minutes after Clay and Vanessa had finished rubbing each other down with an aromatic oil. Having good bases, both opted for fragrance and sensual pleasure over the protection of sun screen, which they avoided for "social" reasons. She had forgotten to unplug the phone before Clay arrived, and its heavy ring caused them to flinch at the same time, then mutter oaths in similar harmony. The couple were sprawled on a king-size canvas mat filled with water. It resembled a water bed but was much thinner and firmer. Water circulated through a chilled holding tank, which kept the mat from getting too hot in the sun. The cloudless sky didn't exactly encourage one to lie exposed to ultraviolet rays for very long, not in Miami at two-thirty in the afternoon. Rather than retreat to the cool interior of Penthouse #9, they remained on the sun deck and took turns shading each other's tender surfaces with their bodies while managing to work in a few other skin games along with frequent massages.

Vanessa thought it might be her husband. Ewen Leetboer sometimes called for no reason other than to find out if she were where she was supposed to be. Clay Redmond had just settled on top of her. His broad physical frame offered a pleasant respite from the sun. Muscle and sinew flared out over her like an umbrella to block the hot rays pouring out of the sky while she warmly welcomed the heat of his penetration. The persistent ring irritated him, nor was Vanessa in the mood for an interruption just then either. She knocked the phone off its stand with a sudden roundhouse swing toward the noise, trying to shut it up. The phone landed on the mat near their heads, cord intact, and at the height of mutual vexation a voice pierced its way out of the receiver.

"Answer it," Clay whispered without stopping. "It may be Ewen. Find out where he is."

Vanessa, lying on her back, was reluctant to interrupt Clay's near motionless but exhilarating thrusts, his masseur-like squeezes and the raunchy touch of his finger as it traced and retraced along the edges of the tiny triangular patch of whiter skin that her Swedish bikini had earlier covered. He beckoned again, reached out and grabbed the phone and plopped it down in her hand.

Her green eyes slithered to half closure. "Yes?" she shouted into the mouthpiece. A second or two later she shouted even louder, "*Silvio*? Silvio who? Who is this?" At the sound of the name, Clay turned his ear toward Vanessa, realizing then who it might be, but he had just spread more oil on her legs and midriff and appeared unable, or unwilling, to shift any further attention away from those areas. After listening for a moment to the caller, Vanessa shrugged a blank look at Clay, then handed him the phone. "Can you believe it?" she cried out, "it's for you, Clay Redmond!" An instant later she jerked the instrument back. "No! It's trouble, I'm going to hang up."

"*Wait!*" Clay responded in a rush, although with a surly—and somewhat apologetic—expression oozing out of his face. "I was expecting a call. My private line is set to forward here."

Vanessa stared harder, twisting her open mouth into a crooked smile. "*You rascal!*" she yelled. "You're back at your rogue business again, aren't you? You should have warned me. Why don't you move all your things in, darling. Bring your genie bottle and live here with me forever!"

Clay kissed her on both sides of the mouth. "I plan to," he answered, murmuring the words with a lusty concentration. While the voice on the phone continued to pierce the air, he seemed unconcerned and lingered to gaze further into Vanessa's face before withdrawing and rolling over on the mat, revealing himself in the naked likeness of a Michelangelo sculpture, except with greater authority around the crotch. Venting the same dreary groan she had sounded earlier, Clay took the phone and covered the mouthpiece with his palm. "Don't worry," he said, seeing that she was still a little troubled by the strange intrusion. "Just a friend. Silvio doesn't know I'm here. Thinks I'm in my office. Relax. It's not one of Ewen's prank calls—honest."

Clay spoke into the mouthpiece. "Silvio?"

"Ah, thank God!" the voice on the phone said. "I was about to hang up."

"Silvio?"

"Yes, Clay, it's Silvio. Forgive the interruption. You have a client with you, right?"

"Uh-huh . . . yeah. But you can talk. What's happening?"

Silvio fell silent for a moment. "Are you speaking from a cell phone?" he asked.

"No, of course not. Private line, secure. What's the matter? Where are you?"

Silvio spoke fast. "In Santo Domingo. Ramón is here. He wants you to fly down tonight. A plane is leaving Miami in two hours. Can you make it?"

"Good grief, man—Santo Domingo? What are you doing in the Dominican Republic for Christ's sake?"

"Something has popped and we are like prisoners here! Ramón needs you to come—very urgent. It's vital you come, man! Besides, my brother is afraid to travel again so soon to Miami. It's safer here, and close. Cuban police continue to patrol the north coast with dogs—and have been patrolling it ever since the Pope came to hear Castro's confession. They are everywhere searching for traitors, Miami gusanos—anyone who looks suspicious—with much presence around Havana and Varadero."

"What do you mean—*prisoners*? Are you fellows in jail?"

"No—worse!"

"Are you sure we can't meet later, Monday perhaps—?"

"*No, no, no!* That will be too late. You remember the name of the Mara Paradiso developer who went bankrupt—Señor Valdez?"

"El Cojonudo?"

"*Sí.*"

"Hell yes I remember. Who could forget a name like that?"

"Well, the man is here in Santo Domingo—for tonight only. Señor Valdez wants to meet you!"

"Are you kidding?"

"Please, Clay Redmond, you must come—and now. We are wasting time, my friend! I will go to Las Américas International Airport in two hours and wait for the plane. It is necessary that you appear—"

"Why?"

"_O Jesús_! Because Señor Valdez will not talk further until he looks into your eyes and satisfies his fears that you will not try to steal his project. _Listen to me, Clay_! He may also do harm to us if you do not come."

"Holy fulano! The guy's got you by the balls. Is that what you're saying?"

"Believe me, yes, El Cojonudo is here in Santo Domingo—_here, man_!—only he must leave in a few hours from this moment. If you do not come, my poor brother will be forced to fly with him in his private jet to Colombia for heaven knows what treatment at the hands of El Cojonudo's torturers in the drug cartel!" Silvio repeated himself in a rush of words that failed to cloak a mood, not of excitement but of frustration, and to no small extent, fright.

"Why does this Spaniard want to meet me?"

"To answer questions."

"What questions?"

"Something to do with his project, Mara Paradiso. He will not say but there is great anger in his eyes when Ramón tries to explain about the Canadian."

"Where are they?"

"In the cave. You know the place where you and Graciela once . . ."

"Okay, okay. All right, Silvio," Clay answered with corresponding directness. "I'll head out now. Be at customs by six o'clock. In the meantime, go have a couple of *añejos* and relax."

Clay dropped the phone back in its cradle and looked around for Vanessa. She had eased away from him while he was distracted with what sounded to her like alarming news. Standing a few feet off in a spicy sarong, she pointed at Clay's attire all laid out on a nearby stand.

"This isn't fair," she said, appearing both upset and puzzled by Clay's half of the conversation she had just overheard. "Our time was way too short. When will I see you again?"

Clay busied himself dressing. "Right now," he replied, "I'm taking you with me but, first, go pack for a couple of days while I call the airport and make us a reservation to Santo Domingo on the next flight."

Vanessa's mouth dropped open. She was stunned over his comment, his rushed movements as he threw on his clothes, and the commanding tone in his voice. Then a glint of daring spread across her face. Her eyes flared with steely brilliance and her mouth remained open for a time as she hedged a bit longer, suspecting that he could, after all, be pulling her leg again.

"Do I have a choice?" she asked in an amused Irish twang.

"No, not if you'd like to dance the merengue in a cave tonight. I'll explain later."

"What about Ewen?"

"What about him? You ask me?" Clay wrestled with his thoughts as he stooped down to tie his shoes. "Okay, let me say it again," he resumed, speaking in haste toward the floor, "I hope the repetition doesn't bore you but, for starters, the man's a world-class chiseler, a crook who robs his friends and partners, even his own wife—robs from *you*, my love—as you've already admitted. In short, Ewen Leetboer is the kind of thief who steals a person's dignity right along with diamonds and any other hard assets he can get his paws on. Around him, 'eternal vigilance' is a useful custom to honor. The bastard deserves every cut and cuff you and I can deliver to his reptilian head. That's what about him."

"Oh, Clay Redmond! Sometimes you frighten me . . ."

Clay tightened his belt. Vanessa had offered the standard disclaimer, he confided to himself, expecting more. As she spoke further, he detected a mood in transition, an easing uneasiness, a quiet and ready resolve underscored in Irish dialect that overrode any deep concerns about the man who treated her like a little dependent pet, a toy, a prisoner to be taken out of her cage only when it suited his private urges or public needs.

For once she was ready to fly away, even for a night or two—whatever time span Clay Redmond had in mind. She trusted Clay's strong sensitive face, his worldly ways and knowledge, which included plenty of street smarts in the mix. The man's love was fierce, all-powerful, complete. He loved the way she wanted to be loved, even when he frightened her. Vanessa could tell the difference without a moment's hesitation, as a woman can always tell about such matters.

Spousal ties be damned, she wanted to be with Clay Redmond, period. He was really her husband in the truest sense of the heart, not Ewen Leetboer. Ewen remained just a paper partner, compliments of an old Justice of the Peace in a town she didn't even remember.

Ewen never captured her heart, only her need of a father figure at the time. Then later he stole her dreams when his evil side began to show and the wealth-crazed monster whom she had married held them, her dreams, in captivity while turning her into a whore instead of a faithful, loving wife.

Nevertheless, an appearance of synergy seemed to exist between them inasmuch as Ewen and Vanessa Leetboer were *viewed* as living embodiments of molecular potency, as complementary co-hosts of those qualities so prized by the business world—sex and power. The accuracy of the view didn't matter so long as there were no public contradictions.

While thoughts raced through her mind, an adventurous spirit began to bubble in her face, which was already flushed to her widow's peak with an infectious jubilance. Clay felt Vanessa's jubilance. He decided to shield her from the details of his plan to snatch justice out of the jaws of a corrupt legal system, just as he had shielded her earlier in the day from the sun's rays. Yet he wanted to make at least a summary statement to ease his own mind if nothing else, to drop a few words to imply the full scope of his intentions; namely, to reduce Ewen Leetboer and his prick life to a state of moribund irrelevancy. Clay hungered to tell her everything right then and there. She seemed ready to listen, eager to squeeze out her own measure of justice. But time was short, less than two hours before the plane took off. His eyes suddenly focused on her clothes.

"Save that sarong for the beach in Santo Domingo," he said behind a cheerful series of glances.

"Yes, my love," Vanessa responded, then rushed toward the bedroom to pack.

Clay called her back for another look. Seeing her flowing red hair, her emerald eyes and Polynesian pose behind the colorful, beguiling outfit, his own eyes opened wide and shifted from glance to ogle, exposing a spirit still amorous in spite of the fact that the two lovers had shared enough intimacies already that afternoon to satisfy most appetites for a week or longer.

"Jump in some soft, stretchy jeans," he said, "and wear that cuddly blouse you had on when I came in. We don't have a minute to lose!"

14

The flight down to the Dominican Republic took a little over two hours. It was dark when the plane landed at Las Américas, a modern international airport set against the sea a few miles east of downtown Santo Domingo. Silvio Alvarez was waiting outside the *aduana*, or customs, checkpoint. He stood alone at the front of a large waving crowd of passenger greeters, dressed in a tropical white suit, without tie or hat but aburst with smiles at the sight of Clay Redmond coming through the line.

"*Hola, amigo—aquí, aquí!*" Silvio cried out in Spanish, showing the elation of someone who might have just witnessed a miracle. "You cannot guess in a million years how thankful I am you made it! I was afraid you would not have time."

"The plane arrived late from New York," Clay answered. He strolled over and shook hands with the excited Cuban, who appeared much calmer than on the phone earlier that afternoon.

Silvio did not notice the woman with the long bushy red hair coming through the line behind Clay until she stepped up between them and smiled in polite deference, then waited while the two men finished greeting each other.

"Silvio, this is Vanessa. She's my friend. She came with me from Miami."

Silvio's face filled over with a stretch of wonder. His dark eyes darted back and forth from her to Clay. The Cuban did not expect a woman to come with his fellow conspirator, nor one so vivid in appearance, so stunning to behold, like a radiant vision further crystallized in detail, but movable, and surrounded with a brilliance that flashes into one's sight and leaves the witness momentarily struck with silence. Silvio swallowed his thoughts then bowed and greeted her with extravagant courtesy.

"Clay Redmond's friends are my friends," he said, straining to hold back any further words of appreciation out of fear he would offend Clay. "Welcome to Santo Domingo, the oldest city of Columbus in the new world and the birthplace of my grandfather."

Vanessa glanced up at Clay, flattered by the attention. "My dear Mr. Redmond, you continue to amaze me," she sighed, shaking her head with obvious admiration. "You have friends everywhere!" She looked back at Silvio. "Thanks. You're very kind. I feel at home already!"

While they were walking through the airport, chatting about things of local interest, Vanessa excused herself at the first sign of a ladies' room. Her companions waited nearby, both appearing enough relieved over the brief chance to speak in private and they promptly put their heads together.

"Graciela would be jealous," Silvio remarked behind a wide grin of approval. He drew himself nearer to Clay and struck a cautious posture. "The lady," he whispered, "does she know our business?"

"Not as we speak," Clay answered with a casual toss of hands. He passed over Silvio's reference to Graciela. "Let's not mention names just yet. She's Ewen Leetboer's wife."

Silvio gaped at Clay. His chin sagged. "Are you kidding me?" he spluttered, then he spluttered some more as he grappled for the right words. "This—this beautiful woman . . . she belongs to the Leetboer *beast*, the—the *pendejo* that you want drowned in a cesspool?"

"Don't worry. It's all part of the sting."

Silvio's brow furrowed. His eyes fixed on Clay, puzzled by the man's soft-spoken, easy manner over something so loaded with dangerous, high-stakes intrigue. Suddenly his face lightened. "Ah-h, yes, of course," he said. "*Ya veo*—I see."

Clay couldn't hide his amusement over the sagacious smear which had at that instant settled on the Cuban's face. "No you don't see," he responded behind his own roguish grin. "The lady has a role to play all right, one which I will explain to her when the time comes. For the moment let's just say she flew down at my invitation, expecting a weekend of fiesta after I've taken care of business with the Spaniard."

"I see," Silvio repeated while still looking puzzled. "Well, the Spaniard is waiting with Ramón at the cave. We must hurry."

Clay took a deep breath and blew out slowly as he thought through the situation confronting him. "What else can you tell me?" he asked.

"Not much. Something is troubling Señor Valdez, though. His anger is strong tonight for some reason. As I related this afternoon, the man insists on meeting you face to face before he will talk further with Ramón and me. You must convince him of your intentions. He insists to leave for Bogotá before midnight. We have only a few hours—"

Silvio shifted topics when Vanessa returned, telling Clay that Ramón had reserved him a room at Hotel Naco, where the two brothers were staying.

"We did not know you would be traveling with a lady," Silvio said, stammering a bit. "But the reservation can be canceled if the lady prefers something along the sea with height and views, perhaps even a busy casino."

"Yes," Vanessa exclaimed with sudden interest. "I'd like to play at least one round of James Bond's favorite game of chance—baccarat!" She ran her arm under Clay's and beamed up at him. "Darling, can we walk on the beach, too, and get a closer look at those strange lights we saw flying in tonight?"

"Ah, yes, the Columbus Lighthouse," Silvio injected when his friend, lost in a gaze back at the woman, failed to answer. Clay Redmond's eyes, the Cuban noticed, were expressing all the consent needed for whatever she might request. "Excellent choice, yes," Silvio continued, relaxing into an easy grace. "You will then like something perhaps nearer the Colonial Zone where there is so much history to discover. May I recommend the Sheraton Santo Domingo?"

"Where is Señor Valdez staying?" Clay asked.

"At El Embajador," Silvio replied. "He maintains a private suite there. Comes and goes as he pleases."

"Naco's okay for tonight. I don't think we'll be getting much sleep anyway, not with the beach, the casino, the Columbus Lighthouse—and the cave of course—on our itinerary."

Vanessa stared at Clay, restraining a smile. "What is this 'cave' you keep mentioning? It sounds a bit scary! Is it full of bats?"

Silvio and Clay chuckled. "That's where I'm supposed to meet this mafia fellow," Clay confided, turning serious. His face took on a grave cast. "Don't be afraid. You'll be safe with us. Right, Silvio?"

Silvio nodded uneasily. "Let us hope El Cojonudo likes to dance," he muttered, crossing his chest.

"Shall we go find out?"

Clay picked up two suitcases but Silvio managed to wrestle one away and strike out ahead, moving at a brisk pace toward the exit door of the airport. They took a cab and the three of them continued a lively exchange all the way to Hotel Naco, a small hotel by tourist standards in the city's residential interior where Clay and the brothers had stayed three years earlier on a mission—a sad mission filled with irony—to commemorate a Cuban anniversary. They had come to pay tribute to the centennial moment when Máximo Gómez and José Martí, in 1895, launched from the shores of Monte Cristi their final struggle for Cuban independence from Spain. It was sad because the event could not now be commemorated inside Cuba; ironic because the freedom that those gallant liberators had fought for through so many long and bloody wars—and which was now celebrated so faithfully by loyal heirs, descendants and exiled defenders—disappeared only sixty-four years later with the coming of communism to Cuban soil and the restoration of inquisitorial justice, despotic rule.

"Give us fifteen minutes," Clay said to Silvio when the cab pulled under the hotel portico. He turned to Vanessa and touched on her bare arm. "Sweetheart, don't let this tropical heat fool you. You'll need your coat when we get inside the cave. Let's check in, freshen up and pull some warmer clothes out of the bags."

She managed a halfhearted laugh, not sure what to expect. "And we'll dance the merengue? Or was it the mafia you said we'd dance?"

"Come on, you brat," Clay answered. He put his arm around Vanessa and they disappeared inside Hotel Naco amidst a rush of luggage-bearing bellboys.

Thirty minutes later Clay and Vanessa came back outside, holding coats in their hands, smelling of soap and cologne and looking quite refreshed and ready for the evening. Silvio glanced nervously at his watch.

"Parque Mirador del Sur," he hollered at the cab driver. *"La Guácara Taína—rápidamente!"*

Vanessa had little time to catch her breath before she was standing in front of an opening carved into the side of a massive rock ledge. Call it a mountainous protrusion located within a city park near the sea. For some time she simply stood there and gazed into the craggy mouth with her own mouth also ajar. At first glance the surrounding façade gave impressions of a theater made up to capture the prehistoric "feel" of another *One Million Years B.C.* movie. Modern features of storefront, architectural accents, and so on, were overshadowed by rustic outcropping of stark naturalism. Yet it was also comforting to Vanessa to see both men and women going in and out, dressed in the casual togs of the present era, shouting, laughing and radiating festive spirits, none of which gave any hint of danger.

"Welcome to the cave," Clay moaned, trying to sound ghoulish. He took Vanessa's hand and led her into the opening behind Silvio, whose nervousness appeared to have intensified now that the rendezvous with the notorious developer of Mara Paradiso lay so close at hand.

Dominicans called it by the name Silvio had given to the cab driver—*La Guácara Taína,* after the original inhabitants of the island. It was a huge cave which the locals dubbed for English-speaking consumers, in loose translation, "Tomb of the Taínos" in honor of the ancient Indian tribe. Clever business minds had turned it into a popular night spot filled with multi-levels of entrepreneurship, including restaurants, bars, casino alcoves, gift shops, floor shows and disco dancing.

"It's enchanting, Clay, it's an absolute dreamland . . . !"

Vanessa blurted with repetitious variations every few feet, wherever she stopped to marvel over the ingenuity with which the cave's vast Stygian interior had been adapted for human enjoyment. Bewitching lights decorated the cavernous walls and high celestial domes. Clusters of stalactites hung in menacingly beautiful arrays above swarms of writhing bodies and other less mobile formations of nature. Irregular surfaces had been ground into smooth sturdy floors, into stairways, benches and counters, even stalagmite-based tables and ornamental adaptations of eye-catching design.

Natural doorways and corridors led them down level after level until they reached the mother lode of enchantment—a spacious, somewhat eerie chamber filled with scores of party seekers and plenty of hustle-bustle. Some of the people were dancing to the music of a merengue band that was gathered together in the lowest part of the cave, which gave the impression of a Grecian amphitheater as it might be viewed from the top tier. The band was going full tilt but barely able to stay ahead of the dancers. Other patrons were sitting at tables scattered about on various levels surrounding the dance floor, dining or just out to enjoy the nightclub spectacle along with their drinks and labored conversation. Still others were crowded around an open bar where they had to scream above the loud music to make themselves heard.

The atmosphere in the dimly lit hideaway was charged with seductive frenzy, and its wild, underground potency had already registered on the faces of Clay and Vanessa. In every way she looked as astonished and amazed as Alice in Wonderland, though no longer frightened. For his part, Clay was thrilled enough to have introduced his woman to such a unique, romantic place, but it was also fun to be back again, and with her.

"A surreal experience . . . oh my goodness!"

Vanessa's voice resounded, but faintly, over the din as they wound their way along. At one point Clay was forced to put his ear down near her mouth to hear, whereupon she delivered a playful bite on his neck, and with conspicuous gusto. "Thank you, my love," she then added, still yelling but apparently not heard by any except Clay. "Thank you for this sweet surprise!"

Silvio had disappeared again, had gone on ahead and pushed through the throngs of happy weekenders to look for Ramón and the Spaniard. Vanessa slipped on the coat that Clay had insisted she bring. It felt good when she overlapped the lapels against her thinly clad front, for the air turned cooler as they descended deeper into the interior.

Clay stopped and glanced about, himself a bit overcome by a sudden wave of nostalgia. "It's still a great place," he shouted, trying to render the words understandable over the noise of the crowd. Someone rushed by and jostled them against each other, which instigated a balancing hug from him and a welcome sense of relief from her now that the mysterious Indian tomb he'd joked about had lost its mystery. "Yep, it's in the air," Clay went on, pulling her closer to let others pass.

"What is, darling?"

"Love."

"Ah, yes! Tell me again the name of this place."

"La Guácara Taína. It's romantic in here tonight, don't you think?"

Vanessa's eyes turned sultry. "Could it be because you didn't have your Irish mistress along when you were here before?"

Clay felt a pang of sorrow as he remembered Graciela there with him a long time ago. It was romantic then, too. "Could be," he answered with a shrug.

"I love you!" she shouted, reaching to gain volume. "I already want us to plan another trip!"

"We will," he shouted back. "At least every year, in March."

"Why March?"

"To visit Monte Cristi again and pray with Silvio and my other Cuban friends for a return of freedom to their homeland. But we'll come *here*, too—to this cave—and even more often if you wish."

"I do wish," Vanessa replied. She squeezed closer and reciprocated his subtle but racy rubs.

Now and again Clay squinted across the main expanse of the cavern, hoping to spot Silvio. After several scans through the audience he caught sight of the Cuban standing way at the back side of the lounge area, his arms engaged in a frantic waggle. With an almost sinister brilliance his white suit reflected the on-off flashes of the disco strobe lasers swirling around the chamber. When Clay waved back Silvio heaved a "come here" sign and pointed with uncommon vigor toward a table farther behind him, near the wall. Clay recognized the lanky profile of Ramón sitting there in the company of three women whose features he could not distinguish at that distance. They were seated a good hundred feet away and in the darkest corner of the chamber. Across from Ramón the hazy outline of a man suddenly came into Clay's view, then another man beside him, both shadowy figures, both heavy-set and peering out into the scene of joyous bedlam like overlords surveying their kingdoms. One of them, Clay figured, would be the feared Cojonudo from Extremadura.

15

"Let's dance across," Clay said. They had reached the edge of the crowded floor at the bottom of the popular nightclub cave, heading toward Señor Valdez's table. The impassioned man commenced to move in the limping step of the others around them. His hand pressed against Vanessa's waist and he felt the supercharged merengue rhythm take hold, evoking sinuous action and becoming evident along softly contoured places softly undulating, as if her entire body had been set in motion by his touch.

With intuitive grace Vanessa followed his lead. "Where did you learn to dance the merengue?" she asked.

"Here—in this country."

"Did a lady friend teach you?"

"Uh-huh."

"Oh? Who?"

"Silvio's sister."

"Oh? Tell me more."

"She was a good teacher."

"I bet. What else was she good at?"

"Many things. I met her in 1980 during the Mariel boatlift. Mariel, you may recall, is a small seaport village a few miles west of Havana."

"Yes, I remember reading about it. Where is she now?"

"In Heaven I'm sure."

"*What*? You mean . . . ?"

"Dead?"

"No!"

"Yes."

"Oh dear—! I'm sorry, Clay. What happened?"

Clay was trying to get into the swing which the other dancers were then executing in willowy, somewhat riotous fiesta fashion. He seemed reluctant to answer her question but Vanessa's eyes filled over with a watery glaze as she scanned his face and waited for him to continue. After a light kiss below each one, each followed by an arms-length, studied inspection, he pulled her closer and eased to the side of the dance floor so they could talk without shouting or getting bumped about by enthusiastic swingers.

"Her name was Graciela," he said with some hesitation. "The poor girl missed out on the boatlift. She wanted to go with Silvio and me but her mother was ill. We, Silvio and I, had come over from Key West in a chartered yacht to pick them up. What a screwy, confused scene it was! Crazy time, you might say. Frightened, desperate people begged us to let them climb aboard—total strangers. After a while it got scary all around. Later, as it turned out, we filled up the boat with them, with refugees. Somehow the chaos didn't keep me from enjoying a few tender moments on the dock, getting acquainted with Graciela. Then, well, the old lady—aside from poor health—had piled up too many Cuban memories to abandon the island. She broke down on the dock, cried like a baby. Graciela refused to leave her."

"You never saw Graciela again?"

"Oh, sure. She used to sneak over to Monte Cristi to see her brother, Silvio. He was already a U.S. citizen and lived in Miami. It was easier to visit in the Dominican Republic. They had a regular sub-rosa business going—dollar smuggling, espionage, and so on—which I participated in just for a chance to see Graciela. U.S. visas were hard to come by in those days. Still are for Cubans. Anyway, we'd meet from time to time over the next few years."

"*Here*—in this cave?"

"Something tells me I should say no," he replied, smirking at the spontaneity of her question and the curious tenor of it. "Most of the time we met in Monte Cristi."

"Clay Redmond, are you lying?"

"Scout's honor. She'd come with a group in a boat across the Windward Passage to Monte Cristi, the closest point to this nation from Cuba. After commemoration ceremonies, or whatever, we'd drive over to Puerto Plata on the Amber Coast, as it's called, and hole up for a few days at Jack Tar Village. That's where she taught me to dance the merengue."

"Oh my goodness! You loved her then, right?"

"Graciela was like first love—very special. Let's say we were both moving in that direction. She—" Clay hesitated, though looking more uncomfortable than nostalgic. His tone shifted. "The

Cuban government reported it as suicide. They said it was triggered by a terminal illness."

Vanessa's eyes swelled with attention. "The mother you mean—?"

"No, Graciela! Silvio and his brother Ramón—you'll meet him shortly—didn't believe it but they had no way of proving otherwise. Party authorities cremated her body. They claimed she'd picked up some kind of contagious disease—AIDS they 'thought'—and hanged herself while in a depressed state."

"How awful! *God*! Was it true?"

"Hell no. But she *had* picked up some State secrets in her work with the underground. Just a kid, too, a beautiful kid of nineteen when it happened."

"Heavens, Clay," Vanessa exclaimed in an outcry so loud that some of the nearby dancers turned and gawked, "this sounds like CIA stuff! Were you . . . ? Were you one of *them*?"

Clay's feet began to shuffle again. He pretended to dance while frozen in place, but they both stood almost motionless for a time, exchanging blank stares. The talk about Silvio's sister took their concentration away from the music.

Vanessa buried her face in Clay's shoulder. He knew from the tense grip on his arms that she was upset, but when she recovered, she pulled back abruptly and broke the silence between them, saying in a quite wistful voice, "Didn't you invite me to dance the merengue?"

Clay bent over and put his face almost against hers. "Are you crying?" he asked.

"No—but close."

Vanessa was also having trouble making herself heard above the loud disco beat and festive babble, which had by then risen to a higher level—a level somewhere close to the steady rumble-roar of a rock concert. "Please don't be angry with me, darling. I feel too good inside to hear any more of this dismal story. Obviously you loved her, as you should have, but you love me now, Clay Redmond, so dance the merengue with your new sweetheart who's right here in your arms and say nothing more about poor Graciela, please . . . *oh please*, not tonight!"

Clay did not answer. With a choreographer's precision, they moved apart and her hips began to sway with his. Her face came alive again with the robust sparkle of a brilliant evening sky. Whether unable or unwilling to suppress it, she threw her head back and gave way to the sensation of sudden rapture. The power of Caribbean music flooded through her senses and coursed through her body and sent the two of them rocking and swaying and stepping in titillating tangents toward, then away, from each other. From hairline to neckline her face blanched at times with uncertainty of movements but continued to throb and reflect such a picture of one in full surrender to raw bliss that Clay forgot for the moment where he was and why he had come to *La Guácara Taína*.

Without appearing in too great a hurry, Clay did manage to keep time with the music while he guided her through the erotic maze of dancers to the other side of the cave where Silvio was waiting. The Cuban looked anxious, rather nervous in fact, which did not escape Clay's notice in spite of the near trance he and Vanessa had fallen into on the dance floor. Silvio was pounding on his shoulder when he did notice.

"Hey, Clay Redmond! El Cojonudo . . . *ay ay ay*! Already I have told you he is not a patient man, my friend. He has put big questions that neither Ramón nor I can answer. In one hour he will leave for sure! Come now please—for the sake of your existence and mine—*Holy Toledo . . . vámonos*!"

Clay's mood had lightened following his tortured conversation about Graciela. He chuckled through Vanessa's hair as he watched Silvio and listened to his comical yet frenetic pleas. "Dearest," he said, speaking straight into the ear of his still swaying partner, "we'll go at it again later, okay? Right now I can't keep these gentlemen waiting any longer."

"Of course you can't," Vanessa answered, gesturing in the calm, sedate manner of a genteel Irish lady, one whose strength of character allowed the inclusion of a distinct, competing tone of amorous intent. To Clay's trained ear her tone seemed to share a kind of delicate vocal cleavage with a voice full of sultry reassertion, a voice bolstered by breathtaking movements in a body overrun with renewed power to mesmerize.

Moments later Silvio, with Ramón's equally anxious but competent help, was introducing them to the fabled father of Mara Paradiso and the rest of his party. When Señor Valdez arose for introductions, his true height became more apparent. He unfolded upward an extra foot, or thereabout, beyond average range, which pleased Clay Redmond because he had prayed for such an ally. The two men shook hands with an air of caution, taking each other's measure in polite but resolute silence. The pause was accompanied by more pressure than either party seemed aware of, for knuckles cracked during the interim, as if the Spaniard's proffered courtesy had seduced Clay's smaller appendage into a snare and left that member of his strategic defense arsenal locked between the jaws of a giant pair of vice grips.

Clay smiled inwardly despite the pain, thinking how well those big strong hands would fit around the neck of Ewen Leetboer and what a gratifying, snappy sound the old Dutchman's "magnificent seven" cervical vertebrae would make when they cracked under similar pressure.

Silvio and Ramón, though, appeared more relieved than Clay to hear Señor Valdez finally speak. "Call me Guillermo," he said in a husky, accented voice that was neither cordial nor indignant. The Spaniard released his hold after a bit of hard staring into Clay's eyes.

What an hombre! Clay thought. He stood back for a moment to observe the big fellow's frame, then lapsed into the stance of a visitor in a museum trying to assess the particulars of a statue. He estimated it to be twice as thick as his own and even more massive and muscular than Marcus Cunningham's. In sizing the man up Clay compared him to a couple of hulks on the Dolphins team—both linebackers and ruthless bruisers—an impression which he expected to prove itself beyond a reasonable doubt when *this* monster tackled Ewen Leetboer.

The Spaniard's killer reputation seemed well deserved if on no other grounds than a terrifying, jet-black, squint-eyed, Saracen glare that radiated from the top of a gladiator-like torso. If judged by the strength and firmness of his grip, Clay decided there couldn't be an ounce of flab on him anywhere. A brute of a man, his fingers and hands were rock hard; his buxom jaws rippled with muscles the moment his broad mouth closed against a savage set of gold-speckled choppers—a frightful sign to parties under his summons and a clear signal that the Spaniard was weighing alternate methods of retribution, though not limited to methods proportionate to any alleged offense committed by whoever happened to be standing in front of him at the time.

"*Who are you?*" the Spaniard asked, glaring down at Clay.

Caught off guard by the abrupt question, Clay rolled his eyes and coughed out a thin laugh. "A broker," he replied following a brief readjustment. "I broker real estate transactions."

Señor Valdez smiled. "Ah, a deal maker!"

"You might say that, yes."

Clay looked around the table. All eyes were fastened on him. He glanced past the faces, one by one, starting with Vanessa, then on to the other man and the three women, at Silvio and Ramón, back at Señor Valdez, and again at the other man. Señor Valdez called him "Pepe." He was smaller than the Spaniard by a few coat sizes but still hefty enough to win most arguments. His features were darker, too. Everything about Pepe looked dark in the dim cave light, everything except his skin. Smooth and shiny, it's pale yellow hue matched the profile of someone suffering from too much nicotine and too little sun. His slicked-down raven hair was combed straight back and pulled into a long, tight ponytail. His fierce, attentive eyes swung to every sound and flared suspiciously whenever anyone spoke other than Señor Valdez, and his expensive tailor-made suit bulged on the left side with outlines of a gun of some sort. The butt was quite visible and he made no effort to conceal it.

A drug lord, Clay thought. *Mafia.*

"Your two friends tell me you have interest in Mara Paradiso," Señor Valdez said. His deep voice sounded as if it were rumbling up from the bottom of a well. "What exactly is your interest?"

Clay looked over at Silvio and Ramón, both of whom remained silent but exhibited enough of a hopeful cast on their faces to suggest that they were relying on Clay to shore up their credibility with this unusual man from Extremadura.

Clay had not anticipated such a hostile reception. He decided to level with the Spaniard, although he didn't want Vanessa involved. For one thing, the situation looked more dangerous than he'd foreseen. For another, she had opened his heart to love again and that fact required an adjustment in plans. He hadn't quite sorted it all out yet but one thing was clear: She would hear it from him before anyone else.

"Señor Valdez," Clay resumed, "we have a common interest, I think. May I be candid with you?"

The big man grunted and poured another drink from one of the several bottles which he had ordered before Clay and Vanessa arrived. With the flair of a generous and attentive host, he insisted that his "guests" refresh their glasses and order anything else they wanted. The three women giggled and chatted among themselves in shrill, excited island patois while he took their glasses and served them himself then waited for them to taste the drinks and give their approval before he refocused on Clay Redmond.

"Of course you may be candid," he answered at last, sneering toward the other man. "Do you mind, Pepe, if Mr. Redmond is candid with us?" Pepe's eyes flashed with sinister effect and fixed back on Clay. "Pepe says it's okay, Mr. Redmond. Please begin by answering one question: What work will this Canadian be doing for you here in Cuba?"

The question shook Clay. He smiled around at Vanessa, who was scrunched up beside him in the close proximity of a devoted wife and seemed to be quietly listening, although she couldn't hide her readiness to dance again. Her attention had begun to wander the moment she sat down, and a bit more than anyone suspected. For the most part, her mind was still racing with the music in the background. Every now and then, if Clay looked at her as he was then doing, she would try to force a show of interest in their "table talk" but, from other appearances, she could have been wearing a Walkman for all she heard. Festivity had not left her body and she continued to respond more to the rhythms of merengue than to the "dilly vox," as she referred to the mix of languages, the giggles and business mutter roiling around their table.

Clay turned back to Señor Valdez. "You mean her?" he said, pointing. "She's not Canadian, she's Irish."

"Not the charming lady," answered the Spaniard. "You know who I mean—the Canadian who left Miami this afternoon in a private plane and flew to Havana with his attorney. Do not play games with me, Mr. Redmond. Informants tell me that you sent him there to arrange one of your 'deals,' as you say. Yes? Already news has come back to me from three different sources. He flew to Havana to hold talks with the bearded one's agents and make bargains to acquire my Mara Paradiso. Your name was mentioned. It was also stamped in several places on papers that this Dutchman from Canada carried with him—papers which my informant took to be a well-documented letter of intent to replace my name in the partnership. Is this true—you sent the Canadian to steal my Mara Paradiso?"

Clay looked around, bewildered. His head swung toward Silvio and Ramón, whose erstwhile happy countenances were then registering much lower expectations as far as any possible benefit from Clay's testimony was concerned. A patchwork of wrinkles had crept into all three faces and each of them exchanged to the other similar expressions of confusion.

"Is this true?" Silvio and Ramón were also asking with their frozen gulps and troubled eyes.

Clay shook his head as if to reconnect some errant circuitry inside his brain, then he held up both hands toward the Spaniard. "I'm sorry, Señor Valdez," he said. "I don't know what you're talking about."

16

C lay whispered an apology to Vanessa and sent her off with
Silvio to dance while he attempted to placate Señor Valdez with
certain disclosures that she shouldn't hear just then, nor in this hostile
setting he hadn't anticipated. She wrenched a sigh of disappointment
over the words of her lover coaxing her away from his side at so
alien a moment, especially into the arms of another man, no matter
how innocent the mission. A thin smear of relief also showed on her
face, for the mood around the table seemed no less strange, was full
of unfriendly currents and made more unpleasant by all the jubilation
that competed from the dance floor for her attention.

References to a Canadian and his attorney sounded familiar
but did not immediately strike her as out of place, since Canadians
were plentiful in Cuba. She gave Clay a biting kiss on his nose and
stepped away from the table, slinging her bushy strawberry hair and

swishing her hips in a defiant fashion as she picked up the merengue beat. Clay followed her movements until she and Silvio disappeared among the swirl of bodies gyrating around them. He felt himself wanting her again in spite of the chilly business winds blowing across the table into his face. The broker's reluctance was evident when he turned back to Señor Valdez.

The Spaniard's flashing eyes, his stiff angry posture and puffed-up visage, reminded Clay of some other Spanish Moors he had met on previous continental jaunts, most often around Cádiz and Granada. They were smart businessmen, those Moors, loyal to their own people but ruthless when revenge spurred their actions. Some were even darkly romantic when they coveted a woman, as Señor Valdez had already shown. Out on the dance floor Vanessa was remembering those flashing eyes, how subtly they fixed on her at times and how they would blink their lustful messages for a moment or two before shifting evilly back to Clay to reinforce words that made her wince to recall. What prompted Señor Valdez to mutter so harshly about a Canadian and his attorney flying into Havana in a private plane? Was it a coincidence, one of no importance? Another rich Canadian no doubt. The feisty redhead, after some thought, hoped it was her husband, for Ewen would not be around that evening when she failed to return to their mansion on Miami Beach and there would be no grueling questions. Furthermore, she didn't care if he never left Cuba, if indeed he really were there.

Clay Redmond braced himself in his chair but showed no strain other than mild annoyance as he absorbed the fierce glares of Señor Valdez and Pepe. The two men looked dangerously impatient as they waited for an explanation, waited to hear Clay tell them why these men—a Canadian and his attorney—were in Havana, plotting with Castro's agents to take over the Mara Paradiso project. Clay mulled through previous experiences with his former partner but soon gave in to a fresh wave of bitterness and began to swear in the low, guttural tones of some irate stretcher-bearer talking to himself about the inequity at his end of the load. After a short, semi-silent ramble through a selection of epithets, he blurted aloud a full repertoire of oaths and slammed his hand down on the table with sufficient force to cause Pepe to reach quickly under his coat and embrace the butt of his pistol. The three island women jumped up in unison and stared in awkward silence at each other, then they commenced a slow, nervous giggle and redirected their stares toward their gentlemen companions. Seconds later they excused themselves and hurried away in pretended urgency to find a ladies' room.

Señor Valdez pulled his glass closer, clutching it, not drinking. Pepe followed suit. Clay blew out a gust of air and glanced over at Ramón, who seemed as terrified and bewildered as he himself felt annoyed.

"Ramón," he said, "those creepy S.O.B.'s, they're looking for you in Havana!"

Ramón screeched back. "Who, man? What creepy S.O.B.'s . . . *quién?*" The Cuban's mouth chomped on his words. His mind, already a hotbed of anxiety, struggled not to betray his person as he ground out some relief from the tension festering in his gut. "What you are telling me? Does Silvio know . . . know *this?*"

"Hell yes Silvio knows, only we didn't expect them to show until next week. Ramón, it's the Dutchman and his dickhead attorney. Those bastards couldn't wait! You've got to be in your office by nine o'clock Monday morning to greet them!"

"What the fuck you trying to pull, gringo?" Pepe wheezed the words out between scratchy coughs. His hand moved with the precision of a cam stroke and locked again around the pistol grip. Without taking his eyes off Clay, he angled his yellow-stained mouth and shouted toward the Spaniard. "*Guillermo, what you want I should do?*"

"You have the silencer, no?" Señor Valdez asked with cool gravity, his voice sounding a bit liturgical this time. "The silencer, Pepe . . . ?"

"It is here," Pepe said. The surly man extracted a piece of cylindrical metal from inside his coat and screwed it quickly into place. "*Cristo*! Who needs one? Not even a bomb can be heard in this noisy cave."

"Yes, very true, Pepe. And who would notice him slumped on the table? Only a sleeping gringo tourist who couldn't hold his rum. Right?" Dressed smartly in a dark suit, Señor Valdez picked at a spot on his sleeve as he spoke. "But the beautiful lady must come with us," he went on. "Otherwise I would worry for her safety. In some strange way she reminds me of my Mara. Do you also have your needles, Pepe?"

Pepe nodded. His fat lips compressed into a sinister mass that seemed to reflect sadistic amusement from imagery then flashing in his brain. "You want me to pop him now," he said with enough enthusiasm to cause Ramón to swallow and roll his eyes.

Señor Valdez glanced at his watch. "Hmmm," he mumbled. "Not yet. We have time. The plane will not be ready for another hour. Pop him on the way out if you must. But, Pepe, first let us hear more. Relax your eager fingers for a while longer, my friend, and allow him—*el hombre de Miami*—his moment of candor."

"But he is a crook," Pepe shot back, speaking in Spanish.

"*Qué hay de nuevo?*" responded Señor Valdez.

"*Este ladrón tiene poco tiempo . . . eh?*"

Clay Redmond had no trouble understanding the two men. At first they came on strong in Spanish, to raise the level of intimidation Clay thought, then after seeing that "the man from Miami" spoke as fluently in one language as the other, they switched back to English. Both men sounded almost comical in their unguarded repartee, as if they were discussing a menu choice with the waiter, yet neither attempted to discourage the other's talk about a "quick end" to the matter, nor propose less violent solutions. Clay had heard such threats before while working with the Cuban underground, some in jest, some deadly serious. He appeared unmoved, although Ramón's taut face and bulbous eyes depicted a man who felt himself trapped in that torrid "cesspool of effluent" which his friend had hoped would flush upon the Canadian, Ewen Leetboer, not him.

"Listen," Clay replied, leaning across the table toward the Spaniard, "forgive me for not realizing your suspicions sooner. The man you speak of goes by the name of Ewen Leetboer, an immigrant from Amsterdam and presently a Canadian citizen."

"Yes, yes, I know," snapped Señor Valdez. "Nevertheless, you are wise not to withhold this name, Mr. Redmond. Please continue."

Clay paused to let the fire in his stomach cool down. "It's damn smart of you to feel that Leetboer is up to no good," he then stated. His voice was subdued and judicial, though not lacking in adversarial timbre.

"Oh? You admit it then?"

146

"Admit *what* for Christ's sake! I admit only that the man is a pirate who dresses in business suits, a looter who'll steal from the Pope if he gets a chance."

Señor Valdez rolled his eyes for a moment, his mouth agape with wonder as he studied Clay's face. He turned and looked at Ramón. The Cuban remained silent but a mask of uncertainty mixed with fright stretched from forehead to goozle, while the rest of his body seemed gripped by a steady repetition of uneasy quivers. Señor Valdez saw the same questions there which he himself had already entertained, questions suddenly fed by doubts about this "deal maker" from Miami. It was enough to inspire fear in the Cuban, yet the Spaniard couldn't help but wonder why the Miamian showed no fear, only insolence and ill humor. He then gestured back to Clay with his big, sun-baked hand.

"Your friend here and his brother speak well of you, Mr. Redmond. Perhaps they are honorable Cubans with no animosity toward me personally or toward my enterprise, Mara Paradiso. Perhaps, I say. You, though, I cannot grant even so much as 'perhaps.' To save your skin and reap great riches for yourself and the international criminal you sent to Havana to rob me, well, would you not have excellent reasons to deceive us all?"

"Let me pop him now, Guillermo," growled Pepe, his hand at the ready.

"Wait, Pepe," Señor Valdez replied, forcing the gun back under Pepe's coat. He glared at Clay. "Answer me, hombre, or Pepe will award you free passage to Hell!"

Clay laughed. "You can't be serious," he said, folding his arms and leaning back in his chair as he stared contemptuously at Señor Valdez.

The Spaniard paused in thought, wondering. *"Perhaps* you can convince me otherwise?" he queried in a suggestive, somewhat taunting voice. "That much of 'perhaps' I give you only because we have a few minutes left."

"Hey, man, I didn't fly down here to debate my honesty! I was hoping to enlist you in a mutually beneficial cause. Everybody knows your project is untouchable—everybody but the Canadian and his attorney. I even explained to him about you and your fearful reputation, but he's no respecter of reputations, nor does he believe Castro will allow you back in the country until the project has been fully developed and his interest liquidated."

"This is true?"

"You damn right it is. Let the Canadian finish Mara Paradiso at his expense. By then Castro won't care who owns the other half. The rest of the world will, though. The smart ones have already placed bets, and they'll be waiting with happy faces for the day you return to reclaim your prize. In the meantime, as you have already heard from the Alvarez brothers, Silvio and Ramón, you'll be protected as a silent partner. What do you have to lose?"

"Ah, yes, I see—a joint venture with you and the criminal! Do you take me for a complete idiot?"

"No, sir. Quite the opposite. But I was looking for a man with balls as well as brains to help me eradicate a walking plague called Ewen Leetboer. The rumor is that you have both. Look, Señor Valdez, the point on which you and I differ is this: Ewen Leetboer does not work for me. He's not even a friend of mine. A former partner, yes, but I have a big score to settle with him. Your Mara Paradiso just happened to come along at the right time. Let me help you protect it."

"If what you say is true, then you have no objection if Pepe fires a rocket into this Leetboer fellow's plane?"

Clay hesitated. "Well, actually I was hoping to take care of that asshole myself."

"You? I cannot believe it. You tell me this lie to save your own skin, right?"

The broker's signature roguish grin emerged. "Okay, go ahead. Take him down. You'll be doing me a fucking great service. Come to think of it, that's not a bad strategy—a rocket. I might use it myself if Pepe misses. Should I succeed in blowing his thieving ass out of the sky one day while he's up there in his corporate jet en route to another partnership coup d'etat, I'll let you know so you won't worry anymore about him screwing you out of your project. Actually, Leetboer thinks he's screwing me, not you."

Some time passed before Clay convinced Señor Valdez that his Mara Paradiso project was in no danger from him and his two Cuban friends. It was the Canadian, Ewen Leetboer, and his scheming attorney, Stanley B. Conover, who needed to be watched.

Señor Valdez listened to Clay's story with varying degrees of suspicion but always with keen interest, and sometimes a chuckle or two. "You do not lie then?" he asked finally in a somewhat less threatening tone. "You did not send the criminal to Cuba—as you say—to *screw* me?"

"No, hell, no," Clay answered, directing his stare at the big man's eyes. "I was hoping he'd screw himself for a change. If you will agree to continue in the role of a developer in trouble, which Leetboer now believes, and with Castro looking over his shoulder, cheering him on, I'm confident he'll fuck up some way. This man's habit of exploiting any form of weakness will overrule, sooner or later, even the healthiest survival instinct. In Leetboer's case, you can count on a temptation like Mara Paradiso to excite his perverse nature long enough to blur the line between your honor and his greed, the line that only a fool would dare cross."

"El Cojonudo's line!" Pepe shouted affectionately. The pistol appeared in his hand again and he gave it a menacing wave toward Clay. "Only a fool, yes, would cross such a line! Are you a fool, gringo?"

"Pepe, put the gun away," Señor Valdez cautioned. His mood turned cheerful, although his robust manner left no doubt that he concurred with the substance of Pepe's warning, if not the style. After a hearty laugh the Spaniard reached across the table and landed a slap of near-bruising magnitude on Clay's shoulder. "We have an ally here, Pepe! I like this hombre, Clay Redmond. Only honest men talk to me as he does." He twisted around in a spirit of consensus and squeezed Ramón's arm as well, apparently quite hard for the Cuban's lips parted over clenched teeth. "You will receive a special commission," he confided to Ramón, "when this transaction materializes. In the meantime, please forgive my earlier rudeness. I had to be sure."

"Of course," Ramón said, exposing a tattered dignity. His clenched teeth parted in small increments and he took on an air of cool Latin reserve, one more evident than Clay Redmond had hitherto witnessed.

"You have convinced me well," said Señor Valdez, turning back to Clay.

"You are a tough man to convince," Clay responded. "It never occurred to me that you could harbor such suspicions after talking with my two friends here, Silvio and Ramón Alvarez."

Señor Valdez chuckled. "Do you wish to know the *one* reason that I trust you now?"

Clay shrugged in modest curiosity as he gazed at the Spaniard. "Only one reason?"

"Only one—but a very important one."

"Then, sure, tell me," he answered, breaking into a wide smile.

"The charming lady who came with you!"

Clay's smile vanished behind a painful facial cast. "Damn!" he said after regaining some composure. "Let me explain something—"

Señor Valdez held up his hands in friendly protest. "It is not necessary," he said. "I have my sources."

"But you don't know who she—"

The Spaniard's hands went up again. "Who she is?" he replied, finishing Clay's statement. "I know she is very beautiful and charming—like my Mara. Please, without meaning to be indelicate, I could not help but observe how devoted to you she also is. What impresses me most, however, is that you are traveling with the criminal's wife." Señor Valdez rocked back in his chair, stone-faced as he paused for a drink. When Clay remained silent, frozen in a rather stern gaze of his own, the Spaniard's dark eyes flashed up suddenly and a thin smile formed around his mouth. "Ha!" he shouted, "It seems you also have *cojones*, Mr. Redmond!"

Vanessa was surprised to find the men laughing and joking when she and Silvio returned. Even Pepe had mellowed enough to absorb a touch of *La Guácara Taína's* fiesta atmosphere, which seemed intact once again. The three island ladies had returned and were negotiating among themselves in heated patois concerning which one would have the next dance with Señor Valdez. Clay's welcome smile provoked another kiss on his nose, a warm, impatient kiss that left traces of red but no teeth impressions this time, nor afterwards as Vanessa's lips touched almost every spot on his face. She appeared utterly blind to other presences around her.

17

After listening to Clay Redmond's description of the Mara Paradiso project, particularly its abandoned equity and distress-sale price, Ewen Leetboer followed up with a lengthy phone call to a certain party inside the Canadian embassy in Havana, along with other "wellspringers" of information on whose behalf he held for later delivery a few tidy sacks of goodies sized to the value of advantages received. As he confided to himself, not to paid informants, he merely wished to consult with more objective sources than a "Miami real estate broker." Since Clay Redmond, the Dutchman figured, had proven himself "ungrateful" by filing a lawsuit against him full of "rude claims"—his personal agent of all people, his joint-venture partner!—and despite the fact that the suit was later thrown out of court for reasons of bribery rather than merit, Leetboer's confidence in Clay's loyalty as a friend and trusted partner, nevertheless, had suffered a backslide. Call it the fate of anyone who winds up on the wrong end of a dispute, often without regard to the worthiness of the loser's case.

Yet, curiously, Leetboer still valued the "ill-tempered" man's nose for real estate, his ability to sniff out solid business deals in a competitive milieu. The crafty tycoon would have altered his generous posture, to be sure, had he realized the extent of his wife's fascination with Clay's nose, too, and its more stimulating competencies, which discovery had delighted her in ways quite far afield from real estate goings on.

Even Leetboer's attorney, who knew the depth of his client's bottom line as well as the old Dutchman's appetite for fallen angels, saw the prudence in a quick fact-finding trip to Cuba. "Give it a look," he advised. They were both Canadian citizens and not subject to travel restrictions to this embargoed nation as U.S. citizens were. Leetboer and Conover could go and come as they pleased. In truth, Washington's embargo against Cuba pleased them quite a lot, for it opened up worlds of opportunities not available to Americans. Cuba, as everyone knew who read the *Miami Herald*, was in the throes of a severe depression. Hence, according to the long-range acquisition strategy and best-fit nomenclature embraced by Clockwork Investments, Inc., the time was right for plucking chickens.

Less than four hours after they left Clay Redmond at the Xanadu Shopping Mall in Miami, Ewen Leetboer and Stanley B. Conover checked into Hotel Nacional, a towering landmark inn located at the curb of the Cuban capital's famed seaside boulevard, the Malecón. On the way to their suite both men commented about the smell of rodent urine that exuded from frayed and faded carpets along the corridors. At least they suspected rodents—and, to their delight, the smell continued to exude on into their quarters. Their mutual sniffs rose in volume and caused them to peer insightfully at each other and chuckle with a kind of cheese salesman's delight, which prompted only a quizzical bystander's glance from the bellhop. As soon as the happy tip-empowered scout departed the suite, the two men put their heads together in a brisk crossfire of appraisals. Their independent observations, both stoked by a keen sense of smell, sent them into vigorous conjectures regarding the need for higher grade accommodations on the island, accommodations such as a development like Mara Paradiso might offer the tourist trade, for instance, if Castro was serious about attracting big spenders.

From an Epicurean perspective Hotel Nacional proved to be a disappointment to Leetboer. From a business perspective it became an instant prime exhibit in his due-diligence folder. Once known as a world-class inn, this erstwhile elegant composition of brick, mortar, glass, steel, exotic hardwoods and Spanish tiles—with its exterior beautifully designed, its interior richly appointed in exquisite fabrics and fine museum-like furnishings and laid out room by room with fabulous views of the sea and city—all combined into one cloistered playground, a benign fortress, an environmentally seductive Margaritaville wherein world travelers might seek luxurious refuge and gather together to unburden body and soul in a paradise abounding in tropical elixirs, aphrodisiacs and other refreshments concocted to pump up one's ego.

Now it had become State booty, one of the many spoils of war that had landed in Castro's revolutionary bag of confiscations. Its expropriated status notwithstanding, the hotel still sat like a European palace on the Cuban shore of the Florida Straits. While traces of better days were daily being overshadowed by signs of unchallenged deterioration and decay, Hotel Nacional yet offered a nostalgic glimpse of the glory years prior to 1959, before Cuba's new dictator introduced communism to the Caribbean and made a lot of people sick to their stomachs, not the least of whom were American investors in Cuban hotels.

Had the invasion been just a Halloween hoax, or perhaps nothing more than a fun-lover's April Fool's joke that got no farther than the foothills of the Sierra Maestras, the dastardly perpetrators, in retrospect, might have become as famous and welcome as the proverbial prodigal son and the event celebrated in annual enactments, in resplendent pageantry, and played out in the streets like a New Orleans Mardi Gras, with blessings copiously bestowed by ecclesiastics, Sugar Bowl queens and numerous other caterers in forgiveness.

But the hoax was real and the loss, cruel. Now this once-gala edifice, when measured against the world stage, stands as any adulterated palace does—a sad reminder of how one man's Oedipus complex had committed incest against a whole nation of brothers and sisters looking for a better way of life only to suffer their asses to betrayal even as they fought and died for change. Like characters in a Greek tragedy, those proud but misguided kinfolk were looking in the wrong direction for salvation and didn't know it until their fat sister sang and moved to Miami.

"You were smart, Ewen, to cut Redmond out of this deal," Conover ruminated later in the hotel lounge.

Dressed in casual garb, in colorful shirts, baggy Bermudas and straw hats profusely adorned with Caribbean decor, they were enjoying rum cocktails at one of the larger tables but too engrossed in their private speculations to notice the stream of gorgeous

Cuban women parading through the lounge in obvious bids to gain invitations to join them, or, for that matter, to join any other affluent gentleman from abroad who might wish to contract for their services. It was late in the third day since they arrived, and, it being Sunday, these two gentlemen had spent the afternoon on a guided tour around Havana, sans female companions, and they seemed much too wrapped up in business intercourse to share the fun or change partners in mid-orgasm.

"Yes, it's all arranged," Leetboer answered solemnly. "My agent, I'm afraid, would handicap me down here. Don't you think he's a bit of a hot-head?"

"Yes—and greedy as hell! That was one big wad of dough you paid him, Ewen! I still say he sandbagged you with that buyer's representation spiel. Buyer's agent my Heineken! The sellers should have paid—like in the old days. But—you know what?—Redmond would have punched me out right there at Xanadu—in Cunningham's office for Christ's sake—if I hadn't handed over that damn commission check!"

The old Dutchman sighed and shook his head in slow, thoughtful swings. His brow furrowed up, imparting a sense of sufferance behind calm detachment that followed into his mouth. "It's unfortunate but, well, what can I say?"

"You're a damn good client, Ewen! You can say that much. He should be kissing your keister every morning before breakfast."

"Yes, something," Leetboer sighed. His face took on more frowns as he continued. "Clay Redmond shows no gratitude, though. What can I say? The ungrateful fellow has much to learn about business."

"He's a fool and a petty thief," Conover added, "and he knows too much about *your* business already. You don't need him now I tell you. After this purchase, there'll be enough deals on your plate to keep you busy forever—and wealthy beyond your wildest dreams. Screw Redmond. Too much discovery took place during that damn trial last year. He'll threaten again when he realizes you've cut him out of this Cuban venture."

"What do you recommend?"

"Action! We shouldn't wait. Let's go ahead like we talked about before."

"I don't know, Stanley. Very risky."

"So's eating a hamburger! Just take him out on your yacht—set up a fishing trip or something—and give him the deep six treatment. You can't let a pissant like Redmond lawsuit you into the poor house."

"Vanessa must not know," Leetboer said.

"Why not? Take her along. Make her an accomplice before she gets out of hand, too!"

"Hmmm. But she seems to like Clay Redmond. Always she defends him when I complain the least bit about his brokerage fees, or *anything*."

Conover harrumphed. "Yeah? Maybe she's sweet on him. Maybe she made a mistake or two herself and needs to pay up."

"What do you have in mind?"

"Teach her a lesson. She gets to watch Redmond go over the rail. Put the fear of damnation in her. Then she'll forget she ever knew him. Besides, who the hell will miss one punk real estate agent? He's not married, he has no kids, his folks are dead. My sources tell me the only kin he's got is a distant cousin, and she lives in Australia. I say we feed him to the sharks—the sooner the better!"

Ewen Leetboer lifted his glass toward attorney Conover. "You're right as usual," he said with a gentle nod. His voice lurched at times, broken and layered with continental accents, but his speech was also quiet and dignified, rather more in tune with the spirit of friendly indulgence than with the sharp, malicious barbs of his attorney.

Conover waved a cocktail waitress over and ordered another round. When she returned with the drinks and paused to try her hand at a little coquetry, he shooed her off with a nasty flourish. Then, falling into a lecture posture, the single-minded attorney held up his hand and spread his fingers wide apart, as he frequently did in front of juries when he wanted to summarize a string of damaging facts.

Seizing the little finger first, he commenced, saying, "Look, Ewen, Redmond *volunteered* the pro forma, right? He stuck the documents in your hand, right?"

"Yes. He gave the Mara Paradiso papers to me. I didn't ask for them."

"No, you didn't have to. They were forced on you by a greedy broker. Right?"

"No doubt he expects something for his work, though."

"Oh yes! Like a hefty piece of the action, by God!" The lawyer grasped his next finger and pulled it into the other. "You signed no papers, you sanctioned no agreements, right?"

"Of course not."

Conover clenched all of his fingers together to make a fist, then banged it lightly on the table. "You see? That was a big mistake on Redmond's part," he chortled, his eyes bulging with insight, his fist continuing to bang lightly down.

Leetboer smiled without parting his lips. "Yes, I quite agree."

"So what are you going to do about it?"

Leetboer shrugged, his voice subdued and calculating. "Like you said, Stanley, Mr. Clayborn Redmond must pay for his mistakes."

A broad grin stretched across Conover's face. "Man overboard!" he shouted into his cupped hands. "No doubt he's stewing over his mistakes right now—but stewing in Miami I'm happy to say, not here. What's the story on that fellow we're scheduled to see tomorrow? You know anything about him?"

Leetboer rummaged around in his briefcase and pulled out an appointment calendar. He studied it briefly then mumbled the name to himself a couple of times before settling on a final pronunciation. "Felipe Jorge," he read to Conover. "Clay told me he was a teacher of illiterate adults but had been reassigned by Party officials to commercial projects. Something to do with his knowledge of computers and foreign banking practices, wire transfers, e-mail, and so on."

"A technician perhaps, not a professional?"

"That is my impression. Jorge will review the project tomorrow and explain to us how joint ventures work in Cuba, then prepare the contract if I decide to accept the joint venture with Castro."

Conover sighed and turned a weary face toward Leetboer. "The agreement won't be written in English, you know. Do you suppose we can get this Jorge fellow to assist us with the interpretation of Cuban documents? My Spanish is a little rusty."

"Sure. A greasy palm, as they say, makes for good business down here, like any place else. My contact at the embassy confided

160

that even doctors are paid by the Cuban government only the equivalent of ten dollars a month."

"Jesus! What the hell must Jorge live on—*air*?"

"Well, under the communistic system some things are free. Medical care, for example. And there are allotments of rice, beans and other basic foods. Of course, according to the embassy, some allotments are not always available, and many medicines. I'm sure a few hundred in American cash will buy whatever we need from Mr. Jorge."

Conover stared at Leetboer with the hard eyes of legal discovery. "Ewen, you're one lucky son of a bitch," he said, breaking into a loud guffaw and sounding jolly enough to set the fair Cuban women into another circulation around the lounge. "Redmond dealt you another goddam angel, Ewen! How does that bastard find these good deals all the time?"

"I must say, he is amazing. Nobody in Miami has such a list of contacts and properties." Leetboer paused and removed the straw hat to scratch his scalp, being careful not to dislodge his toupee. His eyes began to sparkle when he glanced around the lounge and spotted a bevy of beauties perched on stools at the bar, chatting among themselves and rolling sultry eyes from time to time as they slipped into obtrusive postures for his benefit.

"Look it," he said, pointing, his otherwise staid face suddenly aglow with the excited attention of a young college stud who had just discovered a naked co-ed in his bedroom.

Conover turned toward the bar. His eyes squinnied in and out of analytical focus as he studied each one. "Nice," he said. "Very nice."

"More than nice, Stanley. Be honest."

For a brief time Leetboer appeared unable to break away from his fixated stare at the Cuban women. His walleyes depicted a man fully entranced and immensely overjoyed by the prospects of sexual misconduct. A moment later his face glummed over again. "This is good," he said, taking a couple of deep breaths and repeating himself. His voice began to quiver a bit then eased back to its cool and collected timbre. "Stanley, my friend," he went on, "you will need practice for tomorrow. Felipe Jorge must not think we are ignorant of his language or the social graces of Cuba. Go test your Spanish on room service. Make conversation with the bartender and negotiate a discount on two bottles of Havana Club." Leetboer paused again and resumed a delicate scratch around the edges of his toupee before putting his hat back on. "Perhaps, also," he continued, "you will invite the young ladies to visit our suite this evening. My goodness, Stanley, we have been in this cheerful country two nights already. It is time we made bosom friends here!"

"I gotcha," the attorney replied, happy to tack another such matter onto his growing and quite valuable list of confidences. Then with a fiendish quaver in his voice, as if to highlight this added value in the event it might have gone unnoticed, he clucked out a brief advisory, "But you needn't worry about me, Ewen. My lips are sealed. Don't ask don't tell, right? Vanessa couldn't pry my tongue loose with a peavy hook."

"I see," Leetboer said.

18

The next morning Ramón flew out of Santo Domingo aboard a single-engine charter, arranged in haste by Clay Redmond in a desperate rush to get the Cuban back to Havana. "Business is business," Clay had reiterated while he and his co-conspirator waited for the pilot to check out the plane and confirm flight routes. He then added to his mocking imitation of Ewen Leetboer's favorite line a more serious note of warning. "You must be ready to truck tomorrow. Believe me, Ramón, the chiseler from Montreal will be, and he'll come knocking on your door bright and early."

The past few days had been strenuous, nerve-wracking. Señor Valdez, together with his overly pugnacious triggerman, Pepe, left both brothers drained. Now Ramón had to face in just twenty-four hours a new challenge—the "robber of retirements," as his gringo friend sometimes called the man. The Cuban's fake office was ready, though, and the script well rehearsed under Clay Redmond's direction.

It was a brave gamble by any measure, conducting a sting operation right under Castro's nose. When Ramón thought of all the horrible tortures his sister Graciela must have suffered at the hands of the dictator's thugs, his backbone stiffened and rabid eagerness to begin the mission blew away nagging fears over its dangers. Sometimes he wondered whether Clay Redmond would come across with the two million dollars promised to him and Silvio. Did this fun-loving americano from Miami really have that much money? If not, why would he pretend? If so, why would he pay such a sum just to have one old man killed? Were there not many people who would do the job for less? Yes, many, Ramón concluded. Castro himself, absolutely, if Ewen Leetboer tried to screw him the way Clay Redmond said Leetboer loved to shaft a partner—and he'd do it for nothing—provided the Spaniard from Extremadura didn't do it first.

But Clay Redmond was a good friend, a loyal friend, and a man of his word about things that mattered. If he said he would pay him and his brother a million apiece, he would do it. Even a small fraction of that amount would buy the goods needed to wage many blistering attacks on Castro's prize model of justice and prosperity—his sacred *Revolución*! Castro spoke of it with an environmentalist's passion, as if his *Revolución* were a rare living organism vital to the food chain, a blood-based creature that he was nurturing for the benefit of humanity and that he displayed in his showcases to let the rest of the world see the proof of Cuba's achievements in biodiversity. Some had already called it his treasured black mamba; others, an endangered scorpion he'd picked up on one of his Angola tours.

Ramón resented the transition, resented Cuba's fragile democracy falling prey to a nasty curve thrown by a minor league pitcher whose greater ambition was control over people, not control over a baseball. As young and innocent as he was at the time, the sensitive Cuban threw up when the government spun out of freedom's orbit and into a dictator's tyranny. But Ramón did not abandon the island as so many of his fellow countrymen did. He stayed and grew sicker. Only the strongest of the strong could keep the daily dose of Castro's socialistic "boondoggerel" from penetrating into their subconscious lives, let alone conscious. It amounted to a form of mental violation—soul rape—foisted upon the innocent masses. Cubans had no choice but to live under the loins of this so-called revolution, bear its oppressive weight and witness how it held everyone but the *balseros* by the crotch until a tolerance for pain supplanted memories of happier times.

Ramón never lost his memories. He remained strong and determined. He saw Ewen Leetboer as just a means to an end. The old chiseler's fate mattered naught to the Cuban, but Clay's plan mattered because two million dollars mattered. It offered him personal hope again, fodder to nourish his dream of a democratic Cuba, medicine to wipe out a plague festering in the *Capitolio*, pen and ink to cancel a revolution. There was risk, to be sure, enormous risk, but the promised payoff bolstered Ramón's sense of purpose, added ferocity to his quiet Latin dignity and loaded his heart with enough motivation to carry out a hundred attacks. He would also make Clay Redmond proud of the skill and finesse with which he executed his part of the sting.

These were Ramón Alvarez's thoughts as he flew back to Havana. By the time the plane touched down at José Martí airport, he had already begun to feel a strange new mood taking hold.

On Monday morning shortly after nine o'clock Ewen Leetboer sat in his suite at Hotel Nacional pouring over the Mara Paradiso document that he had taken from Clay Redmond back in Miami. Stanley B. Conover was still in bed, still half asleep but struggling to recover from the excesses of rum and fair Cuban women. Just as Clay Redmond had predicted, Ewen Leetboer seized on Ramón Alvarez's telephone number, which, not by happenstance, was easy to spot with its emboldened type and convenient placement next to the Cuban's fake name, "Felipe Jorge." Ramón bit his lip to hold back a laugh when he heard Leetboer pronounce the name *Felipe Jorge* so awkwardly and then ask if he were speaking to the same—the designated party to contact regarding real estate partnerships in Cuba.

"What is it you want?" Ramón answered, his voice crisp and official.

"I am Ewen Leetboer," the Dutchman said, recovering his poise, "from Montreal. A business partner and friend of mine suggested I come to Cuba and take a look at a development called Mara Paradiso."

"Where did you get my name?"

"Well, from my friend—Clay Redmond. He recommended the project for investment. Don't you know him?"

"The name sounds familiar," Ramón answered dryly. "Is he also Canadian?"

"No, no. He's a real estate broker in Miami."

"Oh, yes, now I remember—a rare gringo who speaks Spanish. He asked many questions about Mara Paradiso. I sent him some documents a couple of weeks ago. 'One-party listing,' he called it. My uncle lives in Miami and does business with this Mr. Redmond friend of yours."

"I see. Hmmm, yes, very good. I am also interested in the project. Can we meet and discuss it?"

Ramón hemmed back, as if annoyed, then grunted into the phone. "May I ask a personal question first?"

"Well—eh?—what is it?"

"My instructions from the *Ministerio del Interior*," Ramón continued, rolling his "r's" in the Spanish tradition, "are to inquire into your finances before we release further information. No negotiations will be permitted by the Cuban government until the successful investor deposits five million in the *Ministerio's* Foreign Investment Account. Will this requirement pose a problem for you, Mr. Leetboer?"

"Pesos?"

"No, dollars. Down here we don't like to say *American* dollars, but they are what we must have. Greenbacks."

Leetboer did not answer immediately. He mumbled to himself while performing some mental arithmetic on exchange rates. Moments later he shouted into the next room for Attorney Conover. "Stanley, wake up for goodness sake, wake up now! Get your drunken mouth in here and talk to this man!"

"Perdón?" Ramón said.

"Nothing. The amount surprised me, that's all."

The Cuban sighed and shushed a moist blast of air through clenched teeth in lieu of more graceful sounds of sympathy. It was a technique Clay Redmond had used on the Spaniard in Santo Domingo, and Ramón did not hesitate to follow up with the same curt, unapologetic directness when he spoke.

"It will save time and trouble, Mr. Leetboer, to know the truth before we go deeper into this matter."

There was a ring of finality in Ramón's voice which was not lost on Ewen Leetboer. "I see," the Dutchman said. "Okay, very well. To answer your question, yes, I have the money. But, sir, I must insist my attorney approve the arrangements, the documents, everything. Let us discuss this now in person. Can we visit the site? Cuba is a foreign country to me. I must examine the partnership agreement, must see what I buy before I pay money—"

"You will not *buy*," Ramón shot back. "You only have to *build*. Mara Paradiso comes free to the qualified person who can take the plans and complete them in a reasonable period. If our Maximum Leader approves, you will inherit at no cost one-half of the value that the previous developer put into the project, which, let me tell you, is already greater than you might imagine. The Cuban government, as joint venturer, reserves the other half and will remain an equal partner for permitting further development to proceed."

"And the five million dollars? What will happen to my five million dollars?"

"The five million will be returned to you when you finish the work. In the meantime it will serve as a bond of trust between you and *El Comandante*. It will give our government the necessary assurances, shall we say, that Comrade Ewen Leetboer is serious as well as financially sound." Ramón grew quiet, feeling that his bilingual talents were encroaching too much into the conversation. His pause allowed an exuberant tongue to rest for a moment while he directed several coughs into the phone. "I'm sorry," he soon resumed, "I am very busy. No more talk please. The requirements stand as a matter of record."

By then Leetboer's attention was solidly fixed on Ramón's earlier words, "free, no cost." Clay Redmond was right, he concluded. Mara Paradiso would not require him to put up *any* out-of-pocket other than a good-faith, refundable deposit! He could use the Bank of Montreal's money to finish the project, then unload it on a European consortium for more millions than he could count without his HP-12C calculator.

"Where is your office, Felipe? You don't mind if I call you Felipe, do you?"

"Please, yes, I *do* mind!" Ramón answered crustily. "Just ask my secretary for *El Duque*. It is a courtesy of title my comrades will insist on—and with the Spanish accent."

Leetboer strained to laugh. "Whatever you say, my good sir. Now where will I find your secretary?"

A warm current of emotion began to circulate through Ewen Leetboer's chest while he listened to Ramón give him directions to the *Ministerio del Interior*.

"Shall we meet in one hour?"

"Hmm," Ramón intoned. "Okay, if you insist—but only if you bring a check in the proper sum to certify yourself."

A sharp click followed by a stream of static poured out of Leetboer's end of the phone. He hung up, too, excited about another lucrative investment in the works but feeling a mild displeasure over the snappy manner of a simple Cuban bureaucrat. This Felipe Jorge character did not sound eager enough to the old Dutchman. For a deal of such magnitude brokers back in Florida would be tripping all over each other to get his signature on a contract.

But then, Ewen remembered, Felipe Jorge was a teacher of adult illiterates, not a man of business. For this new work, selling real estate, the government still pays him ten dollars a month. Are these Latin communists so stupid? he wondered. With a few well-placed bribes, Leetboer suspected the whole island could be bought on the "cheapo."

Ewen puffed his jowls in and out, thinking while he puffed. Bleary-eyed himself and running low on testosterone, he alternated listless gazes between the historic skyline outside and Conover's bedroom door inside, behind which he heard occasional grunts, oaths and unintelligible muttering. "For a lawyer you are not very bright either," Ewen said aloud to himself. His words were only a drone, though, drowned out by water gushing from the shower and by his counsel's sporadic, halfhearted forays into Caribbean song.

At 10:45 the Dutchman and Attorney Conover arrived at the *Plaza de la Revolución*, the official headquarters of Fidel Castro and his legion of trustees, body guards, heroes and tested fellow travelers. The two men came in one of the numerous state-run Russian taxis that held sway over the streets. It was driven by a thirty-something local male who manifested a greater eagerness to chat with his passengers than they did with him, since neither could render more than a few Latin phrases. The driver's effort earned him a small tip nonetheless.

"Do you suppose he works for ten dollars a month like Felipe Jorge?" Leetboer asked Conover as they stood on the sidewalk and watched the taxi roll away.

"Yeah," Conover replied grumpily, "plus whatever the poor bastard can knock down in skims and tips without getting hauled before a firing squad."

Conover's face was still puffy and red but he had dressed in his sharpest dapper colors for the occasion and had, by force of habit, duly armed himself with a well-stocked briefcase. His client, not being familiar with the dress code in Cuba vis-à-vis Miami, followed a more conservative bent and swapped out of his baggy Bermudas and flip-flops in favor of dark business attire.

The plaza complex evoked an air of European royalty. Beautiful old buildings graced a park-like setting with monumental elegance, albeit most of the elegance was already there prior to the current regime's bloody take-over. Palms waved in the gentle island breezes, blooms from the flamboyant tree emblazoned the atmosphere with red magnificence, and a bright tropical sun lit the scene with a radiance that showed no partiality to structures or to life's flora and fauna below. Uniformed guards—soldiers in drab olive green battle garb patterned after Chinese military fashions—stood at key spots with their rifles slung at a handy ready over their shoulders. Their heads oscillated in vigilant sweeps across the grounds, stopping only to stare when something suspicious or otherwise curious came into view. Already most of them had their eyes trained on two foreigners approaching the quarters of the *Ministerio del Interior*, one of whom aroused immediate concern, for he was carrying a briefcase big enough to hold many counterrevolutionary devices, including several pipe bombs.

19

A petite, attractive woman of about thirty years greeted the two men just as they arrived inside the quarters of the *Ministerio del Interior.* A wide leather belt with glassy, colorful studs embedded in it was buckled tight around her waist and made her shapely hips even more conspicuous.

"Señor Leetboer?" the woman asked as she approached the two visitors. She looked at both of them with the same questioning eye, glanced at Conover's natty getup and rum-swollen face, then stopped in front of Leetboer as if by telepathic direction.

"I am Ewen Leetboer," the Dutchman said with a generous nod. His arm moved upward with a kind of instinctive grace, though not to initiate a handshake or ready himself to return one if offered, but to finger the top of his hatless head and assess the state of his hairpiece. "I am Ewen Leetboer," he repeated. "This is my attorney,

Mr. Conover. We are here to see Felipe . . . uh . . . Felipe . . . oh what is his name, Stanley?"

"El Duque!" Conover injected with a triumphant grin toward the woman. "And what is *your* name, dearie, may I ask? You seem jolly familiar. Were you at Hotel Nacional last night? In our suite by chance?"

The woman sneered at him and turned back to Leetboer. Her manner reflected the serious demeanor of a modern, no-nonsense female, but the rest of her remarkable presence encouraged far fewer business-oriented conclusions. Creamy skin set against darkly mysterious eyes covered a glut of feminine qualities surrounding the most celebrated points of a woman's body, each being easily conceivable to one's imagination if not already apparent, the whole of which aroused more interest among horny types, especially the *Ministerio's* communist gamecocks, than a eunuch might endure without upsetting biological precedents. Even Leetboer and Conover, in their depleted condition, were drawn into a few lascivious speculations while they listened openmouthed to the lovely Cuban lady in front of them.

"I am your guide," she said in broken English, "El Duque's secretary. He is waiting. Follow me please."

She turned on her heels and began walking smartly across the huge, ornate lobby toward a hallway leading into the interior of the building. The two men shot walleyes at each other, then exchanged a flurry of lighthearted high signs before stepping off in pursuit of the secretary.

Administrators and clerks were busy at whatever it was they were doing and seemed to pay no attention once they saw that the two men were in the company of Comrade Elena. Conover's bloodshot, roving eyes observed at critical spots along the way that some of the older women were wearing holstered pistols. He was still nursing a dull headache from the previous evening's debaucheries and seemed further irritated by what he considered a "gross miscast of authority." The women looked more in the league of house maids than guards, he thought, except for the fact that they glared meanly back at him, were armed, and a few of them slouched in doorways and against walls like lazy, arrogant cops sometimes do who feel their beat a trifle boring.

The woman, Elena, led Leetboer and Conover into a large open room near the end of the building. It was packed with desks, tables, filing cabinets and the usual trappings of a politically correct office. A bust of Che Guevara sat on a pedestal behind Ramón's adopted work space. The nameplate "El Duque" was displayed in bold letters at the front of his desk, and there were numerous pictures, maps and plaques heralding Cuba's history hanging on the walls, mostly it's history of Castro's *Revolución.* Columbus had become a foreigner again, a minor player in the Cuban story.

In reality it was Elena's desk and her office, not El Duque's. Although she was known to be a friend of Ramón's, no one in her office, certainly no one in the *Ministerio,* knew that she was a frequent participant in his clandestine adventures. What they also didn't know was that Elena and Ramón were long-time lovers, not merely friends. Only Silvio and Clay Redmond knew the couple had every intention of getting married when it was safe in Cuba to rear children in the democratic tradition. Elena, because of her good looks, held a high post in the communist government. Based on merit alone, her work was mediocre at best, for she had neither the will nor the desire to waste her talents on five-year plans. It was hard enough pretending to be a loyal communist. Her laudable Miss Universe image simply became a tool to be used in the struggle to free Cuba, a cause in which she and Ramón believed with as much ardor and passion as they heaped upon each other in secret under the persuasion of their personal harmonies. To protect her from jealous officials while at the same time allowing both of them easier movements within the Party structure, Ramón had insisted after Graciela's brutal death that Elena keep their relationship clandestine as well.

For short "performances" she would lend Ramón her office and co-operate in whatever way circumstances demanded. Other comrades took him to be an internal auditor of some kind, there for a few days to check the books, maybe spy on workers and report any suspected "counterrevolutionaries" back to headquarters. Leetboer and Conover would take him as just another grandly titled bureaucrat whose ass was there to be kissed in exchange for permits.

On this day the "sting plan" called for Elena to play the role of Ramón's secretary; that is to say, secretary to her phantom boss, El Duque, who had elected on this occasion to serve his Canadian visitors, on behalf of the State, in the rather ambitious capacity of—loosely translated—"Curator of Real Estate Documents and Commissar of Cuban Partnerships."

When Leetboer and Conover approached his desk, the tall, thin Cuban was giving great concentration to a mound of government papers stacked up in front of him. He continued to read and make notes on a pad until Elena attracted his attention with an airy clearing of her throat.

"The gentlemen you were expecting are here," she said in softer but still broken English. Elena then switched to high-speed

Spanish. "Your target is the older one. The other fellow who is dressed like a Miami pimp will have legal questions for you. Be careful, my love."

Ramón shuffled the papers back into the folder and beamed a healthy appreciation up at Elena. Her coy endearments always made his heart zing a little, which at times tested his willpower, as was then occurring. The Cuban exhaled his passions in a noisy blow and rose stiffly behind his desk and squinted over his glasses at Leetboer and Conover. He had memorized their faces from photographs that Clay Redmond had given to him and Silvio earlier at the Versailles Restaurant and could have picked either one out of a line-up with no difficulty.

"Gentleman," Ramón uttered. His voice was flat, without enthusiasm and a tinge uncivil. He stood like a soldier and stretched his gangly body upward so as to be able to look down at his visitors, who were themselves of average height. "What is your business here?"

Leetboer turned a puzzled face toward Conover, then back to Ramón. "Eh? Didn't we talk this morning on the phone—about Mara Paradiso . . . ?"

"Oh, yes, that," Ramón responded casually, ignoring Leetboer's mewling voice. "Did you bring the check?"

Conover eased into his pre-conference ritual with a grunt. He dropped his Gladstone bag in kerplunk fashion, then followed up with a ceremonial clap that stung Ramón's ears. Moments later the dapper attorney straightened his shoulders and commenced to exercise the muscles in his neck, setting his head in a clock-wise roll while he counted the swings. After several violent weaves in all directions, the attorney's head spun into its normal upright, stationary position, whereupon his watery eyes proceeded to make contact with the Cuban.

"Are you all right?" Ramón asked, visibly alarmed.

Conover's stare hardened. "Relax, young fellow! Just a little something I picked up in law school."

Ramón seemed unamused. "Kindly warn me next time. I was about to summon a doctor."

Conover straightened his shoulders again. "You don't say?" he quipped in a snide tone. "Listen, I didn't expect to hear this kind of baby talk in Cuba, for Christ's sake!" The attorney then stepped forward and leaned on Ramón's desk. "See here, Duque, what assurance does my client have that he won't be pouring money down a rathole?"

The Cuban managed to remain calm. "What assurance does your client need?"

"Well, the economy down here seems a little shaky right now. I would rather the money be held in a Canadian bank. My God, man, we haven't even seen the property yet! What makes you so cocksure we'll buy it!"

"Nothing. The property is not for sale, only the opportunity for a grant of partnership. This multi-million dollar paradise is so special that it will return many more millions to your pockets if you finish building it according to the plans of the creator, El Don Guillermo Valdez. You must prove yourselves worthy of this high Cuban honor. We have not yet found anyone who can."

Conover's head resumed its gentle clock-wise motion while he parsed through Ramón's words. Moments later he glanced over at Leetboer, who had sat down and was pressing idly on his Adam's apple and gazing across the room at Elena. *Ewen's fantasizing about her again*, he thought, not aware that his client was also worried that Vanessa might object if he added another "doll" to his collection. But a certain business froth had formed on the Dutchman's face, too, one suggesting that a "what if" scenario was already in progress, something along the line of, *What if I hire this Cuban sweetie to be my Caribbean sales rep? Set her up in a branch office with all the comforts of home—refrigerators, TV, sauna, pool, beds . . . ?*

The relaxed, inattentive sight of Leetboer caused Conover to mumble an obscenity under his breath and turn back to Ramón in a huff.

"Let's go for a ride," the attorney snapped then shifted into a lighter mood. "Let's take a gander, Duque, at this Mara Paradiso project. We can discuss the check on the way, after I study the partnership agreement. Is it written in Spanish?"

Ramón laughed. "We are not fools here, Señor . . . Señor . . . I'm sorry, I forgot your name."

"Conover, Stanley B. Conover, sir, attorney at law, licensed in Canada, Florida and numerous other countries you probably never heard of."

Ramón laughed again. His eyes flared, exposing well-formed scleras, and his head rocked up and down in short, quick, jerky nods that moved in seriocomic concert with an almost fiendish smile. "But not in Cuba," he reminded the attorney.

"Of course not," Conover barked. "I am not a communist."

Leetboer swung away from his skylarking gaze across the room, rose and slapped Conover on the buttock to quiet him. "Now, gentlemen, listen. We have business to make. My check is here, five million dollars drawn on a bank in Curaçao." Leetboer rummaged in his brief case and extracted a check and held it up for Ramón to see. "Why not leave the check with my banker there? I will place him under strict orders to issue a letter of credit to you once we have a signed partnership agreement."

Ramón's facial expression turned cold and somber. He plopped down and swivelled for a moment in his chair while he rubbed his chin in thought. "A Dutch colony?" he grunted. "Señor Valdez would kill us both if news goes to him that we negotiated away his Mara Paradiso project with foreigners without dollars in Spanish trust. If the things one hears about this man and his temper are true, the *Ministerio* would then need the money to bargain with him for your life as well as my own. It is a contingency we cannot overlook." Ramón paused and glared at the two men, both of whom had taken seats and were sitting on the edge of their chairs, listening in rapt attention. "No, the condition of dollars is absolute," the Cuban resumed. "If, however, your assurances will be better served with the five million on deposit under Mexican authority, then let me inform you that the *Ministerio* has a foreign investment account in Cancún. Otherwise, I must bid you *adios* and have my secretary show you out."

It didn't take long for Leetboer to ask for a receipt along with a copy of a different five-million-dollar check, this one drawn on a bank in Montreal.

"A wise decision," Ramón said. His facial expression hardly wavered as he took the check and examined it. "Good. We have only to fill in the payee line with our Cancún account."

Leetboer frowned. "Look it, Duque, don't you have a rubber stamp with the account name . . . ?" he asked peevishly.

"Oh, yes, we do. I thought you might like to write in the name yourself, since you have already entered 'Mara Paradiso escrow deposit' on the memo line."

"No. I prefer the stamp. It will look more official, don't you think?"

"The point is logical, of course."

"It will also give me proof of the transaction in the event the bank raises questions later on."

"Ramón chuckled. "Not our bank in Cancún," he said. "DXL will deliver it to them tomorrow and I'm confident they'll be very happy to receive a check from Cuba that doesn't—what you say—*bounce*!" He paused and squinted over his glasses at Leetboer. "This is a good check, no?"

"Would you rather have cash?" Conover injected in a nasty tone. The Dutchman quickly pulled his attorney aside and, in few words, told him to "cool it," that he could use his legal skills to squash the deal later, if necessary. Conover continued to voice reservations, however, until the "Commissar of Cuban Partnerships" mentioned to Leetboer that his secretary would drive them to the site that afternoon. Ramón went on to suggest that the two gentlemen might enjoy lunch and a daiquiri or two at Hemingway's favorite haunt, the *Floridita*. They could wait for her there.

"Thank you," Leetboer answered. He gazed across the room toward Elena's desk, as though to shore up his memory with one last look, but Ramón had already waved her out to make arrangements for the trip to Varadero and a guided tour of the Mara Paradiso project. The lecherous stamp on Leetboer's face gave way to mild disappointment. "Oh," he said. Then he winked at Conover, who had brightened somewhat now that his client had assumed full responsibility. "I think we will recognize the young lady. Don't you, Stanley?"

Conover straightened his shoulders. "As long as you think so," he answered, "I'd stake my life on it!"

The collective mood had changed. All three men seemed in better spirits now that the deal had been struck. Ramón walked his visitors to the door and shook their hands with a gusto that seemed out of place, coming from him. Instantly he noticed that their soft, feeble clasps were in sharp contrast to Señor Valdez's steel-trap grip.

"El Cojonudo will squash them like overripe papayas!" he mumbled in a loud burst of glee.

Leetboer gaped at him. "Eh?"

The Cuban stiffened again. "Nothing, nothing. I was just admiring your hands. They are safe havens, like Allstate!" He cupped his hands the way he had seen them do in TV commercials out of Miami, but his guests appeared more perplexed than enlightened. "Oh, by the way," he then added behind an accommodating smile. "Carla, my secretary, will be wearing a green head band."

It amused Ramón to use the fake name and make such superfluous gestures, for he knew that everyone, except perhaps the very old and the very young, would recognize her in other ways. He also knew that Elena would tell him about these two fellows and how excited "Carla" made them. It would give the two lovers a good laugh when they next put their heads on the same pillow.

20

Clay Redmond sat in his apartment office in a post-holiday mull. His mind was in serious ferment. For one thing, it annoyed him that he did not tell Vanessa about his "rat extermination" plan while they were in Santo Domingo. The time was perfect but he could not say the words then. She stuck too delightfully close to him for dismal confessions to come between, and she was so pretty and happy. Why tell her at all? he asked himself. Why run the risk of laying a guilt trip on her and shattering a beautiful spirit?

At Boca Chica beach east of the city, when they were floating in each other's arms, making love in the warm, shallow, emerald-blue sea amidst the dusky glow of twilight, his mouth was sufficiently occupied with other bodily heroics and there was simply no room for talk about third-party intangibles. Later that evening, though, when he tried again to tell her, when they were alone together on the balcony of their Sheraton suite, his tongue took refuge in another intimacy. They had moved over from Hotel Naco the day before. He could have told her then, for he was standing behind her with his arms around her bare midriff and his mouth practically in her ear, yet what was he doing but babbling sweet talk instead. For several minutes prior to turning in for their last night on the island, they stood and gazed at the Columbus Lighthouse—the light of truth Vanessa had called it—but he couldn't tell her then either.

After some thought he decided to hold off until they returned to Miami. Had her bliss-engendering nearness altered his mind or had he wondered too much about the consequences? And what about the nagging notion of whether he really *could* do it? Maybe that was why he hadn't told Vanessa. He wasn't sure himself.

This was another thing wallowing around in his head. There has to be a better way, Clay reasoned, as he had reasoned many times before. The Arab-Israeli model of tit for tat would lead to nothing but endless grief on both sides. Wasn't it enough, quite enough, to loathe the old chiseler, avoid him and curse the evil heart of anyone who would gyp a guy out of his retirement nest egg? Surely it would be easier. Just spend a few minutes loathing, avoiding and cursing every time the urge arose, then forget Leetboer for a while, forget the evilness and go on to something pleasant. The evil one's wife, for instance. She was not evil but scrumptious and gorgeous and dazzling, and she loved Clay Redmond all the way, with or without a nest egg.

So . . . rather than shoot to kill, he told himself, he'd throw a few "get even" punches now and then, benign punches that only knock the wind out (but choppers next if the urge didn't subside). That is, if he could ever catch the thieving rascal alone, without witnesses to corroborate a story believable enough to enable the old rogue and his confederate, Judge "Cotton" Brussard, to pick his pockets again. "*No way!*" Mason Riley would exclaim in a stout defense of his client's rights. "*Those two stinkers will surely haul you back into court on assault-and-battery charges!*" Yes, Clay thought, as surely as your fucking guitar strings will twang at the next gig. In the back of his mind Clay heard the familiar *trust me* refrain from the lips of his attorney and saw those same fat lips then open to expose Mason Riley's all-*un*natural sweet smile of assurance.

"Shit," Clay intoned. He ran his fingers through his thick, sun-bleached hair, mulling. The excitement he felt around Vanessa made him fidget out of a desperate restlessness to see her again after just one day apart. Now the second day was growing long in the tooth, as Wall Street mavens sometimes quip when they feel the time is right for a correction.

Clay lifted the Remington Model 51 out of a hidden compartment under the lap drawer and peered down its dark, death-dispensing barrel for a time, mumbling to himself. Staring. Then he took aim at a colorful and quite puffy spinnaker he saw on a distant sailboat out in the Atlantic, aimed the way a gun-lover will do for the thrill of holding and pointing a real pistol, with no intention to fire. Perhaps, he thought, a half-and-half nonviolent approach really would yield more satisfaction in the long run than shoving a muzzle against the Dutchman's head and sending a bullet through his ratty old toupee. The trigger would not put an end to it. No, because a sense of dishonor would seize his own heart as soon as the other heart stopped ticking. Clayborn Redmond, dishonored, would then have to pay up—and big time this time. Prison aside, he would then have to spend the rest of his sorry life feeling low-down and despising himself for a weakness he never recognized until that fatal moment, and never before had reason to question. The whys troubled him when he considered that, even after the evil carcass lay in rot, locked inside a stainless steel coffin, and even with that devil-bearing box well enclosed within a concrete vault sealed airtight with top grade mortar mix, the late Ewen Leetboer would have won again. But it was worse to contemplate that a mere skeleton would continue to win, that a departed fart would keep on stinking up his mind forever and ever. There would be no retirement for the ill-fated partner, Clay Redmond. *Never—nevermore,* to quote the Raven.

And what about Vanessa? *Oh dearest Vanessa!* The thought prompted Clay to imagine her face, not blazing with the fiery, storybook passion he saw in Santo Domingo or etched with the Mona Lisa look of relief to be rid of the chiseling old bastard, but full of revulsion at the very sight of Clayborn Redmond and his erstwhile "phallic nose" . . . his woman . . . suddenly revulsed because she had been fool enough to submit her heart, her body and soul, to a man who could do such a deadly thing. She would think, *Clay Redmond murdered my husband! He shot dear Ewen, not out of love for me but out of revenge for himself, primitive revenge incited by not a single romantic motive, rotten revenge that reeked of nothing more than a squabble over some little thing called "beneficial interest" in a stupid partnership!*

Nothing noble about that triangle, Clay concluded as he fired imaginary shots at the spinnaker he was tracking across the horizon. "Bang, bang, bang. You're history," he drawled to a phantom Leetboer and then tucked the automatic back in its compartment.

Ramón's phone call interrupted Clay in the middle of his anguish, which had risen to a new high following the Remington's dull, impotent snap against an empty chamber. The Cuban's excitement, though, spilled through the phone and rescued his Florida friend's attention from its morbid drift.

"Hello, Mr. Jones?" Ramón said with loud, articulate distinction.

"You have the wrong number," Clay answered. The broker seemed lethargic and annoyed by the interruption.

"No—wait! This is Felipe Jorge in Cuba. You were expecting my call, remember? Felipe Jorge . . ."

"Oh, yes. I didn't recognize your voice, Felipe. How are things in Havana?"

"*Excellente! Socialismo o muerte* is all the rage down here. We must talk though. Can you travel tomorrow?"

"Tomorrow? To where?"

"Mañana, Mr. Jones! To Mexico!"

"*Qué pasa?* What's up?"

"*Qué pasa?* The shipment of cigars is ready! Because of the embargo you must take possession over there."

Clay hollered up at the ceiling, a kind of cowboy yelp that echoed through the apartment. He feared surveillance by Cuban authorities and had suggested to Ramón in Santo Domingo that they scramble their conversation whenever a phone call from the island became necessary. They would couch incriminating facts in innocent terms but not hesitate to incriminate others with misinformation when circumstances called for it. They would also ad lib in liberal doses, use fake names, and otherwise leave a confusing trail for eavesdroppers to follow. Within the shifting context of their creative dialogue, the critical message would make sense only to them.

Reference to a "shipment of cigars" lifted Clay's face out of its somber cast. Right away he began to pick up some of the excitement he was hearing in Ramón's voice. "Hot damn!" he yelped. "How many in the shipment?"

"The total sum as we agreed!"

"You mean five . . . ?"

"Yes."

"Good. I'll need time to settle the invoice."

"No problem. The great thief from Canada consented to finance the shipment just as you predicted he would. I couldn't believe my eyes! Now I cannot believe my brain. Do you think there is even a tiny chance his check will clear?"

"Sure," Clay answered after another loud hoot. "The old swindler is too crafty to let a check bounce in Cuba. Besides, he's got so much money he won't even miss this little dab now that it's out of his hands. But—*goddam*—how he hates to let go! Are you familiar with terrapin power, Felipe?"

"I have heard rumors about terrapins," the Cuban replied with a chuckle, "those with certain features of a horse's turd." His quiet dignity had been derailed by a rare streak of jubilance brought on by their charade and by the success of his con job. "They tell me one can chop the reptile's neck away from the body and the head will not turn loose whatever is in the mouth until salt turns to rum. Something like that."

"The rumor lives in Leetboer. I suspect our two-legged terrapin does not believe he has yet parted with his money. Otherwise, he wouldn't have turned loose for rum or salt. You told him the Cuban government would refund the deposit later, didn't you?"

"True, the way you instructed. But still the task did not seem a small one for the man's arm to lift the check and pass it over to me. To watch him struggle, one would think this tiny paper weighed five hundred kilos."

"You're right about that. You got him to turn loose, too. What a clip joint you must be running, Felipe Jorge! I would love to have been one of those ubiquitous flies on the wall down there, watching you and your lovely *camarada*—Carla isn't it?—sell him Mara Paradiso."

Ramón's laughter crackled with an air of raucous pride that he seldom showed to anyone. *"Sí, Carla, mi camarada,"* he said between chuckles. "Maybe we perform another of these stings one day, after the embargo is lifted, then you can come here and I will show you how easy it is to steal from a rich tourist."

"But first, now that you've talked him into financing the conspiracy, let *our* rich tourist show you how easy it is to steal from Castro. What a partner, huh?"

"True in every detail. Such a thief can steal the beard right off Fidel's face. There is no embargo with Canada so the robber of retirements, to use your words, is free to come and go as he pleases. Americans suffer more from the embargo. Like a fox, Castro pretends it is a misfortune for Cuba yet all the goods in the world are available to him, legal merchandise from every country but the United States—and even there if the price is right, for cash. The problem, though, is that our Maximum Leader has few dollars. He cannot pay and so he uses the embargo to make excuses for his failures."

"Would you say Castro loves to hate the embargo?"

"You have spoken a great truth, Señor Jones. Oh yes. The embargo is like a woman of the street he embraces for his pleasure, only he is the whore."

"To hell with the embargo. I wish I could go to Cuba any time I want. Fuck! Where are those two bastards now?"

"There are many bastards in Cuba, amigo. Of which two are you speaking?"

"The great ones—Ewen Leetboer and Stanley B. Conover, Castro's new partners."

"*Ah, esos dos bastardos.* They went with Camarada Carla to inspect Mara Paradiso."

Clay's voice rose. "And you're not with them?"

"It was her solution to drive them to Varadero. She went with them alone. I could tell they have a great lust for pretty women, those *lobos*, so I let her convince me—too easy perhaps—how much more important it was to put their minds on other wonders than Mara Paradiso and the problems they will soon encounter with the Spaniard, Don Guillermo Valdez."

Clay spewed a hearty burst into the mouthpiece, his first laugh since picking up the phone. The crew monitoring this call must be getting an earful, he said to himself, convinced and even hopeful that Ramón's phone *was* bugged. No doubt everyone of those assholes would give a year's salary—which is not what even a cotton chopper in Alabama would call a substantial sacrifice—to get an eyeful as well, to learn the identity of the mystery woman, Carla. To find out that she and Elena were the same person would drive those who had seen Elena crazy with lust. All would think the same thought and cross themselves as if in obedient gratitude for the blessings of a personal saint: how fortunate that Camarada Carla is none other than the lovely traitor Elena, they would think, and what pleasures might befall them, they would rush to imagine, from the simple trade of their silence for a little *"buen tiempo"* with her.

The corrupt image of suspected eavesdroppers, amusing at first, forced Clay back into an earlier somber mood. He remembered Elena from bygone days when he and Graciela were the hot-couple topic. Now it was Ramón's and Elena's turn to stand in the spotlight. But the risk was great, too, and it bothered Clay when Ramón briefed him in Santo Domingo about his scheme to use her office. Over there Ramón seemed more confident about the risk. Now, with only his voice to judge by, Clay felt the Cuban sounded less so despite attempts to camouflage their identities.

"She'll be safe, you think?" Ramón asked, turning serious.

"If she can handle their ogles and dirty, tasteless wisecracks," Clay told him.

"But, amigo, what about . . . dirty, tasteless intentions?"

"Knock it off. You know the answer—a big fat NO, at least none her pure heart will accept."

"Perhaps I should have gone to Varadero with her."

"No, Felipe. You did right. She'll keep them off-balance, and with class and grace. It's important now that you get me the check . . . gars. Check on it, I mean."

Clay's slip of tongue and quick cover-up brought a smile to Ramón's face. "Yes, check the checkgars, the *checkgars!* I will phone you later tonight with further instructions," he answered and hung up.

21

Around two a.m. Ramón phoned Clay's private number again. "At last we can talk without codes," he sighed, sounding a bit whipped. "I am now in Cancún but I have worried the whole way about my lovely Elena."

Clay mumbled sleepily, checking his watch. "You had me in a stew, man. Look what time it is!"

"Did I wake you?"

"I was catnapping. Figured you'd call back sooner. You hung up so quick, like somebody had a gun on you."

"Are you worried, too?"

"No, not about Elena," Clay answered. "For a while, though, I was worried about you. So the Great Houdini has already made it to Cancún? May I assume everything is still on track?"

The Houdini comment forced a laugh out of Ramón. "Yes, fine," he said. "No problem with our plans. It's . . . it's that my lovely Elena . . . she is still with the two crooks . . ."

"Relax, Ramón. She'll be safe enough. Women are not the primary interest of those assholes, I tell you, even such beauties as your lovely Elena."

Clay had ordered pizza and stayed put in his apartment for fear of missing Ramón's second call of the night. A few critical points were left dangling and the accumulation set off a queasy discomfort inside of him that soon prompted a slew of pessimistic thoughts. Something must have gone awry, Clay kept saying to himself, since Ramón had cradled the phone so abruptly and without explanation. But when the Cuban called back, and after the first few words, it was apparent that he merely had to leave in a hurry to catch his ride and did not want to give away a critical itinerary to some puke-face wiretapper.

"Very well, amigo. I trust you," Ramón replied. "You know these lechers, they are not dangerous, right? They will not harm my lovely Elena?"

"They're not the type to rape a woman, if that's what you mean. A man, though, now that's another matter, especially if he's got 'ets' hanging off the end of his ass."

"*No comprendo.* I'm sorry, Clay, but your profanities do not always make sense to me."

"No matter," Clay said, yawning. "Think of it this way: Ewen Leetboer likes to screw men out of their, uh, *assets.* Stanley B. Conover likes to help him, likes to watch. On a purely physical plane they're quite harmless fellows. It's Castro and his military machine that worries me the most. If the old warrior finds out that

Leetboer deposited five million dollars into your hands instead of his private coffers, he may not approve the partnership."

Ramón howled. "What an understatement you have spoken! *May not approve the partnership*? Are you kidding me?"

"You don't think so?" Clay said, gently baiting him in an effort to restore the Cuban's humor.

"No way, José! Because there would be no Leetboer left to approve. The man would become quickly kaput, as they say in Russia, or somewhere! Mara Paradiso would remain an orphan, right?"

"I'm afraid so."

"El Cojonudo would like that!" Ramón chortled. "It will save him the trouble of introducing a machete to the lecher's throat."

"Yeah," Clay agreed in the middle of another lengthy yawn, "although Leetboer might suffer a worse fate if Castro gets to thinking his new Mara Paradiso partner has somehow cheated him out of five million dollars. No severed, cleanly hacked neck then. We don't want to be around when Fidel comes to that conclusion. Keeping the old Dutchman alive to experience the torture on a daily schedule, year in and year out, would be the ultimate punishment, not quick kaput. That's why I say your lovely Elena has more to fear from Castro and his military machine than from Leetboer and his crooked attorney."

"Yes, but such is the life of Cubans. We must live with soldiers and police in our face all the time. So what else is new? Maybe I should have followed your advice and used a Tropicana dancer instead of my Elena for so dangerous a mission."

Clay sighed. "No, you did right I tell you. Elena puts all of those buxom broads at the Tropicana to shame. Thanks to her you got the check. Thanks to you you still have it. Good work I say. Payday is not far off. Now, about that bank account. We must act fast to clear Leetboer's draft. By the way, I'm much relieved that you made it to Cancún okay. Unknown couriers in situations like this can give a guy diarrhea in a hurry. Tomorrow—" Clay glanced at the clock on his bedside table. "Fuck, it's already tomorrow. Anyhow, your personal delivery will eliminate the risk of losing our, shall we say, good-faith deposit."

"Very true. There are many thieves who handle the mail these days. Whether in Cuba or Mexico, a check of this dimension would not survive even one hour."

"Uh-huh. And a raft would be too slow. Agree?"

"Yes, and dangerous for the check," Ramón answered in the same mock-serious tone. "I don't think the ferries to Cancún are running from Cabo de San Antonio either."

"Scope it out. We may need alternate transport later. Daily runs would be nice, I think, and practical for our purpose. By the way, how did you get out of Cuba this time?"

"Easy."

"The hell you say! But you're in Mexico. You haven't had time to walk or swim. Don't tell me you managed to line up a flight?"

"Bingo! Is that the right word?"

"It could be. What did you line up?"

"The DXL plane! It left Martí at ten-forty tonight. Thanks to your MasterCard and the extra cash it has provided, the pilot agreed to accept a bribe and rent one of his uniforms so he could take Felipe Jorge along as a co-pilot trainee."

"Well I'll be damned," Clay said wearily. "Felipe Jorge, huh? That character is becoming quite a scoundrel. Doesn't he ever stop to piss?"

"Why? You have equipped him well—a passport, visas, all kinds of fake papers, and of course this very powerful MasterCard."

"Okay, okay. So the DXL pilot smuggled you out of the country. Is that what you're saying?"

"You know it is the only way. A legal visa is a rare thing in Cuba. Remember? Unlike you there in Miami with all your freedoms and liberties and great airports, I cannot just jump on a jet and fly to Cancún whenever I please, not without our Maximum Leader's permission, which, as you are well aware, he does not often grant to those who steal from him."

"Yeah, and even to those who don't. Leetboer will soon discover this. All right, good. I'll give you a ring after the next plane lands. Do you have a place yet?"

"The DXL pilot suggested Casa Maya."

"A luxury hotel?"

"*Sí.* But it is only a few dollars more according to the pilot. He will share the room."

"And the cost?"

"No. The room was part of the arrangement of co-pilot."

"How generous you are with my MasterCard," Clay grunted. "Okay, I'll call you from the lobby. We can talk in the restaurant. When the banks open I'd like to touch base with the boys at Banco Mar. My guy there is an expert at laundering money. I'm confident he can work a speedy clearance on the check, particularly if he gets a small percentage."

Ramón whistled into the telephone. "Banco Mar is a very big bank in Mexico," he yelled, almost screeching. "Do you have an account with them already?"

"A small checking account," Clay answered, "for travel convenience. Ewen Leetboer's deposit, though, must go in a different account altogether, one that can't be traced back to us."

"Clay Redmond, my honored friend, you are truly a genius!" Ramón replied, pulling the phone away from his mouth to soften a robust, jubilant shout. "For another small percentage, as you say, I am equally certain that this courtesy of an untraceable account can also be arranged. Correct?"

"Yeah. Now you're catching on to the tricks of the trade. If all goes well we'll have time to stop in at Bogart's for a couple of tequilas before the plane leaves, say around six or seven? I'll have a few things to go over with you once the bank deal is settled."

"The DXL pilot tells me there is Cuban music at La Brisa," Ramón hinted.

"Okay, La Brisa. I'll be in the bar in case we have to split up at the bank for some reason. Or maybe I'll go for a walk on the beach. Who knows? Somewhere."

"You sound a little strange, my brother. Is everything all right?"

"Sure," Clay lied.

"Sure?"

"Approximately perfect. Copasetic."

"Truly?"

"Truly."

Ramón waited for further denials but when Clay offered none, he spoke jauntily into the phone. *"Salud,* until you arrive.

Then I will find you wherever you decide to be. This is what I told my lovely Elena some years ago when I expressed a desire to take her to Cancún. She was afraid of getting lost here and separated from me and I told her, 'No, Elena. Cancún is not yet like Havana. It is a young city designed with Mayan integrity.' This is exactly how I phrased it and would you believe she laughed at me?"

"Really? Why?"

"For wanting to take her to a place less beautiful than Cuba!" Ramón answered, lapsing into another hearty chuckle. "She then requested Paris."

"Remarkable."

"Remarkable? What is so remarkable about Paris?"

"Not Paris. It's your great spirit, the sound of it. Ramón, you mustn't worry about Elena. Too bad you couldn't invite her to come along with you now that Cuba isn't as beautiful as it once was. Maybe she'd accept this time."

"No, she would only laugh again. Sometimes my Elena is a fantastic joker."

"Show her the MasterCard. Flaunt a little of the cash you're about to inherit. Knowing the pay scale in Cuba, she probably was just trying to spare you an embarrassment. Anyhow, you'll have other opportunities, and soon I trust, to express your desire again."

"Oh, no," he responded, "not even for a vacation! Never will I insult her with another offer of travel to a less beautiful place! To her Cuba will always remain number one, even with Castro there. The country is something deep in her heart."

"Elena is no fool," Clay said. "She'll change her mind after Cuba regains its freedom."

"Perhaps," Ramón sighed. "In the meantime I will continue to hope she will at least one day accompany me to Miami. We have so many friends there now." Ramón's voice faded into a whisper, then nothing. But his pause was brief this time, with only hems and haws to break the silence. Clay seemed to know what was on the Cuban's mind and so he waited with cagey patience for him to spit it out.

"Your woman Vanessa . . ." Ramón went on, stammering a bit as his voice returned. He then proceeded smoothly into the issue that Clay had suspected. "She will be with you?"

"No."

"No? Why not? If my Elena is successful in not being harmed while she holds the interest of the lechers, your woman will be alone for two more days. Maybe longer. Is this not another fortunate occasion for you to travel with her?"

"No. It would not be in good taste."

"Good taste? What do you mean? You have taken the lady already to Santo Domingo!"

"Yes, hell—and I meant to tell her down there."

"That's different. El Cojonudo kept us too busy with his threats. Where is the problem now?"

"Here, with me. She still doesn't know yet. It would seem sneaky not to tell her now that we've gone this far."

"Then tell her!" Ramón shouted, forgetting for the moment his own concerns about Elena. "If you can trust her, I mean. After all, she is the man's wife. Can you trust her?"

"Yes."

"Then tell her. She will only want you more."

"There isn't time now, not in Miami. I want to tell her at Bella Mar where we first met. So . . . later it must be."

"Ah, yes. Later, a favorite time with many people." Ramón eased into a deeper chuckle than the other ones. His eyes suddenly bulged into grossly protuberant balls of light and dark and his head nodded in those jerky little movements that he had served up so effectively to Stanley B. Conover the day before. A thin 'gotcha' smile eased into the facial mix and for a moment it appeared as though Ramón were staring straight at Clay instead of the hotel wall in front of his telephone.

"My brother," the Cuban blurted, "I think maybe you are in love again! Yes, I think so—"

"Go to sleep," Clay answered, cutting him off."

He hung up the telephone momentarily to break the connection and called the airport to make reservations to Cancún. The next plane would leave too early for a leisurely breakfast at a decent hour, but coffee and rolls aboard the flight sounded rather yummy right then.

At 2:58 a.m. Clay set an alarm and turned off the light by his bed. Like Ramón, he was also worried about a woman. Even if he decided not to pull Leetboer's plug and send the old chiseler on his way, leaking vital fluids and crawling feebly toward his eternal night, he, Clay, must still face up to the fact that his sting operation had so far lessened Vanessa's future estate by five million dollars, plus accrued interest, and even greater losses might follow. How would she feel about that? he wondered. How would she feel about a lot of things? Divorce, for instance, if not widowhood.

At least Vanessa shouldn't have to endure the miserable ordeal, Clay told himself, of being screwed by Ewen Leetboer ever again. Emancipation from that loathsome experience was worth something, the distraught broker figured, and he carried these thoughts with him on his drift into yet another oasis of darkness where he hoped to snatch two more hours of sleep.

22

C lay Redmond made it to Cancún okay but didn't return the
next evening as planned. His Banco Mar contact had been sent
unexpectedly to Acapulco to straighten out some accounts there and
would be delayed a few days, maybe longer. Clay decided to hole
up offshore on quiet little Isla Mujeres near Cancún and wait. He
welcomed a break anyway. The recent pace had drained him. But
he also needed time to reflect, to plan, to sort things out without
distraction, even from Vanessa.

This Mexican two-step had to wind down soon, though,
before Leetboer caught on to the sting and canceled the check. If the
old Dutchman stayed true to form, he'd return to Miami and immerse
himself in a separate intrigue for a while. Such a detour would
provide Clay Redmond with all the wiggle room he'd need, thanks

to Silvio, who kept the broker advised of Leetboer's movements in and out of Cuba.

Ramón, full of anxiety over the safety of his secret love, Elena, could hardly restrain a joyful yelp when Clay suggested he not go with him to Isla Mujeres.

"You brought the check," Clay reminded the Cuban. "I'll take it from here. Besides, you're worried sick about Elena so why park your ass in Mexico and wait for that banker to get back when you're needed in Cuba?"

The message hit home. Without argument Ramón donned his rented co-pilot's uniform and headed back to Havana aboard the DXL plane, which had just returned from Mexico City and other points of delivery. Once airborne, and in almost every breath, the restless Cuban repeated a vow of mortal revenge if any harm came to Elena, or even a fear of harm, while she was on the mission.

"Holy mierda, Clay is worried too!" Ramón fumed, scolding himself with repeated outcries. "What a great danger I have placed her in!"

The Cuban could not conceal his distress. Once off the ground, he began to thrash in his seat without regard to the delicate navigational instruments within easy reach of his arms, both of which he occasionally put in motion to knock down phantom likenesses of Ewen Leetboer when they sprang up in front of him, often just inches beyond his nose. Now and again he would force himself to relax, or to appear relaxed, then after he could sit still no longer, he'd ruminate in fits and starts and chat in loose—sometimes incoherent—discourse with the pilot as they flew over the Gulf of Mexico. What seemed to him a precarious situation for Elena continued to swell larger in his mind, frequently mushrooming into ruinous scenes and inciting outbursts against Leetboer and Conover loud enough to spark several stealthy glimpses out of the corner of the DXL pilot's eyes. Ramón had dislodged the regular co-pilot, who seemed quite happy to leave the noisy cockpit and go join a couple of female "camp followers" in the cabin.

"You seem troubled, Duque," the pilot soon remarked. "What could possibly upset you after experiencing such a flamboyant place as Cancún? The women there are magnificent, are they not?"

Ramón's face wrinkled over. "No, but my fiancée is," he sighed. "Perhaps you were having a flamboyant experience in Cancún, but I was suffering in my heart the whole time, knowing she was giving two thieves a private escort—thieves who may also be killers!"

"Forget her," the pilot answered with a smart, businesslike wave of his hand.

He was a seasoned professional from Panama and a part-time snitch for Castro in matters pertaining to overnight deliveries in and out of Cuba and the secrets his packaged cargo held. Opportune moments rarely escaped his keen eye for detail. Unhampered by low moral character but, to the contrary, aided by it, he had begun to see some profit in live cargo as well. This younger man in the co-pilot's seat seemed in the pilot's mind to be overly virtuous yet guilty of something in spite of his snooty rejection of a friendly blow job.

"Find another fiancée, my son," the pilot added in a sorrowful pitch, as a father confessor might utter. "There are many excellent choices in Havana as well as Cancún. Why would your woman escort thieves and killers anyway? Is she crazy?"

"It was my foolish belief she would be safe with them," Ramón replied. He had calmed outwardly but his voice was heavy with remorse.

The pilot grunted. "Then you must be also crazy."

"Yes, too much crazy. I should not have allowed her to drive them all the way to Varadero—"

"Your fiancée drove two killers from Havana to Varadero . . . in a car?"

"Of course a car. What do you think, a goat wagon?"

"She was alone with them?"

"Yes!"

"What kind of car?"

"A Chevrolet . . . 1956 . . ."

"With slick tires I bet. Is the car a sedan, with a comfortable, roomy back seat perhaps?"

Ramón squinted at the pilot. "Why you ask such questions? She drove them under orders from the *Ministerio del Interior* so they can look at this half-finished resort called Mara Paradiso and exchange agreements with each other about how much the property is a steal. So fucking what?"

"*So fucking what*? Listen, my innocent, unlicensed co-pilot, I will tell you so fucking what." The pilot paused to turn on the automatic controls. "For an instance," he resumed after briefly observing the plane's performance, "she is now alone with two killers, right? There are no ministers present, right?"

"Fuck you," Ramón said.

"With every mile I think these two thieving killers have been looking at her also. Can you not wonder how true this is?"

Ramón's eyes closed, his face erupted into a picture of agony. "*Yes, damn them!*" he wailed. "It would be impossible not to look at so desirable a woman."

"You see? You must find yourself another virgin to marry and forget this one. The killers will surely not leave you even a taste of her chastity."

"Fly the plane!" Ramón snapped. "You have no concept of my Elena!"

The pilot, not sensing the depth of Ramón's anguish, continued to amuse himself with further taunts. "Oh, so it is your Elena? Yes, now I see. Now I see more clearly with the name. Now I see your Elena with them, driving the 1956 Chevrolet for the killers to look at a place called—what you call this resort?"

"Mara Paradiso. The name is not important."

"*Paradiso?* Oh, yes, this name is very important! How could such a name not suggest the many pleasures available in the Garden of Eden? It will bring thoughts to mind, a man's thoughts. On the journey back to Havana they will be overcome with these thoughts. They will be overcome enough to remove the lady's clothes, perhaps without a struggle, because, being killers, they have guns and must be handsome devils. Otherwise, they would be impatient to have her right away in this place you call Mara Paradiso. Ugly killers would not be looking at unfinished properties when they have a beautiful señorita in the car beside them. They would be eager to finish with her instead, much too eager to turn away and look at bull dozers and hammers and dirty hombres with beards."

"You are thinking with your cock, old man," Ramón said, bristling. "Believe me, there would be a struggle. My fiancée is a tiger."

"Very good! Oh, yes, yes. It will encourage the handsome killers more to make their passes. A fighting woman arouses a man, like a fluttering bird arouses a cat."

Ramón stared hard at the pilot. "You are a pig!" he shouted. "*You are a mad pig!*"

"And after they have had their little fun," the pilot went on, not pausing to let Ramón speak, "they will leave her in a ditch—naked, bruised or maybe even bleeding her tiny life away . . ."

The pilot's words stunned Ramón. For a few seconds the Cuban seemed frozen in a glare through the cockpit window, as if he were seeing somewhere in the sky what the pilot had just then described.

"*Holy mierda!*" he cried out again, "*I will kill them both!*"

"Who, Duque? Who will you kill?"

"The two fucking Canadians! Now please shut that pig mouth and let me think—"

Ramón's eyes then turned their glare back to the pilot while his hand extracted a nylon cord from inside a pocket. Suddenly, with the agility of a commando, Ramón rose and slipped the cord around the man's neck and tightened it with a fierce jerk.

"*Aargg . . . aaugh!* W-what the hell—!" The pilot's windpipe flattened, his voice barely intelligible. At the same time, his eyes began to bulge and flash unfettered fears that a skyjack was underway or, worse, that the CIA had finally caught up with him.

Ramón sneered down at the defenseless pilot. For several minutes the Cuban played out some of his anger with the cord, tightening it and releasing the pressure in slow spurts over and over again while issuing his own taunts. Then moments before the distressed man looked on the verge of passing out, Ramón growled in a tone so direful it seemed to send a chill over the autopilot as well, for the aircraft's wings began to dip menacingly, first one way and then the other before stabilizing.

"What the hell you ask?" Ramón blurted. "Listen, asshole, I will tell you what the hell is. You must not concern yourself with these two killers. These two killers will face their own eternity of hell tomorrow, perhaps not so long after you. Their sins are many, yes. These killers, these robbers of retirements, these defilers of women have no more than a few hours to continue their treacheries. As for you, you have a big mouth, a filthy mind. You show no respect for mothers and daughters and you ask too many questions for a simple pervert. Now it is time for you to listen, you obscene old fool. One more thing—you can place another bet along with the slick tires. It you will be more certain to win, provided you do not bet against the perfect truth of the next words you hear: *Listen, you piece of shit on Castro's balls! Some would say your life is 'hanging by a thread.' I say perhaps only by the noose around your fat neck. But what does it matter now? If I knew how to fly this whorehouse-above-the-clouds, you would be already dead!*"

23

"What you think, Stanley?" Leetboer asked without looking at his attorney.

Conover lifted the new broad-brim straw hat he had purchased from a street vendor in Havana some days earlier. Perspiring from every pore, he nevertheless tried to strike a cool and collected pose as he wiped across his brow with his forearm. "Beautiful," he replied with a stir of enthusiasm. "There's a ton of equity in the ground already."

"Yes, Stanley, but Mara Paradiso is huge. There are many equities left to complete."

"Not much really if you forget the Rolls Royce touches that crazy Spanish developer tacked on. Hell, Ewen, with all this cheap labor down here, you can finish out the rest and sell your share of the project by next Christmas."

"You think that quick, eh?"

"I do, damn right I do."

"Why you not say it then, Stanley? If you believe your words, go on and say Mara Paradiso is a prize. Tell me it will be a sweetheart deal for Ewen!"

Conover threw his head back and uncorked a defensive laugh, one of his rabbit-in-the-hat tricks he often extracted to fend off unexpected pressure. "If you don't forget about Redmond!" he countered in a boisterous tone, giving Leetboer a stern legal eye and a raised finger pulsating with cogency. "We have to take care of that jerk before he gets wind of the five mil check you turned loose back in Havana. Sure as hell he'll demand a commission."

Leetboer tugged at his Adam's apple while he thought. His dull gray eyes opened beyond their usual half-mast slit, not suddenly, but in a cautious progression that soon took on faint glimmers of omniscience. "I may not wish to sell," said Leetboer as his outward gaze widened and he lapsed into a more circumspect stance.

Stanley B. Conover stared at the side of Leetboer's turned-away face. "Okay," he muttered, then sucked air through closed teeth for a moment before resuming. "Keep it, keep your little gold mine. That's better yet—income streams forever. But remember where you are."

"What you mean?"

"I mean this is commie country. Different rules."

"Ahhh. You *do* think I am being foolish, yes?"

"Only foolish if you give Redmond a slice of the goddam pie."

"I see. Then you will not abandon me down here if there are investigations about his disappearance?"

"Hell no—to the contrary," Conover retorted, giving the air a vigorous jab. "If you'll set me up with a twenty-five percent stake, Ewen, I'll take care of Redmond myself, plus all your legal headaches, all the crappy stuff, till the merry end. What the hell—I'll even try to cut a deal with Castro to bring gambling back."

Leetboer looked down at his feet. "I see," he said.

The two men were standing on a promontory above the Mara Paradiso project, overlooking an ambitious sprawl of unfinished structures poking through a seemingly deserted landscape. Some buildings rose out of a thick tropical jungle that had already encroached upon them after a few months of idleness. Even the charming old-world spires, in place on several and reverently celestial in their skyward stretches high above the palms, were not exempt from the aggressive, take-charge onslaughts of Cuban flora nor beyond the reach of curious howler monkeys Señor Valdez had imported from Costa Rica. Other structures were scattered amidst grassy knolls on hillsides, left to weather undisturbed in their shell condition but still exuding a unique character which, one might say, was a bit on the order and style of fanciful castles under construction by competitors in the gaming industry. Buildings nearer completion and with their elegant Mediterranean architectural design in fuller evidence were set like jewels against the stunning beauty of blue-green waters and white sandy coastline.

"Let us think how to do this work," Leetboer mumbled. "First, I will send for my 'Republican Guard,' as Saddam would say. That is, my crew in Canada . . . the foremen, my best men."

"Yeah, you'll need somebody to supervise the locals. Let's check with that hotshot back in Havana, Felipe Jorge. He can put us in touch with the original workers."

"Ah, yes, him—Felipe Jorge. Good idea, Stanley. Perhaps he will know the best ones to hire back."

The old Dutchman was overwhelmed with awe as he viewed the rich expansiveness of what had already become *his* resort. To borrow words used by real estate pros, he had *moved in.* As for the "defaulting" party, Señor Valdez, Leetboer gave the Spaniard's misfortune not a whit of thought beyond his usual philosophical summary whenever defaults occurred. "One must pay for his mistakes," was all Ewen Leetboer had to say about this presumed delinquency as well, although he repeated it several times to mollify Stanley B. Conover, whose exuberance for the "windfall" project had grown by the minute but was now and then counterbalanced by an outpouring of compassionate disbelief. *The poor bastard,* Conover would sigh, wondering how anyone could walk away from such a development, cold turkey, with so much already invested.

"Damn beautiful, Ewen," the attorney then repeated, after paying final homage to Señor Valdez's impoverished status. He could no longer hide his enthusiasm for Mara Paradiso either now that Leetboer had agreed, albeit tacitly, to cut him in for a quarter of the take. *Fuck Redmond,* Conover scoffed under his breath. *I can play the broker scam game, too.*

When the sun beamed through a thin layer of clouds, the aquamarine waters seemed to wash and wave their beauty straight into Ewen Leetboer's enlivened eyes, bestowing upon their dull grayness as much sparkle as might a school of sequin-clad mermaids swimming past in a squeaky tight, siren-like formation.

Sensing that he might have let himself get too carried away in front of Conover by the enormous profit potential he saw in Mara Paradiso, Leetboer put the fire out in his eyes and, without forewarning, resumed his staid business manner. "Where is the girl?" he asked, swinging his head in search of her.

Elena was perched on the fender of Ramón's pre-revolutionary Chevy 210 a few yards away from where the two men were standing. "Carla is here," she answered sleepily.

Leetboer stepped closer to the vehicle. "Oh, miss, can we come again tomorrow, yes?"

"Heavens—!" Elena shrieked, frowning. "Another trip? We have traveled here three times already! What more is there to see?"

"The rain. Tomorrow it will rain."

"A shower maybe."

"Good. Even a medium shower will tell me things about the soil. Now, miss, tomorrow you drive us back again. No more talk."

Leetboer moved up to the car door. Before he opened it all the way, Elena slid off the fender, perking up but holding a twinkle of annoyance in her eyes as she glanced at him. She had on a somewhat frayed pair of jeans, and it was apparent that their distressed condition came honestly from legitimate wear rather than from factory theatrics. Without further comment she proceeded to stretch a bright yellow headband around her dark Latin hair. Afterwards she gave the sleeveless blouse she had changed into earlier a good fluffing to fan the hot air underneath, then, to escape more heat, she tied the bottom end in a double knot around her waist, exposing a neatly recessed navel and a midriff that dieters mostly dream about. As the Cuban woman walked toward the driver's side, she began to chide Leetboer in a playful, less abrasive tone.

"If it is so difficult to remember Carla's name," she said, pausing to get inside the vehicle, "perhaps you should not return tomorrow."

Leetboer's dead pan hardly flinched. "Oh," he muttered. "What a statement over a name." His gaze softened. "Are you angry with me?"

"No, only worried for you."

"Worried? My goodness—why?"

"Because you forget things."

Leetboer's gaze softened further and his dull eyes began to take on a friskiness. "I see," he said. "Maybe I buy you some roses when we get back to Havana. Maybe I try to remember Carla's name better. Would that please you?"

"Roses?"

"Yes, roses. Red and white ones. And yellow ones, of course, beds of them on some acres with lodgings in the middle where you can live and work for me . . . ."

Elena laughed after hesitating, not knowing whether he might be serious. "Look, Mr. Leetboer, you are a nice man but luxuries have no place in Cuba for ordinary Cubans. Just answer me this one question: If you are so quick to forget what you have already seen after three visits here, do you think it is wise to undertake such a complicated construction as Mara Paradiso?"

Stanley B. Conover jumped in the back seat, clucking to himself over the exchange between the other two, which sounded all in good humor now that he owned a stake in the deal. The unflappable attorney had also moved in.

Leetboer eased onto the front seat. His face was still animated from the exhilaration that finally came over him during the last of the three site inspections. Or so Elena concluded until his gaze continued its meltdown over her body, spreading its watchful pour in slow exclusivity from banded hairline to painted toenails while other oscillations about his head began to speed up and set off a rapid succession of blinks, as if his autonomic nervous system had engaged itself for some defensive purpose other than clearing the eyes of a mote. Quite spontaneously he reached over and touched her smooth bare arm above the elbow and gave the underside nearest her breast two or three quick squeezes, perhaps with less promiscuous intent than Elena's sudden shiver implied. In fairness to both parties, the advance was either a clumsy grope or a whim to satisfy some dogged impulse that was urging him to confirm the reality of such an eye-popping distraction.

"I think we remain over here in Varadero tonight," Ewen Leetboer said to the Cuban woman. "It is late. In this old rattletrap and on these roads Havana will take several hours more. Do you know a place?"

Elena retracted her arm and gently pushed his hand away. "Many. There are hotels for tourists not far from here," she answered with matching directness. "I drove you past them when we first arrived some days ago, and again on the second trip. As I said, sir, your memory is not good."

"Good? Hmmm . . . goodness," he stammered, his wrinkled face further bedeviled by sudden recall. "Then I will arrange a suite. You will share it with us, eh?"

Elena gazed at him for a moment in silence, reflecting on the "rose estate" and the squeezes under her arm. "Cubans are not allowed to stay in tourist hotels," she explained with quiet dispassion. "But do not worry. I have a friend here in Varadero, a good friend from childhood days. She will take care of me."

"*Perfecto!*" Conover hummed behind a new spurt of energy. "Can she take care of us, too?"

214

Elena studied their faces for a moment, not missing the obvious. *"Qué babosos!"* she muttered under her breath, and with a huge frown that suggested another conflict. "First, let me be honest, gentlemen. I could get in much trouble for this arrangement. My friend too. Our tourist laws are very strict. But, to answer your question, yes, maybe."

"Yes maybe?" exclaimed Conover. "Now what the crap does that mean—*yes maybe!* We don't give a rat's ass about your screwy tourist laws, sweetie. Can you or can't you? Will you or won't you? Pesos or dollars?"

Elena rested a hand under her chin in a fretful pose. "I will talk with my friend," she said after an agonizing silence, "but you must protect me from the police if they come."

"Sure, sweetie, I'll protect you," Conover hummed, adding a courtroom flourish of fingers, some of which ended up on top of Elena's head, stroking her hairline. "What are friends for? Right, Ewen?"

"Right, Stanley."

Elena cast a puzzled look at Ewen Leetboer. *Why does he yield so easily to his attorney?* she wondered. The Cuban woman pulled forward, away from Conover's "mucky-fucky" hand, as she would later describe it to Ramón. To keep her tour-guide role intact, though, she made a tentative effort to chat and sound pleasant while examining her own face in the rearview mirror.

"This good friend I know will cook for you and provide a bed," she went on, reddening her cheeks with a few quick pinches. Then she gave the two men a coy wag of her finger and added, "A bed for sleeping, señores. None of this—" Elena executed the universal gesture.

"Fuck you," Conover said.

"No, never, no way! But the cost will be the same. You must give American dollars, too. Cuban pesos are worthless. Cuban girls are not."

A late-model Toyota Land Cruiser pulled up beside the Chevy, blocking Elena's exit just as she was ready to pull away. She gave the vehicle a quick scan to determine if it was a rental from Hertz or another agency or whether it bore any governmental or military identification. She found no clues and decided that it belonged to one of Cuba's Olympic athletes or to some lucky comrade with relatives in Miami. The man at the wheel, who was dressed like a chauffeur, pressed a button to roll down his window and spoke in Spanish to Elena while motioning over his shoulder at someone in the back seat.

"Qué pasa?" the Cuban woman asked, staring hard at the driver. He shrugged at her inquiry and continued to motion with his thumb lowered toward the person behind him. Elena strained to see the shadowy figure in the back seat but a clear view was obscured by deeply-tinted privacy glass in the windows. The engine was still running. With some further straining, she made out the form—a man in a suit as dark as the glass she was trying to look through sat motionless in the comfort of a cool interior. His eyes were pointed straight ahead, not at them at all and seeming unconcerned about the fact that his big four-wheeler was blocking the way.

Leetboer still had his mind on further flirtations with Elena and showed no interest in what he considered to be an easy traffic matter to resolve. In stony contrast, Conover sat upright with his eyebrows in a nasty crumple, urging Elena to ignore the intrusion and drive on.

"I cannot back up or turn for the trees," she said softly so as not to be overheard by their unexpected visitors. "Neither is the other side of the road safe for the car . . . and—look what lies ahead—the *cliff*!"

"Then talk to them!" Conover huffed. "Tell that asshole driver to get his rig the hell out of our way—like *P.D. pronto* for Christ's sake!"

Elena forced a chuckle to hide her frustration as well as inject some much needed calmness into the situation. She got out of her car and began to complain in loud colloquial Spanish as she rounded the hood of the Land Cruiser and stomped toward the driver's window. There followed a short exchange between her and the driver, who appeared to be just a mouthpiece for the occupant in the back seat. Elena turned her fiery stare to confront the other party behind the driver. A stout gangster type with Latin features was reposed among the trappings of a luxurious, custom interior. While he might have appeared relaxed and friendly to some, Elena winced when she took a second look. A stark, still silence hung over him with the sinister prescience of fog in a horror movie. His face was scary, too, reflecting the blank, cold cast of a ruthless brute; and his beady eyes, which had not wavered in their hard-and-fast glare since she stepped up to the window and looked in, seemed ready to burn a hole straight through her skull. His hair matched the raven blackness of her own, and it was slicked back into a long pony tail. The only thing moving was smoke from a cigarette stuck between his fat lips.

"Good afternoon, Elena," he finally said in a low, even voice. A geeky smile eased out of his yellow-stained mouth.

Elena stared at him. Then a few tense moments later her eyes locked on a pistol butt protruding from under his coat. "No, no," she replied, mildly startled but trying not to show it. "I am Carla . . . Carla from the *Ministerio del Interior.* Who are you?"

The man nodded and held up a photo of her. "Elena," he repeated with quiet firmness, "Ramón's woman. Do not lie."

"Who *are* you?" Elena asked again, sounding less defensive after hearing Ramón's name.

"I am Pepe. The woman who is Elena in this photograph will be safe with me."

"Oh, *Pepe—yes, yes!* I'm sorry. I did not realize who you were. Ramón told me about you."

"Listen—!" Pepe interrupted himself to take the cigarette out of his mouth. He then tapped the end somewhat ceremoniously on the rim of an ashtray before discarding it. After a brief interval of more hard-staring silence, he extracted another cigarette from a silver case in his coat pocket and used it to point at the pistol, which had just been further exposed. Elena acknowledged Pepe's gesture with a flurry of nods and listened with rising trepidation while his low-key monologue continued.

"Ramón has been detained in Havana."

Elena's eyes widened along with her mouth. "Detained?" she gasped. "Tell me—*qué pasa?* What do you mean? By whom detained?"

"The police. There was an incident at the airport. A pilot was strangled. Ramón's brother in Miami phoned the Bogotá office for help. You know him—Silvio. He said Ramón was delirious with fear for his Elena and I was sent here to protect you and to arrange his release. Tell me, are you in danger now?"

"Do not think of me please! Ramón—is he hurt from the crash?"

"The plane landed safely at José Martí. A woman passenger, perhaps the pilot's mistress, told the police that Ramón strangled the pilot and left the plane in a rage. Do not worry. I will convince the police that this fool pilot was eating Mexican enchiladas with his mistress and one lodged in his throat. Like faith, bribes can also move mountains."

"O Dios mio!" Elena screamed, cupping her mouth and almost collapsing against the driver's elbow propped over the window opening.

"Sí," Pepe said without the slightest whiff of compassion. "And after you pray to heaven for your man," he continued, speaking low as if in a church and employing the same smooth, easy tone he had just used to inform her of her safety and of Ramón's detention, saying, "please tell the two miserable thieves in the classic motor car next to us they are trespassing on El Cojonudo's property. If they are still here when I return from Colombia, I will shoot out their eyes."

24

Señor Valdez spent several more weeks in Colombia after Pepe returned from his emergency mission to Cuba. His business interests there were drug related, of course, as they say most all business conducted in Colombia these days is, one way or the other. Then he flew to Miami and checked in a towers ocean-view suite at the Fontainebleau. Pepe came along, too, and stayed with him for a couple of nights to catch up on the sleep he'd sacrificed while in Colombia in favor of increased vigilance. Under new and urgent orders, the loyal accomplice was soon dispatched back to Cuba to further reward certain officials for their courtesies to the prisoner, Ramón Alvarez, a.k.a. Felipe Jorge, during his detention. There was also the important business of keeping an eye on Mara Paradiso and the Canadian. Pepe's visa had not been canceled. In spite of Señor Valdez's reputation for mayhem, which prompted new regulations to safeguard foreign investors, including curtailment of "El Cojonudo's" travel privileges in Cuba, Pepe's dollar diplomacy made him a welcome liaison.

The hotel was a great place for the Spaniard to relax after dealing with a backlog of nasty problems in Cali and Medellín, even Bogotá. Some of his compadres down there had become "too much greedy." The subsequent "loss" of their services, however, had only a minor impact on staffing, for fresh recruits, new graduates and a standing army of "up-and-comers" were always waiting in the wings for a chance to prove their salt. What really hurt Guillermo Valdez, though, was having to put his Mara Paradiso project on hold while the violators of trust were punished and stolen cash retrieved. Meanwhile, there were the chosen standbys not yet so greedy itching to fill the shoes of the ones who no longer needed shoes. In time these replacements would become overly greedy, too, and the cycle would continue. Greed and treachery among dedicated drug dealers were balanced by justified suspicions among the cartel bosses, some of whom were occasionally found guilty themselves. Señor Valdez considered these traits nothing more than normal components of the job description and, like the trade itself, were best maintained out of sight if not out of mind, at least *his* mind. The latter was simply impossible, for Señor Valdez assumed them, the greed and treachery traits, to exist in each of the traffickers in spite of his warnings, his background checks and, later, the horrific examples arranged by Pepe, who demonstrated in graphic detail how to lose one's shoes and what it really meant to be "forced" into early retirement.

For the two men, Guillermo Valdez and Pepe, it was a great relief to get back to Miami, away from the thieves, embezzlers and betrayers in Colombia. If only Guillermo's dear Mara were with him to enjoy the love they had shared from childhood, how happy he would be in Miami during this otherwise dismal stopover. Now he had to settle for memories. Nothing else remained. He privately resented the other women whom he invited into his suite. Nevertheless, they were nice and he treated them with respect for relieving the pressure around his pubic arch, but none of them ever managed to soothe the ache in his heart for his beloved Mara.

Guillermo Valdez had powerful friends in Miami's exile community, some whose influence reached all the way to the Cuban leader's inner circle.

"What shall we do with this Canadian land pirate?" he said one evening to a trusted ally, Vicente Coto, a devout contrarian regarding Fidel's legacy. In every way, Coto felt entitled to make criticisms, for he had already paid his dues with half a lifetime in the dictator's prisons.

Coto's friends say he had grown smaller in jail, had suffered too much hunger during all those years in the Cuban dungeons. Certainly he was a gaunt figure compared to Señor Valdez. Lighter in complexion, too, not having any Moorish strains, although some of the lightness in his skin could be attributed to several dark years in solitary confinement. As strange as it might seem to those familiar with his background, Coto looked more the worldly man of leisure than a lowly "gusano" or "counterrevolutionary traitor," as Castro had branded him. Unaffected by day-to-day pressures, he had learned to accept things with equanimity. His easy, affable manner brought deeper respect from those who knew him, for they had also heard the stories of treatment in Cuban jails from others like him and felt he had every reason to hate. Yet, in spite of a desolate half-life, he still walked around Miami with a carefree, almost innocent air and somehow, miraculously, managed to radiate enough Latin "machismo" to turn a woman's head. His thick silvery hair and scarred but quietly handsome face showed no signs of bitterness because of the cruel prison existence he had endured following Castro's post-revolutionary purges. To the contrary, Coto projected the same sort of happy, kind, non-grudging face as Nelson Mandela, who also knew something about prisons and how they could sap one's life away unjustly.

The two men were having dinner at the Fontainebleau's celebrated Club Tropigala, where they often met to refresh their family's long-standing friendship when Señor Valdez happened to be in town. The setting was marked by prosperous customers, a holiday atmosphere enriched by grand entertainments, spectacular musical revues and exotic performers from all the major genders.

"Why not bury him under the cornerstone," Guillermo Valdez's guest replied between appreciative glances at one of the ladies at the next table. Her congenial smile had caught his eye.

Señor Valdez grunted. "Impossible," he said while jousting the air with his fork just above Vicente Coto's hand. "That horrible act would haunt me. It would be like burying him next to my dear Mara. *Impossible!*"

"Ah, yes," Coto responded softly. "Of course, Mara. I forgot. Forgive me, my old friend, I have been too long behind the wall—Fidel's *muralla*. Your beautiful lady was alive then." Vicente Coto chuckled to himself over the stir he had caused in the big man sitting across from him. "But listen, Guillermo, there are many suitable landmarks in Cuba waiting to claim the remains of such a man as you have described to me this night."

Señor Valdez's huge head moved in a slow nod of acknowledgment, not agreement. His penetrating stare and dark, sun-beaten but smooth Moorish face bespoke the earnestness of serious inquiry, even though his friend seemed unchallenged by the question and not at all troubled by the solution he had proposed.

"You would kill him then?" Señor Valdez asked.

"No, not me, not Vicente Coto. But El Cojonudo would. Your reputation demands it, Guillermo."

Señor Valdez raised his lips, forcing a brief sneer of a smile. "Now *you* listen, Vicente, listen to your friend who is sitting in front of you. My reputation requires more than a Chicago-style conclusion. The man who would adulterate my Mara's monument does not deserve swift justice."

Vicente Coto winked at the lady at the next table and turned back to Señor Valdez. "True, but how will you accomplish such a revenge? Castro will not allow you back on the island. The Canadian is there now and may never return to Miami. How can you succeed under those conditions?"

"No problem. How did you get out of the Cuban prison?"

"I told you already. The man you asked me about earlier this evening—Clay Redmond—he came with Jesse Jackson and persuaded Castro to release me. Several other prisoners were also released that same day, including a nephew of Máximo Gómez. It was like a miracle from God."

"You see? You have already given me the answer."

Vicente Coto rolled his eyes back from the lady to Señor Valdez. "Did I?" he said, puzzled. "And what answer did I give?"

"This fellow who helped free you, Clay Redmond. He is the answer."

"Oh? In what way, Guillermo?"

"In every way! There is much ill will between him and the Canadian. At first I thought they were in league and courting Fidel to take over Mara Paradiso. Then I saw the Canadian's wife in Santo Domingo with Redmond. Ahh, such a beauty! For her, Vicente, I'm sure your deal maker from Miami will take care of my problem."

"But Clay Redmond is a real estate broker, not a killer. You will need a ruthless man for such a task. Pepe, for instance."

Señor Valdez chuckled and wiped around his thick mustache as he weighed a swirl of thoughts. "How well do you know this Redmond fellow, Vicente?"

"Well enough. He brought me back from Cuban hell, didn't he? No gringo I know around this part of the world is a better friend of the Cuban people. He even helps me from time to time with investment decisions here in Miami. The man is no killer, Guillermo. Clever yes, and strong as a bull, but he would not harm a flea. His business is what you just then remarked—saving people, not abusing them."

Señor Valdez shrugged. "We are not talking fleas tonight, Vicente. If the Canadian puts one finger on my Mara Paradiso, he is no less than a dead rodent—*un ratón muerto!* My discussions with Clay Redmond in Santo Domingo convinced me he feels no love for rats either."

"A very proper deduction, Guillermo. Come to think of it, on one occasion I did witness—when we were coming out of Cuba from the prison—I do recall now how my friend showed some irritation with a Cuban official. There was a brief absence of love then, too."

Señor Valdez's dark eyes came to a sudden focus on Vicente Coto. "What happened?" he asked, again gesturing impatiently with the fork.

"The official spoke unkindly to me at the airport, ugly talk. He was chiding me and calling me disgusting names. You know the words—*gusano, traidor, hijo de la gran puta, culo, chingón,* and so on. He was speaking in Spanish but he did not know that Clay Redmond was fluent in the language. My friend kept me from making a scene, fortunately, for the guards would have removed me back to the prison. I think that was what this crazy official wanted—to interrupt the diplomatic process and throw me again into the dungeon. He knew my family and hated me because my sister would not marry him."

"What about Redmond? He did nothing else but hold you and prevent you from making a fool of yourself at the airport? Is that all?"

Vicente Coto managed a warmhearted grin and turned his head toward the lady at the next table. A young platinum blonde with an escort, she nevertheless seemed intrigued by him.

"Wait, Guillermo. Let me finish please," he said calmly. The lusty set in his eyes faded as he turned back to the Spaniard. "You see, the official not only did not know that this gringo was fluent in Spanish, but the idiot did not know that the gringo was also fluent with the martial arts. With one quick movement Redmond silenced him, and to such a perfection that the fool was left unconscious in the arms of his subordinates. No one saw it because Clay Redmond moved so fast and so privately that the fool's attendants thought he had fainted from the pressure of all the curious people crowding around to see the nephew of Máximo Gómez before he and the rest of the prisoners boarded the plane. Can you believe this, Guillermo? Can you believe that Cuba's monstrosity of a dictator held this fine man in prison for twenty-five years for no reason but a difference of views regarding the merits of his repugnant revolution?"

"What an insult to the honor and bravery of Máximo Gómez," said the Spaniard, scowling in sympathy with his friend. "Such an outrage must be addressed."

"Truly. And here he was with me in the airport. Here was the bloodline of Máximo Gómez being forced into exile and begged away from his homeland by strangers. The single other choice was to stay in Cuba and die in prison. Oh, such a travesty, such a meanness!"

"And die he would," Señor Valdez remarked sadly, "but *only* the nephew, the meanness never. What were you going to tell me about Redmond?"

Vicente Coto tensed up and fell silent for a brief time while he sorted through some unpleasant memories. "Yes," he soon resumed, easing back into a smile, "as I was about to say, Redmond conducted himself like the famous invisible man of the cinema. He struck but no one saw him strike, not even me and I was standing beside him. No doubt the blow was very painful, for the official collapsed on his feet then fell over with the slow grace of a stalk of sugar cane after the machete passes."

Guillermo Valdez's laughter rippled through the dining room and sparked another robust wave of his fork. "Ah, Vicente, my friend, you have been very eloquent in proving my point a second time. Clay Redmond will find a way to deal with the other rat, too!"

Coto's smile twisted into a frown. "Why you not perform this duty yourself, Guillermo? With those big powerful hands around the Canadian's neck, it would snap like a dried worm parched by a week in the Cuban sun. In the old days you would have been too eager for this 'justice' you speak of to allow another man to enjoy the pleasure that, by every common measure, belongs to El Cojonudo."

Señor Valdez stabbed a chunk of beef with his fork and lifted it into his broad, gaping mouth. He chewed for a moment, staring at no one across the busy dining room, then focused back on Vicente Coto. "I am tired of killing, Vicente," he said wearily. "It has become a bore. Already this past month, in Colombia, I have put many men in graves for their foolish crimes against me. Enough, Vicente, enough killing. For one thing, old friend, at this moment my need for personal justice is satisfied, if only in partial measures. For another, I would be afraid—if my hands reached to Varadero and touched the Canadian—there would be at that instant a bloody desecration of the earth around my Mara's monument. If you will permit me still one more reason, let me add that I refuse to allow even a drop of his filthy blood to stain the beautiful pictures and thoughts that daily visit my head. As for Pepe, he would have acted last month if I had so much as winked approval. He was right there at Mara Paradiso with his weapons, only a few feet away from the thief. As you heard me explain earlier, I had sent him on a different mission and he was wise not to take the action then. You see, Vicente, even though it would have been very easy, I cannot have the blood of this land pirate pig on Pepe's hands either. A big publicity for all the tourists to read about would not be good for my business in Cuba. Yes, my friend, Clay Redmond is the answer. He will find a way to satisfy my need for justice without doing harm to Mara Paradiso."

After a studied glance into the fiery face of Señor Valdez, Vicente Coto eased into a rhythm of soft chuckles, interspersed with a scattering of broken grunts that soon sent both man into a siege of laughter. "Very well, Guillermo," Coto injected a bit later. "Your decision appears unshakable. I can only confirm that you have chosen properly the best man for this action. How he will satisfy your desire for justice I cannot say, but, trust me, if those are your instructions, you will receive full satisfaction before this wretched business ends."

Vicente Coto chuckled again and turned a warm, beseeching gaze back toward the blonde lady at the next table, who was waiting with her own wink.

25

*D*earest, how completely you have dominated my thoughts these past weeks! What more can I add to what I've already said but a thousand kisses for all the sweet words you whispered in my ear down in the tropics and all the fabulous places you showed me, not to mention those joyously wicked proofs of a man's virility and how persuasive each was in exposing the deepest secret passages into a woman's femininity. Our stay—our truly marvelous stay—in Santo Domingo was wonderful. I wanted more, to remain there for a much longer time, maybe forever, but condescended to the practicality of the arrangement. Don't you think the love we made on the island was almost as glorious as the love we made in my apartment ages ago? I really do mean ages, yes. And why do you think? Well, because it seems ages right now, yet only a few weeks have passed since we returned, since I last saw you.

You were so ready for me that night after the cave, weren't you? You couldn't wait another minute once you got me back inside Hotel Naco. Nor could I. You were such a rogue, though. My charming rogue who stole my heart so quickly, so completely. As you Marines say, "Wham bam, thank you, ma'am!" But then we had the following day to look forward to, all day, and some fine, whole days and nights after that. Now we do not have the luxury of spending a next day in each other's presence, a bitter loss. Still, we do have a kind of maturity of mind and a sense of forever that adds years to our brief acquaintance, "stretches" it back into our past and makes me feel that we have always known each other because of what seems already an exclusive life together, because of . . . as you once said . . . a vibrant, positive confidence in a love that surely must have marked us for each other during our childhood.

Consequently, my dearest, don't you think our armor (need I add "amor"?) is simply superlative and that we are equipped to withstand these long droughts of separation with less discomfort than other lovers might feel? Lately I've even caught myself having a bit of erotic fun just thinking about you coming back to me. To anticipate the "next time" feeds my heart with strength, floods my mind with a galaxy of visions of your face, your magnificent nakedness, and sends shock waves of ecstasy to tantalize the imprisoned part of me that you so masterfully unlock when we are together. What better way to be reminded of the pleasure that another rendezvous with you, my love, will bring!

I write this now because the phone may no longer be safe. Do not call me here either, nor at the apartment. A man has come almost every night since Ewen returned from Cuba and they talk until late, well after I have gone to bed. The man is a private detective

231

I think, or a criminal of some sinister ilk. Perish the thought he's a business partner, as Ewen tries to make me believe. I've never seen the toady's gruesome face before but all of a sudden he's everywhere I go. He's huge, too, a monster. Something tells me this woman is being watched.

Oh, my darling, I must find a way, I must be with you again—and soon! I'm frightened. It has been too long that our lips haven't touched. Yes, I know it's my fault, but I have to be very careful now. The fox is acting like a hawk and has employed this oversized detective to follow me. Yes, I'm rather certain that's what the ruddy blighter is doing. Oh, why did you have to go to Mexico and leave me in this dreadful mess? Would you believe that "His Highness" demanded just this morning that I join him later in Cuba? He has already been there three times since you left, and he's leaving again tomorrow with his stupid attorney. Of course I said no but I can only wonder what will happen next. Without you, I'm sure nothing good.

Hurry back, my darling. I loVe you.

Vanessa did not sign the letter, but she did enlarge the "v" in love. Twice she read the hurriedly composed script to herself. Wistful smiles forced her lips to pucker at times, as if the memories stirred by some of the lines were so vividly real in front of her that she wanted to embrace them, not let them go. The references to Ewen Leetboer also made her smile, but grimly. After a long, noisy sigh she enclosed the page in an envelope and stuffed it in her purse for some later action.

It was ten in the evening before she gave in to frustration and flopped down on her bed. Clad in a thin, loose nightie, she lay half under the sheet for a while, listening and thinking and hoping Clay Redmond would walk in the door right then. If not, she would forgive him anyway, for she feared he must still be in Mexico. Otherwise he would have arranged a tryst already. Even talking to his answering machine made her feel better. She would leave another message when she calls his office the next day from one of the public phones at Bloomingdale's. During her meditations, she bitched about tapped phones and even considered responding to the devilish urge to call from Penthouse #9 and rave on passionately into Clay's recorder. What a really great scoop for the big creep down stairs to report!

Vanessa pulled the sheet up to her shoulders and commenced to probe in her bushy red hair with mounting exasperation, pretending annoyance that she couldn't find Clay Redmond's strong hands buried in it. He would know how to keep the tresses out of her eyes and away from her lips. When Vanessa grew tired of her pretensions, and even more tired of the surrounding silence, she turned on the television and set the timer so she could drift off while watching some light, sleep-inspiring show. Ewen Leetboer was still downstairs "plotting" with the stranger. Not even Stanley B. Conover seemed to be included in Ewen's private meetings with this man, which she thought peculiar. Ever since his first trip to Cuba, abrupt as it was, Ewen Leetboer had been acting much too odd for her taste. Too secretive and non-communicative, even rude and preoccupied in ways as strange as the mysterious matter that appeared to have him so absorbed.

At the end of her hour of nightly recap, she sighed a wish that he would go away with his secrets and never come back.

A few days later, after Clay Redmond's contact at Banco Mar returned from Acapulco, the two men flew straight to Montreal, or as straight as one could fly, considering the obligatory stop in Atlanta. The banker, who had his own contacts, took enough time-outs in Acapulco to make arrangements for a pickup of the five million in U.S. cash, pending receipt of the check and a verifiable signature. Pursuant to prior verbal agreements between the parties, i.e., in more formal terms, an "unwritten memorandum of understanding," a small unrecorded token of appreciation would be awarded on both ends for expediting the transaction, plus travel expenses of course.

A greater amount of time than Clay Redmond expected had elapsed since he left Miami, most of it on Isla Mujeres waiting for the banker to return and set up the strategy sessions. It wasn't easy to slip five million dollars in cash across three borders. Then again, it wasn't too hard either. This sting operation was still a big deal, though. During the idle hours spent in Montreal, Clay managed to reach Marcus Cunningham at Xanadu and plant a seed concerning the "endangered" Ewen Leetboer and his whereabouts.

"It's like this," Clay said, speaking from his hotel room, "Your new Xanadu associate, in his rush to property instead of judgment, has set upon a risky course down in Cuba."

Marcus Cunningham guffawed. "I hear everything is risky down there, pal. Is the old smoothy smuggling dope now?"

"Not that I know of. But Leetboer's little island adventure could end on a tragic note. My spies tell me he's trying to rip off Castro."

"Fat chance of that. Hey, pal, you called at the right time. I've got news for you. Listen—"

"So help me, Marcus, it's true."

"Yeah? I didn't realize they were going steady. What's Castro to Leetboer other than a crummy dictator?"

"His latest partner."

Cunningham snorted into the phone. "You wouldn't bullshit me, would you?"

"Nope."

"You mean they *are* going steady?"

"Yep."

"Unbelievable!"

The hoots and bellowing laughs from Clay's burly friend were so jarring that Heather Ambrose stepped to the door and peeked in his office, her pretty face pulsing with clerical readiness. Cunningham waved her away and continued his phone conversation with Clay Redmond.

"So Ewen is trying to rip off Castro, huh?"

"That's what they say."

"Hey, pal, the odds on that matchup will make a neat fit in the no-brainer mold. At least it'll sound like good news to Frank Creuthop. Just between us roosters, I don't give a cock's wattle what happens to Ewen. Why you telling me all this stuff anyway?"

"*Hey*—I thought you ought to know! Okay?"

"Thanks, Clay. I wasn't trying to be cute. Something's come up and your news sort of fills in the cracks. Yeah, it's beginning to make sense now."

"How so?"

"Well, until yesterday I hadn't heard a peep out of Ewen Leetboer since he bought into Xanadu."

"Bet Creuthop was glad to see him."

"No, Ewen didn't show. But his wife did and Frank sure as hell enjoyed seeing her! What a rubberneck he is! How in the wide world, I wondered, could anybody as big and fat and crotchety and ossified as Frank Creuthop possibly get it up but—*son of a bitch!*—he was staring at her and all of a sudden his dick starts to poke through his pants like a teenager's right there in front of the poor gal. It was embarrassing! For a moment I thought old Frank was having another one of his seizures and his blood somehow got to circulating through the wrong arteries and rejuvenated his manhood. Anybody else would think the old fart had swallowed a bottle of Viagra."

"Hold it, Marcus," Clay said, interrupting. He switched the phone to his other ear and puffed into it. "Are you talking about Leetboer's wife . . . *Vanessa?"*

"In living color, man. *Wow!* She dropped in and introduced herself. All I can say is Ewen Leetboer's one hell of a fool to be screwing around with Castro when he's got her day and night, night and day, inside his mansion. What a dish for Christ's sake! By the way, she talked about you, not him. What's going on?"

Clay hedged a moment, then, "Uh, I owe her money . . ."

"You lying bastard!"

The broker didn't like to hear Vanessa being used as a conversation piece. Most of all he didn't like having to lie about her, having to pretend she meant nothing to him.

"What did she want?" he asked Marcus, adopting a cool broker's manner but burning inside to hear the answer.

"I'm not really sure. Sounded like the little lady had to go to Cuba some time this week. Or decide to go. I couldn't tell which. Ewen's over there now, she said, and he wants her to bring some of his work crew from Canada across the Straits on their yacht. And you know what else he wants?"

"The world?"

"Yeah, right. But listen to this: The lady flat-out told me he—*Mister* Leetboer she called him—wanted you to come along and help run the boat! Why would he even allow a stud like you on board with her? He hates your guts, doesn't he?"

"Business is business with Ewen. He's not above using her to draw confederates—another one of his bait-and-switch tactics. Most likely he wants me to translate a little Spanish for his work crew."

"Good point. His wife did make a few complimentary remarks about your bilingual expertise. Said she'd feel more comfortable with you along, especially if the Cuban Coast Guard hauls up beside the yacht and starts interrogating Ewen's construction workers. She didn't say as much, but I figured not a one of the dumb asses could speak the first damn word in Spanish. She only hinted that Ewen hasn't yet hooked up with a local guy he can trust."

"That's just it—there aren't any. He doesn't trust anybody, nor can he afford to. His problems will multiply down there. You see, Ewen bought the foreign rights to a big bankrupt development over in Varadero. He thinks he's fifty-fifty with Fidel now. Everything's in Spanish—the blue prints, the surveys, the title, the partnership agreement, Castro's commie manifestos—*every fucking thing.* For a guy who loves to screw his partners with fine print, he'd be in hog heaven if this development were any place but Cuba."

"Your deal, I gather."

"Yeah, I put him on to it," Clay said. "For whatever it's worth. I don't think Castro will allow Ewen to pay a commission to a Miami gringo, though. Might have to work something out with him on the side."

"Might, huh? You *might* get screwed again, too. Good luck. What do you think you'll see this time, Ben Franklin's face on a few thousand C-notes or Ewen Leetboer's ass, once?"

"Ewen Leetboer's ass is the *last* part of him I want to see," Clay responded, joining in his friend's laughter. "But I'll take an arm and a leg for starters."

The broker camouflaged his remarks with humor to soften the literal substance behind them. His rule was to deal honestly with friends, although a kind of courtroom allegiance sometimes came into play and "judicious" restraint forced him to reserve pieces of the whole truth when total candor seemed unwise, unwelcome or dangerous.

Cunningham continued to joke without sensing the irony. "You're too easy on the crook!" he yelled. "Stick it to him before he sticks it to you for Christ's sake."

"Now that you mention it," Clay Redmond said, thinking of his Ka-Bar, "that's not a bad idea."

"Yeah, let the prick have it. Don't fuck around."

"Okay, big guy, I'll do my bloody damndest to follow this advice. You're right, he owes me. Maybe a few bales of C-notes under the table would help rebuild my retirement account. It could use a lift. Whatever I can squeeze out of the weasel-fingered skinflint will be nothing he'll miss or remember the next day. He's loaded, Marcus, unlawfully loaded."

Cunningham burst into another loud cackle. "Some money freak, huh? *Fuckarino!* He must have packed away one hell of a stash. His wife didn't say much about that, like she knew but didn't know. Hey, give me a number where you can be reached and I'll have Heather run it by her place. Phone's out of order she says. Can you believe that? The lady's phone is on the blink and she lives in a fucking mansion on South Beach!"

"You can't get through?"

"Nope. At least nobody answers. According to Mrs. Leetboer, she can't talk on the phone either, which is why she came to Xanadu."

"Really? All that distance across town just to use your phone? Gimme a break, Marcus."

"Okay, smartass. You want to know what I think? I think she drove all the way over here to find out where the hell you are! She needs a first mate for that yacht, remember? The Florida Straits, remember? Like PDQ! What really sounded fishy was her insistence that you not try to get in touch with her. She'll call you once I produce the magic number. The sweet way she insisted, incidentally, was enough to make a lonely guy go somewhere and jerk off, but let her explain it first. That part didn't make sense to me. You know how mystery muck goes over with women. I just hope she's not using you, too. Now what's your goddam phone number, pal, and how long you gonna be in Montreal?"

26

Silvio Alvarez drove El Toro to Miami International Airport to meet Clay Redmond. The broker was coming in late from Cancún, not Montreal, as first planned. At the last minute he decided to set up escrow accounts for Silvio and Ramón in the Mexican bank and make deposits there rather than chance another border crossing with undeclared cargo. Aside from that bit of precaution, the banker needed the money in Mexico to put the final creases on his "laundry" service. Not to be outdone, Clay needed to keep the currency in his sight until the accounts were opened and a signed receipt issued.

Weeks earlier Clay had phoned Silvio from Isla Mujeres to advise him of an extended delay, then suggested he pick up the Jeep.

"No sense paying a daily parking charge while I cool my heels in Yucatan for God knows how long," Clay had groused to the

Cuban. "Besides, Silvio, you'll need an extra set of wheels to keep tabs on Ewen Leetboer. You know where the key is. Just don't run over the louse, not even if you have to brake for him. That honor still hangs high on my own option list."

Silvio twittered a quiet laugh into the phone without answering. Sometimes, like his brother Ramón, he didn't quite know what to make of this fellow conspirator's instructions. Even when Clay confessed he was only kidding, a suspicion usually remained for a while to plunder the Cuban's mind. *Perhaps my gringo compadre was not truly kidding,* Silvio would think later. But, either way, he felt the laughs were worth the wonder. No sleep was lost before other issues muscled his doubts aside.

That evening the bright lights of Miami looked especially good to Clay as he gazed out the plane's window. He was home again, always a welcome event after a layover in Mexico. The sight of Silvio waiting in the terminal, though, stirred memories of Santo Domingo, not home. Down there a couple of months earlier he had met Clay under similar circumstances at Las Américas, where the Cuban was decked out in a tropical white suit, pacing around the customs gate with the same nervous expression on his face. Here in Miami, not having the glaring eyes of Guillermo Valdez and his hatchet man, Pepe, to contend with, Silvio had switched back to fashions of subtropical Florida—light slacks and a loud short-sleeve shirt that flashed paradisiacal themes. The only thing missing was that pretty redhead walking beside his friend.

"The money is in Mexico," Clay told Silvio on their way to the parking garage, after a few delicate queries.

Silvio's lower jaw dropped. With a deafening shout the Cuban jumped upward and came down forward, spun on his heels and stood in Clay's path to stop him, then calmed and met the broker's stare head-on. *"All of it?"* Silvio gasped. His expression shifted from jubilance to grimace to counter unfavorable news, if any.

"Five million less the two bankers' cuts."

The Cuban squatted and leaned against the bumper of the nearest car and executed a flurry of Hail Marys. Some moments later he rose and, before speaking, squinted hard at Clay, his eyelids slithering to near closure.

"You have returned with a worried face, amigo. Are we with problems still?"

Clay looked back at him with the same probing eyes. "Not me," he said after a bit. "I'm fine. What's the latest on Ramón? Is our poor brother still in jail?"

"No. *Hermano* is okay. To tell the truth, he is better than okay. Pepe pulled strings with the Cuban police and Ramón—well, they released him."

"Ah—good. Where is he now?"

"Wait, there's more. The next day after the release, and at the request of Señor Valdez, Pepe took Ramón and Elena out of Cuba."

"Where to? Miami—they're here?"

"No. Back to Santo Domingo."

"Are you kidding? Why would he do that?"

"Pepe says for love."

"Now you're jiving me, Silvio. What the fuck is going on with Ramón?"

"Honest, amigo, it's true! Listen. Would you believe the great El Cojonudo has a big heart?"

"Well, I know he's got big hands that squeeze hard."

"Yes, very big ones, like his *cojones* in the rumors. Listen, amigo! This giant from Extremadura, this terrible Spanish Moor who kills enemies with his teeth, sent Pepe from Colombia to fly them in his private Learjet. Then, as if the rescue was not enough, he insisted Ramón and Elena remain as guests in his magnificent suite at El Embajador."

"Sounds fishy, Silvio. Valdez must be up to something."

"No. The man wanted nothing for this courtesy, only that his two lovely guests, as he called them, relax in safety and enjoy each other while ' . . . Clay Redmond *destroys* Ewen Leetboer'."

"Bullshit. He didn't say that."

"Honest—to the letter! Ramón swore to me on our mother's spirit these were the Spaniard's exact words. Señor Valdez knows everything of our sting!"

Clay cracked a thin smile, unnoticed in the dim airport parking garage. The month away had infused him with strange, scrappy feelings.

"Does Señor Valdez know *exactly* what's at stake here?"

"Yes!" Silvio answered, pounding his hands. "He knows—and *exactly,* even about the five million dollars."

"Does he know exactly what we still might do?"

"Quién sabe? Who can say? My guess is methods do not concern him, only results."

The two men walked on to the Jeep, swapping questions and answers in rapid exchanges.

On the way to drop Silvio off at his latest hideout in Little Havana, Clay stopped at a quiet lounge just off *Calle Ocho.*

"Let's talk over a drink for a few minutes," Clay said, sliding from under the wheel and onto the sidewalk before Silvio could object. He knew the Cuban favored shadows over limelight when they were in Miami together plotting intrigues.

Silvio's grimace, which had not completely disappeared, intensified. He remained in the Jeep and motioned Clay to the window. "Are you sure you want to talk in there?" he asked. "News of our business would bring a good price on the black market. Castro has spies all over the city, man!"

"Who pays attention in bars?" Clay answered with a shrug. "Anybody can write his life story on a napkin and what do you think will happen if he leaves it on the table along with a tip? The tip goes home with the waitress; the life story is left for the janitor to publish in the nearest Dumpster. Not to worry, my friend. Let's have a nightcap. This has been a long month. Actually too long—and too fucking much of it spent in Mexico."

Silvio put on dark glasses and followed Clay inside. It was past ten and only a few customers were still nursing drinks. After satisfying the Cuban's preference for a table with the least light and traffic around it, a cheeky cocktail waitress took orders for two Cognacs in large snifters and whirled away with the urgent rush of a runner on a relay team, clasping the ticket book across her breasts as she darted around tables in pursuit of the bartender's outstretched hand.

While the two men waited for their drinks, Clay Redmond turned serious again.

"I've been doing a lot of thinking," he said.

"Yes, I can see. And what are these thoughts tonight, my brother, that have you so upset?"

"Leetboer's back in Cuba."

"Good. Let him stay there with Fidel and search for his deposit."

"No, Vanessa's involved now. He wants me to help her sail his yacht to Varadero."

Silvio hemmed. "That's even better, no?"

"No. The stupid ass wants me to take a crew over so he can begin work on Mara Paradiso. Any day now the shit's gonna hit the fan, *big-time*. Apparently he still doesn't suspect he's been screwed out of five million bucks. Aside from that dubious likelihood, he knows the embargo is still in effect, that I can't travel to Cuba, not legally anyway."

"But his crew—are they not Canadian citizens?"

"I suppose. Most of them."

"So what is the problem? The red-haired lady with the beautiful green eyes will be with you. What could be better for Clay Redmond? All you have to do is remain on the yacht with her and sail it back to Miami after the Canadian workers go ashore with their equipment. Simple. In and out—the way we brought to Key West in 1980 many refugees from Mariel." Silvio paused to sigh over the memories aroused, then continued. "Maybe you can rescue a few *balseros* along the way. This would make the Miami Cubans very happy."

Clay joined in Silvio's chuckle, but soon the horrible fate of Graciela crossed his mind and he shifted back to Ewen Leetboer. "The Dutchman doesn't need Clay Redmond. At first I thought he wanted me along to translate, but then I remembered that one of his crew is Portuguese, an expert sailor who speaks Spanish like a native. Name's Arturo. He sailed the yacht down from Montreal last year, with Leetboer sometimes at the wheel, showing off to Vanessa the whole way back to Miami. She later told me about how miserable the trip was."

Silvio scratched around in his thick black hair and took a sip from the snifter. "You are right, amigo. There is a puzzle here. Is it possible he feels guilty over the theft of your retirement and wishes now to honor with a 'piece of the action', as you say, your service of bringing him Mara Paradiso?"

"Ha! If anything, the chiseler wants to make bloody sure I'm cut out of the brokerage picture. No doubt he's getting daily advice from his kiss-ass attorney on how to do it. It's downright comical."

"Comical?"

"Yes, because I never expected a commission out of the Mara Paradiso deal, not even a share in the partnership. How could I? It was a fucking scam from the start. All I wanted was closure on the sting."

"We have that now, right?"

"Not quite. We haven't heard from him yet. I want to see his face when he finds out. I want to see what a chiseler's mouth looks like when it's gasping for air and whether those greedy hands will reach out to comfort even his own desperate heart when I quote his famous line, 'You gotta pay for your mistakes, Ewen, you old horse knocker. Business is business.'"

Silvio gloomed over. "What about El Cojonudo? He wants you to *destroy* the Canadian, not just rob and torment him. Have you settled on a plan for this duty?"

Clay smiled and worked the muscles in his jaws. "Cheer up, Silvio. We have his money. *Big money* and he doesn't even know it yet. Am I satisfied? Can't say for sure. Maybe. Maybe I'll find out on that trip to Cuba with Vanessa." Clay paused. *I have robbed him of his wife, too,* he thought, *and the sad bastard doesn't know that either.*

Clay continued aloud to Silvio, "On the other side of the equation, Señor Valdez wants blood more than a rich partner. As I said earlier, don't you think it really is comical?"

Silvio grunted. "What is better for a laugh will be the face of Ewen Leetboer when the Cuban police come to Mara Paradiso and arrest him and his workers for sabotage."

Clay chuckled. "Sabotage?"

"Yes—or something even worse to justify so huge a capture of foreigners. Counterrevolutionary mercenaries Castro will call them before he passes sentence."

Clay Redmond turned quiet and gazed around the lounge. "Yeah," he said, nodding in slow agreement with his lips pooched out.

Silvio watched Clay for a few moments, waiting for him to repeat his own charges against Ewen Leetboer, and, for laughs, perhaps suggest more Cuban punishments. Clay, though, continued his idle surveillance of the lounge, and Silvio soon took advantage of the silence to sneak off to the john. When he returned, Clay gave the table a mock karate chop.

"Let's forget about Castro for now," he said, his voice low but intense and resolute. "The old windbag must still be in the dark, too—the same as Leetboer."

"What are you thinking, amigo?"

"Just this. Valdez is rushing things. I thought we agreed in Santo Domingo that he would sit back and enjoy the fun, give Leetboer time to ship in building supplies, crank up the bulldozers,

247

maybe even add some value to Mara Paradiso before politics took over and shut him down."

"You're right on this point," Silvio replied, "but remember the other point: Señor Valdez is not a patient man. The concept of Mara Paradiso came to Cuba as a memorial to his dead wife. One of her ancestors was a Conquistador here. She loved Cuba, and everybody on the island who had ever seen them together—her and the Señor I mean—knows he loved her more than the world itself. You have already heard the stories from Ramón and me about how investors suffer misfortunes from the hands of El Cojonudo every year because they, the investors, are foolish enough to trust a communist to guide them to good investments—and even more foolish to choose Mara Paradiso from the dictator's list! Now it is our turn—but *not* to be foolish."

Clay pressed against the tip of his nose with his index finger as he listened. "Are we being foolish to continue?" he asked suddenly, dropping his hand.

"What other choice is there?" Silvio answered in a loud whisper. "Amigo, we must not offend the Spaniard with delays! Ramón and Elena may be in danger if we do not proceed as he wishes. Señor Valdez treats them well but they are still his hostages."

"Uh-huh. You may recall, brother, that I wished it first. Now that I've ripped the chiseler's ass off for a change, something inside is telling me to let it go, *no mas*. Sure, I'll have some fun needling him about his loss, but nothing, not even his scalp, will give me a happier moment than just walking away with Vanessa."

Silvio leaned back and cut his eyes around the lounge. The place was almost empty. Even the cheeky waitress had slowed to chat with the bartender. The Cuban looked back at Clay and a brief smile replaced the grimace. "Or sailing away perhaps?" he added. "But before you go on your honeymoon, Clay Redmond, we have work to finish."

Clay gave the brandy a good roll in his snifter and watched the beads form, then he waited until they vanished one after the other in slow, silent bursts that signified good booze.

"*Muy cómico,*" he said.

27

E wen Leetboer's yacht had the smell of foreclosure all over it. A luxury craft from stem to stern, it came into his possession when a former partner failed to meet a deadline on his mortgage payment. Another slam dunk for Stanley B. Conover, another ten cents on the dollar for Clockwork Investments, Inc. And so it went. The transaction appeared to be humane enough, though, looking at it from one angle, without cynical forethought. Here was Big Brother at his best, some would say, a fairy godfather holding out a protective shield to save a partner's butt. How sweet, they'd murmur, their faces bursting with approval. From most angles, to expand a bit, that protective shield somehow dominated the visual afterglow to all parties but the victim caught in the sly old Dutchman's default trap. Only his victims wound up truly knowing the score. Business being the business that it was in Ewen Leetboer's enterprising mind, he considered himself just a struggling entrepreneur making his way in the world, swimming hard to stay afloat and above the drowning rats who would pull him under with them if he lost his head and got sentimental all of a sudden. Then there were the heartless crooks trying to screw *him* out of *his* money. He had to fend them off, too. It was all in a day's work, a page in the high drama of just making a living. "Nothing like a Hinckley Sou'wester 70 to make the struggle worthwhile," Conover would kid when Leetboer poor-mouthed about the lawyer's fees. The Hinckley meant no more to him than his little red Lada rusting away inside the garage at the South Beach mansion. Ewen Leetboer was a collector, not a boat person. "People must pay for their mistakes" remained his most reliable, mind-easing catchphrase. The collection process demanded it, even if he had to assume full responsibility for ten such magnificent ships as a Sou'wester. Boat slips didn't come cheap either, not at Coconut Grove anyhow. The whole rotten business of "making people pay for their mistakes . . ." was almost like charity work. Or so Leetboer confided during his feel-good moments.

Clay Redmond found Vanessa's letter in his mailbox the next day after his return from Cancún. *"Dearest,"* the postscript read, *"you've been gone soooo long! Plans have changed. Did Mr. Cunningham give you my message? I told him I needed you desperately to go with me to Cuba. The yacht needs you, too. Ewen is still over there. Right now you're the only one I know who can run it, the only one I trust at sea. Heather Ambrose dropped by with the good news. You will be here in just three days, she said—and rather without a hint of personal interest I was pleased to note. The poor girl. If she only knew the passion that news of hers stirred in my heart—Oh! Darling, I'm delirious with joy! The thought of having your big strong arms around me again makes me almost faint from the rush of happiness filling my heart. Please meet me Friday at the yacht in Coconut Grove. That is, if you make it back. I dearly hope you can be there by nine with your Top-Siders on (no boots please), ready for a week at sea. You're in for a big surprise, sweetie pie—and oodles of loVe from, Yours and Only Yours."*

Clay relished the way Vanessa expressed herself to him—direct, open, loving—but he held in check for the rest of the day the temptation to phone her. It was already Thursday and her warning about tapped phones, eavesdropping and a "stalking stranger" who was practically living at the South Beach mansion raised the hairs on his neck, rekindling the scrappy mood he'd felt the night before. But how fortunate for the stranger that some little protein in Clay's system gave him enough pause to hold off for another day. A call would put her at risk, he figured. That smart aleck Dutchman probably had Caller I.D. installed on every phone and all the lines tapped, including Penthouse #9 at Bella Mar. *Something's going on in Ewen Leetboer's noggin,* Clay mulled, and he vowed to whatever gentle spirits hovered around him, if any, not to trip the old chiseler's motherboard, at least not before he'd revealed his plans to Vanessa. Friday at nine sounded safe.

Vanessa waited below deck. Clay knew his way around the ship just as he had known the way into her apartment. *How like my darling rogue to help himself to a key to the engine room,* she mused lovingly while doing some last minute primping in front of a mirror. Some of Ewen's crew from Montreal had already arrived and were loafing around the dock, drinking their morning coffee out of big Styrofoam cups and rapping with each other, sometimes too loud, while they waited for a call to come aboard. The ship's mistress, above all, did not want anyone on the yacht until Clay Redmond showed up and she'd first had a chance to spend a few precious moments with him in private. She dared not greet her roving lover in public. The sight of an out-of-control embrace in full view of the men would, like "flashes" of old, convert to breaking news and find its way to Ewen Leetboer with the speed of e-mail, if not cell phone. Nothing untrue about the story, just the spin some turkey might put on it to score points with his boss. True or not, she knew it wasn't the sort of news to write home about. At least not yet. Vanessa had other plans for Ewen Leetboer's forward-bending ears.

"Hello, sailor," she cooed, sounding like Heather Ambrose but rushing like her passionate self into Clay's arms the moment he stepped inside her private cabin. Vanessa was clad lightly in togs meant to protect against the sun more than from the hands of seafaring harassers. Her red hair had grown longer but still hung down her shoulders in the same alluring, bushy masses, a feature that Clay remembered with as much clarity as dreams can lay open to a hungry heart. Neither could he help but notice that her eyes were still full of their emerald green dazzle. All in all, it took them less than a minute to peel away the layers of clothing and get down to bare skin. As if he had performed such an act on stage a thousand times, he scooped her up in his arms and moved like a South Seas chieftain toward the bed only to be overcome by her almost savage caresses. His knees buckled and caused him to stumble, clodhopper fashion, upon the bed with her under him. Vanessa's arms remained locked in place, her grip unbroken by the fall. Undaunted himself, Clay began some devouring of his own, and with the same ravenous intensity that she was applying to every part of his body that her lips could reach.

"It's amazing," he said later, after they had pulled apart to stare into each other's eyes. "I can't get over how much I've missed you this past month. *Ay, mi Vanessa,* you have become the very life's blood of this sailor. There's no turning back now. To hell with the Ten Commandments."

"I know," she answered, rolling on top and resuming her kisses between words. "When you touch me I'm overcome with joy, not guilt. You're my everything. I love your pretty shirt, unbuttoning it, getting under your salty jeans, your . . . *Oh God! Let's do it, I can't wait any longer either!*"

Just as she eased him inside her, a grim, barrel-shaped man of about forty years of age, and with a camera in one hand, opened the cabin door with the other. He was *big* but he didn't make a sound. From the looks of it, his nose had been broken at least once. The rest of his face bore a tired, indifferent cast but otherwise reflected the alert blankness of a cat's. It was a "heavy" face further camouflaged by a dark, full beard. He stood there a moment, erect and dutiful, spying around with the zest of an oversexed voyeur, then, after a couple of shots of the two of them together, he backed quietly out, gawking over the shutter and snapping angles in wild confusion as he went. Engrossed as they were, Vanessa and Clay didn't sense a presence until the camera flashed. They rolled apart just in time to see a huge, shadowy form retreat through the entryway and leave both lovers shaken but also furious for not taking time to set the dead bolt.

"Who was that big yo-yo," Clay groaned, jumping up and covering Vanessa. As he stepped over to secure the wide-open door, she screamed.

"It's *him,* it's that horrible snoop!"

"Stay put," Clay said. He threw on the basics and bounded out the door in pursuit of the intruder, leaving Vanessa in a rant, gasping her Irish fury with every breath.

Leetboer's men were still waving their Styrofoam cups and babbling among themselves when Clay Redmond jumped off the yacht and broke into a fast lope, his shirt untucked and flapping in the breeze. They shifted focus and turned their eyes on the chase. Further up the pier, on past Clay, the big fellow whom they had just seen come off the boat in a similar hurry had reached the parking lot and was about to climb into a van when Clay grabbed a handful of his hair and yanked him to the ground.

"Okay, son of a bitch, what's going on?" Clay growled at the prostrate man. "Gimme that damn thing."

He didn't wait for the man to hand the camera over but reached down and applied a little "pressure-point persuasion" to pry it loose, then stuck his shoe on the man's big roly-poly gut to hold him down while he examined the camera. It was a Nikon Lite·Touch, the kind Clay sometimes used in real estate to get wide-angle photos of properties.

"So. Panoramas, huh?" Clay said in a mocking tone.

The man lay still, looking up at Clay through tired, nervous eyes. "Yeah, whatever . . ."

"You packing?"

"Packing?"

"A gun."

"Oh. No. That is, yeah. It's in the van . . ."

Clay frisked him for a weapon. Finding none when he rolled him over, he took the man's wallet out of a back pocket and examined it briefly, smiling at times as he flipped through the contents. Seconds later Clay's face tightened, grimacing hard; his Top-Sider sank deeper into the man's gut. "What kind of porno freak are you? You trying to piss me off or what?"

The man grunted and struggled to get out from under Clay's foot. "No, I'm free lance . . . the *Herald . . .*"

"Don't give me that crap. You're a fucking snoop for Ewen Leetboer. A private eye with an expired license. You're lucky my foot's not on top of that sick nose. Talk fast, big boy, or it will be!"

"Okay, okay. It isn't you, it's the woman. My client hired me to follow her, find out what she's up to. Who are you anyway?"

"Kiss it. What name did he drop?"

"Gosh, mate, go easy on the tummy please. I just had an operation!"

"You're about to have another one. *Who?*"

"Not you. You're crew, right? No, not any of the ship's crew. It's some hotshot Miami real estate guy who wears cowboy boots and fancy Cuban shirts."

Clay laughed and offered the man his hand and pulled him up. "Not Clay Redmond, by any chance?"

"Yeah, that's the name. You know him?"

"Uh-huh."

"Can I have my camera back now?"

Clay laughed again and extracted the film. He stuck the roll in his pocket. "Sure," he said in a quasi-polite tone, giving the man his Nikon. For a brief time Clay stared hard into a pair of shifty eyes and added, "The next time I see you anywhere near the woman you've been following, I'll toss your little joy box in the bay—and your big fat ass right along with it. You read me?"

The man swallowed and pawed at his neck, as if to adjust a tie that wasn't there. "You're playing with dynamite, mister" he said. "My client—"

"Say it, dammit, say Ewen Leetboer!"

"Hey, don't get excited, mate. You already know it's him, or you seem to. He's building a case, protecting himself from his wife. She's after his fortune, if you know what I mean. Extortion, blackmail, whatever the bitch can get on him. Redmond is in it with her. Hey, maybe I don't include you in my report. Okay? Understand? I'll swear it was Redmond with her."

Clay glared at the man in the piercing style of Señor Valdez, causing him to fidget and stammer even more. A quick chop across his thick neck sent him crashing to the ground again. "Maybe she's not a bitch," Clay said. "Are you saying Leetboer doesn't care if I get in bed with her? Doesn't care if she's sleeping with any of these other guys? It's just this dude Clay Redmond he objects to?"

The heavy man rolled his eyes up at Clay and rubbed his neck. "See here, you don't have to get violent," he moaned, giving Clay a pain-filled squint. "I could have you booked—"

"Yeah, and I could break your nose again."

"For God's sake, mister, I'm trying to do you a favor. Why get mixed up in a family matter?"

"Answer!"

The man twisted his neck a few times, testing for movement gingerly while noting the ready position of Clay's tough, calloused hands. "That's about the size of it," he grunted. "You better be glad you're not in his shoes. Or boots, right?"

A big motor home loaded with kids had just parked two lanes over and the occupants were pouring out and rushing past them on their way to the docks. Clay pulled him up on his feet again so as not to attract attention.

"Go!" Clay barked, giving the man a hard push. "Remember what I said: stay away from the woman. If you cause any harm to come to her, I'll feed your balls to my paper shredder. Now beat it!"

The man stared back at Clay for a moment, at his brawny frame and grim, cowboy face. "What's your pitch in this, mister?" he asked timidly. "I mean, you're not in on it, too, are you? I mean . . . *oh God!*" The snoop's head suddenly dropped. A comical disgust resonated in the snorts and moans that soon followed. "I should've . . . *aw shit!* You're *him,* you're Clay Redmond, right?"

"Get the fuck out of here," answered the broker.

28

S tanley B. Conover was dead serious about his promise to his client, a rarity in these times, coming from a member of the bar who had signed no incriminating documents compelling him to "take care of" a certain party. His fertile imagination worked overtime. He had laid it all out to Ewen Leetboer in a kind of "plea bargain" session, i.e., he offered a picturesque crime scene in exchange for a hefty stake in Mara Paradiso, laid it out at the very height of his euphoria arising from visions of a twenty-five percent ownership in the luxury development and further reinforced by a beggar's belief in the honesty and integrity of his benefactor-client, who, as it turned out, had not committed anything to paper either. Conover even seemed eager to make Ewen Leetboer a present of Clay Redmond's head. Just a figure of speech, he would insist if asked under oath, for there would be no *head*, by itself, to present after he got through with the "greedy, client-robbing, son of a bitchin' broker," as the irascible attorney phrased it. No body either. Nothing, not even a fiber or a smear of shit or any other sample worthy of a DNA test. Less evidence, by Conover's measure, than a cremation would leave.

Ewen had made the job easier when he offered to lure Clay Redmond to Cuba on his yacht, *Noche Buena,* a real dreamboat which he intended to rename *Holland Days* after the designated go-between had delivered on his end of the bargain. Not only would a fresh name wipe away deck stains resulting from, as Ewen Leetboer presumed, the attorney's sloppy, unprofessional clean-up of the crime scene but would cast a bit of glory in the direction of his native land, giving perennial honor from port to port to the enterprising spirit of fellow lowlanders.

Missing persons in a foreign country were not always found, nor, for that matter, much believed to be lost unless they chose to be. Anybody lost at sea "should have known better," a caution that Judge Brussard had already immortalized on behalf of Clay Redmond's trusting nature, elevating the concept to "material fact" during the courtroom ripoff of the broker's retirement nest egg. By the time the Coast Guard got wind of a castaway, there would be no need for a search-and-rescue mission. The statute of limitations applied as much (common sense says *more*) to a person overboard as to a person under suspicion of having put him there, regardless of whether he, i.e., the party consigned to the depths, had been humanely launched with a biodegradable life preserver or roughly clothed in a lead-lined rucksack.

"The yacht will dock in Varadero tomorrow," Leetboer confided to the attorney after getting his daily phone message from the "snoop," as Vanessa called her husband's private dick. "Redmond will be aboard."

Leetboer drew a deep breath and took a languid gaze around the hotel lounge. While holed up at Hotel Nacional, the two men had spent the last three days scouring Havana, seeking the whereabouts of one Felipe Jorge or anybody who could lead them to him. Even Jorge's assistant, the Cuban "doll baby" known only to Leetboer and Conover as *Carla*, had also dropped out of sight, or at least had not reported in for work since the day after they returned from Varadero in the Chevy 210, with Pepe's big honking four-wheeler evermore present in the rearview mirror.

Later, when they realized Carla was also missing, Conover vented his fury every time Leetboer mentioned the message from Pepe that she had passed on to them. "That goddam guy in the Toyota Land Cruiser scared the hell out her," he snarled. "She's hiding out, afraid to go to her office. Can you imagine the nerve of that little bandido fart telling us we were trespassing, that he'd shoot out our eyes when he came back from Colombia?"

"It was a strange encounter," Leetboer replied. "The fellow had drugs in his system for sure. Or something to give him courage to say those things. Maybe a kook trying to impress a pretty girl."

Some officials unfamiliar with the name suggested Felipe Jorge might have been "transferred to the cane fields," a common practice within the Party that required no advance notice and, by standing custom, brooked no delay. The "shifty" Cuban's sudden disappearance, though, continued to plague Leetboer's tightly ordered mind, where there was no room for coincidence. It also prompted Conover to make numerous phone calls and visits to other authorities inside the *Ministerio del Interior* without so much as finding anybody who even *knew* Felipe Jorge. Nor was the Canadian embassy much help. Leetboer's contacts there disavowed ever mentioning the name, much less providing a dossier. It was some other chap named Ramón Alvarez, they insisted, a name Leetboer remembered seeing on the Mara Paradiso brochure Clay Redmond had shown him back at Xanadu. The Dutchman had then, without comment one way or the other, discounted Alvarez, considering him just another of the broker's numerous allies, perhaps a fellow agent in cahoots to wrangle a big fat commission. The embassy staff's insistence only reinforced Leetboer's belief, setting off fears that Redmond had somehow gotten to them with bribes.

Neither could the embassy locate Leetboer's banker in Montreal, who quite unexpectedly had taken leave for Switzerland on a combined business-skiing vacation and left no itinerary or emergency phone numbers behind for his colleagues to pester him with annoying interruptions during his absence. Or so he explained in a note left on his desk.

Even the Dutchman's attempts to enter the Revolutionary Palace and to see the head knocker himself met with more annoyance than success. The police were always so aggressive and rude whenever strangers sought an audience with their revered Maximum Leader.

Stanley B. Conover had not yet allowed the full import of Ewen Leetboer's concerns to overshadow his dreamy musings about Mara Paradiso. He watched Leetboer size up the lounge decor for the umptieth time, then quietly admitted to himself, but not to Leetboer, that his stake in the Caribbean empire might be in need of further shoring.

"I told you I'd take care of Redmond," Conover intoned in a jittery cadence, half smiling as he spread his hands over the table like a tired conductor seeking finality to a Mendelssohnian scherzo.

Leetboer shrugged. "Very good, Stanley," he said, his dead pan at half mast. "We have other grounds now for the actions you proposed."

"Oh? And what might they be, pray tell?"

"I'd rather not say. The matter is a private one."

Conover's mouth popped open as he watched his client squirm away from his sharp legal glare. "What's going on, Ewen? You hiding something again?"

"I said it's a private matter. *Okay?*"

"Baloney! Spit it out. So what if it's a private matter. I'm your fucking attorney for Christ's sake."

Leetboer reoriented his head to view the lounge decor from a different angle. The deadpan flag rose a few notches; his face took on a robust, angry flush. *"Vanessa . . . ,"* he managed to blurt in a halting, venomous whine before stopping, as if the subject were too painful to continue.

"Vanessa? What about Vanessa? You said she was coming. Is she bringing the yacht over here or not?"

"Yes . . ."

"You did say Redmond will be aboard, right?"

"Yes, it is confirmed," Leetboer answered, relaxing a bit. "The yacht sailed out of Biscayne Bay an hour ago. My confidant followed with binoculars, watched Redmond at the helm until the yacht disappeared."

Conover burst into a broad grin. "Hey—ho ho—hot stuff! What the deuce are you worried about?"

Leetboer looked at Conover with blank eyes. "You are the one who is worried, Stanley. I am not."

"No? Well, you sure as hell don't look exactly thrilled. You're not getting cold feet, are you?"

Leetboer stiffened. "No. No, but . . . okay. I tell you now in strict confidence so you will understand why you must not fail. Agreed?"

"Shoot."

Leetboer cracked a thin smile, eying Conover with amusement. "Shoot, yes, and straight, like John Wayne. My confidant—"

"Just a minute. I've been meaning to ask you about him. Or is it a her? Gimme some background on this character. Don't you know you can get your tail in a crack messing around with these wacky informants? Frankly, your silence here has been—if you don't mind my saying so—insulting as hell . . ."

Leetboer appeared annoyed but tried to hide the depth of it behind a waxy grin, although the effort failed to soften the dreary, expressionless cast on his face. "His name is Karl Skepe," the Dutchman said without further explanation as to the man's credentials. "Mr. Skepe confirmed what you already suspected. He caught them in bed together—on the yacht."

"Run that by me again—caught *who*?"

"Vanessa and Redmond."

"*Jesus Christ*! Did Skepe get pictures?"

"Yes, but Redmond took the roll away from him by brute force. Karl said Redmond roughed him up pretty bad—used judo, karate, something like that."

"Yeah, I can imagine. Redmond is a dangerous man, Ewen. He would have busted my skull back there in Cunningham's office if you hadn't stepped in and okayed that fucking commission."

Leetboer nodded and pulled on his goozle while he continued to gaze around the lounge. "Let us do it," he said. The Dutchman's voice sounded decisive, although quiet and with the soft-spoken authority of someone ordering a ham sandwich on rye. "For obvious reasons I cannot put myself on the yacht but will remain in Havana in the event of an inquest. The job is yours alone. Everything is in place as we discussed. Arturo will go with you to do the sailing work. You will see that Clay Redmond never gets back to Miami, yes? Am I correct in thinking this? You will take care—"

"I got you covered," Conover snorted, interrupting Leetboer with a solid pound on the table. "Hell, yes. I can hardly wait to read the missing persons report. We're partners now, right?"

"Excellent, Stanley," Leetboer responded, ignoring the question. "Now let us talk on other matters for a change. I am a little bored with so much news about Clay Redmond."

"Fine. You don't mind if I ask about your little lady, do you? What's the game plan there now that we know whose side she's on?"

"*Game plan*? Is that what you call it?"

"Come on, Ewen, get real. You can't afford to turn a blind eye now. She was balling Redmond for Christ's sake!"

"So what? There is other fucking going on. We have to locate this man Felipe Jorge."

"Yah! Yah!" Conover chortled in a mocking tone. "Ho ho ho, Felipe Jorge. He is one cool customer! I knew from the gitgo there was something slippery about that asshole. Nobody seems to have the faintest idea who the hell he is."

"Perhaps he lives among friends and they are protecting him. Everybody seems to know his other name, though."

"El Duque?"

"Yes, him. Perhaps we should focus on that name instead of Felipe Jorge."

"But they all swear El Duque plays baseball for the New York Yankees. A star pitcher. He floated over on a raft awhile back and is definitely a *persona non grata* in Cuba now. Don't waste your time looking for him. The other one, the phony El Duque, well, he could be anywhere. If the slimeball wound up with the whole five million, though, you can forget about combing the cane fields in sunny Cuba. Try the rain forests of Borneo instead."

The two men sat in gloomy silence for a while. "Perhaps I should send for Karl Skepe," Leetboer sighed finally, staring out at empty space.

"That might be a waste of money as well as time," replied the attorney without altering his own vacant gaze. "What could Skepe do for us down here? Take pictures? Get his ass kicked again?"

"It was just a thought, counselor. I am somewhat puzzled by how quickly we were mislead."

"They saw us coming—yeah—a couple of *patos*, as Cubans call the Yankees."

"Or maybe they were waiting for someone else and made a mistake. The Cuban lady who drove us to Varadero in that old clunker was too pretty for clerical duties. She belongs in Hollywood, acting great scenes, seducing producers and directors—"

"Or hustling some rich dude like you, eh Ewen?"

"Now, Stanley, enough of that. Tell me, seriously: how could we have been so stupid?"

"You mean hungry—hungry for a piece of the bitch! Oh, the bitch . . . Carla somebody! You got to admit she charmed the balls right off both of us. That is, until that jerk scared her shitless. She got all limp and pale after that, and so did my hard-on."

"Hmmm," Leetboer mumbled, suddenly exposing a glint of admiration. "A beautiful piece of machinery, nevertheless."

"The word is *chicanery*, I believe. Okay, maybe you're right. Maybe you better put Skepe on their trail."

"I have already."

Conover sighed, feeling deceived again. "Whatever."

"You see, Stanley, it was a team effort, like baseball."

"Fuck baseball, Ewen! Those two monkeys tried to swindle us out of five million dollars!"

"You think . . . *swindle*? Honest?"

"Sure."

"I don't know. According to my contacts at the embassy, Felipe Jorge was only recently a teacher of illiterates for a monthly salary of ten dollars. Where would he learn to perform such deception so fast?"

"Probably from the illiterates. Christ, man, don't be so nonchalant about it. You should have put a hold on the check right after that bandido kook showed up and threatened us. Now we gotta find Jorge before he tries to cash it! To allow a stolen draft to get all the way up to Montreal without your final blessing would only make the bank look klutzy and you foolish."

"The check has been already cashed, Stanley."

Conover's eyes flared. "Huh? Say that again."

"You heard me. It is true. A message came while you were singing in the shower. Listen, what we have to find is where the money went. If Castro has it, then I must presume he will honor the Mara Paradiso agreement we signed in good faith with his agent, Felipe Jorge."

Conover remained silent for a moment, digesting the latest facts in the case. "Don't presume too much," he soon replied, his tone turning dour. "They say Macho Man Castro has a nasty disposition. This damn Felipe Jorge story might really piss him off."

"But we have papers, official documents stating terms and conditions. Aren't you my lawyer in these matters? Did you not advise me properly?"

"For crying out loud, Ewen, the papers are written in Spanish. I haven't had time to sift through all that gobbledygook yet. But don't worry. You're protected. I slipped in a contingency clause. It'll give you the standard out in case you don't like the deal. Furthermore, you can bet your sweet ass—"

"Thieves do not honor contingency clauses, Stanley," Leetboer said, unable to hide his impatience. He rose without waiting to hear any more of Conover's excuses, lifted a four-folds wallet out of his brief case and began to shuffle through it with a money counter's attention. After inventory he extracted ten ones in U.S. currency and dropped them on the table, then spoke across the lounge to a poised group of cocktail waitresses. "We will return later," he called out, not knowing whether any of them could understand a word of his Dutch-accented English but certain that they could all speak in dollar terms. A chorus of "*Gracias*!" came back from the group, one of whom hastened over in a swishy stride to retrieve the gratuity while the others looked on like venture capitalists whose cut was all but sliced. On his way out Leetboer noted with mixed emotions that for most Cubans, including Felipe Jorge, the gratuity amounted to a month's wages.

An hour later the two men arrived at the Revolutionary Palace to try once again to see the President, Fidel Castro, and take up the matter of the Mara Paradiso project, first rights, the five-million-dollar good faith deposit, and so on. Most likely the meeting would be short, Leetboer surmised, and—in the interest of both parties—sugar-coated with a lot of give-and-take. He and Conover had all day tomorrow to make it to Varadero in time to greet the yacht, *Noche Buena*.

29

"*Vanessa, we gotta talk!*" The words gnashed through Clay's teeth the moment he came bounding onto the yacht's spacious deck following his encounter with the "snoop," Karl Skepe. He was breathing heavily from the brisk trot back, not to mention the chase and the ensuing weighty fray. His shirt was still unbuttoned and hanging out, his thick sandy hair, disheveled.

Vanessa raced to his side, scanning for signs of blood as she spun around him. As if still in doubt, she lifted his shirt tail and peered for a moment, then arranged his hair back in place. "My darling, you aren't hurt . . . ?"

"No, I'm okay. I presume he's the turkey you wrote me about—Ewen's secret agent. Right?"

"*Yes*! You can thank your lucky shamrock he didn't pull a gun out of his baggy pants. I shudder to think what orders Ewen may have given him. Oh, Clay, I'm so sorry for this outrageous intrusion! The nerve of that creep—and on your first day back—*aarrgh*! Heavens yes let's talk. I'm *petrified* with—"

She broke off after noticing that the four masters from Leetboer's loyal team of overseers had moved down the pier and farther away from the yacht where there were benches under a canvas shade. To the last foreman, they appeared as absorbed in events aboard the yacht as they still were in the contents of their Styrofoam cups, yet they also seemed pleased enough to watch from a safe distance rather than move into the line of fire merely to pick up a little more audio. Vanessa, employing subtle movements with hands and eyes, motioned for Clay to follow.

Back inside the cabin she closed the door and locked it with a snappy click of the deadbolt. Turning to Clay and exchanging gazes for a moment, she collapsed in his arms and hung there, corpse-like, with her eyes closed until Clay gave her one of those famous Tarzan joggles, playfully checking for signs of life. Then a smile emerged and the brilliant emerald glow in her eyes opened to him. "First things *last*," she cooed almost in a whisper. Without warning she shot upright and pushed Clay back across the bed. His Top-Siders never left the floor but his feet went high in the air, sockless. Before gravity brought them down again, she stripped off his jeans. "*You rascal!*" she then screamed, "You see now what happens when you abandon me for so long? I've been worried about you and aching all over these past many days—actually *yearning* like a silly, frightened child, wanting your arms around me, protecting me, dying to be with you and away from all this ghastly business that—*thank God!*—you have now witnessed! Oh, Clay, I could just *kill* Ewen!"

Clay Redmond acknowledged every charge with a compliant nod. His earlier pique dissipated and he turned quietly companionable, even gracious and cooperative while under attack and not at all loathe to object when she disrobed him. Vanessa's blood was in a fine boil, Clay surmised, so he tossed his shirt on the floor and proceeded to undress her while she fumed. After a pause to admire beauty in the raw, a magical moment that put him in a daze, ex-Marine Redmond eased his hand against her mouth. "Quit beating your chops," he said. Then he coaxed her into position over him, which ended all complaints for several groan-filled minutes.

Later, when she pushed up to look at Clay and tell him about the "incredibly loving feeling" he had unleashed inside her, the pile on top of her head came undone and a thatch of radiant red ringlets fell across her brow, shrouding her face and intermingling in loose masses with the thick tangle on his chest. He reached up and parted her hair for a better view of the "colleen twinkle" he sometimes saw in her eyes when they made love, but Clay Redmond could say nothing even though his lips continued to move in gulpy silence, the way a man's will who shows a readiness to speak but whose thoughts seem locked on a different tack.

Vanessa sensed that he was struggling inside. "What is it, darling?" she asked in a hushed, uneasy voice. The blissful sheen was still evident on her face, but earlier glints of anger and a touch of fright were also beginning to cloud her eyes again. "Are you worried about that creepy snoop?"

"Uh-uh," he grunted, panting a little. "Not really."

"What is it then?"

"I can't talk. You took my breath away."

"Phooey! More likely a cat got your tongue."

Clay heaved a deep sigh. "No, you swallowed it, ma'am. But, speaking of cats, this one's out of the bag now. We have to believe that Ewen will know our little secret before dark."

"What happens when we get to Varadero?"

"Who can say? Maybe nothing. *Maybe* . . . if we're lucky."

"Perhaps we shouldn't go there now. It might be unpleasant, even dangerous."

Clay pulled her head closer and kissed her gently on the lips. "As bad as it sounds, my instincts are telling me to go ahead as planned. Otherwise I won't know what Ewen is up to. He asked for me *before* the snoop dropped in on us clicking that damn Nikon and packing an expired detective license, so my old partner must have something in mind other than male pride and the honor of his gorgeous wife." Clay paused and stared for a time at Vanessa. "To complicate matters," he continued, "so do I have something in mind, which makes the trip—his asking for me, I mean—seem a bit too convenient. Spooky even."

"What on earth do you mean, darling?"

"Simply this: A month ago I would have jumped at the chance to meet Ewen in Cuba. As you might guess from what I've told you, a sudden, unexpected encounter on foreign soil—soil already tainted by a dictator and therefore perfect for burying dirty rotten thieves—would have fit like a glove in my plans. But now—?" Clay Redmond paused and exhaled. "Remind me later to tell you about a sting operation my two Cuban friends and I have in the works. At the moment I'm more concerned about how the rest of that little ambush is unfolding. If Ewen is on to me I've got to know it before he knows I know it. I wanted to tell you in Santo Domingo but wasn't sure whether the screwy game I'd set in motion in Miami would hang together in Cuba, and even less sure he'd play by my rules. Apparently he doesn't yet realize he's *playing*, not by my rules anyway, but at some point the cold hard facts will bite him in the tush and he'll either scratch his crack in silence or send that jack-leg attorney to the courthouse with a bag full of writs, subpoenas, motions—you name it—each one designed to chunk me in the brig for the next twenty years."

Vanessa pushed herself up again and slapped Clay on his shoulder. "Are you trying to frighten me?" she asked softly but smugly, putting on a bemused face. "You sound *awful*, darling!"

Clay chuckled and gave her a tight, fondling hug. "Listen, lady, are you forgetting your husband ripped off my interest in a piece of land that I had earmarked for retirement?"

"Please, *sir*, you told me this already. I didn't forget. How could I? He was telling me, too."

"Yeah? What was he telling you?"

"That you had filed a suit against him."

"Is that all he told you?"

"He never shares details with me. I had no idea who was right and who was wrong. Not then I didn't."

"Now you do?"

"Oh, yes," she said, kissing the tip of his nose. "Isn't it as plain as this big sexy beezer on your face?"

Clay tweaked his nose a few times after she gave it a light thump, then kissed her back. On the neck first, then on each breast. "I like to think so. What do you think?"

"I think I love you . . ." she sang in a shy, lilting voice.

"You *think*?"

"Yes, like the lyrics in the song—so sweet and honest. But, darling, it still puzzles me why the court didn't rule in your favor. How could the jury be so stupid?"

"There was no jury. Just good ol' Judge Brussard."

"Then how could the judge be so stupid?"

"Not stupid—corrupt. Ewen bought the dickhead—and it wouldn't surprise me a bloody bit to find out that my own attorney was cuddled up in the same plot. I can't prove it but all the signs pointed to a guy—yours truly in this case—who'd been fleeced like Mary's little lamb."

"You?"

"Me."

"*Fleeced?*"

"Yeah, right down to my fucking suntan. For a long time all I wanted to do was get even some way, *gut* the chiseling bastard, take back what was mine and go on with my life. Then I met you. Everything started to change."

"Are you glad?"

"Glad?"

"Glad you met me?"

"More than you'd believe."

"Then what else changed besides everything?"

"Well, let's see . . . where shall I begin . . . ?"

"At the beginning, of course," she said, giggling.

Vanessa was still lying astraddle Clay, listening as he spoke into her ear while stroking her hair. Now and then she would rise up and stare in wide-eyed disbelief into his face, looking very much like an innocent, naive girl who was hearing for the first time a story packed with romantic fantasies but also peppered with the teller's dark, unsettling hints of deathly mayhem. While she was quick to admit she hadn't heard much about the lawsuit before, only bits and pieces, and most of it from Clay himself, she felt relieved on noticing the tone in his voice. It seemed different this time when he talked about the suit. Clay Redmond was not as angry now.

"Don't feel guilty!" she gushed. "Listen, I've wanted to *poison* the scheming monster. I thought about it, not once but many, many times."

Clay joggled her again when she tried to make light of his confession. "Okay, maybe you *thought* about it," he said, his eyes blazing up, "I have a 'contract' on the guy. The plan's in motion as we speak. Christ, Vanessa, don't laugh. I'm serious. It's an old saying that sometimes you have to take the law into your own hands. In my case it's not the law I'm taking in hand, not a *just* law anyway. It's a *duty*. Do you watch the fights?"

"Fights?"

"Boxing."

"No, hardly ever. Boxing is a cruel sport, if one can call it a sport. Why do you ask *me* such a question?"

"The referee. He advises boxers before they touch gloves, often uses the same short, pithy phrases fight after fight—"

"What sort of phrases, darling? Tell me."

"Okay, one I like is, *'Protect yourself at all times.'* That's what I saw myself doing—protecting myself, my dignity, my sense of who the hell I am, my sanity. Also my hard-earned cash."

"Goodness! How do you do all that and still fight?"

Clay smiled, amused at Vanessa's probing curiosity. "How do I do all that?" he repeated. "Easy. By drowning a rat gnawing on my retirement account. The court won't do it. Listen, my sweet, that scoundrel owes his life to you."

"I'm sure Ewen would not agree."

"Of course not. I've tried to tell you for a long time but just didn't know how—afraid I'd lose you, I suppose. Afraid you'd think I used you to get back at him. Yeah, I admit it. I wanted Ewen Leetboer *d-e-a-d*. Sorry. But's it's the truth."

"Oh, my darling! You really do mean it, don't you? Oh, my heavens! Yes, you mean it." Then she shifted and broke into a gale of laughter. Clay pushed her head off his chest and studied the anguished expression on her face, the frightened gleam in her eyes. "I-I'm so ashamed," she resumed. "I too was afraid. I knew you hated him for what he did—him and that horrid attorney. After you came to the apartment that day and we made love for the first time—*oh!*—a moment of sublime angelical suspension, full of Heaven's glory! Forgive me, my darling, but I cannot just now think of enough words to praise *that* time. Anyway, I became terrified—and lived in terror for weeks!—wondering if you might come to hate me one day because I stayed married to the pig. I tried to think of ways to get away from him so we could be together whenever we chose. At first I didn't believe it was wise for me to give up my advantage as his wife. Like you, I wanted to be *paid* for the miserable existence I was having to endure, the false, utterly lurid life I was forced by his—and my own—selfishness to live. Then after Santo Domingo, and later while you were in Mexico, I decided that nothing was more important than being with you. We wouldn't even have to get married. We'd be together whenever and wherever we wished, without fear or guilt. If you had not agreed to go with me on this voyage, I would not have bothered to come even to this marina. Now, with you, I feel safe. I will simply tell him when we get to Cuba."

"Tell him what, sweetie?"

"Tell him I want a divorce. Right? Clay, I can't stand the sight of the man around me anymore. Let him keep his money. He has made me hate wealth and what it can do to a person's mind. I don't believe I can bear to live in the same house with him a day longer! Promise me you will not commit violence against Ewen, though. Clay, *you mustn't*! If you do, I will surely lose you to a great stone prison far away from me, a place full of steel bars and troubled men. Or, worse still, I would lose you to your own little private insane asylum, another world hidden by a conscience too stricken to allow me to live with you and too stubborn to let you live even with yourself. Gosh, Clay, I don't really have to ask him for a divorce, do I? No. I'll just send him a note saying, *I hereby divorce you, Ewen Leetboer, you pig*! Our marriage was nothing. Only a few mumbled words by some yawning old man in his slippers who barely had his robe tied properly. All we need do now for the revenge you seek is *leave*. Let's not go to Cuba. I've saved some money, darling. I can also sell my apartment. You know its value. Millions. Yes, we'll head this yacht straight for the Canary Islands, a charming place in my mind where I've always wanted to live. For a few moony years at least. Or you can come back to Ireland with me and we'll raise sheep and live in a sweet little cottage by the sea—"

Vanessa began to cry. Clay pulled her head back down on his chest and let the soft, muted sobs continue. "You're so dear," he sighed. "But we have to be smart now. Ewen has something in mind. Maybe it's a good thing this time. Let's wait and see. We'll pretend the snoop didn't turn loose his little nugget of golden dirt after all.

Not yet anyway. Now why don't we just tack on across the Florida Straits and deliver this cargo? Then I'll speak to Ewen about us."

"*Oh god!* Do you have a gun?"

"A gun? What about the small arsenal he installed in the aft cabin last year? Isn't it still there?"

Vanessa chastised herself with a rap on the head. "Of course," she responded grittily but in the next breath added, "Wait—that's his private quarters now. Ewen keeps that room locked tight as a drum! I haven't the foggiest where he hides the key either."

"Okay, no problem. But to answer your question, yes, I have a gun, a small pistol. It's in my bag over there. You can't imagine how many times I've wanted to use it to—" Clay hesitated for a moment then went on. "—to settle old scores, blow away *thieves*, defend damsels in distress. Those sorts of things."

Vanessa wiped her eyes and smiled back mechanically, not catching the hidden meaning and apparently not interested in lovey-dovey talk right then. "Well, if you insist on going to Cuba, let's get *Noche Buena* underway. But after we reach Varadero, I don't want to wait around for the old snail to come belly dragging in tomorrow afternoon. If we leave now, we might still make port by dark. He's never on time you know, so please don't stay overnight to talk with him about us. Tell him later if you must, years later. Remember the note I said I would write?"

"You're serious about that Dear John letter, aren't you?"

"Oh, Clay, already it sounds wonderful! We'll drop the men and their stuff off. Let them think we're going back to Miami to pick up more supplies, then after we motor out of view from shore, we'll unfurl the sails and set the yacht on a course for some faraway place. Okay, darling?"

Clay didn't respond immediately. He was thinking about Señor Valdez and the widely recognized risk that befell men who ignored his "requests" such as Silvio had recently delivered. Why was the Spaniard now insisting that he, Clay Redmond, pull the trigger on Ewen Leetboer? It struck Clay as curious, another ironic twist, since he had lately begun to turn away from the notion of murder in the first degree. The broker was also thinking about the five-million-dollar sting fund sitting in a Mexican bank. With two million already set aside for Silvio and Ramón, he would need to draw on the balance, surprise Vanessa with an equal share and make her a partner in this evolving alliance. Unfortunately, all paperwork required for transactions abroad was back in Miami tucked away in a storage vault.

When Vanessa prodded Clay for an answer, he looked up and saw the earnest plea in her eyes and replied, "Aye, aye, skipper."

Left unsaid was his belief that a little more time would resolve the conflict.

30

Varadero lies a few degrees westerly of a due-south course from Marathon Key, a hundred miles distant. Miami's Chambered brass probably sees this renowned tourist hot spot as a serious competitor, although not a one of them would admit as much, at least not out loud. Being a little under two hundred miles away, give or take a few, Varadero sits closer to Miami than Havana does. Clay Redmond remembered when the place was just a quaint little fishing village, offering no sights that anyone would cross an ocean and pay money to see. With Vanessa along, he looked forward to the trip as much as any hot-blooded tourist from Spain, France or Italy.

After lunch the broker rounded up Ewen Leetboer's four "team leaders." Arturo, Ewen's Portuguese sailor, stood meekly among them, which was something of a surprise, since he could handle the yacht quite well. Clay figured Ewen had something else in mind for him other than navigation. Maybe the chiseler didn't trust the Clockwork men around his wife. But, as Clay remembered, Vanessa didn't trust Arturo to sail the yacht. She had insisted to Leetboer that Clay do it himself, with her help—and none from those workers, those "brazen oglers."

When Clay Redmond called the men aboard, each one of them gave off a matchless (and cleverly honed) sigh of relief to find that the trip was still on. They had heard the stories about Cuban women and, again, each one tried to "out-macho" his cohorts by jumping onto the deck with the surefooted likeness, and cockiness, of an old salt in pursuit of a tropical night of cha-cha-cha. While Clay motored *Noche Buena* out of the Coral Gables harbor, heading for open sea, Vanessa put the men to work at any little job she could think of to keep them busy and out of sight. Their eyes bothered her, the sidelong glances and inquisitive, sneaky peeps. At times she'd laugh inwardly. *Maybe that's what Ewen told them to do*, she'd reflect. *Maybe he wanted more snoops around to keep their bloody eyes on me. Maybe these men tattle more than build . . . .*

"We should've left at daylight," Clay said when, later, Vanessa dropped by the helm with some nibbles. Her face brightened at the sound, any sound from him just then for she needed to hear the deep, soothing voice of this lovable guy, Clay Redmond. *Her* guy he was, and it would seem that she was forcing an act of bravery upon herself by cuddling up to him in plain view of her husband's tell-all clockworkers. She didn't much care any more. She also wanted to smooch a little but, fearing it would compromise Clay's authority in the men's eyes, she decided to slip in her kisses when this curious crew wasn't looking.

Clay talked on. "We'll never make it by dark," he noted again, unaware of the bittersweet thoughts rushing in and out of Vanessa's head. "I figure about twenty hours, which means we'll reach port tomorrow afternoon just in time to be greeted by the latecomers, Ewen the Screw and Stanley B. Funkybutt."

Vanessa squinched up her nose at Clay, half smiling. "Can't you keep the motors running, darling? Speed things up a bit?"

"Let's go with the wind," he answered, objecting with a polite show of teeth and a friendly finger glide along her open waist. "Sails and motors don't tango like we do, honeybun."

The day was getting away from them already, most of the morning shot. Clay Redmond knew they would be sailing all night. The light wind didn't bother him other than the fact that it bothered Vanessa. She wanted to go faster. The Irish lady didn't relish a face-off with Ewen Leetboer, especially not him, this soon after Karl Skepe opened her cabin door and saw his boss's wife in bed with Clay Redmond. Vanessa began to expand on the big man's character whenever she talked with her lover about that awkward moment of discovery. "Surely that monster snoop," she fumed at one point, "surely the bloke didn't waste a minute getting to a phone and blabbing the news to his likewise bloky boss!" Though he didn't say so, Clay Redmond suspected that Ewen Leetboer, for some time now, had known more than he let on, had long since put two and two together and, thanks to his "steel-plated rib cage and galvanized stomach," had accepted the bitter result with the aplomb of an Old World patriarch. To save face he would probably say nothing about it. Not right away anyhow. A consummate conniver, the Dutchman might rather pick a time to suit his best interests, which had nothing to do with love or even betrayal but everything to do with bottom lines and positions of strength at the bargaining table. Jealous-husband rage was not his style. Too physical, too sticky, too short on the good stuff like counter offers, leverage, defaults, *honest* screwing. Monkey business was not the same as a businessman's business. Nor would he ever repeat the odious term after an "is" just to beg a question or belabor the obvious, at least not in the gutsy, ready cadence employed when he repeated the motto he lived by and invoked in praise of the true kind of business so instructive to careless victims of his capital gains trident.

Business is business Leetboer would drone on such occasions. Nothing more, nothing less. While the faithful practice of it continued to do wonders for his bottom line, and even though he seldom passed up the chance to "buy into" a little light-hearted hanky panky on the side, he viewed monkey business in a more solemn light. Some would say in about the same light as he viewed the stock market: a gambler's milieu honeycombed with crooks and cocksuckers and far too risky for serious wealth accumulators like himself.

As the yacht sliced deeper into the Atlantic currents, Clay Redmond's thoughts turned moodily to Silvio and Ramón. Together, the three men had made the crossing many times. The sound of waves slapping their ethereal blueness, their liquid innocence, against the hull, opened his mind to those days when Graciela was still alive and things were different on the island. How many rafters had since died while trying to get to Miami, he wondered, knowing the answer already. *Too many*. How many had been swallowed up by "troubled waters," as Simon and Garfunkel used to sing about, *swallowed up* as if the sea itself wanted to make a point using human life as the fodder of choice, a point about the price of freedom, its value, its worth, confident that such points are better made to a grieving public when the wrong lives are allowed to perish.

Clay Redmond stayed close to the helm for the rest of the day and through the night. The Florida Straits was always full of ships going to and coming from the Panama Canal, as well as other ports on this side of the locks. *Noche Buena's* autopilot didn't give way to such dangerous traffic. Eyes and ears still remained, for small ships, the best and most reliable watchdogs within the shipping lanes.

Vanessa joined Clay at the wheel as much as he would let her, brought him food and drink more often than he asked. At times she'd stand by to give him a potty break or maybe massage his neck when he yawned and looked tired. If the wind picked up too much, she'd take over while he went forward to trim the sails. Later in the evening, under the cover of darkness, her hands ventured down from his neck, around his broad shoulders, into his vigilant but easily subdued erogenous zone, bringing arousal into play for brief intervals to keep him awake. The rest of the time, and in between times, they simply talked. After the men retired to the guest cabins below deck, the two lovers spun out their fantasies to each other in soft urgencies, contest-like, to see who could paint the most affectionate images of whatever future their respective fates might allow them to share. Around midnight he sent her off to bed.

"Maybe you should let Arturo help you," she said before leaving.

"No. He's afraid you'd complain about him again to Ewen."

"Blarney! Then I'll stay."

"Go to bed. I want you fresh tomorrow."

"And what about you, darling?" she asked in a sultry tone. "You'll fall asleep! My arm cannot possibly reach from the cabin, nor your—*this!*—to it. Really, shouldn't I stay?"

A dull waning moon had just risen but gave off enough light to expose the emerald gleam in her eyes, which dazzled Clay for a moment. "Not to worry, sweetheart," was his answer before kissing her goodnight. "I'm awake now." Then, adopting her sultry tone and spicing it with a Spanish flavor, he added, *"Ay, mi amor!* O sweet colleen! My *'this'* owes you one—a very *beeg* one which you may claim *cuándo, cuándo, cuándo* we make bed together."

Late the next afternoon Clay Redmond eased the yacht into the slip at Varadero. The four workmen, each one (but Arturo) eager to show off new skills picked up on the way over from Miami, made the vessel fast with generous loops of half hitches along a wooden platform on its port side. Arturo was first to leave. The other three men tried to follow suit and leap up on the pier like their Portuguese shipmate, but they soon settled for a safe, landlubber's wobble instead. Ewen Leetboer greeted them with effusive presence, provoking astonishment all around as he shook each hand with a gusto one usually holds back for friends not seen in years.

By some incredible prescience Vanessa foresaw her spouse standing at dockside, waving *Noche Buena* into the slip he had reserved at Varadero's not-so-quaint little harbor of foreign registries. So she was less surprised to see him actually there on the pier than she was to see the big, hokey, hail-fellow-well-met, skin-stretching smear of a smile on his face. It brought instant relief, perhaps because the usual crocodile version was, oddly, not evident. *Maybe he doesn't know yet*, she thought. In spite of vague doubts, she saw no sign of anger about him, not even in the wary, pacing movements back and forth on the dock as the yacht approached the berth. Yes, the fool was just excited, glad to see familiar faces. No, Ewen Leetboer didn't show the slightest awareness that his wife had been caught on top of another man, naked and deliriously screaming in concert with ecstasies unknown to him, nor did he appear any different, except friendlier perhaps, from the man she'd confronted at other times over lesser causes, clearly nothing to compare with even the least weighty times when minor arguments would turn raucous and often rise to ear-splitting pitches. Most of these were occasions having to do with her allowance—i.e., *money, money, money*—and her use of the term "my darling apartment" rather than the cold preference he would garble out in reply, the insipid "our unit" term. Quite often, to get her goat even more, he might insist on adding the income-producing adjective "rental" in between, inciting loud wails of invective from Vanessa. *Maybe Ewen's a bit horny*, she thought after allowing him a brief hug. His old Dutch fondle somehow worked its way into the embrace, which caused her to pull back, out of his grasp, and chuckle to herself over the stiff, bony attempt. Nevertheless, she was glad to see that her snub had not affected the jubilant mood her spouse appeared to be in. Even more odd, the proud Dutchman seemed unaware that her chilly reaction took place in front of the men, including his idol, Stanley B. Conover. Such an embarrassment, whether intended or not, usually put her at risk of some immediate, painful reprisal. *What has happened to Ewen?* she wondered. *Why is he being so nice?* Consumed by a brief rush of pity, Vanessa was almost moved to hug him again.

But Ewen's sneering attorney was there, too, and the sight of that blowhard and his rotten, know-it-all, "leechy" visage, his curved-down mouth and puffed-up lids in partial closure over bloodshot eyes, made her want to heave into the harbor.

The four men brought over from Miami were not "snoops," as Vanessa imagined. They were nothing more than Ewen Leetboer's key men, his construction team that embodied all the expertise needed to oversee the evolution of complex developments, his loyal protectors who would bring together an army of local labor—*cheap* labor Ewen Leetboer was happy to note during his frequent calculations of profit—and guide them toward completion of a pearl within a Pearl of the Antilles—the Mara Paradiso project. Leetboer took a fancy to the legends surrounding his new venture, in particular the one about Mara Paradiso being a shrine to a beautiful woman, a shrine made famous by the love of her husband, the inimitable Señor Guillermo Valdez. Being a businessman equal to his reputation, Ewen Leetboer was quick to recognize the importance of a vigorous advertising campaign to extend the legend into the breasts of all those romantic duffers who would come and spend money at his resort, perhaps buy overpriced condos there and palatial homes even more overpriced. Such legends would indeed make the place famous overnight. But he hadn't yet heard the stories about Mara Paradiso's infamous side, the side protected by the avenging spirit of a Spaniard known by the fear-inducing sobriquet, *El Cojonudo.*

Stanley B. Conover did not join in Ewen Leetboer's high-spirited welcome. He stepped backward to a piling and leaned on it in a slouchy, hands-in-pocket manner while his client charmed the crew with small talk and a flood of familiar references to their specialties, each of which he was counting on them to put to good use, and soon, on his behalf. The attorney seemed more interested in what Clay Redmond was doing, for his bloodshot eyes followed along as the broker rechecked the mooring lines and gathered up loose items around the deck before joining them on the pier.

"Well, well, Mr. Redmond," Leetboer bubbled, giving the broker a hearty chub reminiscent of Middle Eastern customs. "It seems I am in your debt once again. How can I ever repay you for all this kindness? I trust you had no problems with the yacht?"

Clay had followed Vanessa, ready to defend her if Leetboer and his loyalists turned violent. The chub caught him, Clay, by surprise and nearly provoked a martial arts reaction, but the Dutchman's gleeful tone relieved the tension even though the unusual presence of it came as still another surprise. Clay just stood still and let his former partner engulf him with a grand display of cordiality.

"No problems," Clay replied after a dragging silence. He backed off a couple of paces and searched Leetboer's face for any signs that the old Dutchman might not be as happy to see him as he appeared. "*Noche Buena* is a great ship, a real beauty, worthy of a full-time cook, if not a captain," the broker added, somewhat in jest.

Leetboer bobbled up and down with excitement. "You like her, eh?"

"Very much. Wish I could afford one just as fine."

"I see. Really, you like her, eh?"

"Really."

"Go ahead, Ewen," Conover shouted from the piling.

"Yes," Leetboer said, swinging his head back and forth between the two men. "Yes, of course. I am in your debt, Mr. Redmond. You must let me pay you—"

Clay Redmond shrugged. "If you truly feel indebted," he said, interrupting in the same gentle vein as he was hearing, "maybe you wouldn't mind letting me take this yacht out every now and then. You know, for a week or so when you're not using her."

Leetboer's smile widened. "A week, yes? Like a time share you mean?"

"Yeah, you can call it that, a time share. I'd love to take a six month's cruise in this baby, starting today, starting right now and sailing all the way to Guadalcanal!"

Clay was still standing in a semi-combat posture, his arms akimbo, his face twitching with the uneasy smirk of a poker player who'd just raised the ante. Ewen Leetboer looked over at Conover. The attorney was nodding and twisting the kinks out of his neck, as if preparing to mount a courtroom rebuttal. The Dutchman twittered a laugh then, closing the distance between him and Clay, slapped the broker on his shoulder and guffawed. "Yes," he said, "perhaps another partnership, eh?"

"Uh-huh. Even with a written agreement, hey? Maybe in simple English this time, not Conover's English . . . hey?"

"Hells bells, as the hippies talk, why not? You have proven your value. Look what a treasure you put in my hands in Miami this year already. Look it—*Xanadu*, for goodness sake!"

"Yeah, a nice little plum. Nothing compared to this Cuba deal, though."

Leetboer blanched for a second, then, "Ah, Cuba! For sure here in Cuba! Mara Paradiso, look it! Yes, what a jewel! Ah, Mr. Redmond, are you joking with me?"

"As a matter of fact I am," Clay answered, holding his smile in tow.

Leetboer studied the broker's twitching face for a brief time, then turned toward Conover, who was still slouched against the piling. "Stanley," he barked, "you must draw up papers for Mr. Redmond's time share. Give him fifty percent interest in *Noche Buena*, with stipulation he will serve as captain of the yacht during all exercises of time shares, including my own. Further to the subject, you may as well start his rotation with the first six months beginning as soon as we sign the papers."

Conover snarled and stopped nodding. "Okay, but you know what I gotta do," he shouted, peering wild-eyed at the four men as though he were addressing them. "Gotta get back to Miami first. The legal stuff is in storage—you know, encrypted on a floppy. I'll need my computer to unlock the draft model, et cetera, et cetera."

"How much time will you require?" Leetboer asked, smiling.

"Practically the whole damn week, Ewen, counting travel. Don't look so damn gleeful about it either. I'm not flying!"

"Very well. You can leave right away on *Noche Buena*. Since you do not like the plane, I'm sure my wisely reformed partner will be happy to sail you to Miami for this important work. Then return here with the partnership agreement, you and Mr. Redmond, and I will sign it and my wise partner can be on his way to Zanzibar, or wherever it is he likes."

"Let's get going then," Conover bellowed with a loud handclap, pushing away from the piling. His Gladstone bag then came into view and caught Clay Redmond's notice.

Leetboer turned back to Clay, grinning with renewed intensity. "Is that agreeable with you, Mr. Redmond?" He resumed his hold on the somewhat bemused broker's arm, giving it a few cordial shakes as he waited for an answer.

What's he so fucking pumped up about? Clay wondered. *And why is he calling me 'Mister' Redmond like we just met?* The broker had caught a whiff of the same smelly agenda that Vanessa appeared to be catching, setting off cosmic glares between them, yet Clay felt his insides more shaken than the limp appendage Ewen Leetboer had extended to him and was then shaking his hand so joyously as he continued to yell out orders to Conover.

Clay Redmond was shaking his head, too. His ruddy face continued to twitch but lines of restraint and wonder were fast replacing the earlier poker-player smirks. "Look, I said I was kidding. Okay, Ewen? Thanks anyway. I don't think I can afford the legal work—court costs and so on, if you know what I mean. Sounds like Stanley wants to make a big deal out of it, as usual."

Conover's lids popped fully open. He stared hard at Ewen Leetboer and mumbled something under his breath, then the jaded attorney flashed some of the old eyebrow language at his client, not a wiggle of which was lost in transit.

"I will take care of Stanley," Leetboer replied, his focus shifting back to Clay. "Stanley is my expense. Look it, the paperwork will be small—and only for your protection. I'm self-insured, as you know. You are not."

Clay Redmond took his cap off and brushed through his thick mane. He glanced around for Vanessa, his face red and stony from the pressure of mounting mistrust slithering around in his head. She had stepped back on the yacht and away from the strange, frenetic behavior of her husband and his attorney. When she saw Clay looking at her, she heisted her shoulders and winked coolly at him, back and forth, from one rolling emerald eye to the other. The message had the force of a blinking yellow light on the edge of a world-class pothole.

"No, Ewen, I can't let you do this. Forget it."

Leetboer's mouth sagged. "I see," he then mumbled sadly, followed by a few thoughtful hems. "Yes, I see. However, that bit of modesty is too generous for you to extend to me. I am a rich man, Mr. Redmond, and getting on in years! I feel beholden to you, not just for sailing my yacht over here and bringing my wife and valuable foremen, but also for all your help in the past, your guidance in real estate matters, in other of my investments, and so forth and so forth. Yes, I owe you something more lasting than a check for seaman's services, for goodness sake. Take it as inheritance well deserved, a gift perhaps not as gratifying as the one Judge Brussard should have awarded you earlier, but valuable nevertheless. For me it is just another atonement I am now begging a good friend to permit."

Clay gazed back at Vanessa. She had moved behind the helm, sitting in Clay's seat, listening without appearing to be listening. Her Canary Islands dream was beginning to show up again around her mouth and eyes, Canary without the yellow blinking lights. Clay could tell what she was thinking. He turned to Leetboer but paused and began to ruffle the hairs on his neck as he squinted in thought.

"If you insist, how can I not accept?" Clay Redmond responded, humbling himself. "I'll need some sleep first. Shall we get underway, say, around midnight or will tomorrow noon be soon enough?"

The twinkle in Ewen Leetboer's dull gray eyes increased. "Midnight will be fine," he answered.

31

A little after midnight *Noche Buena* motored out of Varadero's dimly lit harbor and disappeared in the darkness, sails hoisted. Clay had slept for several hours before the roll and pitch of the yacht awoke him. His head was aching and felt strange. He looked at his wrist. His trusty Timex was not there but judging by the size of the waves he guessed they had been at sea for some time. "What is going fucking on!" Clay muttered, his voice unsteady. "Arturo—?"

The broker crawled out of the bed he and Vanessa had made love in two days before, the one where Karl Skepe had photographed them locked together, moaning, wailing undecipherable sounds like a band of impassioned Paiutes. He had slept in his clothes. When he tried to open the door he discovered that it was barred from the outside. "Son of a bitch," he grunted, his speech jerky and full of slurs. "Well, well. Looks like I'm locked in. Some joker must be playing games—!"

Clay banged on the door with the side of his fist then listened in between knocks. Not a sound did he hear other than the lonely, frightening roar of an enraged sea. He pounded hard with the leg ends of a chair, shouting as loud as he could until he grew weary of the effort. The door was made of steel but it also seemed welded to the jamb. Every attempt to force it open failed. Clay sat back down on the bed, mulling. "*Conover*—!" he muttered this time. Things were still not clear in his head.

Vanessa was last seen at the Cuban restaurant where they ate dinner the evening before. Under protest she left with Ewen Leetboer afterwards, then only because Ewen promised to get her back to the yacht in time to join Clay Redmond on the return voyage to Miami. She wouldn't hear of remaining in Cuba even for one night without Clay somewhere close by, although she didn't say as much or explain why she refused to stay over. Just what Ewen had in mind for her to see—another condo perhaps—was not disclosed either when he coaxed her out of the restaurant, so Clay, feeling deserted, drugged and barely awake by then from lack of sleep, or so he thought, couldn't even remember making his way back to *Noche Buena* or taking off his wrist watch or getting in bed or closing his eyes to grab some shuteye before putting out to sea. Too much rum he concluded, except there was a different feeling inside now, a hazy muddled feeling unknown to him. Throughout dinner Ewen never let up on the jolly, saccharin manner he had displayed earlier at the dock. Vanessa wondered if her spouse hadn't been sniffing coke.

Clay did remember that Conover had excused himself earlier, had left the dinner party under the pretext of gathering personal effects needed on the trip. Clay also remembered that Conover had his Gladstone bag with him, at his feet, when *Noche Buena* arrived that afternoon. Conover was not a forgetful man. His personal effects traveled with him and they traveled in that bag, a veritable working man's cornucopia well stocked for all accommodations. *Was he lying?* Clay rolled the question around in his mind for a bit. He never doubted the man's ability to shade the truth, cover up facts, gloss over miscarriages, and so on, but there was usually a fairly transparent reason when he did resort to legal chicanery, which was often. In this case the reason wasn't clear to Clay Redmond and the question begged itself: *Why?* Clay knew from experience that some attorneys harbored a streak of jealousy toward brokers whose income exceeded their own. In short they resented having to load up a closing statement with a five-digit commission, payable to some "ding-a-ling landmonger"; six digits turned them blue. Clay Redmond figured a prick like Conover would stretch his legal skills to the limit to scuttle a multimillion-dollar deal such as he specialized in. But that couldn't be the problem here, the broker concluded. No big deals were pending. The screw job set off by Conover's default traps was behind him.

After a short rest Clay Redmond began to bang on the door with greater force. He figured it was lashed tight at the knob with a rope or small cable. When he pushed hard, there was some give and a rattle or two but nothing more. The door held fast.

Clay checked the valise he had brought aboard back at the Coconut Grove Marina, finding everything in place but his Model 51 .380 automatic. The gun was missing. Slowly it occurred to the broker that Ewen Leetboer and his attorney might have somehow learned of the sting operation and the plot to do away with one or both of them. Was it true? he wondered, and had they taken precautions, a preemptive strike maybe? A pang of suspicion began to escalate in his already aching head. Only Vanessa knew, or at least she was the only one within spitting range of Leetboer's ear who *could* betray either party. Clay's mind raced. Would she? he asked himself. *Vanessa—a narc?* It didn't seem possible. Her love was too obvious, too deep, too sincere. If she betrayed *him*, then nobody was safe anywhere; not even the Pope's prayers could override the force abounding within Temptation's sellout zone. "*No, not Vanessa,*" Clay howled at the walls, *"no way!"* But suspicion continued to gnaw at him. Ben Franklin's view of the matter suddenly popped into play: *Three can keep a secret if two of them are dead.* Then the line in a Jimmy Buffett song, *Some people claim there's a woman to blame but I know it's my own damn fault.* He shouldn't have told her. After all, she was the Dutchman's wife and stood to lose everything she'd hoped to gain by submitting herself to the lecheries of the old goat—*everything!*—if the plan went awry and her involvement discovered. *Did the bastards beat the truth out of her?*

Suddenly the door swung open and Stanley B. Conover was standing in the hall with Clay Redmond's Remington in his hand, grinning one of his most repulsive courtroom grins. The attorney's expression rose to a kind of morbid delight when he saw Clay's eyes widen in wonder, if not shock. Somehow the "mangy attack dog," as perceived at that moment, reminded Clay of Pepe.

"So you finally woke up, did you?" Conover said.

"Clay rubbed his eyes. "What time is it?"

"Late. I must have given you a little too much of my, shall we say, 'after dinner' concoction back at the restaurant. It's almost morning if you must know."

Clay stumbled toward Conover, shaking his head to clear it of confusion. "What's the gun all about?"

The attorney raised the pistol and waved it at Clay. "You tell me," he said. "I found it in your gear." Clay shook his head and moved closer. "Stay back, Redmond! Don't get footsie with that Karate crap either, I'll dump this clip on you."

The broker squinted at Conover and moved backward a couple of steps. He staggered then slumped down on the edge of the bed, puffing like an exhausted tiger. The dope he had been served unawares still had a grip on him but perhaps not as much as Conover thought. The attorney seemed nervous too, Clay noticed, more than a man should be with a gun in his hand. Conover tried to cover up by acting tough and using hood lingo but the façade was weak and pocked with the style of an amateur killer. Clay chewed over a few options: *Maybe Leetboer found out about the sting. Ramón wouldn't tell them . . . but Pepe . . . ? Has the bank traced the check yet . . . ? Shit! Guess the old Dutchman knows I'm in on it. What did Skepe tell him . . . ? No, not Vanessa . . . !*

Conover eased into the room and pressed his way along the bulkhead, keeping a good distance between himself and Clay Redmond. Then, waving the gun again, the attorney motioned Clay toward the door. "Let's go up on deck," he said, roughening his voice. "You need some fresh air. I'd like you to have a clear head when you leave this boat. I won't say how you'll be leaving it; we'll get to that later. Here's a hint though: you'll find the scenery great; that is, if you happen to like a mackerel's view of things."

Clay pretended not to understand. He appeared utterly befuddled, as if a zombie had taken possession of his mind and left him too absorbed to plod through any matter at that moment other than Conover's initial command to go on deck. Outside, he walked past Arturo with a drunken cast on his face, never looking straight at the Portuguese. Arturo said nothing. The bedraggled sailor had his hands full plowing a safe course through twelve-foot seas. Engrossed in his struggle, he seemed oblivious to the presence of the two men and kept to his courageous tussle with a stubborn helm.

When they reached the deck, Clay lurched along to the starboard rail. At the first opportunity he grabbed a halyard to steady him. He hung there for a few minutes and just breathed. Conover, hugging the mast, looked on and made foul wisecracks, unaware of the effect the cool night air was having on Clay's lungs. The broker felt renewed power returning to his body. His memory was still a bit fuzzy, especially about the evening at the restaurant, yet he was clear-headed enough to know that it would be smarter to continue the drugged act for a while longer. Conover pointed to the nose of the yacht. "Up there!" he snarled with a pathetic twist on his face. "Watch your step, Kung Fu. I'd hate for our champion broker to fall over just yet. We'd never be able to find you in these turbulent waters. Now that would be a first-class pity, don't you think?"

"Now that would be a fact," answered Clay Redmond, slurring.

The two men made their way to the bow of the yacht, struggling to stay upright as Arturo had been struggling to steer the yacht into the wind. They stood apart for a brief time staring at each other. The silence was awkward but telling.

"Okay, Redmond, this is it. Jump in."

"How's that? I can't hear you."

"You heard me all right! Jump in the fucking sea for Christ's sake!"

Clay smirked away his drunken act. "Screw you!" he said. "You must be crazier than I thought you were."

"You bet I'm crazy—crazy to see you go for a swim. Look, Redmond, here's the deal. Either you say bye-bye and jump over like a good boy and practice your overhand stroke or I'll say bye-bye and plug you so full of holes you'll look like . . . like . . ."

"Yeah, I know—Swiss cheese, right?"

"Exactly. You won't be able to swim with all those holes taking on water. That is, unless you can swim *under* water, swim all the way back to Miami holding your big nose. Miami's quite a ways from here you know, a good sixty or eighty miles I'd say. What'll it be, hotshot?"

Clay poked a pinkie down his ear and jiggled it hard for a moment then scratched the side of his face while he considered Conover's instructions. "Stanley, you sound a little out of character to me. Got to hand it to you, though, you're slick. Who would have thought it—Stanley B. Conover, a hitman! May I ask why you're doing this?" Clay paused and chuckled and waited for a response but Conover only pushed his lips out like a mad camel. "Actually," Clay resumed, "I know why, don't I? You're following orders, right? All that talk about a time share was bullshit."

"Don't sweat it, Redmond. You shouldn't have played touch with Ewen's wife."

"Oh, so that's it. Skepe tattled on us. Yeah, I see. Figured he would." Clay stiffened; he felt normal again, wide awake and steady on his feet. Conover's crude reference to Leetboer's wife stung him inside but it also relieved him. "It's about honor," Clay muttered aloud to himself, "not the sting, not the five million."

Conover hollered over at Clay. "Okay, rummy, what's so funny?"

Clay's grin expanded into a loud laugh. *"Him!"* he yelled, pointing at the attorney. "Stanley B. Conover is funny. He's about to get screwed by his boss and the poor slob doesn't even know it."

"My, my, how full of shit you are tonight! Okay, Redmond, go ahead and get it out of your system. Have your little laugh. No harm done. You're a dead man anyway."

"What's Ewen gonna do to Vanessa?"

"Nothing you need to be concerned about. It won't be pretty, though, since you asked. If you can stay afloat long enough, you just might bump into her."

The distance between them was no more than ten feet. Clay had a grip on the bow rail while Conover, his legs spraddled comically, was trying to balance himself without getting too close to Clay Redmond's lethal foot. Clay's eyes were focused on Conover's movements, waiting for a chance to attack. At that moment Nature accommodated him by sending a huge wave crashing onto the yacht. Conover was swept nearly over the gunwale but managed to hold on until the water cleared the deck and the yacht stabilized as well as it could under the stormy conditions. Clay grabbed a lifeline and moved toward Conover. It was still a long hour before dawn, with poor visibility because of constant sprays, even though each man's eyes had adjusted to the dark. Clay Redmond could see his heirloom automatic still in Conover's hand. For a change it was not pointed at him. Conover was cursing and wiping the salt water out of his eyes when Clay stripped the gun away. With casual ease Clay jerked the attorney to his feet and tied the lifeline around his waist.

Conover crouched and covered his head. "Don't kick me, Redmond, don't kick me . . . *please goddammit!*"

"Kick you hell, I'm gonna knock your ass overboard with my fist, you wimpy prick!"

"No—*wait!*" Conover yelled, opening his eyes for a quick peep then banging them shut again and readjusting the arm cover over his head.

Clay clasped the attorney by a shock of hair and pulled him out of his cringing posture. "Stand up, Stanley. Look me in the eye while I decide what to do with you."

"Oh God," Conover groaned. "I thought you already knew!" He laughed hysterically for a moment. His mouth was full of stutters as he said, "You're no killer, Clay Redmond. Look here. Why did you tie this lifeline around me?"

Clay pressed his nose hard against Conover's. "So I can cut it loose when you fall in," he growled.

"But you said you were going to *knock* me in—!"

"I changed my mind. What makes you think I want your cruddy blood on my hands anyway?" He pulled back from Conover's nose and snorted a lazy chuckle on seeing a broader view of the terrified expression on the attorney's face. "Ewen Leetboer must be more senile than I imagined," Clay resumed, "sending a gutless fart like you out to bushwhack me." Clay rammed the pistol against Conover's stomach, setting the attorney into a spasm of coughs mixed in with desperate pleas for his life. "You know, Stanley, I'm awfully tempted to just slice you open—Charley the Tuna style—and feed your sorry ass to the crabs!"

"Listen, Clay, it was a joke . . . for Christ's sake, a joke! I'm serious. It was a goddam joke, my friend—honest! Ewen only wanted to put a scare into you, that's all. He was terribly hurt when Skepe phoned in the news."

"What news?"

"You know—about you and his wife . . ."

"Yeah, Ewen looked all broken up back in Varadero, didn't he? Old Ewen's such a kindhearted, considerate fellow, right? Why he picked up the whole tab at the restaurant tonight—or was it last night?—or when in the hell ever it was. I can't remember. Anyway, he didn't act like the typical Dutchman, now did he?"

"That's true, Clay, very true. You really hurt the man, you're like a brother to him."

"Uh-huh, I'd lay money on it."

"Listen, he wants you to have that time share. Let's go on to Miami and I'll fix up the docs just like we discussed in that godforsaken place back there—"

"What godforsaken place was that?"

"You know, that damn Cuban tourist trap."

"Varadero? The home of . . . *Mara Paradiso*?"

"*Oh Jesus*! You know, you know . . . yes, exactly—!"

"Keep talking."

"Yes, yes! You'll have your time share all right—!"

"Keep talking!"

"Yes, yes, except it won't be a time share now. Ewen wants me to have the other half but I'll throw that in, too. Sailing makes me sicker than flying for Christ's sake! To hell with yachts—you can have it all. I'll fix everything. Then we'll head back to Cuba, sign the papers with Ewen and you can take this fucking boat to Guadalupe—or wherever. It'll be yours lock, stock—"

"Shut up." Clay rammed the gun deeper into Conover's gut. "Where did he take Vanessa?"

32

"Please enjoy where you are, dear Elena."

"I'm sorry, I cannot."

"Neither can you leave."

"But, why, Pepe?"

"I have told you already. It is my duty. Señor Valdez wishes you and Ramón to remain here as his guests. He has his reasons."

Pepe and Elena were alone in Señor Valdez's suite at Hotel Embajador. She was homesick and made that fact clear at least once a day. Ramón usually went to the Casino by himself, since Pepe would not allow both of Señor Valdez's "guests" to go out together unless he went along also, and Pepe was not always in the mood to play chaperone.

The casino became a daily stop, a routine, for Ramón. The distraught Cuban hoped he might bump into a fellow exile and pick up something new to pass on to his brother in Miami. Like Elena, he was also restless, maybe less homesick but more eager to learn of the fate of the Dutchman. When Clay Redmond followed through on his part of the deal—that is to say, "destroyed" Ewen Leetboer, as Señor Valdez had so tactically put it, then he and Elena would be released. He'd take her to Miami, set up their home in exile there and tie up any loose ends still dangling from the sting operation. Ramón did not know, nor did anyone else know other than the assassin himself, that Ewen Leetboer had put his own plans in motion to deep-six Clay Redmond. Their goals were definitely *not* of the "mutually exclusive" type.

"But we have stayed a long time with you," Elena sighed, "many days now, and to what purpose but to live like tourists in this magnificent hotel and waste away from too much idleness. Pepe, you have been nice, a better friend than we have a right to expect. I am grateful for what you and Señor Valdez have done to save Ramón from Castro's awful prisons but we have work to do. There is no work for us here in Santo Domingo."

Pepe strolled to the balcony and looked out over the Colonial District. Activity on the street was light. The sun hung near the western horizon. He would leave the suite with Elena in less than an hour and join Ramón for more games, then dinner. The gangster's dark, shifty eyes took in the street scene as methodically as he would scan an approach to a cocaine drop-off site, searching for signs of double crosses and CIA traps.

"Santo Domingo is also magnificent," he said, not turning away from his outward gaze, "equal to your Havana in many ways. Please try to enjoy your stay here."

"Santo Domingo is a foreign city to me, without meaning."

"Listen to me, my child. Your sweetheart will not be safe in Cuba under the present government. He killed a spy in the service of Fidel Castro, a ghastly affront to the leader and one that is considered a counterrevolutionary act by every authority in your country, deserving of the firing squad. My bribe freed him for the moment but his act of defiance against the Revolution will not go unpunished if he returns and shows his lost innocence in public."

"You mustn't worry for us, Pepe. We have connections with the underground in Cuba. Our friends there will protect us."

"Please, no more about this matter. We must leave now and find Ramón."

Pepe was awed by Elena's beauty but beauty alone was not enough to shake his mind free of fear. This woman was taboo, not to be touched by anyone whose hands she did not welcome, and she welcomed no one's hands but Ramón's. Fear of the wrath of El Cojonudo kept Pepe's mind sealed, his cock as limp as knitting yarn. No temptation this side of Eden could force him to make the slightest advance or commit even one tiny innocent flirtation. Elena seemed to understand this unspoken code of loyalty. She no longer showed her former uneasiness around Pepe. Ever since the incident at Mara Paradiso when he threatened to "shoot out the eyes" of Ewen Leetboer and his attorney, and frightened her nearly to death as well, he had conducted himself like a seasoned diplomat, a gentle harem guard, if not always a perfectly gentle man.

Ramón was pulling the slots in the hotel casino when they found him. Pepe stood back for a bit and watched him feed quarters to two machines as fast as he could switch from one to the other. It was a way of quelling an inner rage. A big jackpot merely brought the Cuban a few minute's relief from the agony of living in limbo.

"What have you won today?" Elena asked Ramón, stepping beside him and rubbing his shoulders while her eyes fastened on the three spinning wheels that were then filling her face with excitement as she waited to see which of the colorful symbols would land on the pay line.

Ramón snorted at each drop. Without taking his eyes off the machine, he answered Elena out of the side of his mouth. "Nothing big enough to bribe our way out of Santo Domingo," he sighed, "but there is a joker sitting at the bar who is big and who has been annoying me with his stares."

Elena glanced over and scanned the line of customers crouched on bar stools, settling on the largest man in the crowd. He was sitting near the end of the bar, with an open view of Ramón and the only person who bothered to look their way, looking much too often to suit Ramón Alvarez.

"The heavy one in the yellow shirt?" Elena asked.

"Sí. And with the disgusting beard. Not easy to miss such a monstrosity of human flesh."

"Do you know him?"

"Never have I seen the person. See—he is staring again!"

"Perhaps he knows you from some place. You are becoming quite a traveler, my dear."

"Yes, and I am ready to travel away from here!"

Pepe moved up closer, listening. He had donned his dark glasses on leaving the suite and the intensity of his own stares did not show. "Ramón," he said, "you look disturbed, my boy. What troubles you today?"

Ramón turned as Pepe approached them. His head sagged at the question. "Nothing, Pepe, nothing. It is nothing. You know I can no longer keep secrets from you."

"But I do not insist on knowing everything, only some things."

Ramón winced. "Tell me again what things are they . . . ?"

"Things that will help me keep you and Elena safe. It is my duty to protect you."

"Which requires a very broad knowledge—*de todos los planes*—right?" Ramón leaned on a slot machine and wearily shook his head at the floor. "Pepe, you know already the one matter that troubles me the most. You rescued us from a miserable fate but why are we held—me and my lovely Elena—in Santo Domingo like prisoners? You have taken our passports, our money, my MasterCard. I cannot even make a phone call without you standing next to me with your fingers ready to yank the cord away . . ."

Elena slid her hand up and down Ramón's back. "Pepe does not wish to talk more of this, Ramón. Tell him what troubles you now—the fat man over there who is staring—"

"*What is this*?" Pepe said in a raspy whisper. His head swivelled for a moment; his hand flew up from his side and came to rest half in and half out of his jacket, aligned for easy access. He turned back to Ramón. "Who stares? Show me him."

"There," answered the Cuban.

The man looked off when Ramón pointed in his direction.

He twisted around on his stool and resumed sucking on a straw that poked out of the bartender's latest serve.

"*El Gordo* in the yellow fishing shirt, with the owl neck, you mean, with the hairy face of a bear?"

"The same."

"Wait here," Pepe said. He moved quickly, before the big fellow could turn around again, and came up close behind him, almost touching. Stools on either side were taken, so Pepe stood quietly in place, peering at thick, wind-blown, dirty hair and a hulking spread of body that smelled of sour sweat. *What woman would go to bed with such a pig?* Pepe thought. When the bartender spotted Pepe standing and peering through his dark glasses, seemingly toward him, his chin thrust forward and he jostled his head and rolled his eyes in the customary attitude of one poised to take and order over the heads of seated customers. When Pepe did not at first respond, the beckoning bartender moved closer and spoke to him. Pepe's steely eyes were riveted on his quarry and he paid no attention to the bartender. He even seemed irritated by the repeated call of his name and broke away from his preoccupation only long enough to signal a drink preference, which was known as he was known by many of the employees at Hotel Embajador.

"Excuse me." Pepe rubbed against the man when he reached over his shoulder to take the drink from the bartender. The mafioso's touch was light. His frisk was complete in a matter of seconds, causing not a stir of awareness from the unsuspecting party on the stool. Pepe felt no hard objects either and saw nothing suspicious poking out of that huge yellow shirt other than a camera, which was hanging from a strap looped around the man's thick neck. The shirt was so full of pockets, though, and the man's lower body so sprawled in loose-fitting clothes, Pepe couldn't really tell if he was armed or not. Nor was Señor Valdez' trusted lieutenant much concerned; it was enough to watch the big man's hands and be ready to shoot him if he pulled a gun or knife from under one of the folds of flesh his untidy garb concealed.

Pepe swigged the drink and banged the glass down in front of the man then tapped him on the shoulder. "Will you come with me please?" he said softly but with a firm and official ring.

The man spun slowly around. "Do I know you?" he asked behind a quizzical smirk that somewhat parted his chin whiskers.

"The question will be answered in the proper order. I have already asked you to come with me. Now, please . . ."

"Who the hell are you?" the big man said, looking amused as well as startled by the blunt request.

"Come with me please," Pepe repeated.

"What do you want?" answered the man in a sterner tone.

"I want you to come with me—and *now*."

"Are you . . . police?"

"Yes, come."

"Do you have identification? There must be some mistake—"

Pepe pulled back the lapel of his coat, exposing a holstered pistol. "No mistake," he said. "Here is my identification." The mafioso spoke with a low, ominous growl filtering through his voice. "Now if you will please remove both sides of your enormous ass from the stool and come with me, I will not kill you in this room in front of all these tourist gamblers."

The man threw his head back and laughed. "Oh, shit, who let you in here anyway?"

Pepe's hand shot out suddenly and jabbed a small blade into the man's chest and extracted it with a vicious twist.

"*Ouwwwchh! What the fuck . . . you . . . doing . . .* ?" the man yelled, clutching the bloody spot on his shirt.

"Relax, funny man. I am only showing you where the first bullet will enter," Pepe said in a remarkably calm but piercing voice, a raspy but almost docile voice that stood in stark contrast to his earlier growls and to the stricken glaze on the man's face. "Right here over the heart. The second one maybe will go higher . . ."

Grabbing onto the man's yellow shirt, Pepe wiped the blood off the blade. It was a short blade, filed down to horrify more so than inflict mortal wounds, and had not pierced more than an inch, but the big man acted run through to the spine.

"*Jesus Christ*—!" the big man gasped. He thrashed and moaned and, for a brief time, glared wild-eyed in frozen silence at this "mad assailant" in front of him who had begun to wave the blade again, waving it like a teacher would wave a pointer at diagrams on a chalkboard, Pepe waving his knife as if in search of another site to jab.

"Ah-h, yes, higher . . ." Pepe muttered, "maybe up there on that great neck of yours—"

"*Wait!*" the man shouted, his face no longer flushed red from derisive laughter but pale and colorless and wracked with fright as well as agony. "Where do you want to go . . . *Jeez—I can't believe this*! All right, all right . . . lead the way—"

"No, you lead the way," Pepe replied, easing behind the man and jabbing him in the buttock with the blade when he moved too slowly away from the stool. "Over there where the handsome young Latino is waiting with his beautiful lady. Go and stand in front of him. From there you will be able to see the whole person and tell us why it is you like to stare so much at him. Are you a queer?"

The man did not respond. Pepe led him past Ramón and Elena, motioning for them to follow. They walked to a quiet nook and stood for a moment facing each other.

"Do you know this bobo?" Pepe asked Ramón.

Ramón scanned him a second time. "No, but surely he must know me after so many rude glances! Would you believe this two-legged *caballo* even snapped several pictures?"

"I will handle the matter," Pepe said, not waiting to hear more. "It is my duty to protect the guests of Señor Valdez, as I have been telling you for several days. Do you believe me now?"

"I believe you, oh yes, Pepe. Truly I believe you now!" Ramón appeared eager to yield, considering the man was of an awkward size. The Cuban turned to Pepe, whose eyes had not abandoned their intense focus. "You are the boss, okay? My admirer is all yours, all five hundred pounds of him. Go with your instincts."

"And you go back to the suite with Elena. Order room service. I will handle this matter and join you there later."

Ramón protested. He wanted to hear what Pepe's captive had to say. Pepe agreed and together they pumped him until he refused to talk further. Finally Pepe shooed Ramón and Elena away. The mafioso waited for them to pass out of sight then turned back to the heavyset man, scowling as he folded the blade and put it in his pocket. As if by automation his hand moved inside his jacket and grasped the pistol and pulled it into view. "Listen to me, hombre. Why did you withhold the full truth from my friend?"

"No, honest, I told him everything!"

"Everything but who is paying you to carry out these criminal acts. Tell me now! If you lie I will shoot away your manhood. If you lie a second time I will kill you quickly before there is a third lie."

Pepe's evil visage shocked the man. Suddenly he showed an eagerness to talk. "Ewen Leetboer!" he practically shouted.

"*Hijo de puta*!" Pepe grunted. "The land pirate?"

"If you say so. Look, mister, I was only hired to find your friend and keep an eye on him until my client gets here. That's all. I don't know the details—don't want to know—but I did hear them talking about dumping somebody at sea. Not your friend though; they wanted him alive, him and his girlfriend."

"They? They who?"

"Leetboer and the other guy—his attorney."

"There was no one else?"

"Only Leetboer's wife."

"Describe her please."

"Gorgeous, red hair, late twenties or early thirties. Not the kind of dame you'd expect to see married to an old duck—"

"She was with these two plotters?"

"Yes but she didn't look happy about it. They're staying in one of those tourist hotels in Havana."

"Which one?"

"Nacional, the big one."

"When do you expect him here in Santo Domingo?"

"Tonight, around ten. Maybe earlier. He flies his own plane."

"You have no other mission?"

"None. I'm just a bloodhound."

"Tell me again your name."

"Karl Skepe."

"Your wallet and passport please."

The big man hesitated but the sudden motion of Pepe reaching inside his jacket for the pistol put him in a rush to cooperate. Here . . . here they are . . ." he stammered, shoving the requested items toward Pepe's busy hands.

Pepe, agitated by the man's delay as well as his sneaky business and piratical clientele, rapped him across the jaw with the gun before stuffing it in his belt. The man, Skepe, flinched miserably but once the weapon was out of Pepe's hands, a surge of courage spurred him into bolder action than he had shown during his tussle with Clay Redmond. In a sudden swift movement he brought his heft against the mafioso. Using his huge gut, Skepe pinned Pepe to the wall and was fumbling for the gun when a bullet struck him in the neck, struck in about the same spot Pepe had pointed to earlier with the blade. Skepe slumped to the floor. Pepe was holding another gun, Italian make already equipped with a silencer which he had tucked in his belt at the center of his back.

Pepe returned the "emergency" pistol to its location and holstered the one that had distracted Skepe. Apparently no one had noticed or bothered to investigate the commotion. The mafioso brushed himself off, stone faced and silent. For a moment or two he gazed through his dark glasses at the expanding puddle of blood on the floor. The bullet had clipped an artery. Skepe's mouth was still moving in slow, labored gasps, forcing some of the blood to flow across his lips along with a few garbled words. He seemed to be begging for confession. Pepe bent down and listened until a cold silence enveloped the man, then, sounding a soft grunt, Pepe rose and stepped around the puddle and moved in a casual stroll toward the lobby of Hotel Embajador.

33

With Pepe detained downstairs, Ramón lost no time placing a call to the Xanadu Shopping Mall. It was late and he feared the office would be closed. The crisp, feminine voice of Heather Ambrose relieved him, although he sounded a bit frantic to her and not the kind of call she cared to take right at five o'clock.

"Please slow down," she said, interrupting Ramón's burst of questions. "Now tell me again what it is you want."

"*Jesús!*" Ramón shouted. "Okay, I tell you again, I tell you I must locate Clay Redmond. It is urgent, I must speak to the Xanadu person there who is his friend."

"I'm his friend."

Ramón hesitated. "You are the owner?"

"No."

"Then, please, may I speak to the owner? Clay advised me, in case of emergency, to speak only to his friend who is the owner of Shopping Mall Xanadu . . . in Miami."

"That will be Mr. Cunningham, the managing partner. Let me see if he's still here. It's after closing hours, you know."

"I'm sorry. Forgive me the intrusion but I am not in your country at this time and the message I have for our mutual friend, Clay Redmond, cannot wait for tomorrow. Please—it is of grave importance that I speak to this Mr. Cunningham. Yes, Cunningham is the name. I see it here in my notes . . . ."

Heather cradled the phone across her shoulder and looked over at Marcus Cunningham. Marcus was standing in the doorway to his office and, on hearing Clay Redmond's name mentioned, had ventured out to pick up more of the conversation. "What is it?" he asked, wrinkling his brows in puzzlement.

Heather shrugged. "Someone with a Spanish accent," she answered. "He thinks you may know where Clay is. Maybe you better talk to the man. He sounds desperate."

Marcus Cunningham took the phone from Heather. "I'm Cunningham," he grunted into the mouthpiece. "What's this about Clay Redmond?"

"Are you the owner of . . . of the Shopping Mall Xanadu?"

"If you're looking for space, we're full up. Long waiting list. And, yes, I'm the owner, one of them."

"Thank heaven!"

"Who the hell are you?"

Ramón stiffened for a moment, expecting neither the question nor the brusque tone. Then he forced an inner calmness and began to speak in his old Cuban dialect that flowed somewhat smoother. "My name is Ramón Alvarez, a friend of your friend, Clay Redmond. I must get critical information to him right away—information he must have. Can you help me?"

"He's in the book. Call him."

"I did. No answer, only a strange Christmas message, *Noche Buena*, and hymns. My brother told me Clay Redmond went to Cuba—"

"Oh, yeah. *Noche Buena* is the name of Ewen Leetboer's yacht. He hired Clay to sail it over there. Clay left Miami last week."

"My brother says he is overdue back."

"Then your brother knows something I don't. Clay's not too hip with schedules."

"Please, Mr. Cunningham, this is urgent! Clay Redmond may be in great danger."

"Danger? Now what the hell's that supposed to mean? Clay's a real estate broker, not a buccaneer. He's a big boy, too, and knows how to take care of himself."

"Exactly right, I agree. But, Mr. Cunningham, you are also his friend. Will you not offer protection if he needs it?"

"Protection from what for Christ's sake?"

"From enemies, from attackers with weapons."

"Ha! I pity the poor bastard who tries to attack that guy. I've gone a few rounds with him on the mat. Clay's a black belt. What are you trying to tell me, that he pissed somebody off, said something nice about Castro down at The Versailles?"

"Hardly so simple as that, I'm afraid, Mr. Cunningham. This Ewen Leetboer is looking for Clay Redmond the same as I am, only he is looking to do harm."

"Ewen Leetboer? You gotta be kidding!"

"I am not kidding, Mr. Cunningham. Clay Redmond is in danger. I must find him first, I must warn him. The land pirate Ewen Leetboer hired a killer—"

"Ewen Leetboer hired a *killer*? What the hell for?"

"You must ask Clay Redmond this. It is a personal matter."

"Holy fuckaroly!" exclaimed Marcus Cunningham, blowing hard into the phone. "Why didn't you say so earlier? Clay's supposed to be aboard that so-called Christmas yacht—you know, *Noche Buena*. Check the marina at Varadero. Where are you now?"

Marcus heard a sharp click on the other end of the line, the click of a lost connection. He slumped against Heather Ambrose, nearly knocking her out of her chair, and shouted hello into the phone a number of times before hanging up, sounding more agitated with each shout. "Damn phone," he growled as he walked back into his office. A short time later he reappeared in a rush and banged the outer door shut. For a moment he stood in thought, facing the Venetian blinds that were still quivering from the sudden closure, muttering to himself, then, like a frustrated squad leader, he spun around and trained his stare on Heather.

"*Heather!*" he shouted, drawing up his arms in a contentious pose.

"What are you thinking?" she shouted back.

"That phone call just then—shit! All of a sudden I've got this funny feeling that Clay may be in some kind of trouble after all."

"With Ewen?"

"Yeah. Frank Creuthop would love that, wouldn't he? Ewen Leetboer taking on a black belt, trying to hurt Clay Redmond—*Jesus H . . . !*"

Heather did not seem pleased with Marcus's bluster over such a serious matter. She sometimes fantasized about Clay Redmond and never doubted, even now, that she could easily develop an addiction to him if Marcus weren't around. "Just what kind of 'hurt' are we talking about here?" she said without looking up at Marcus.

"Damned if I know. That fellow on the phone just then dropped three words on me—*danger, killer* and *harm*. In my book they add up to some pretty fucking serious hurt."

Heather waggled a tentative smile. "Ewen seems like such a nice man though, so gentle, proud and dignified—the very essence of nonviolence. He's too old for that sort of thing. He's certainly no tough guy either, the kind to go around beating up people. The caller sounded a little paranoid to me. Why would Ewen even *want* to hurt Clay?"

"I haven't a clue but I can't sit here with my thumb up my ass if Clay needs backup. Call Coconut Grove—the marina where Leetboer parks his yacht. See if you can get a number. There's got to be a cell phone, a two-way radio, an e-mail address or some way to contact the skipper when that frigging boat's out to sea."

"Are you serious?"

"Quite! I just remembered, just put two and two together. That was Ramón Alvarez on the phone, one of those Cuban brothers Clay eats chicken soup with over at The Versailles. They're like family, I mean—and might have been if their sister hadn't got snuffed out by one of Castro's goon squads. Something's going on, Heather. Clay's about to get screwed again. I can feel it, I got this funny fucking feeling deep down in my gonads. Call the operator. Clay may have more than one cell phone. See if you can't get a trace on Alvarez's number while you're at it."

"You really are serious, aren't you?"

"Hell, yes, I'm always serious! You know that."

"Sure I do."

"Don't get cute now. After all ol' Clay has done for me and this great piece of real estate, the least I can do is sound an alarm, pass the word from his Cuban *hermano* that the Dutchman is after him with his dick at full mast."

"Oh, Marcus—" Heather said, laughing and frowning at the same time. "Clay thinks Frank is the target, not him. I still can't figure why Ewen would be after Clay. They settled the law suit, didn't they?"

Marcus laughed. "A law suit is never really settled, my dear."

"Well, it just doesn't make sense. If they were still partners, okay, I can see that. At least there's room for a few misunderstandings to crop up now and then. But this 'hurt' business bothers me; they're not violent men. I think they would talk out their differences like gentlemen."

"Oh, yeah? Like me and Frank do, huh?"

"Ewen and Clay are not partners anymore, Marcus!"

"But w*e* are, Ewen and me. Either way the mop flops I've got a stake in the outcome. Clay put Ewen onto a hot property over in Cuba. Got to be a cut in the deal some way. Maybe there *is* a partnership angle after all."

"For your sake I hope there really is. You don't need another distraction. Those two guys, if they haven't already, must simply force themselves to find a way to get along. I don't want to see either of them hurt. I'm fond of both."

"You are, huh? Well, you're just a natural-born sweetheart, my love. You don't like ugliness, you're positive, optimistic, angel

321

through and through. I respect that in you and admire you for it. You don't have to soft-pedal Frank Creuthop, though. He's more than a 'distraction,' as you say. You and I both know he's a pain in the ass. Remember all the days when I wanted to bash his head in, to throttle him permanently, to shut down his loud mouth forever? How many times have you heard me say I've had it up to my eyeballs with that old fart?"

"Several hundred."

"Yeah. Some people don't make good partners."

"But, Marcus, Clay Redmond and Ewen Leetboer do! Clay has knowledge and skill. Selling real estate is his business. Ewen loves to invest in real estate. He has great wealth. They seem perfect for each other. Why not good partners?"

"Why not? Because Ewen's greedy. He cheated Clay out of his 'retirement nest egg,' as Clay phrases it, which is a sneaky way of saying 'Fuck you!' Then Clay sued Ewen, which is a benign way of saying 'Drop dead!' Either way, they're now obligated to hate each other's guts, which is a not-so-promising way to carry on a partnership. Now make those calls please."

Pepe came back to the suite at Hotel Embajador while Ramón was talking on the phone to Marcus Cunningham. To Ramón's annoyance the mafioso activated the speaker phone and sat quietly listening until he became bored with the exchange and unplugged the line. "You must not give locations, Ramón," he said calmly. It would only endanger you and Elena. Who was this rude man anyway, not a friend to place confidence in surely."

"A friend of Clay Redmond. Pepe, I wish you would not cut me off at such critical moments. Mr. Cunningham was about to tell me where Clay Redmond is."

Pepe grunted amicably. "No problem. I already know where Clay Redmond is."

"You do? How do you know this?"

"El Gordo with the staring eyes told me before I sent him away. It is a serious matter all right. The land pirate's lawyer has orders to kill your friend from Miami while he, the land pirate, continues to rob us all. Señor Valdez, of course, will not allow such a theft."

"The lawyer . . . *kill* Clay Redmond? Ha! Not a chance. He knows only retainer fees and some legal terms. I believe it was the big hairy one—my admirer in the yellow shirt."

"El Gordo?"

"Exactly. The Dutchman employed *him* to do the killing. Why did you send the monster away?"

Pepe grunted again. "It was a courteous gesture. Listen, we have a plane to meet. The land pirate is flying here to take you and Elena back to Cuba. No doubt he will bring assistance equal to the task."

Ramón gaped at Pepe, his mouth hanging open for a time. "You are kidding me again, I think, yes . . . ?"

"No. I do not kid, Ramón. It is true."

"But why, Pepe—?"

"The matter is complicated, even to me, and I know many intrigues. Ewen Leetboer is traveling with his beautiful wife and some of his guards. Ramón, you must help me persuade this Dutchman to release her. It is not my duty to kill him."

"Ahhh. *¡Qué mujer!* I still cannot believe she is the wife of that old man—Ewen Leetboer."

"His prisoner is more the truth. Soon she will be a victim along with her lover."

"I suppose you are now hinting of Clay Redmond?"

"Of course the broker. He is her lover, no?"

"Who can say? He has not made such a confession to me."

Pepe smiled. "The land pirate will also take her life when he learns that Clay Redmond is dead. It is an old torture: Kill the unfaithful wife's lover, then present her with his head and let her live with the reality awhile before her own execution."

"I don't understand, Pepe. Clay Redmond is alive! Why are you trying to make me think he is not?"

"Do you know he is?"

"I know the man. He *cannot* be dead!"

"Good," said Pepe. A brief smile returned to his face. He nodded at Ramón and lit a cigarette. "Please bring Elena out of the shower and let us go to the airport."

34

By morning the sea had calmed and *Noche Buena*, under less turbulence, continued to glide along the route back to Varadero. Stanley B. Conover, tied to the mast, cursed one spray after another during most of the trip. To the utter limits of his stamina he rolled and thrashed with each crashing wave and, in gruff torrents, followed up with a barrage of court-house huff that poured out of his mouth in a stream as foul and irreversible as the steady vomit of salt water pouring along with it. Even his screams for help, his hoarse pleas, fell on deaf ears. Arturo would have none of it. He remained at the helm under orders from a new captain whom he had come to admire, as one fellow seaman to another, in spite of criticisms his boss had advanced in Varadero. The Portuguese was indeed an able sailor, a loyal worker, too, as well as a realist who saw no advantage in a confrontation with Clay Redmond, not after seeing Conover with a gun pointed at the broker, attempting to force him to jump into a raging sea. He had also witnessed Clay's bold pursuit and masterful conquest of a man twice his size back at the Coconut Grove Marina. He wanted no part of that seagoing cowboy.

"Sail the yacht back to port," Clay told the Portuguese after securing Conover. "I've got no beef with you, Arturo, but that shithead roped to the mast just tried to kill me! You must have seen it." Clay eyed him, waiting for a reply. Not getting one right off, he prodded the Portuguese again. "You did see it, didn't you? Come on—speak up for Christ's sake!"

Arturo still didn't answer, seeming confused, disoriented until Clay impressed him with a sharp clout on his shoulder. "Yes—the pistola!" he gushed. "I'm—I'm sorry, Señor Clay, I did not know. Neither could I help you. He would only shoot me as well! The man must be crazy, no?"

"Very much crazy, yes, but not as crazy as his client."

"His client? You mean Señor Ewen . . . ?"

"Yeah, that asshole. Conover has no other clients. Just Ewen Leetboer. Your boss also, right? Are you happy with him?" Clay kept talking, ignoring Arturo's gaping, ready-with-answer mouth. "That old bastard sent his prick lawyer on this mission of villainy. You see that, too, don't you?"

"Yes, I—I see that now." Arturo answered quickly to avoid another clout. His eyes remained fixed on the forward deck, his hands glued to the wheel. "Señor Ewen he is the boss, yes, but after tonight, to tell you the truth, I am not so happy with him."

"A boss to beware of I'd say. Might be a good time to start checking out new jobs. Appears this one has turned a skosh too treacherous to last much longer. If you like, assuming we make it back to Miami alive, I'll mention you to a friend of mine who's been looking for somebody with your kind of seaman's savvy to run his yacht."

"Thank you, Señor Clay. I'm sorry, I'm . . ."

"If you're worried about the money, don't be. Whatever Leetboer pays you I'm sure my friend will top."

Arturo kept repeating himself, apologizing, attempting to explain his actions but choking up and stuttering until his face filled over again with the anguished features of a tortured soul. Then almost as quickly as he'd lost control he seemed to regain it, as evidenced by a sudden haste to speak in more measured tones. "I did not know, Señor Clay," he said. "I was told you were too sick to pilot the yacht. They informed me nothing of treachery, not a word about this feature of the journey, only the urgency of bringing papers back from Miami." The skin on Arturo's face, dark and weathered with wrinkles, began to smooth out as he eased his grip on the helm. "You may consider Señor Ewen no longer my boss."

Clay searched Arturo's eyes for a moment, then touched him on his shoulder in a gentler, more reassuring manner. "Good," he said, easing his Model 51 into Arturo's jumper pocket. He winked at the Portuguese, mumbling, "Watch my back, amigo, and wake me up when you spot land."

Arturo smiled away his anguished face, aided by a head that bobbled to some inner rhythm. He seemed relaxed and full of gusto for the first time since leaving port. Clay went below to Vanessa's cabin. He lay awake in bed for a while, unable to sleep from worrying about his sweetheart. Leetboer's latest surprise had caught him off guard. Did the old Dutchman blow a fuse because Vanessa grounded what little dick he had left, gave herself to the plaintiff, not to the victorious, retirement-nest-egg-sucking defendant? Conover turned out to be what Clay already knew him to be: a predictable whore. No surprise there other than "*Why him?*" Why did Ewen send a scam artist to do the job? Conover had no balls, no experience in out-of-court homicide, not at close range anyway, just a big fat ego behind his thick blockhead and lots of greed in his otherwise anemic gut. It seemed a contradiction that simple infidelity could turn an experienced adulterator like Ewen Leetboer into a mad killer. Maybe, Clay reflected, maybe in a sudden rage, yeah. Anybody could. Maybe on the spur of a red-hot moment that dedicated old moneygrubber really could pull a trigger to safeguard his trove. But this blotched attempt to dump him at sea was driven by a grisly will to commit nothing short of premeditated murder, the same as he himself had already given great thought to and left hanging, at least until Señor Valdez reopened the issue with his own shocking request. Now the idea of "destroying Ewen Leetboer" was beginning to take on legs again and this time Clay Redmond had suddenly been handed the most time-honored, unsolicited reason of all: self defense.

"To hell with Ewen Leetboer!" Clay shouted into the empty cabin. He buried his head in Vanessa's soft feather pillow, thinking. "I can't kill the dumb ass," he mumbled some minutes later. "He's not worth it. Señor Valdez will just have to find another hitman." Clay fell quiet for a moment, his face drawn over with self-disgust. "Who's the dumb ass anyway? Ewen's got all the money so how dumb can *he* be?"

The broker drifted off to sleep. Hours passed before the gentle sloshing of waves against the hull woke him up. He lay on the bed for a while, thinking about Vanessa, where she was and what sort of danger Leetboer had brought to her. It was impossible to think of this bundle of heaven, whatever the circumstances, and not imagine her body cuddled against his own, their arms and legs entwined like vines in a jungle, their hearts pumping out inexhaustible passion for each other. It was also annoying that Conover had to cross his mind in the very next reflection. What to do with that son of a bitch? he groused to himself. Then when he glanced at his watch, he sprang up as if powered by his shout, *"Holy damn, I've got to find her!"* Clay had slept in his clothes. He rushed up on deck and looked around. The sea was calm, the yacht hardly moving. An eerie quiet hung over the ship. The broker found Arturo in an awkward slump against the cockpit wall. The Portuguese appeared to be dozing, or conked out drunk. Fortunately the autopilot was on and still holding at 165°, the preset course to Varadero. Clay shook him awake.

"Where the hell's Conover?" the broker shouted angrily.

"Gone—!" The word shot out of Arturo's mouth as if forced out by Clay Redmond's harsh, booming voice, before the Portuguese's eyes had even opened.

"Gone? Gone where? Wake up, Arturo, wake up and talk to me before I break—!" Clay paused and moved closer for a better view of the man. Something wasn't right. Arturo looked dazed, not drunk. The sailor's eyes cracked as he felt around the top of his head, rubbing gently and moaning. There was blood on the side of his face. "Gone," he repeated. "He grabbed pistola. I could not stop Señor Stanley. He hit me with something when I turned from him to alert you. I do not remember after that."

"He took my gun? He took the dinghy?"

Arturo began to stir, although with some hesitation, seeming afraid to move too quickly lest some part of him come unhinged. "Yes," he mumbled. "Yes, early this morning he worked loose from the mast and came to me with tears in his eyes, begging for my help against you. I refused to assist with his criminal business, but he would not stop pleading. After some time and more tears Señor Stanley became convinced of my decision and then insisted to escape in the lifeboat. When *Noche Buena* came in close to shore, he lowered the boat into the sea, tied it to a stern cleet, came back to the cockpit and asked for the loan of the cooler, which he knew had food and water in it. Without waiting for him to plead further, I looked away from his pitiful eyes and turned to get you. In an instant he struck my head with a club of some kind—"

"A blackjack," Clay said. "The sneaky crudball! No doubt he meant to use it on me earlier." The broker handed Arturo his handkerchief. "Here," he said, motioning at the blood on the Portuguese's face. Clay gazed out over the water, searching for the missing dinghy. "I don't see a thing. Stanley must have jumped ship hours ago."

"What time now it is?"

"Twelve-fifteen."

"He been gone long time, plenty long to disappear."

Clay shook his head. "The crazy fool," he said. "I didn't think he had the gumption to pull a stunt like this. He could get his sorry ass killed out there."

Arturo forced a chuckle. "It was pitiful to watch his eyes begging for my help," he said. "In his final moment of fear, Señor Stanley chose to face the dangers of the sea. He did not wish to face you again. During the several minutes he was begging, and even once on his knees, he told me you were going to break his neck with your foot before we reached Varadero."

Clay grunted. "Another crummy exaggeration," he said. "Go get yourself doctored up. I'll take her on in from here."

An hour later, under escort, Clay followed a Cuban Coastguard cutter into the harbor at Varadero. A dinghy riding low in the water was tied to the Cuban ship, its small Evinrude still in place. The letters *Noche Buena* were only partly visible across the stern, the rest submerged. "The crazy fool," Clay murmured. On a wave from the Cuban captain Clay brought the yacht into the berth where it was moored the night before.

"What will happen now?" Arturo asked the broker after he had secured the lines. His dark leathery face was once again filled with stress lines.

"We wait here for the *guardacostas*," Clay answered. "They'll have more questions. I have some of my own."

"Perhaps we should have continued to Miami."

"No, I have to find Vanessa. Arturo, can you tell me anything about where Ewen Leetboer might have taken her? Think, for Christ's sake. You were with them."

Arturo's eyes bulged out. "But, Señor Clay, they did not consult with me about their plans, only ordered me to sail the yacht since you were ill."

"Since I was drugged you mean."

"I'm sorry, I was not aware of their intentions."

"But you were eating with us at the restaurant. You must have heard something while I was out. Think!"

Arturo rubbed his scalp in a strained effort to resurrect some elusive memory. His face went into contortions after he forgot and rubbed too vigorously over the knot on his head where he had been hit with the blackjack. "*Ay yi yi!*" he moaned. "There was a call—Señor Ewen's cell phone—I think you were in the *baño* then. Anyway, he left the table to talk in privacy but when he returned two minutes later, I overheard him whispering to Señor Stanley about a five-million-dollar thief his agent had located in Santo Domingo."

Clay's head swung around, facing Arturo. "Did you catch a name?"

"A Latino name only, Felipe something. Does '*Air Clockwork*' mean anything?"

"Yeah, that's the name of Ewen's jet. What about it?"

"Nothing. Just that Señor Stanley could not go with him to Santo Domingo. You were ill and Señor Stanley, with my help, brought you to the cabin below—"

"Shit!" Clay mumbled before Arturo could finish. "I was drugged, dammit."

"Of course. Anyway, Señor Stanley remained on the yacht with me. That is why Señor Ewen took the other men on the plane. Señor Stanley already had his assignment to Miami."

"Think, Arturo! Did Vanessa leave the restaurant with Ewen?"

"Yes, finally."

"What's that mean?"

"She did not want to go with him. The lady was concerned for you, because you had passed out at the table. She spoke harsh words and refused to leave until Señor Ewen promised she could return to the yacht later."

"Then they left the restaurant?"

"Finally. We also left, Señor Stanley and me, with you between us unable even to hold on to our shoulders. We had to support you the whole distance, which was not a short one. The *camarero* thought you had consumed too many Cuba Libres."

"Bullshit," Clay Redmond said.

The Cuban captain suddenly appeared with two armed aides. Without waiting for an invitation, he stepped onto the yacht and approached Clay and Arturo, who had moved away from the helm and were sitting in folding chairs on the open deck. The Cuban official wasted no time on pleasantries, although he acted polite enough, which effort was somewhat masked by a dignified courtesy befitting his rank in the Cuban Coast Guard. Clay stood up with his passport ready.

"You are from Miami?" the captain asked after a brief examination of the document.

Clay nodded. "I came over to pick up the owner of this yacht. He's a Canadian citizen."

"What is his name?"

"Ewen Leetboer."

"Where is he now?"

Clay looked at Arturo and grunted. "We think Santo Domingo."

"When will he return?"

"Who knows? Maybe tomorrow, maybe never."

The captain eyed Clay for a minute or so, then consulted a memorandum attached to his clipboard, smiling intermittently as he read it and mumbling some of the words to himself before staring back up at Clay and Arturo. "This yacht is no longer authorized to moor here," he said in the tone of an official announcement. "You must go from this port, take the boat away and leave Cuban waters.

Otherwise this handsome craft will be confiscated and you and your comrade, arrested."

Clay Redmond gave him a sharp, perplexed look. "What for?" he said coolly, gritting to restrain himself.

The captain shrugged. "For ugly crimes against the Fatherland. What you think? Even murder perhaps."

"*Murder*?"

"We found a dead man in your lifeboat. An autopsy will be performed tonight. If you are still here when the report is finished, you will be detained with uncertain consequences."

"Look, Captain, how about some help here. I'm having a tough time trying to understand what the hell's going on!"

The captain chuckled. "Do not try to understand, at least not tonight. Tomorrow when you are miles from Cuba you can reflect on your good fortune and maybe come to understand how blessed you are to have such a powerful friend."

For a brief time Clay, his face sobered and blank, could only watch the captain chuckle. After a bit the chuckle became contagious, causing the broker to shake his head in a hopeless gesture and chuckle back. "What friend would that be?" he asked, his low voice sounding of frustration more than curiosity.

"Come, Mr. Redmond. Do not be coy with me. You should be very proud that it is El Cojonudo who speaks so well of you, not those *gusanos* in Miami!"

35

Two nights earlier Marcus Cunningham and Heather Ambrose enjoyed a lavish dinner together at the Versailles, to celebrate a victory they thought. Heather had found a cell phone number assigned to *Noche Buena* and, after a confusing exchange with Arturo, had managed to coax the Portuguese into waking Clay Redmond and putting the instrument in his hand.

The conversation was a bit breezy at first, and full of rejoicing, remindful of three lost souls who had stumbled upon each other after weeks of wandering in the wilderness in search of a familiar face. The broker did not bother to tell them all the gruesome details of his journey since leaving Miami with Vanessa. Other matters took on fresh urgency the moment he heard Heather describe Ramón's frantic call. Clay kept stressing that he needed to get to wherever Leetboer went that night in Varadero after leaving the restaurant. "The sneaky scoundrel forced Vanessa to go with him." Clay shouted angrily. "Arturo tells me he overheard talk about a trip to Santo Domingo."

"Who's Arturo?"

"Ewen's yacht skipper. But he's on my team now—an okay guy, by the way. If Ewen flies to Santo Domingo tonight, he'll most likely take Vanessa with him."

"That's nice."

"Nice hell! Your new partner has other things in mind!"

"Doing things with her, you mean?"

"No, doing things _to_ her. And Ramon for good measure."

"I can't help you with that one, pal," Marcus answered back without appearing overly concerned. "Maybe they just wanted to find a cozy little spot to enjoy some tender moments together."

"Tender moments—ha! That old dog wouldn't know a tender moment if one bit him in the . . . high heather."

"Hi yourself you big hunk," Heather cooed, looking a bit puzzled over a second greeting, and more so when Clay apologized.

Marcus glanced at his secretary and winked. "If you say so," he said to Clay Redmond. "By the way, pal, where the dickens are you?"

"At sea."

Marcus shushed a loud blast of air through his teeth. "Yeah? Now that covers a whole lot of H_2O, fellow. Can you hone the geography down a bit?"

Clay's chuckle was labored. He expected some such "smartass" crack, as he silently tagged Marcus's rejoinder. "Just got run out of the Varadero harbor," he drawled. "*Noche Buena* must be about twelve miles off shore now, heading east."

"What do you mean 'run out'?"

"The captain of a Cuban coastguard patrol boat suggested that it would be in my best interest to get the hell out of Cuba."

"Why—because you're American?"

"No. Call it a goodwill gesture on the captain's part, inspired by El Cojonudo."

"El who?"

"I'll explain later. Anyway, this captain said either leave or go to jail for murder, so I left."

"What the hell are you talking about? *Murder*! Are you off your rocker, Redmond?"

"I was, actually, but I'm back on track now. A few nights ago Leetboer's attorney slipped me a Mickey strong enough to drop a horse but then he's the one who showed up dead yesterday. The Cuban cops think I might have killed him."

"Holy shit—now you really aren't making sense! Stanley Conover? Conover's *dead* you say? Baloney, baloney, Bronx cheer."

"Hard to believe, I admit. He was such a monster thorn in my side. How could I be so lucky, I keep telling myself. Yes, Marcus, it's true. Not a mark on that slippery snotwad though, which figures. No bullet holes, no bruises, nothing so indelicate as that. Like he'd gone to meet his celestial Lord while asleep, happily dreaming up another ripoff scheme to put in motion on behalf of his terrestrial lord."

"Hey, pal, cool it with the Lord yak. You listen to that coastguard guy. This murder crap sounds bad. We're talking about

Ewen Leetboer's attorney, man—his master closer, his next best thing to a national security advisor! Take it from your Xanadu fan club, Redmond. Get the fuck away from Cuba. Circumstances being as is, twelve miles out still sounds mighty damn close."

"If it'll ease your mind, I'm waiting for my copter ace out of Largo to hoist me off this yacht. Got to get to Santo Domingo fast. Got to find Vanessa. She's with Ewen . . ."

"What's wrong with that? He's her husband for Christ's sake! Let him take care of her."

"That's just it. Her husband *will* take care of her. But I'm hoping he'd rather take care of me first."

"What the hell—are you talking *guns*? Real guns with bullets?"

"Something deadly. I hate to disappoint you, Marcus. I know you kind of like ol' Ewen. He's such an easygoing, pleasant chap compared to Frank Creuthop, right? Yeah, ABF—anybody but Frank. I hear you. Okay, friend, now you hear me. Plug this late-breaker into your mainframe: that old sidewinder is after me through her! Forget the wife role. Vanessa is his hostage, a prisoner, bait. He figures I'll come looking for her sooner or later, and in the meantime he'll have his little cadre of beefeaters standing by with their guns and knives, poised to save him from my sneak attack. Get the picture? The Dutchman's not far off in his thinking either. I'm cruising down the Florida Straits now, waiting for dark and a chance to get back inside Cuba in case my copter ace doesn't show. There's a small airport in Varadero. Somebody will fly me over to Santo Domingo. Got to find her before he does something crazy."

"You're in a kooky mood yourself, Redmond. Come on back to Miami and wait Ewen out. What've you got to lose?"

"Vanessa for one thing. She picked up some hush-hush stuff on this trip, knows too much and is hellbent to quit the old goatsucker even if it means sacrificing all rights to a piece of his fortune. He'd rather bury her in a cane field down here than suffer the humiliation of a public split, not to mention losing a good size chunk of his estate through a divorce settlement not engineered by Stanley B. Conover. Or, more to the point, risk having her blab his secrets, his assorted skullduggeries and private sins to the D.A. in Miami."

Marcus laughed one of his I-know-where-you're-coming-from laughs. "Sounds like you're sweet on the gal," he then said cutely. "Are you?"

"The short answer is, 'none of your business.' Now will you please help me get word to the Cuban brothers?"

"How? I don't know jackshit about any of this cloak and dagger razzle-dazzle. I'm only a lowly landlord."

"Go to Versailles. Any waitress there can put you in touch with Silvio if you can convince her you're doing a mercy errand for me. He'll know if Ramón is still holed up at Hotel Embajador."

"Santo Domingo?"

"Right. The hotel people won't say, won't give out the suite number or any names registered in or going to it. Mafia security. Ramón's a 'guest' there, I've been told, but he could be in danger himself. He needs to be warned. Maybe Silvio can get through to him. One or the other of those fellows will surely know where the Dutchman is hiding Vanessa."

Heather butted in. "Clay darling, can't you call Silvio on your cell phone?"

"Conover must have tossed it over the gunwale the other night along with the rest of my gear. Missing in action. As for the yacht phone, I've tried, sweetie. No answer. You'll have to run him down the old-fashioned way."

She took some addresses and numbers Clay read out while Marcus probed for more details.

"Listen, Clay," he groaned after the broker kept mentioning Ramón and repeating the need to warn him about a possible visit from Ewen Leetboer, "We've already talked to that Cuban. Like I said earlier, he called here all upset, screaming half English half Spanish, looking for you. He seemed to think you were the one in super-grave danger."

"Yeah, he was flat right about that," Clay replied. "I think the danger he had in mind, though, might now be passing on to him."

"Which is?"

"Long story. No time for it here. Ramón must have been trying to warn me about Conover. That shyster was definitely on a homicide mission. Ewen's up to his old tricks, has turned into a giant hot gnat all of a sudden, as if he can't get enough blood just by screwing his partners. Where was Ramón calling from? You never did say."

"The Cuban didn't say either. He did let us know he was not in the States at the time. The phone went dead just as I was in the middle of asking him for the usual Joe Friday facts."

"Fucking phone," Clay muttered, bumping the cabin bulkhead with the heel of his hand. "Find Silvio. He'll know how to get in touch with Ramón. Can you call me back, say, in an hour?"

Marcus looked at Heather over the rim of his glasses. She was listening on the other phone and gave Marcus a quick up-and-down nod. "Okay, pal," he answered, "We'll do our damndest to locate Brother Silvio. Just between us old shuckers here at Xanadu,

340

though, we're more concerned about you. That Ramón brother scared the hell out of us. Now you've gone him one better. Conover is dead—*murdered* I distinctly heard you say—and there you are in the middle of the ocean telling me his favorite client in all the world, one of my mall partners no less, is gunning for you. Does that mean Ewen has reason to believe you whacked his attorney and he's pissed off about it?"

Clay Redmond held his tongue for a moment, then, "Nice try, Marcus. No, I didn't whack the geek, although I'm not all broken up over the present state of his health any more than I'm sorry that his wonderful client might be in serious trouble with the law. I'm not sure what that old Dutchman is thinking. If I ever get my hands on the son of a bitch, though, I'll let you know."

"Okay, pal. You'll hear from us ASAP."

Marcus hung up the phone but Heather was still holding her extension. Quickly she blurted into the mouthpiece, "Be Careful, Clay," sounding as cautionary as Miss Kitty when Matt was readying himself for a hard ride and plenty of action.

Pepe and his two "guests," on their way to the airport, stepped out of the elevator into the lobby of Hotel Embajador. The police had already arrived and were busy roping off the crime scene.

"Hey, look," Ramón said, pointing at a crowd gathering at the entrance to the casino. "Something is going on in there."

Elena wheeled around to join a line of gawkers, shouting back and motioning for Pepe and Ramón to follow. "I want to see why is it so many police have come to the casino."

Pepe overtook the Cuban woman and spun her around with a yank. "It is nothing," he said. "A thief maybe has robbed one of the tourists. We have no time for this. *Vámonos!"*

Pepe assumed that somebody had stumbled over Karl Skepe and sounded the alarm, but he had no feelings about it one way or the other. It was just a homicide investigation. His mafioso mind had already ruled out any sense of guilt, for the death of thieves and snitches was a common thing in his world, not worthy of further thought once the offender had been silenced.

They left through the main entrance, Pepe walking behind in a slow macho amble, not to avoid attention or even to attract it but out of respect for the dictates of an attitude steeled in the cauldron of high crimes and misdemeanors. Twice during the short passage through the lobby, he condescended to break his stride and haul back on Elena and Ramón when they raised a voice or showed too much interest in the commotion stirring behind them.

A taxi was waiting at the curb. The driver, a friendly chap eager to serve, seated his fares and proceeded to maneuver around two police cars that were parked beside him in the middle of the street. The vehicles were unattended but their motors were running and a strobe light was flashing on top. An ambulance rolled up just as the taxi pulled away.

Ramón and Elena nudged each other when they saw a team of medics pile out of the ambulance. The men were moving in double time, each carrying some bit of life-saving equipment or other. The last two rushed inside the hotel's main entrance pushing a wheeled stretcher. Ramón leaned forward and spoke to the driver. "What's the big deal in the casino?" he asked.

The driver twisted around with a cheery smile on his face, champing to share his knowledge. "A gambler was attacked," he said in Spanish. "They found him on the floor, blood everywhere!"

"Who attacked him?" Ramón pressed, also in Spanish.

"No one knows. The police are searching for the killer now."

"Ramón, forget this," Pepe said in English. "Do not make a pest of yourself with questions." The mafioso turned to Elena, who was sitting in a pout with her arms folded across her front. "Tell him, Elena, tell your man we have other matters before us, matters that will demand every attention in a short few minutes."

"Ramón, shut up please," Elena said, her eyes not moving out of their hot vacant stare, her voice flat and unconvincing.

"The man was not Latin," the driver said. "A foreigner."

"What did he look like?"

"Like *El Diablo*! He was a big one, big—*muy grande*!—with a filthy beard."

"A big devil?" Ramón turned and squinted at Pepe. "A big devil!" he repeated almost in a laugh. "Imagine that, Pepe!"

The driver hardly paused. "Yes, a very big one. I saw him earlier today talking with the *conserje*. For sure the doctors will need plenty of help to get him on the stretcher."

Elena's eyes began to flash. "Pepe, do you know about this?"

Pepe snorted and took a cigarette out of his silver case. He glared back at Elena as he was lighting it, then at Ramón for a moment before extinguishing the flame. "Forget this," he said to both. "Who cares about one big devil? We have your Miami friend's woman to rescue from the land pirate." Pepe's eyes suddenly fixed on the rearview mirror. "Perhaps the driver, who seems so much infected with his talk, will inquire for us about *El Diablo* and reveal the answers to your questions when we return tonight with the lady."

Something about Pepe's Mediterranean face, his hoarse but measured voice squeezing through a pair of tight fat lips made the driver uneasy enough to shift his attention back to the road. The shock of seeing Pepe's sinister aspect in the rearview mirror was too much. *Those beady eyes . . . staring so hard in the glass!* The gabby little fellow's head shot forward, his own eyes refocused, his mouth closed and so remained for the rest of the trip.

36

Earlier that afternoon the helicopter Clay had been waiting for swooped out of the clouds and circled the yacht for a few rounds, then settled into a hover after the pilot saw Clay standing on the forward deck waving him closer. A tall mast and billowy sails kept the craft from setting down, but transfer in the air was easy enough for two seasoned combat vets. Extra fuel was hoisted up to top off the chopper's tank. Minutes later Clay was aboard, too, en route to Santo Domingo. His last words to Arturo were, "Take the yacht on to Coconut Grove. When Marcus Cunningham calls back, tell him Silvio came through."

The chopper pilot, one of Clay's Marine buddies, lost no time setting his course, one he apparently seemed to know by heart. As if by migratory instinct he simply "beat his wings" along the Cuban coastline, staying far enough out to avoid triggering

Fidel Castro's MIG fleet into motion, then over the Windward Passage for an emergency landing at Guantanamo to take on more fuel. After consoling the air traffic controller, the O.D. and other lords of base security, the two men grabbed a quick bite at the only McDonald's in Cuba and rapped bittersweetly about Viet Nam while they ate.

"You know, Bobbett, you're still a renegade," Clay said as they walked back to the hanger. "I'm not complaining but I bet you didn't even file a flight plan."

"Safe bet," Bobbett answered. "Classified trip, right?"

"Always. No passenger list either, huh?"

"None of that shit, ol' buddy. You know me. Hey, you still working Cuba for the Miami front?"

"Not this time." Clay paused, then added, "Emergency R & R." He laughed inwardly, wanting to tell about Vanessa but deciding to let his lie stand. The less his friend knew the less chance of getting swept into a murder trial later.

About that time Bobbett got busy checking his instruments and didn't follow up. When he did resume he merely said, "No need to get permission for overflights across Haiti and the Dominican Republic. I'm not gonna overfly either one."

"You have to drop me at the airport in Santo Domingo, don't forget."

"Well, yeah. So maybe I'll just skirt the edge of that little jewel town. No problem."

The pilot continued to follow the coastline, hanging out a few miles, but he stayed close enough to make it to the beach in case of mechanical trouble.

The flight was one of the few things of late that had worked out okay for Clay Redmond. The broker, barred from reentering Cuba with the yacht, knew he had to stay with it or jump ship, as it were. Yet the alternatives made him sick. After he pulled out of Varadero, he'd considered sailing back to Miami and lining up a twin-engine Piper, but that scenario pointed him in the wrong direction and might further hogtie him with unforeseen delays. The thought of sailing on to Santo Domingo didn't quell the queasy feeling in his gut either. That trip could take two, maybe three days and time was a commodity the broker refused to trade away. Vanessa was in danger. He felt it the moment he came out of that dope-laced hangover, which, he later concluded, happened to have its own silver lining. That is to say, it was the final act in the shifty, fraud-filled life of the late Stanley B. Conover.

But Clay's dilemma worked out fine for his war buddy. While the freewheeling entrepreneur took the charter for old times sake, he was also delivering the copter to a buyer in Puerto Rico. He'd land in Santo Domingo only long enough to let Clay off and gas up again.

"These birds are great on the battlefield," he said cheerfully, "but they don't have the range for good offshore R & R use."

"Put some fucking hustle in this chopper, Bobbett," Clay grumped. "An extra grand if you drop me down before ten."

"You got it, Redmond. Piece of cake."

When Ewen Leetboer's three associates stepped out of *Air Clockwork,* Pepe was not surprised. He figured them to be the sort of people he most understood. He saw them as mercenaries, not construction workers, which the mafioso would have readily advised had it been suggested that they were merely the Dutchman's crew leaders. Their heads swung around too cautiously for blue collar types. They patted themselves in places like cartel men in Colombia did, checking their armor as dutifully, as automatically, as they would check their flies when they left the john or saw a pretty woman heading their way.

Pepe, shaded by a high hurricane fence, watched and adjusted his own strategy as the occupants deplaned some yards away. Ramón and Elena, given no other choice, stood waiting beside him. It was dark along the fence, shadowy where they were standing, with only a few dim bulbs burning around the building at that late hour. Most of the employees had gone home for the evening.

"That's him," Ramón whispered, "the middle skinny one in the suit—there next to the woman!"

Pepe's eyes were already locked on his prey. "The land pirate, yes. I remember him well from Mara Paradiso."

"Who could forget such a Quixote?" Elena whispered, muffling a laugh. "Pepe, what are you going to do now? You cannot expect us to help you fight them. They surely must have guns. We should leave before your land pirate recognizes Ramón and me. Even you he knows. Then we will all be faced with much danger."

"Wait here," Pepe said, shushing with his finger. He stepped out of the shadows toward the gate as Ewen Leetboer's party approached. "Excuse me," he said to all of them. "I have been sent to meet someone. Perhaps among you is that person."

Surprised by the sudden encounter, the man in front flung his hands out to stop the others. "Check the main airport," he said rudely. "This is a private strip. We're not expected." He laughed then waved the others ahead. Ewen Leetboer was holding Vanessa's arm in a tight clasp but otherwise following along like a timid member of a tourist group. When he started to pass, Pepe stepped closer, blocking his way.

"Excuse me, sir," he said to Leetboer, his voice still hoarse yet more polite than the taxi driver had heard. "The lady with you, I think, may be that person."

"*Oh my God*—!" Vanessa shrieked in a sudden frenzy. She inched up, peering through the dim light. "*You*—! You were in the cave . . . the cave last summer . . . ?"

Pepe smiled. "Ah, *gracias*," he said. "I am flattered that you remember."

Vanessa tilted her head and smiled nervously. "What is it you want?" she asked, her pretty face flushed with both joy and regret that she had dared to mention the cave just then.

"You," he answered, "*la mujer pelirroja*. Forgive me the intrusion but I have been instructed to escort the lady who is Vanessa to Hotel Embajador where she can wait in comfort for Señor Valdez. It is my duty to protect this person until he arrives."

Leetboer's associates, sensing a curious situation unfolding, surrounded Pepe. As if pleased with the action of his men, and bolstered enough to step casually in front of the mafioso, Leetboer clicked on a small flashlight and studied Pepe's face. "Eh?" he mewled after a bit, then broke into a fretful murmur. "*You*!" he howled several times before managing to voice his thoughts in a somewhat more controlled flow. "Ha! Too bad you made such a poor impression on me at Mara Paradiso."

"My terms were generous," Pepe responded at once. "Even now with your forces beside you, it would be wise not to violate them."

"Eh? Look it, buster, I do not answer to people who would shoot out my eyes . . . for goodness sake!" Turning to his men, he hunched his narrow shoulders irritably and droned, "This man is a kook, a pothead who has threatened me twice. Use him for your amusement, only do not be so nice in your games as you were with the broker. I will wait with Vanessa in the terminal."

Two of the men rushed Pepe, grabbing his arms on both sides. Pepe watched them take their holds without offering any resistence. To the contrary, he turned limp and cooperative and smiled at their stern, protective action as if he knew all the moves, each of which was acknowledged with an approving nod. After the Dutchman and Vanessa disappeared inside the tiny private-plane terminal, a dimly lit facility adjacent to Las Americas International Airport, the third one began to pummel him in the gut, the ribs and, when Pepe slumped backward, savagely in the groin. Ramón and Elena watched through the chain links with their eyes locked in a wide terror-stricken gape. Each was thinking the worst as they backed deeper into the shadows.

"Wait," one of the men said. "Let's get this bozo over in the bushes. We can't leave him here next to the plane. The cops will impound it."

As two of the men took hold of Pepe's arm and proceeded to drag him through the gate toward the nearby shrubbery, the third man moved ahead to pick a suitable spot. Seemingly from out of nowhere a sudden blow across his neck sent him crashing upon the concrete path. The other two, hearing the noise, turned around but were not fast enough to do their partner any good; the phantom foot was faster. They did not see more than a shadow of it, a swift swish of powerful motion, before they too were lying unconscious on the concrete.

"Clay Redmond!" Ramón shouted from behind the fence. "Oh brother—*mi hermano*! What space in heaven did you fall from? *Dios mio*—!" The excited Cuban ran up to Clay and hugged him with hearty Latin fervor. Elena came bouncing up as well and added her own embraces, for she had not seen Clay in over a year and his sudden appearance at so critical a moment presented her with an even greater reason to greet him lavishly.

"*Clay Redmond*!" she screamed. "Ramón said it. You were sent by the angels to save us. What a heavenly blessing!"

"You're partly right," Clay said. "I dropped down in a helicopter across the way." The broker bent over Pepe and checked his pulse. "He's alive."

"Of course I'm alive," answered Pepe, rolling up on his haunches. "Do you think three such fools could harm me?"

Elena's joy in seeing Clay spilled over to Pepe when she heard his hoarse, somewhat saucy voice. All traces of her earlier pout vanished in a hail of glories. Ramón had slipped into a state of speechless awe after seeing Clay Redmond manhandle Ewen Leetboer's three guardians, but his dark Latin face was full of smiles nonetheless.

Clay took the mafioso's hand and helped him to his feet. "After all that pounding you must be hurting somewhere. Let me help you back to the car."

Pepe pushed Clay's hands away. "*No necesito*," he said, lighting a smoke. "Those animals did not hurt me. I am wearing protection like the boxers. Also like the CIA and football players."

"You're lucky. I know these men, Pepe. They were about to stick a gun down your throat. If they'd gotten you behind that shrubbery, they would have plugged you for sure."

Pepe grunted. "Not a chance. I was waiting exactly for them to take me behind that shrubbery so I could kill them safely. I have my ways, the same as you." He glanced at the three men on the ground. "Perhaps it is not too late."

"No, Pepe!" Elena screeched. "Let us tell the police about them."

Pepe grunted again. "The police like to ask questions, my dear. Señor Valdez cautioned me as a favor not to invite such officials into his private affairs." The mafioso kneeled beside each one of Ewen Leetboer's so-called "construction foremen" and extracted their weapons, following up with a hard whack across each skull with the barrel of a Dirty Harry special. One of them began to writhe but his effort merely earned him another hard whack, a gesture that was quickly extended to the other two men in equal measure. The action was fast and brutal, causing Elena to shield her eyes from the scene. Clay and Ramón hardly had time to wince at the gruesome sight before Pepe was back on his feet. "Now we place them among the shrubbery," he said with the easy, observant aplomb of an interior decorator. "These men are big and heavy; you may help me in that task if you don't mind."

"Leave them where they are," Clay said.

"Not hide the bodies?"

"Why us? We haven't been here. Right now I'm more interested in finding Vanessa. Did she come in on this plane?"

"Yes," Ramón said, relieved to hear himself again. "Ewen Leetboer forced her to accompany him into the terminal."

"Ramón, you and Elena stay out of sight. You, too, Pepe. I'm going to get her."

Pepe grunted. "And the land pirate? What will you do with him? Is the thief of Mara Paradiso not your primary mission?"

Clay's face tightened in thought, knowing what Pepe meant. "I'll deal with that mission later," he said. "One body at a time."

The mafioso nodded and blew out a thick pall of smoke. "After three bodies," he said, motioning toward the trio lying in a heap near his feet, "what is left but the fourth? You will bring a marvelous satisfaction to Señor Valdez with that delivery."

"Wait out front," Clay responded over his back as he moved through the shadows toward the terminal.

37

"Stop, Ewen, you're hurting my arm!"

"Then come, woman! We must go to that place—a hotel."

"Without your bodyguards? My goodness, you're getting brave all of a sudden. Is it because you sent Clay Redmond off on a wild goose chase?"

Ewen wiped his mouth. "The name is a distant memory, my dear. Perhaps you should also forget about Clay Redmond."

"You wish!" Vanessa blurted behind a contemptuous grin. She jerked her arm free and walked to one of the windows. It was dimly lit outside but she managed to see dark forms swinging their arms in a furious struggle. At that moment from her vantage point it appeared that Pepe had no chance against them. She hoped he would not be hurt and wondered why he had approached them so daringly. Leetboer watched with her for a brief time before he turned and started for the front entrance, which was opposite the one they entered.

"Stay if you like," he said. "You should know, however, that my men have orders not to leave you alone, orders to take you back to Cuba, orders they no doubt are anxious to obey. Arturo will soon return to Varadero with the yacht. We will all meet there and I will show you Mara Paradiso. By the way, the men also have been granted certain 'liberties' to amuse themselves with a good chase if you try to run off."

Vanessa wheeled around, glaring. "You bastard!" she yelled. Then calming a bit, "You said Arturo. Why Arturo? Is Clay not—?"

"No. I'm afraid the broker has deserted us. Too bad."

Vanessa sneered at him. "You're crazy," she scoffed, believing that her spouse was just trying to irritate her.

"Look it, Vanessa, do not worry. You will be safe with me. Come. Karl Skepe is waiting at the hotel. He has found the other thief, perhaps a criminal confederate of Clay Redmond's." Leetboer paused, thinking, his head bent down. *Hmmm. It will be better to link them!* "You may know this thief," he went on, looking up at Vanessa. "Perhaps you have seen them together."

Vanessa bristled again. "Why do you say that?"

"Well, for goodness sakes, Vanessa, considering how cozy you have been with the broker . . . ?"

"You bastard!"

Leetboer forced a thin smile. His dull gray eyes began to glitter with impatience. "Come," he repeated. "Come and confirm this man or I leave you to the dogs outside!"

An agent at the end of the room was putting the finishing touches on a mound of paperwork. He stood behind the counter, occasionally glancing over in the direction of the lady when her voice rose angrily. Then he would cut his eyes toward the man but only for a moment before turning back to his work. Neither paid any attention to him until, suddenly, Vanessa dashed toward the counter.

"Sir," she shouted as she approached. "Call the police. This man is annoying me."

The agent raised up, startled, then squinted with tired, blinking eyes at the man across the room. Leetboer smiled and lifted his shoulders, as if to gesture his innocence with a shrug. "She is my wife," he declared behind a glum smile. "What can I say?"

The agent, a pudgy fellow of about fifty years, looked back at Vanessa. He remembered his poor dead father's advice concerning pretty wives and the trouble they could bring to a foolish man. This one standing in front of him with such a beautiful but pleading face made him shudder to behold. *"Estoy ocupado,"* the agent responded. *"Tiene problemas matrimoniales. Tengo informes que cumplir. Ha llegado tarde. No me moleste por favor."*

Vanessa gritted her teeth at the disquieted man then put a seething stare on Leetboer. "Okay," she said after a bit, walking toward him, "I'll go. But I want you to know, Ewen, that I am leaving you once we get to the hotel. Whatever business you have there for me must be quick."

Leetboer grabbed her roughly by the arm and pulled her through the entrance door. "Don't be so hasty with your plans," he snapped. "You will leave me when I say you will leave me. That time has not yet arrived."

"Ewen—!"

"Quiet now. No more talk."

"You're hurting me, Ewen. *Stop it!"*

Ignoring her pleas, he pulled her out to the street and waved to a passing taxi. Less than a minute later Clay Redmond came running around the corner of the building. The cab was pulling away when he spotted Vanessa and Leetboer in the back seat. It picked up speed and shot out of sight and left Clay in a fruitless hustle to overtake it. Seeing no other conveyance, he raced back to the scene of the recent scuffle. Ramón and Elena were standing over the three bodies chattering furiously in Spanish about their predicament when Clay rushed up and grabbed the Cuban by the shoulders.

"Ramón, they got away!" he cried out. "Quick—where would they be going in a taxi?"

"To Hotel Embajador!" Ramón shouted back. "Ewen Leetboer thinks that is where he will find you know who—Felipe Jorge."

"Leetboer believes that imposter is in town, huh?"

"*O sí!* His pimp found me and the next thing I know he is dead and the Dutchman himself is in Santo Domingo with a small army."

"Skepe? Skepe is dead?"

"Completely."

Clay was silent for a moment, then, "A damn bloody coincidence, I must say."

"Coincidence?"

"Yeah, Conover and Skepe were on the same side. Who would clip them?"

"Not Felipe Jorge, not El Duque . . . !"

"Don't joke about it," Clay said. The broker managed a smile even though the gesture looked born of more grief than joy. "Saving your butt is the reason I'm down here. Ewen Leetboer wants all three of you clowns!"

Ramón returned Clay's anguished smile, apparently under less stress for he remained jovial. "No doubt the crook wishes to steal back the check."

"Where's Pepe?"

"He went inside the land pirate's jet, to examine the cockpit. Pepe flies the plane for Señor Valdez you know."

"Gotta get to that hotel," Clay yelled. "How did you come?"

"Pepe has a taxi waiting around the corner."

Clay rushed through the darkness to the plane. "Pepe," he hollered up toward the cockpit.

"Is that you, gringo?"

"Yeah. Leetboer took off for the hotel. He's got Vanessa."

"So what? She is his wife, no?"

"The lady is in danger. I'm going after her."

"Truly? The land pirate will harm a lady you think?"

"This one, yes. I'm sure of it. Wait here, guard the plane so the crook can't fly out in case he slips past me again."

"Go gringo," Pepe hollered down. The mafioso stuck his hand through a side window, waving it in snappy motions as if annoyed. He'd been listening to the pitched voices below and had already decided he must stay with the plane. Leetboer would surely come back for it after discovering that Skepe was dead. Whether the woman would come back with him was another matter. That particular matter, Pepe was saddened to think, seemed to hold greater concern for the Miami broker than the primary mission assigned by Señor Valdez, namely "destroying" Ewen Leetboer.

Even though the two matters were not mutually exclusive, Pepe saw no reason to reverse the priorities. The slippery land pirate might evade capture, he surmised, whereas the beautiful woman would be easy to find and save. "Take my taxi," he grunted down after some hesitation. "Ramón will show you. I stay with the plane, yes, and you stay with my two Cuban guests. See that they do not, how you say, *defect*. It is a talent very plentiful in their country these days."

"Not to worry, Pepe," Clay said, making a victory circle with his thumb and forefinger. He started to leave but Pepe hollered down again and stopped him.

"Listen, gringo, you have already earned the respect of Señor Valdez. To some degree you have also earned mine. For your sake, then, and for the peace of mind you must now bring to Señor Valdez, do not allow the land pirate to escape. But *listen* to me: do not kill him here in Santo Domingo either. Señor Valdez has advised me of another plan for the land pirate's final destruction. *Comprendes?"*

Clay bounded away shaking his head without answering. He wasn't exactly sure what Pepe meant by a "new plan," but for the moment his attention was fixed on Vanessa and rescuing her from the greedy old thief who had forced her to accompany him on still another of his wealth-accumulating missions. The fate of Conover and Skepe was rattling around in the back of Clay's mind, too. Very strange, he concluded.

"So Skepe is really dead?" Clay asked a second time, as if he couldn't believe it. "What happened?"

Ramón, with the taxi driver's help now that Pepe was no longer riding in the vehicle, began to reveal the details of the big man's "execution."

"The killer vanished!" the taxi driver injected dramatically after Ramón stammered on that point. "It was a mafia hit from the Caribbean underworld! The police are looking for him now—the slayer!"

"Him?"

The taxi driver craned his neck to see Clay's face in the rearview mirror. "Yes of course *him*. Surely no woman would attempt to murder such a gruesome monster as this one."

"Drop us at the side entrance," Ramón interrupted, "and wait around the corner as before. We must not intrude on the police while they are investigating crimes."

"Bueno," the taxi driver replied, appearing very happy with his fares and their seeming gratitude over his revelations.

"Stay with the cab," Clay said to Ramón and Elena. Then, in a sudden swift move, he jumped out while the driver was still rolling along in search of a parking space and ran inside the hotel. It happened so fast the two Cubans didn't at first realize he had departed. Their heads swivelled barely in time to catch a glimpse of the broker dashing out of sight.

Elena peered at Ramón. "I cannot sit here and wait," she said. "Clay may encounter great danger in there."

Her lover nodded. "Fortunately our brother knows how to deal with great danger, but, very well, let's follow along, only don't let the land pirate see your pretty face or we may encounter great danger ourselves." Ramón turned to the taxi driver. "Park over there," he said, jigging his fingers back and forth toward a vacant spot. "If you wish to be paid, please be content not to budge one inch until the man who just left us sitting here like dummies returns."

The cabbie, aside from the fact that he was by habit quick to notice a fare running away without paying, was nevertheless unprepared for the sudden turn of events. He mumbled under his breath while bringing the vehicle to a stop along the curb a short distance from Hotel Embajador. "No problem," he answered minus his usual ebullience. A half-hearted but obliging smirk slowly spread over his face as he pushed his cap forward, flicked on the radio and laid his head back against the seat.

Clay Redmond paused at the edge of the famous old hotel's ornate lobby, although his eyes stayed focused on the guests, not on the esthetics of Trujillo's grand creation. The body of Karl Skepe had already been carted away and the police were allowing the casino to resume operations, except for the immediate area where Skepe's body was found lying in a pool of blood. Clay scanned faces in rapid-fire fashion. Leetboer and Vanessa were not in the casino or the lobby. The broker, not wanting to draw attention, moved around at a casual pace as he worked his way to the reception counter. The clerks were all busy with the check-in line but a well-dressed man soon came out of the adjoining room and approached.

"May I help you?" he said in smooth Castilian.

"Yes," Clay answered in kind. "I'm a friend of Señor Guillermo Valdez. You know him of course?"

The man's eyebrows lifted. "Of course."

"He sent me to find a certain gentleman who he thinks might be in the hotel at this time."

The man to whom Clay was speaking and who turned out to be a senior employee with sweeping authority, looked carefully at him for a moment without answering. "Señor Valdez you say?" The executive searched Clay's face as he spoke.

"Yes."

"Señor Valdez is a friend of yours?"

"Yes, that's what I said."

"What is the gentleman's name you are seeking? Is he a guest here?"

"His name is Ewen Leetboer. He may not have registered yet but I'm almost certain he came into this hotel less than an hour ago."

The executive looked askance and rolled his fingers musically on top of the desk while he digested Clay's request. His face puckered in thought. "Where is Señor Valdez now?"

"In Miami."

"You say you are a friend of his?"

"I said that, yes."

"Señor Valdez sent you to find this man?"

Clay frowned without answering. "Perhaps he has already gone up to the suite. Can you tell me the number please?"

"Aha," the executive laughed uneasily, "you are the second person tonight who has inquired about the Valdez suite. Is this Mr. Leetboer accompanied by a young lady by chance, a very attractive young lady with striking red hair?"

"Uh-huh."

"I see," the executive said, which reply, curiously, reminded Clay Redmond of the man he was trying to find, the Dutchman. "Excuse me for a moment please while I consult with my assistant. I seem to recall him speaking of such a party. Yes, our security guard was involved. If I am not mistaken, they entered the elevator not long ago with one of the local police from the casino. Is something wrong?"

"What's the room number for Christ sake—?"

Clay's gruff voice caused the executive to flinch "I'm—I'm sorry, sir. Señor Valdez insists on his privacy. We have strict orders from him not to release to anyone the information you are requesting. Since he is your friend, you no doubt have knowledge of his . . . shall we say, *firm* character. Surely you must know how stupid and dangerous it would be for us to violate his trust."

The executive began to fidget a little faster as he looked into the tough, resolute face of Clay Redmond, as if he sensed another danger standing, almost too quietly, in front of him, one that he dare not challenge any more than he would challenge the will of Señor Valdez. Unable to hide his nervousness, the executive backed away, whirled and disappeared inside the room from which he had emerged earlier.

"Hey—!" Clay Redmond shouted.

Too late. The executive vanished before Clay could ask anything further. "Crap," the broker muttered then stepped to the end of the long reception counter. His eyes resumed a careful scan of faces as people moved in and out of the elevator and around the lobby. It was obvious to him that Leetboer had bribed the house detective as well as the police and now had recruited them into his service.

Then he wondered about Vanessa, how she was holding up, whether she had been injured by Leetboer's rough treatment. How strange he felt, chasing a man all the way to Santo Domingo whose wife he meant to take for himself. Hardly a moral act, although he couldn't help but doubt the morality of tying the knot with a person one didn't truly love. Or what might be viewed with equal sadness, having tied the knot under the presumption of true love, the person maybe loses that love along the way yet hangs on to the trappings even to the point of self-deception, not to mention dual misery. Either way, Clay thought, true love of the mutual sort must be rarer than hens' teeth, as his grandmother used to whisper in his ear when he'd bring in a fresh date. Morality issues notwithstanding, Clay felt blessed. He loved Vanessa and she loved him. Each loved the other with unfamiliar passion; they were true soul mates; they belonged to each other as if they had grown up in each other's shadow, from barest youth, mesmerized by the mood and smack of daily attentions. Having each other *now* had become the only important thing left in his shrinking world. Too bad they hadn't met earlier when they were both single, free, unencumbered. Too bad they weren't the childhood sweethearts they already seemed to be, for they would not have passed through all those many years of darkness alone. This curious twist, rather than boosting his thirst for vengeance by providing a deeper reason to send Leetboer on his way to the Promised Land, where partnership pickings might be even better than in Miami, caused the broker to experience a sudden wave of compassion for the old double-crosser. He laughed inwardly at himself for having given so much energy to a pursuit that had now lost its meaning. Sweeter impulses seemed to have trumped all desires but sharing life with Vanessa and making her the centerpiece in his own, and forever. The wait was almost over. His soul mate was here in this hotel. He could "feel" her loving presence and "hear" her muted screams for help.

Amidst his reflections Clay managed to spot Ramón and Elena ducking behind a heavy screen of shrubbery near the elevator, which, even there, was remindful of the lush decor of Leetboer's patio where he had enjoyed a memorable luncheon in Vanessa's company, thanks to his old partner's generosity. Seconds later the broker slipped up behind the two Cubans and put his arms on both, setting off loud gasps before they turned and recognized him.

"Relax," Clay said, sounding a gentler tone than either expected to hear, since they'd ignored his instructions to remain in the taxi. "Now that you've come, take me to Señor Valdez's suite."

38

Clay Redmond felt a little stupid for having hassled the hotel official over Señor Valdez' suite number. In the excitement since arriving in Santo Domingo he'd almost overlooked the fact that Ramón and Elena had been bottled up there with Pepe and knew exactly where the suite was. But much to the broker's surprise the hassle proved rather enlightening. The executive aroused his curiosity. The man was hiding something. What, Clay wondered, lay behind the façade of protecting the privacy of Señor Valdez? Perhaps the Castilian smart-ass had allowed himself to be seduced by Leetboer's cash and was now afraid he himself had been exposed as a violator of that privacy. Anyone acquainted with Señor Valdez would judge the consequences to be dire indeed. Clay decided to check on his theory later in the event Vanessa was not inside the suite.

"The land pirate expects to find only one face up there he knows—mine!—and he will want very much to separate it from my neck." Ramón spoke with dramatic flourish. He pushed the elevator button for the top floor and tried to chuckle away a gnawing fear. "Yes, Clay, Felipe Jorge is Leetboer's target. Would you not go after such a thief yourself? Pursue him across the Caribbean?"

"Tell him your real name if he asks. Show him some ID. It's been awhile since he last saw you, then only for—what—less than an hour? You're dressed like a street bum now, not a flashy communist peacock. He may not recognize you in those duds."

"Listen, my brother, Pepe allowed me no time in Cuba to pack. He convinced me with his pistol to board the plane immediately after I was freed from jail, without even a toothbrush, so is it fair to hint that my shirt needs a replacement, that my *pantalones* are falling apart from overuse? Besides, the land pirate will recognize Elena for sure regardless of what she wears. Then he will connect us and right away point his cheesy finger at me and shout, "Aha! Felipe Jorge, the seedy swindler of my five million dollars!"

Clay threw up his hands in a gesture of surrender. "Okay, but wait by the elevator. Keep it open and ready. We may have to chop-chop the hell out of here."

"What will happen to us, *hermano?*" Elena sighed, stepping up and grabbing Clay Redmond's arm to restrain him. Her contorted expression coaxed a troubled sort of beauty out of her face, a beauty stripped down to its sensuous essence and not usually so apparent under the circumstances. She continued talking as both men listened; their silent vows of protection echoed loud in the gritty set of their jaws. "Señor Leetboer must be very angry to bring so many men to this country to find Ramón and me."

"Maybe nothing will happen," Clay said. "I'd feel better if both of you just went on back to the taxi and waited."

"No," Ramón replied. "We want to help. It is part of the sting. Cha-cha-cha, okay?"

Clay Redmond took a long, probing look at the two Cubans, then shrugged. "As you wish. But Leetboer brought a hired gun upstairs with him. Best you hang back till I sort things out."

Ramón's eyes rolled. "But you and Pepe silenced the hired guns already. No? Aren't they lying dead in the airport shrubbery, with Pepe there to prevent any miraculous recoveries?"

"Not them. Leetboer added a local cop—maybe more—to his swat team since he arrived in Santo Domingo."

When the elevator came to a halt on the top floor, Clay Redmond clicked the "door open" switch and stepped out into a wide, darkly lit corridor. No signs of human life anywhere. "Wait here," he repeated, jabbing his finger lightly into Ramón's stomach. "If they're in the suite, my business shouldn't take but a few minutes."

"Cuidado!" Elena whispered. Her smooth Latin face erupted again in a swirl of worry lines. Streaks and creases formed over the smoothness and seemed to accent even more a kind of virgin purity, an undefiled beauty made oddly more beautiful under stress, yielding a loveliness and innocence that less perilous times might never disclose.

Moments later Clay Redmond, holding the Valdez key in his hand, stood at the end of the passageway and in front of the door Ramón had described. The door was bulky, thick and solid, fashioned from tropical hardwood. Some wretched artisan, working for peanuts no doubt, had carved one of his masterpieces into the center, a delicate face evoking the grievous sanctity of the *Pietà*.

Above that imposing likeness, the words "Angel Mara" were emblazoned in classic scroll across the width of the door. A spyhole had been worked into the letters to make viewing more comfortable from inside for the taller Señor Valdez while the decorative camouflage and height rendered it unnoticeable to visitors on the outside. Clay spotted it immediately, though, a detection skill born out of his booby trap and reconnaissance experience in the Marines. He extracted a stick of gum from his shirt pocket and chewed on it for a brief time then mashed the wad over the hidden eye. After three sharp raps on the door he moved to the side and waited. The broker listened for a moment but heard no sounds coming from within. He rapped again, harder. Nothing. This was not Penthouse #9 at Bella Mar, yet a romantic wave of the moment conjured up pictures of Vanessa standing behind these walls at Hotel Embajador, waiting in voluptuous suspension as she had done in Miami, waiting with her heart in her mouth to hear the telltale clatter of the key and the door to open. Clay tossed the Valdez key up and down for a bit, the key that Ramón had tried unsuccessfully to retain for his own heroic purposes, then shoved it into the lock. A nostalgic glaze spread thicker over his face as he "harked to the tintinnabulation," as Poe might say. For a time he lost himself in a few sweet reveries, in blissful thoughts of the woman he hoped to find behind the door. Moments later he pulled the key out and pushed it back in to hear the sound again, and to listen. With his ear to the adjacent wall he caught the swoosh of a faint gasp, a throaty utterance of alarm followed by the noisy bolt action of a gun, then the tinkle of something metallic, like bullets, rolling around on a glass-top table farther back in the suite. At least he knew someone was in there, someone waiting to ambush Ramón most likely, someone not expecting *him* at any rate.

The knob began to turn from the inside. A male voice called out both in Spanish and English, "Who is it? *¿Quién es?"*

"Room service," Clay Redmond answered in a musical tone.

The door opened and a potbellied, rangy fellow peered out. He was not wearing a coat but the holster strapped to his chest, to which was attached some sort of official-looking badge, suggested he might be the hotel's house detective or someone connected to the local police and now under the employ of Ewen Leetboer. "You're not room service!" the man said with an ugly sneer.

Clay observed the holstered pistol for a moment. "Oh, I'm sorry," he exclaimed, drawling. "How clumsy of me." He pretended to examine the key again, flipping it end over end a few times before turning back to the house detective. "Sir, you better check with the hotel manager. My key matches *this* suite number, it opens *this* door. You must be in the wrong room."

The man grunted a profanity, holding his sneer in place and putting a grisly stare on Clay. "And you must be loco! If you're not looking for a roomful of trouble, I'd advise you to get the hell out of this hotel!" He started to close the door but Clay Redmond's boot blocked it. The man spied down at the floor, then back up at Clay's smiling face as if puzzled by the antics of this cocky intruder. Signs of rage began to flush even brighter in his already beefy-red face.

Clay held up his finger. "Wait. I really did mean 'room service,' okay? Let's just say I'm offering service to a lady in distress who's in this room." The broker paused and relaxed against the door jamb, his face as placid as Lake Louise, his boot unmoved.

"Who the fuck are you?"

"A friend of a lady. To answer the question you should have asked, yes, I am looking for someone in particular."

"Who?"

"As I said, a lady."

"Describe her. Does she have a name?"

"Well, she's a woman if you know what I mean. *Y qué mujer!* A woman of exceptional beauty. She has the most gorgeous, flaming red hair the Holy Triangle ever graced a head with. Truly. And, by the way, the lady's name is Vanessa. Does she happen to be inside this suite by chance?"

"Go away before I lose my temper. There is no lady for you in here."

"May I see for myself?"

"Damn your insolence!" The house detective snorted like a cornered boar and reached for his pistol. Clay kicked the door further open, knocking the enraged man flat on his back. In a flash the broker's boot came down hard on the house detective's arm, which blunted his struggle to get at the pistol still in his holster but launched a bellicose yell for help. Clay reached down and jerked the gun away and then stepped back. Just as the man scrambled up on his feet, the broker delivered a sharp chop across his neck, sending him to the floor again, this time unconscious.

A uniformed policeman crept into the foyer from the interior of the suite and grabbed Clay from behind in a bear hug and tried to wrestle him down. Both of Clay's arms were pinned against his body but his hard, rough hands had not been deprived of all wiggle room. In fact, as Ramón Alvarez might have noted, they were perfectly aligned to administer a "macho squeeze" to the attacker's *cojones.* Suddenly the attacker's bear hug gave way to greater urgencies.

Releasing his grip, Clay whirled around and struck him in the solar plexus with a crushing blow followed by a crack over the head with the house detective's pistol. The policeman fell across the house detective, still coddling his testicles. Clay took his gun, too, and walked into a sumptuous suite almost as roomy as a tobacco barn and every bit as lavish as an Iraqi palace. Señor Valdez sure knows his onions about living well, Clay thought, observing the decor.

Suddenly Vanessa came screaming out of the kitchen. *"Oh, Clay, it **IS** you! Oh my darling—you're really here, you're alive!* She flew into his arms and began caressing his face all over.

"I am now," Clay said in between kisses. "Alive, O yeah!"

"Damn that Ewen! He's so cruel—*oh shit!*—I could just kill him. He made me think you were dead!"

"Not entirely true, not yet anyway. I told you he was a conniving, compulsive asshole. Where is the crook?"

"In there, in the master bedroom searching for a weapon!"

Clay glanced toward the door then back at Vanessa. Their eyes froze in mutual admiration, both seeming unmindful of the crisis swirling around them. Her hands pressed against his face to verify the reality once more. He felt the heat of her passion blend with his own, causing his blue eyes to blaze up and his lips to meet hers. They sank into a long and devouring kiss, as if it might be their last.

Even as they broke away, they held their gazes, not seeing or even caring that Ewen Leetboer was standing close by them in one of the adjoining antechambers with an automatic in his hand.

"How charming," the Dutchman said finally, shattering the lovers' engaging silence. Then all three of them began to swap glances with each other. Leetboer's dull gray eyes soon came to rest on Clay. "Under the circumstances, Mr. Redmond, I can't very well welcome you back."

"No need to," Clay replied, turning and speaking as if to Vanessa. "I've already been welcomed."

Ewen remained calm. He held the gun down toward the floor and did not attempt to threaten with it. "Forgive me if I don't seem shocked to find you and my wife embracing."

"I never supposed you would be," Clay responded. "I hereby credit you with the good taste to see things as they are."

"Yes. But I am shocked to find you in Santo Domingo, alive and, from all appearances, quite well."

"Really? Why shocked?"

"I heard you fell off the yacht during turbulent weather and perished."

"Where on earth did you pick up such a rumor?"

"From my attorney of course—your shipmate, remember? He claims you lost your footing on the deck of *Noche Buena* while attempting to trim the sails. When I asked why he didn't rescue you, he said he couldn't because the sea was too rough. Stanley told me you were simply swept away in front of his eyes. I had no reason to doubt his word."

"Interesting. So Conover is spreading lies again—this time from the grave."

"What do you mean?"

"Don't tell me you're out of touch, Ewen."

"Perhaps I am. Please update me. How did you survive?"

"Easy as *not* falling off a yacht. It's your beloved attorney who perished at sea."

Ewen Leetboer's mouth sagged into an ugly gaping hole. "Stanley?"

"None other."

"Come, come, you're kidding me . . . ?"

"Now I'm shocked, shocked that you didn't know. Are you saying that you heard the news of my supposed demise but nothing of his?"

"Why should that surprise you?"

"It doesn't. But it does suggest that he told you things that he couldn't possibly have told you, not after the fact in any case. The turkey never got back to tell you that his plans didn't quite pan out. Or did he? Anyway, he was found in the lifeboat, dead, after botching an attempt on me."

"Stanley? No, I don't believe you." Ewen raised the automatic and pointed it at Clay as he spoke. He looked nervous and awkward holding it.

"Where did you get that gun?"

"I collect guns. You know that."

"Uh-huh. Well, it looks familiar. Wouldn't be a Model 51 Remington, would it? Can't be many of those babies still around."

Ewen Leetboer held the automatic up and examined it for a moment. "So what if it is a Remington model as you say?" He appeared puzzled by Clay's notice but quickly recovered and looked up again. The broker stepped in front of Vanessa. He seemed unalarmed as he watched Ewen bend his bony elbow upward and point the gun back at him. "My dealer advised me that this 'baby,' as you also say, is very effective at short range such as we now have between us, Mr. Redmond, so please don't try to be a hero to impress Vanessa."

"Thanks for the warning," Clay answered. "By the way, does that Model 51 have any prominent etchings on it, like my initials for instance?"

Ewen held the piece up closer to his face and scanned it carefully. "Hmmmm. So what is proved? Perhaps you took it from my gun cabinet last week. You could have etched them here while aboard the yacht, eh?"

Clay Redmond chuckled and started walking toward Leetboer. Vanessa locked her fingers around his belt and followed. Ewen Leetboer, however, felt an immediate resentment of the broker's confident stride and straightaway thrust the automatic forward, as if to fire. After an uneasy pause and with mounting displeasure, he yanked on the trigger once, then twice, then a third time. A panic seized him when the gun didn't go off.

"Stop it, Ewen!" Vanessa cried out, straining to see over Clay Redmond's shoulder. She had never observed her spouse with a weapon of any sort in his hand. These were things he collected and put in his gun cabinet and looked at through glass doors. Or was his ability to threaten, maybe even murder with one, another of the many aspects of his character she had not yet seen? At that moment she began to wonder whether he was just trying to scare them or if he intended to take revenge for her betrayal.

Leetboer backed against a chair, the pistol still pointing at Clay Redmond. "Do not come closer or I will shoot," he bluffed. "Remain there—both of you!"

Clay continued to move toward Ewen. The Dutchman kept squeezing and jerking on the trigger to no avail. The gun remained stubbornly silent. Clay's face, though, was turning into a serious masque of anger with each step. Stanley B. Conover had passed on grim stories about Clay Redmond's mastery of martial arts and how dangerous his open hands and feet were in an altercation. "He's a trained killer," the attorney had cautioned on several occasions in the past. Since the court trial Ewen Leetboer developed his own well-rounded fear of the broker, applying gentle psychology in their dealings to avoid physical violence. While the old Dutchman specialized in other forms of violence, violent thievery for instance, trained killers he wanted no part of. Clay Redmond's knowledge of the Miami real estate market, however, had been worth the risk.

In desperation Ewen lowered the Remington to his side and slumped into the chair behind him, spluttering, "Look it, Clay Redmond, you can take her. What do I want with the hussy now? Take her and leave."

Clay lifted the gun from Leetboer's hand without a struggle.

"Get yourself a new attorney," Vanessa said, stepping out from behind Clay and wrapping her arm around his. Her tone was calm again, without rancor. "From now on you and I will deal through them—exclusively."

Ewen Leetboer did not answer. His head was hanging low, as if it might soon drop off his neck and land on his feet. A wave of pity swept through Clay Redmond as he looked down at his erstwhile, crumpled partner. He said, "By the way, Ewen, the safety sticks."

"Yes."

"Yes. The darn thing never did move easy."

"Yes."

"Yes. Took on a lot of salt water the other night, too, after it wound up in the lifeboat with old 'angle eyes' Conover. Guess it really started acting the fool then."

"Yes."

"Yes. I knew how to make it work but you didn't. Neither did Stanley. Bless my dear old aunt's heart, though. She knew how—and a whole lot more. She may have saved my life—and yours as well."

"Yes."

"Yes. But your ace of aces, that dandy spitballer of an attorney, sure as hell missed out, didn't he? By the way, I know how *he* got hold of my pistola. Yeah. But *you*? Oh, my, Ewen. Did one of your boys loot Conover's pitiful little lifeboat after that poor old pathetic fuck had no further use of it? No? Well, the best I can figure, somebody meant to shove a killjoy finger through his escape plan. Imagine that. Gosh, Ewen, such a ringer fills a fellow with utter curiosity so be a good guy and educate me."

Leetboer looked dazed, unable to speak. Clay waited for some reply, even another feeble "yes," but when the Dutchman held his silence, the broker resumed. "Sorry, Ewen, I didn't mean to spoil your day. Remind me to ask you later how you managed to kill that tricky prick. And why. Right now I'd like for us to go to the airport. I have a friend out there who's dying to meet you."

39

"How can you make business with this repulsive character?" Pepe asked Ramón. They were sitting inside the cockpit of Ewen Leetboer's plane. "What is the big 'check' he speaks of in such a confusion of words?"

Ramón's cool Latin blink suddenly accelerated. "One of his investments I think."

"Investments? In Cuba? Ha!"

"I think so."

"Mara Paradiso perhaps?"

"Perhaps."

"Perhaps, eh?" Pepe studied Ramón's face for a moment. "Then perhaps we can no longer be friends if you continue these deceptions."

Ramón laughed uneasily. "Deceptions? Why do you question my integrity, Pepe? I tell you everything, don't I?"

"Don't tell me everything. Tell me only what the check is and why the land pirate whined so much to you about it."

"He thinks I am another person."

"What person?"

"Felipe Jorge."

"Perhaps he has a reason to think this. The land pirate would not write you a check for no reason, would he?"

"A check?"

"Yes, a check. Ramón, didn't the land pirate write you this check he speaks of?"

"No, not me."

"Then who? Felipe Jorge?"

"I think maybe the *Ministerio del Interior* . . . ."

"You look nervous, *Cubano.* Does Pepe make you nervous?"

"Pepe makes my head ache with questions. Will you please stop this inquisition? I am telling you the truth!"

"You are telling me the truth, eh? Then why do I get this funny feeling you are also lying?"

"No, never would I lie to you, but these are matters of confidence. You would not ask me to betray a confidence, would you, Pepe?"

"Of course not. Only tell me about the check. Does it concern Mara Paradiso?"

Ramón wiped his brow and sighed ruefully "I think so."

"You think a lot for a Cubano, don't you?"

"Es necesario!" Ramón's response burst out with the force of a football cheer. "Thinking is essential in Cuba to avoid trouble and remain alive." He glanced at his wrist. "My watch has stopped, Pepe. What time is it?"

"Time to hear more about this check."

The Cuban threw up his hands, rolled his eyes and let loose a volley of sounds that dragged with frustration. "Okay, I tell you. But first you must promise to help me convince the land pirate I am not Felipe Jorge."

"No problem. He is now convinced. Felipe Jorge cannot be you. He is a friend of mine and I know who are my friends."

Ramón laughed at Pepe's unsubtle wink. *"Excelente!* I'm sure he will believe you once you show him the silencer in your coat."

"The check, Ramón . . . ."

"Yes, of course. The check is a real one but also a joke."

Pepe frowned. "If the check is real it cannot be a joke. Talk sense, Cubano. What is the amount of the check?"

"Five million."

"Pesos?"

"Dollars."

"Holy Papa! No wonder the man whines to you."

A wave of pride swept through Ramón and he felt a desire to be more candid with Pepe, to talk further about his triumph over Ewen Leetboer. "You can call the check a deposit," he said with pedantic delight, "a token of good faith to prove the land pirate's honorable intentions, something like a down payment—"

"A down payment? On what—his sorry life? Can you translate for me what he says? The fool cannot talk even with the intelligence of a *morón."*

"Señor Leetboer is no fool, Pepe. The man truly believes his five million dollar check has secured for him a partnership with Fidel Castro and the legal right to finish the development of Mara Paradiso." Ramón scratched his cheeks and puffed under raised brows as though the Dutchman's belief might have merit.

Pepe's eyelids eased together to form two narrow slits through which his black, piercing eyes seemed more exposed and sinister than ever. "Is this the part about the check that is a joke?" he snarled, his voice roughening in perfect complement to the sour cast on his face.

"Ha!" Ramón cried out, clasping his hands together like a bordello matchmaker. His earlier nervousness had given way to a look of mock smugness. "Yes and no."

"More bullshit talk! How can 'yes and no' be the answer to something real?"

"Like this: The land pirate believes his check has bought for him everything of Mara Paradiso. That's a yes. To believe it yourself, that's a no."

"El Cojonudo will not believe it, that's a fact. Where is this joke check now?"

"In Mexico I think."

"In Mexico? Pfft! How can that be? Castro would never allow it."

"You're wrong, my friend. El Jefe does not know the check exists."

"You joke again. Fidel knows of every existence in Cuba."

"Not this one."

"Ramón, Ramón! How can you speak of such a ridiculous exception with so straight face? You are a long-suffering native of the island, amigo! *Jesucristo!"*

"It is the truth I tell you! The check materialized out of a beautifully executed sting. You know what a sting is, Pepe?"

"From a bee, yes," Pepe shot back, his tone still rich with bluster and disbelief. "Ramón, you talk as much riddles as that pathetic crook does. Save your explanations for Señor Valdez. His presence will no doubt inspire more acceptable stories from everyone."

"Señor Valdez—where—?"

"Here."

"Here—in Santo Domingo?"

"Here is here, is it not? He will arrive on a charter flight very soon, before the sun rises perhaps." Pepe fell silent for a moment, suddenly lost in reflection. His grim face softened and he resumed, though he had to speak above his own robust chuckle. "Ah, Ramón, what a magnificent pleasure for El Cojonudo to join us and greet this miserable land pirate whose tail right now is so much caught in a very big crack."

"I'm sure the greeting will be a cordial one," Ramón answered, lapsing into an even livelier chuckle.

"You do not think we will see a test of wills, do you?"

"Heavens no, Pepe. The land pirate has no will at the moment. Did you notice how humbly he answered Clay Redmond's questions after they came aboard the plane?"

The two men nodded back and forth in friendly chatter for a while before leaving the cockpit and joining Clay Redmond, Vanessa, Elena and Ewen Leetboer in the cabin. Leetboer appeared a bit more animated, as well as coherent. Conditions favoring a bribe always brightened the Dutchman's outlook. His speech had picked up its old-world rhythm following the disastrous events at Hotel Embajador. A sense of craftiness started to twinkle in his dull gray eyes, a facial feature often mistaken for congeniality by observers. He even began to hope out loud that he might bring his former partner back under control with the promise of a "phenomenal" interest in Mara Paradiso. Unfortunately for him, Pepe and Ramón were entering the cabin about that time and the mafioso overheard the two key words lisping out of Leetboer's mouth. " . . . *Mara Paradiso . . . .*"

Pepe didn't bother to sit down. He grabbed Ewen Leetboer under both arms and lifted him straight up, causing the Dutchman's toupee to come loose when his head hit the ceiling. Pepe shook him hard while he was suspended in air. When the hairpiece landed on the cabin floor, the mafioso stepped on it and ground his shoe a few times before he dropped the speechless man back into his seat.

"You must not talk of Mara Paradiso!" Pepe growled into Leetboer's face, his nose only inches away. "Never let those words pass through your crooked mouth again."

Ewen Leetboer's face froze in shock. After Pepe moved away and took a seat some arm's lengths distant, the Dutchman remained as still as a statue for what seemed several minutes to the others who had been caught up in the short but impressionable fray.

"Here, Mr. Leetboer," Elena said, retrieving his hairpiece from the floor and handing it to him. The Dutchman twisted around in his seat, his face aglow with a mixture of fear and embarrassment which seemed to intensify as he glanced along the smooth, outstretched arm of the Cuban woman. With a shrug he took the hairpiece then tried without much success to undo the damage caused by the grinding action of Pepe's shoe. After a bit he gave up and placed it back on his head. The hairpiece was still somewhat misshapen but no one laughed or commented.

"Thank you, Carla."

Elena sat back down, nodding as if to say "Save your gratitude, old boy. I'd do the same for a dog." Vanessa gave the Cuban woman an approving pat on the shoulder, not so much to salute her initiative but to acknowledge a tender moment of humanity. She followed up with an affectionate squeeze on Clay Redmond's muscle above his elbow. The broker, whose arms were folded at the time, reciprocated without unfolding and delighted her with a secret fondle. Thrilled by her lover's touch, Vanessa held his hard, heavy hand tight against her breast for a moment, unobtrusively she thought, before she let him take it away. Ewen Leetboer, though, picked up on their sex play, for he was the sort of man who always took quick notice of signs, or links, between targets of opportunity worthy of blackmail, graft or, for that matter, any allied form of advantage; but, like the gracious onlookers who'd witnessed his embarrassment earlier, he said nothing and revealed not a twitch of pang. In his mind he had already divorced his lovely but unfaithful wife. Stanley B. Conover, bless his departed soul for showing enough vision to prepare the necessary paperwork ahead of time, had saved the estate from another nasty round of litigation.

Other issues were beginning to encroach upon memories of Pepe's outburst. For instance, where were his men, his loyal guards? And Karl Skepe? No one had yet mentioned their sad fate, and he hesitated to ask about them for fear of squandering an element of surprise. At the moment the Dutchman's principal regret was that he did not have Attorney Conover at his side to handle the legalities of assault and battery. Obviously he hadn't brought enough men along from Miami. Neither had he hired a sufficient number of local mercenaries to protect him from all the unexpected dangers he had encountered down in this hostile land, with no telling what still lay ahead. His mind began to hum with remorse. He had underestimated Clay Redmond. The broker, whom he had considered a man unwisely trusting and overly hot tempered, was now the coolest, most trustworthy, two-fisted fellow around him. Why had he foolishly followed his "business-is-business" rule when certain Chapter 11 "adjustments" could have been made to protect the able partner Clay Redmond had proven himself to be? And Conover's vision aside, why had he let the attorney talk him into such an idiotic, short-sighted scheme as killing the goose that had already laid so many golden eggs for him—his broker—just to save a piddling commission? Mara Paradiso wasn't worth it. Neither was Vanessa. As matters stood, the Dutchman concluded, Clay Redmond was. Not only did the broker deserve his weight in golden eggs but Karl Skepe's as well.

Clay Redmond whispered to the mafioso to accompany him outside for a private chat. The broker still felt uncomfortable. Señor Valdez wanted one thing and he wanted another. Now the Spaniard was wanting something else again. All Clay Redmond wanted was Vanessa, wanted to take her and head for Miami, outfit the yacht and sail into a new life. The two men ambled along in silence until they were quite beyond earshot. Clay said,

"What's Señor Valdez got in mind, Pepe?"

"Ah, gringo, do not put to Pepe such a question. Who knows the mind of El Cojonudo?"

"You do."

"No. No one does. Sometimes not even Guillermo himself."

"Did I not hear you correctly? Didn't you say just a few hours ago that Señor Valdez is no longer insisting that I bring him Ewen Leetboer's head on a platter?"

"Do not worry yourself over this minor change of plan. For the present the land pirate's head must remain attached to his body."

"Just for the present, huh?"

"Maybe longer, until Señor Valdez takes his satisfaction of looking into the crook's eyes. Perhaps then he will insist again the head come off."

"Okay, fine. But don't count on me. I won't take it off," the broker said to Pepe. They had moved a distance away from the plane and were walking back and forth in an adjacent parking lot.

"You won't, gringo? You would refuse El Cojonudo's wish?"

"I won't 'destroy' the man, no. Wasn't that the word Señor Valdez used?"

Pepe studied the broker's face carefully. A glaze had settled upon it that the mafioso sometimes saw in Señor Valdez's face, a vagueness, something deep within the Spaniard that suggested he might be possessed of a conscience after all.

"I see," he said to Clay Redmond.

"You see what?" Clay answered, being reminded of Ewen Leetboer's bad habit of seeing but not seeing.

"I see in your soul already that you have no stomach for this execution."

"It's more a matter of heart, Pepe. I was pissed off as hell when Leetboer screwed me out of my interest in that tract of land in Miami. It was the centerpiece of my retirement program. I wanted to get even, I wanted blood. Now the anger has left me. Frankly I can't help but pity the old asshole if you care to know the truth."

"You pity him, the man who robbed you?"

"Yep. Losers affect me that way sooner or later, no matter how big of a son of a bitch they are."

Pepe grimaced, clacked his teeth together and slapped his forehead. "Oh gringo, you tire my insides with this kind of talk! Señor Valdez will arrive shortly. Give him your excuses. It was his commandment that the land pirate be *destroyed,* yes, and I advise you to be careful with your change of heart. His was a change of plan only."

40

Silvio Alvarez didn't feel much at home around the Xanadu Shopping Mall, not like Clay Redmond did, but he had promised the broker (*Hermano,* as the Cuban sometimes called him) when they talked on the phone that morning to take a message to Marcus Cunningham. Silvio's thick black hair was in as much need of a comb as the shopping mall magnate needed to relax and lose a few of the signs of high anxiety that showed so clearly in his face. Clay Redmond would've been touched. He didn't have many clients who exhibited such a flattering level of concern for him, certainly not Frank Creuthop. Frank, whom Heather Ambrose referred to with euphemistic restraint as Xanadu's "de facto factotum," happened to be in the office when Silvio arrived. The Xanadu partner was occupying a wide, "double-lane" recliner that Marcus Cunningham, much to his regret, had allowed the "old walrus" to donate to Xanadu's furniture pool so as to make visits more comfortable, not to mention longer. The sight of the big man's flab spilling over the armrests, as well as other excesses of flesh pushing through openings under them, irked Marcus Cunningham, although not nearly so much as the continuous sound of the partner's loud, "busy-body" voice.

"Ah—thanks for coming, Silvio!" Cunningham bellowed out, rushing to meet him at the door when Heather announced his presence. Marcus appeared much relieved by the interruption. Heather would tease her revered boss later for looking so overjoyed when she opened the door, for springing up so "cutely" out of his chair and whizzing around the desk, as he always did when such chances arose to break away from Frank Creuthop, even for a five-minute piss call. The magnate glanced miserably at his mall partner, who had settled his great spread of buttocks deeper into the recliner, and said, somewhat grudgingly, "Frank, meet Silvio Alvarez, another of Clay Redmond's Cuban connections. He's the brother of the man I mentioned to you earlier."

Creuthop stuck his heavy arm out without a budge from any of the rest of him. "Pleased I'm sure, Silvio." He gave the Cuban a dead-fish shake followed by a long, critical once-over as he caressed the tip of a Cohiba Robusto which he'd helped himself to out of Cunningham's assortment of Havana cigars. "For God's sake, Silvio, tell Marcus how to get in touch with his real estate broker! That's all he can talk about lately."

Silvio gave Creuthop a sharp but noncommital gaze then took a seat on the couch toward which Marcus Cunningham was pointing. Marcus sat down on the other end.

"Where the hell is Redmond?" the magnate asked straightaway. "Is he okay, safe I mean?"

Silvio's teeth flashed with a sparkle of indulgence, a frequent reaction when others voiced concern over the broker's safety, knowing how devastating a black belt could be with his hands and feet. "Clay sounded first class on the telephone," the Cuban replied, shying away from the first question. "He instructed me this morning to thank you and the lady out there . . ." Silvio paused and pointed toward the front office. " . . . to thank you both for helping him find my brother Ramón. They are together now."

"Hey, that's great!" exclaimed Marcus Cunningham. "Where did Redmond find your brother?"

"In Santo Domingo. Clay says please do not be alarmed by his silence, for he is traveling with others and telephones are not always available."

"Guess that means he's still in danger, huh? You know what, Silvio, maybe I should tip off the police down there, ask them to check on him. Redmond might be in deeper shit than either of us think. Who do I call?"

Silvio hesitated before answering. "There is no jurisdiction where he is."

"No jurisdiction? Now that *does* sound scary! What other good news do you have for me today?"

Silvio had already shown an obvious reluctance to talk openly to Marcus Cunningham while another party was sitting like a giant laughing Buddha in the center of the room. Clay had not briefed him on such a curious personality as Frank Creuthop, so he skirted and tiptoed along during the conversation, giving just enough of Clay's message to prompt the Xanadu magnate to ask "safe" questions and avoid those he didn't want Creuthop to hear answered. At one point

Silvio slipped and blurted out, "Clay mentioned only some risk, a little . . ."

"Oh shit!" Cunningham bellowed, his face wrinkling over again. "Risk, huh?"

"But pleasures were mentioned also!" Silvio quickly added. "The Caribbean is full of them, our dear friend said, which you will hear about later. These were Clay Redmond's words. He also added that when the day of return comes, he will bring a bottle of Dominican rum for toasts to your good health and to continued success with Shopping Mall Xanadu."

"Well holy damn! Frank, will you listen to that! Redmond's sitting on a powder keg down there. It wouldn't surprise me to find out he's got guns pointing at him from every direction. Probably does, yeah—guns probably already shoved halfway up his ass—and he's worried about us, wants to bring rum and say a toast! What a guy!"

"Speaking of guys, what about our distinguished alien partner?" Creuthop asked in a churlish, mocking tone, referring to Ewen Leetboer.

"Aha! Are you about to confess you give a flying fuck?"

"Pffsshit! Of course not. Just wondering. Don't see how it would be unchristian of me to wonder if he really might have a gun shoved up his ass, as you say. You know yourself, Marcus—and you, too, Silvio—that devils nowadays travel with truckloads of dirty money to take over shopping centers like Xanadu. I'll just bet my chair that Xanadu's resident Lucifer is up to his sharp red horns in drug traffic!"

Silvio gazed blankly at Marcus Cunningham, not knowing how to respond. Marcus read the signs and shot a hard look at

Creuthop. "Knock it off, Frank," he snapped, then turned back to Silvio. "Frank is referring to Ewen Leetboer in case his conservative compassion confused you. Any news there?"

"No, nothing. Clay did not mention him."

"Too bad," Creuthop said, blowing a big cloud of Cohiba smoke into the air. He peered at Silvio for a moment. "You wouldn't know where that devil is, would you?"

Silvio shrugged. "The last news I heard of the man he was in Cuba. Something about an investment there. Clay was giving details when we lost our connection this morning."

"Lord Jesus," Creuthop sighed.

Silvio's entrepreneurial spirit rose suddenly, sensing a vacuum he might fill. "I perform investigations, Mr. Creuthop. Do you wish to hire me to find him?"

"Hell no! I don't care where the carpetbagger is as long as it's not in Miami. That cuss missed our last board meeting and I was wondering if maybe he'd gone off and died."

Marcus Cunningham forced a laugh. "You old fart, tell Silvio the truth. You never wonder a minute about Ewen Leetboer. You only *hope* about him. What you mean is you *hoped* he'd gone off and died, you *hoped* he had a gun shoved up his ass."

Both men chuckled, each casting a saucy glance at the other in a rare acknowledgment of mutual accord. Creuthop's raucous, abusive exchange with Marcus Cunningham, which followed, made Silvio edgy, as if he'd stumbled into the presence of another El Cojonudo. Clearly the man in the recliner was even more massive than the Spaniard, but his mass appeared soft and fluid, not muscular and hard, and it hung in repulsive folds over his belt. He looked lazy, too, and probably could not achieve victory in battle even with a child. Frank Creuthop did not frighten him in the same way that Señor Valdez did. It was more like fear of an insult, something he would have to ignore or, as a point of honor, address. Both prospects left him feeling uneasy. To him Frank Creuthop was simply not a pleasant man to be around.

Marcus Cunningham noticed Silvio had inched up on the edge of the couch. "Wait a minute," Marcus said, gently nudging the Cuban further back in his seat. "Don't go yet. Gimme a number. I need to talk with Redmond."

"There is no number. He was using a pay phone."

Marcus frowned and pushed his lips out. "Last month when Clay called from the yacht, come to think of it, he did mention Santo Domingo. Yeah. Was in a helluva hurry to get there, too."

"*Sí.* Hurry, yes. Only this time he hurried to leave there."

"Where's he heading now? You never did say."

"Neither can I say with precision. Some place in Colombia was all Clay could tell me."

"South Carolina?"

"No. South America."

"*What?* What the hell is it with Redmond! He never said anything to me about going down there."

"But he did say not to worry."

"Yeah, I know. Then he mentioned 'risk' in the same breath. Something's not right, Silvio."

"What are you worried about, Marcus," Creuthop interjected, not content to be squeezed out of the conversation. "The man sent word he's having fun."

"Bullshit. Redmond would've invited me along if that were true." Marcus stared back at Silvio. "Is your brother with him?"

"As a matter of fact, yes. My brother also is having fun."

"Yeah?" Marcus Cunningham said, chuckling and relaxing a bit. "Sounds like they've got women in their midst!"

"And some investors. Clay is trying to make a deal with one of them."

"Some rich tourist perhaps?"

"More than that."

"Yeah? Who?"

"You ever hear of Guillermo Valdez?"

Cunningham's eyes bulged. "Yeah, I've heard of him. He's the big macho guy building that swanky complex over in Varadero. Or was before he went bankrupt. Got kicked out of Cuba, right?"

"Rumors to that effect, yes. All lies. Señor Valdez left Cuba for personal reasons. He is not Cuban, by the way."

"No?"

"No."

"Right. Clay was telling me about that project not long ago. It had a name, a catchy name like Martha's Vineyard or something. What was it?"

"Mara Paradiso."

"Bingo—that's the one. Ewen Leetboer got interested in it for some reason, wanted to buy the whole thing—I mean, like, *thousands* of units . . . million dollar pads, upscale all the way!"

"Jesus God," Creuthop muttered.

Silvio's teeth flashed again. "Señor Valdez would never allow anyone to buy his property."

"But, Silvio, didn't he lose the property? I heard Fidel Castro took it over. Nationalized the whole kit and caboodle."

Silvio broadened his smile. "No one owns land in Cuba anymore, you're right. The communist government forbids it but Castro will accept partnerships as long as he is in control. Mara Paradiso is unique. Fidel only thinks he nationalized it. He has tried many times to entice foreign investors into partnerships with him so they will come to Cuba and breathe life into the fantastic vision that the real owner has created. So far Fidel's efforts have been futile. Señor Valdez is not Cuban, that is true, but he is still the true owner, he is still a Spaniard of great prominence in Latin America. No one will touch his project, his Mara Paradiso, for fear of offending him. It would be like spitting on the grave of his dead wife. Everybody knows the danger there. The ghost of her conquistador ancestors guard the land, according to legend, for terrible things happen to those who trespass."

Creuthop grunted. "You see, Marcus? Redmond is down in that part of the world trying to get some poor dumb asshole to sign a another one of his mean-spirited contracts. That's what turns him on. He's having fun all right—like he did with us here at Xanadu. Oh God! I wish to high Heaven he'd never brought that infernal snuff devil into our partnership!"

41

Señor Valdez, an able pilot with credentials dating back to his youthful apprenticeship in the drug trade, took control of his own plane and sent Pepe to fly Ewen Leetboer's, both aircraft being Learjets and similar in operation. Clay Redmond and Vanessa, by invitation, accompanied the Spaniard while Ramón, Elena and Ewen Leetboer, by direction, went with Pepe. The destination was assumed to be the Miami International Airport, but once in the air each plane's compass needle swung subtly toward the south. At first neither Clay nor Vanessa noticed the shift in course. The two planes flew out of Santo Domingo late in the evening and, after a short time in flight, all marks of civilization disappeared except for a few faint flickers from fishing boats and freighters here and there. Besides, as Señor Valdez anticipated, the couple showed less interest in his instrument panel than in the 'make-do' privacy the aircraft's interior decor provided. Once in their seats their eyes locked on each other. Had their hearts been housed in a tinderbox, the jet would have quickly burst into flames. In a spirit driven by unspoken harmony they proceeded to embrace and fondle under the shroud of the cabin's darkest corner, and with a focus much too dedicated to allow questions to arise concerning a route already fixed in their minds. It was as if they finally were heading toward that "sweet little cottage"—a dreamy love nest that Vanessa had spoken so passionately of earlier—and didn't care about anything else. Also, Señor Valdez cleverly distracted them with his voyeur-like squints back into the cabin, his busy head swings and continuous chatter, which of course was the Spaniard's intention.

They had been aloft for almost an hour before the moon, then in it's fourth quarter, caught the lovers' eyes as it rose out of the sea. The thin golden crescent, hovering low on the horizon, enhanced the romantic atmosphere, evoked some oohs and ahs from Vanessa, but to Clay Redmond it suddenly looked out of place.

He eased to the cockpit and dropped into the co-pilot's seat, his face reflecting a somber curiosity. Señor Valdez grinned and turned away when Clay eyed him. "What?" the Spaniard asked, staring obliquely at the instrument panel. "You have a question, yes?"

"I do," Clay answered. "What bearing are you on?"

"Bearing? Why do you ask? Are you a student of navigation?"

Clay shrugged, half grinning back at Señor Valdez's profile. "Astronomy is more the issue. I was just wondering why the moon is over there instead of over here. Assuming we're on the way to

Miami, shouldn't it be on the right side of the plane instead of the left? It's rising, you know, not setting."

Señor Valdez chuckled deep in his throat but did not look at Clay. "I can see you are no fool," he said. "You notice details, important details, and I am impressed with you for that reason."

"Why are we flying south?"

Señor Valdez cleared his throat. "Just a short detour, an emergency landing shall we say."

"Are you taking us into drug country?"

"Please do not be alarmed. You will be safe with me. Later I will arrange passage for whatever destination you and the pretty lady wish. First, though, Pepe must attend a little business during this brief stopover. While he is occupied, I would like to hold serious discussions with you about a matter close to my heart. There are things for you to see after we land. Then we talk."

"Sure, no problem. I still would like to know where the hell we're heading, though."

"We are there already."

"Where?"

"South America!" the Spaniard yelled. "Look below."

Clay peered out the window. The moon was still faintly visible but dawn had lit up the sky with breathtaking shades of pink and lavender, sending enough light to see land, with forest green in every direction ahead of them except for a line of snowcapped peaks in the distance. The broker sat in silence for a moment, studying the turned-away face of Señor Valdez. "South America, huh?" he mumbled. "Well, sir, that's a big hunk of real estate. Can you narrow the location down to a country—or a city maybe?"

"Even more narrow than you ask—a mountain range! I have a place in the Andes, *una finca perdida,* a secret spot high among the slopes and valleys of that magnificent *cordillera* you are now witnessing, with many hectares of—as you gringos say—'farmland.'"

"Complete with a private airport I bet. And perhaps even a coke lab or two, huh?"

Señor Valdez stared straight into the broker's eyes. His grin widened. "Of course. It is the style in my business. But do not think in those terms. You and the lady will enjoy a touch of Eden as my guests. For practical reasons, however, I cannot reveal the . . . coordinates. My competitors and enemies you see."

Clay Redmond's head wagged in 'I-can't-believe-this-shit' mode. The news addled him and he fell back into his earlier silence and listened to the Spaniard describe the treat awaiting him and Vanessa. She heard her name and came forward and leaned on Clay's shoulder. Everything sounded so grandiose, elegant, serenely wild.

"You're very kind to us," she said to Señor Valdez during a pause. The emerald hue in her eyes flashed with a fervorous blaze, a spark from inner depths that adventurous undertakings tend to ignite and bring to the surface of an eager face such as hers was at that instant. "I don't care where we are or where we're going. Just please don't put me in the other plane with Ewen Leetboer."

"You must not worry over such a contingency," the Spaniard answered, then lapsed into a loud, gaping laugh that exposed most of the teeth in his huge mouth, some of them glittering with a similar golden richness as seen earlier in the moon, which by then had risen quite high in the sky and given over its radiance to the sun. "No, no.

Do not allow fears of that land pirate to trouble your pretty face with anxieties. I have other plans for him."

Ewen Leetboer, a consummate survivor, found himself in much need of that virtue before the plane flew out of Santo Domingo. He boarded in the smart business style of a pompous merchant on a global buying trip, even smirking at times as though the harsh commands, the jerks on his arms and clouts to the most vulnerable and tender areas of his body—surely the forced departure—were merely links in a charade, all a big joke being enacted by the mafioso to amuse his 'guests,' as he persisted in calling everyone but his fearsome boss, Señor Valdez. Except, the Dutchman thought, the drama seemed more directed at him alone. It also seemed less a joke when Pepe pushed him rudely into a cabin seat and handcuffed his wrist to a crossbar. Still, he did not resist or complain. Buttressed by a robber baron's cast of mind, he forewarned himself that failure to cooperate would be met with even more abuse than these 'hijacking jackasses' had put upon him already. Thus he tried to gather strength by recapturing some of the old, more comfortable realities he dearly craved right then. Surely he had never experienced such an assault, such a criminal detention, and he wailed in bitter silence for justice, for legal counsel, for another Stanley B. Conover to come along and answer his prayers and save him from all this lawless treatment endured back in the hotel at the hands of that ingrate Clayborn Redmond and then by those two Hispanic hoodlums at the airport, especially the bigger one who kept thumping him on the head as if he were a mischievous kid, calling him 'land pirate' and accusing him of trying to steal Mara Paradiso.

"Felipe," he cried out to Ramón Alvarez in a burst of despair.

The Cuban was sitting behind him and next to Elena, who was asleep in his arms. "Please do not address me by that name," he answered in a gritty but soft voice so as not to wake her. "What is it you want now?"

Leetboer's face had lost its old untanned pallor, had turned red with grievous fear and, in a visual nutshell, seemed aboil under the heat of a tortured ego. "You speak that crazy pilot's language," he wailed. "Tell him I am in pain and need a doctor. Some of my ribs I think are broken. He must land the plane at once. Tell him now, Felipe."

"I tell *you* now I am not Felipe Jorge! My name is Ramón Alvarez."

"Very well. Only tell him for me. I will pay you."

Ramón eased his arms from around Elena, got up and spoke some whispered words to Pepe. A short exchange ensued between them. As expected, the Cuban's message from Ewen Leetboer evoked only sneers and loud caustic remarks from the mafioso. When Ramón returned to his seat, he leaned over and said to Leetboer, "The pilot advised me that we will be landing shortly. You can visit the clinic then. He said medical attention is one of the benefits you will receive for services to El Cojonudo."

Leetboer's gaze was full of puzzlement. "Services? What services does he mean? I have not provided any services to that kook, to Co . . . ho . . . what's-his-name, whatever it is."

"It is better you forget the past, Mr. Leetboer. Pepe speaks of the future and, I must tell you in all honesty, his convictions sounded plenty strong to me."

"But I do not provide services to anyone. I receive them and pay for them."

"Pepe says not to worry. In your new assignment you will also provide them."

The pain suffered by Ewen Leetboer permitted him only a tiny smirk. "I see," he said. "The mystery is solved. It appears these bandits want a ransom of some ridiculous amount. So that is what he means by services, eh? Very well. Ask him how much."

Ramón stared wide-eyed at Leetboer, shrugged, then rushed back to the cockpit to confer again with Pepe. When the Cuban returned, his dark eyes bore such a happy twinkle that the Dutchman's agonies seemed to lessen. "Pepe says you may keep your checkbook closed. El Cojonudo requires only your services."

Ewen Leetboer stiffened. "Does this Conudo fellow know that he and that crazy pilot in there may have crippled me for life?"

"He does, trust me. You are lucky if that is all."

"Bah! And he still expects me to grant him some sort of privilege?"

"Services only. Pepe just confirmed it."

"I don't even know what he *thinks* I can do . . . ."

Ramón laughed. "Señor Valdez is aware of your many talents and achievements, Mr. Leetboer. I'm sure he will come up with something that brings credit to your legacy."

Ewen Leetboer groaned and rubbed gently on his rib cage. "I cannot work in the dark. Neither can I work with broken ribs. When may I ask does he expect me to begin playing this extortion game?"

"Very soon was my conclusion. But be careful with such words when you talk with El Cojonudo. His patience is easily offended. For your own safety you must do as he says. You must provide services beginning very soon, and you will receive proper instructions as you perform the services."

The place Señor Valdez described was more than the single villa he occupied. It was a compound of villas, a village in fact, a community of residents living in separate quarters but sharing a common purpose, not unlike a regimental camp where soldiers trained and executed orders without question, with unwavering loyalty. Here was *Campo Bello,* a well-deserved name for his village but also the name of a famous presidential landmark further north which the elusive Spaniard adopted to confound narcotics agents. Here the level of elegance was considerably greater than one would find in a regimental camp, of course, if not the spirit of camaraderie.

Señor Valdez surprised his staff by appearing to enjoy the role of host. Something about Clay and Vanessa fascinated him. He felt close to his own love, his Mara, when he was around them. He therefore wouldn't allow the servants to escort his guests as they usually did when the Spaniard invited in some of his trusted cohorts and business associates from Spain and other places. Vicente Coto, the long-time family friend, had himself spent a few months there after his much heralded release from Castro's prison, recuperating from twenty-five years in hell and learning to make love to Heaven's worldly women again. Some of the Cuban inner circle still boasted to their leader about the Spaniard's hospitality. And there were many others, but not a single visitor ever managed to find the way back to Señor Valdez's lofty jungle retreat, although some had tried after copping pleas with overly zealous prosecutors. Those luckless few managed only to lead themselves to their doom, together with whatever troop was foolish enough to follow.

Ramón and Elena had the pick of several guest cottages. Elena selected one with colonial scroll work, a small interior patio and lots of Spanish tile smuggled in from Seville. Ramón laughed at her choice and tried to get her to admit that other places than Fidel's "Fatherland" were also beautiful, but she merely returned his laugh.

"Fidel has no Fatherland," she told him. "He belongs nowhere, not even in this dark jungle with the other wild animals he so much imitates with his executions."

"This little cottage made you smile, though, I thought. Don't you find it beautiful just a little bit?"

"Yes, Ramón, yes."

"You see? There are other places in the world, too, that you would find just as charming."

"Perhaps. But here I like. It reminds me of Cuba. Why go to these other places to be reminded of Cuba when I can live in Cuba and see every day how beautiful our precious island is?"

Señor Valdez left the two Cubans to their discussions. He walked away with his heavy arms around Clay and Vanessa, pulling them along as if they were his children. It was no surprise to either when he insisted that they take one of the suites in his villa so that they might visit more and talk in private. "My place is secure," he assured them. "The only bugs are in the canopies outside and they do not spy for the CIA."

42

They had breakfast on a secluded terrace that reminded Vanessa of places she had visited in Spain before she married Ewen Leetboer. She loved the open-air effect, the lush tropical environment and the infusion of some of it with a bit of the old world's ambiance. After a tasty omelette prepared by a Chinese chef, Señor Valdez steered her and Clay into the villa's drawing room and suggested that they continue their talks in there. He led them toward a massive picture window behind which was artfully positioned an elongated, curvaceous couch equally as plush, if not as provocative, as the one in Bella Mar's Penthouse #9 that had put Ewen Leetboer into such a frenzied buying mood some months back. After hearing Vanessa exclaim so ecstatically over the scenery around the terrace, the vigilant Spaniard thought they might also enjoy a more expanded view of his private world, including alpine lakes and forested mountains, many of which were still topped off with snow left over from the winter and seemingly so close as to form a part of the villa's immediate grounds.

"Betcha old Zeus never had it so good on Mount Olympus," Clay said, taking it all in with a cool, surveyor's eye.

Vanessa erupted with sighs. "Oh, darling, are we in Heaven or what? It's sooooo gorgeous! Can you imagine our sweet little cottage perched in the middle of a stunning dreamland like this?"

"Yeah—easy enough. I can also imagine a place by the sea, one where sparkling waters put us to sleep every night lapping the edge of a white sandy beach only a few steps from our door. Can't imagine, though, not having mentioned it before."

"Oh, you have, my love. Many times. Turquoise waters like in the Caribbean, right?"

"Uh-huh."

"Bring the coffee here," Señor Valdez told one of the domestics, ignoring Vanessa's and Clay's private tete-a-tete. "And a platter of Chin Lee's pastries. Then leave us in peace, mariposita. No interruptions."

The domestic, a pretty Latin girl of twenty or so, curtsied and ran off with her rosy cheeks in a tight perk, as if secretly thrilled with this latest assignment from her godly overlord. Clay watched her retreat and thought of Graciela, who was both lithe and lovely like that and radiated a similar cheery face whenever he slipped into Havana and showed up at her mother's door. He turned back to Señor Valdez. The Spaniard had taken a seat farther down the couch along the curve where they could see each other as they talked. "It must be quite a challenge, Guillermo, to bring a spread like this out of the ground in the middle of a beautiful nowhere. You've raised the concept of 'fabulous' to a higher level with this place."

"You think so, eh?" Señor Valdez said, smiling. Clay didn't often call him by his first name and he viewed it as another positive sign.

"Take it from a real estate man who's seen a lot of places. This one tops them all."

The Spaniard's smile rippled further across his face. "Wait until you see Mara Paradiso."

"We look forward to it," Clay answered, grasping Vanessa's hand and gazing into her eyes with the sort of searching scrutiny that seeks a blessing's amen.

Señor Valdez fiddled with his mustache while the couple cooed in each other's ears, then when they looked back at him his face had turned somber. "Forgive me for being so direct, Clay Redmond, but the Creator endowed me with very little regard for games of the tongue. The land pirate—let me tell you why I changed my mind about killing him."

He paused and gazed at Vanessa, wondering how much Clay Redmond had told her about their designs on her husband. No matter how she felt about the man, old world chivalry prevailed. To him it seemed indelicate to talk in her presence about killing someone so close, someone who had shared the same bed with her, yet she never flinched when Clay appeared as eager to address the issue as he did. Señor Valdez relaxed, although he decided he would not mention Ewen Leetboer by name unless his guests did.

"You mean about *me* killing him, don't you?" the broker replied.

"At the time that was my wish."

"Only you wanted more than just a simple, uncomplicated murder. You wanted him *destroyed*, right? I mean, really messed up!"

"Yes, that too. Again, loose words for which I apologize. I should not have spoken them. You see, I was furious when that thief set his criminal feet on my property."

"It was a hoax," Clay explained. "The guy had no authority."

"Yes, I know that now. But so what if he had no authority! It was his evil intentions I resented. He came to Mara Paradiso to rob me of the millions of dollars already in equity there."

"I know the feeling, if not the millions."

"That fool still thinks he is in partnership with Castro. What a joke. Anyway, the other point I wish to make is this: just by *thinking* himself the true developer of Mara Paradiso he profaned the memory of the woman I have loved since childhood. So, yes, I *did* want to destroy that cockroach, that repulsive defiler of sacred assets—and ASAP, as executives in the trade world say. Since you had good reasons to feel the same—and were in fact already deep into your sting intrigue—I decided to see how far you would take your work."

"Not far, as you observed," Clay responded with a labored grin. He paused and pointed at Vanessa. "This dear lady here changed my mind without knowing it."

"Aha. Even in Santo Domingo when I first saw you two dancing together I knew this would happen. Beautiful women have great power over the men who love them."

"Gentlemen—*please!*" Vanessa shouted, blushing and turning away in a fit of annoyance.

"Oh now do not hide such a pretty face," Señor Valdez teased. "The famous Beast of fairytales was not the only one to fall under the spell of Beauty's power. All real men will at one time or another. I am no exception. Ah, but such happiness this power brings when true love comes with it! For instance, my Mara also possessed great beauty and a heart as pure and kind as any angel's. She would not approve of killing even a fly in her name. In the heat of my anger her visions would come and chide me in my sleep. Her sweet presence floated around me all the time, growing stronger beyond my own fury as the project began to emerge out of Cuba's fruitful earth. It was easy to see that her spirit desired only peace and love to touch the monument I was building in memory of her unforgettable self. I had no power to resist her charms, nor would I want such a power."

"I wish I could have known her," Vanessa said, visibly moved by the Spaniard's glowing tribute to his late wife. "I'm sure she was a remarkable person."

"Lady Mara's paradise sounds plenty remarkable too," Clay added. "You really must invite us over to see the place after the embargo is lifted."

Señor Valdez shot Clay Redmond a cornered-fox look, as if he had been upstaged by the broker's words. "Perhaps I will," he said, stammering a bit. "Perhaps even sooner. The embargo cannot stop what is ordained. First I have to make peace with Castro."

"That shouldn't prove difficult. He's desperate for dollars."

"Then he will be especially fond of mine when I promise not to kill any more of his investors. That is, if I can convince him my heart has truly changed."

"Has it?"

"Indeed. My heart is full of forgiveness."

"You weren't always so forgiving of encroachers, were you? Like Ewen Leetboer, for instance."

"No," the Spaniard said, clinching his jaw at the sound of the Dutchman's name and fixing his eyes on Vanessa. She appeared unmoved so he continued. "In the beginning some killing was necessary of course, for there were many robbers out to take whatever plunder their hands could seize upon. Selective annihilation became my way just as it was the way of Mara's ancestors, the *conquistadores,* who also took treasures themselves but never as thieves. They took to honor Spain. Those courageous and principled men transformed the world with their destinies of exploration, which is not the way of thieves."

Vanessa listened with acute interest. She hoisted the coffee cup to her lips again when the two men raised theirs toward her in a gesture of toast. For a refreshing moment she savored the taste, the aroma set free by this treasured alpine bean, which, though perfect in itself, did not reach the tantalizing heights set off by the precious gleam she was then seeing in Clay Redmond's eyes. She would remember his look when they made love again and reward him for the sweetness she felt from it, but at that moment other passions were toying with her head. "Subtlety and cleverness in the light of day," she sighed, tossing her hair and setting a mass of redness in motion, "has become the new style of thieves, hasn't it?"

"They're good in court, too," Clay added after Vanessa's comment evoked the memory of Judge "Cotton" Brussard. "Ah progress! Make way for the modern criminal. These guys can now pick up acquittals for themselves and their cronies 'on the merits,' as the legal hawks say, the merits being intimidation, bribery, strong-arm stuff. The more ruthless types fall back on murder in a pinch—and occasionally for old time's sake or just for the pure hell of it."

"Oh Clay darling—" Vanessa sighed again, and with a deeper, lingering heaviness, knowing where his thoughts were. "Guess you're entitled to a bit of cynicism. Heavens! Thieves were doing unconscionable things to you right inside the halls of justice, weren't they? I had no idea and yet I was living with one of the worst of them. It's scary."

"Sounds sort of like a terrorist culture might be taking root right under our noses, huh?"

Señor Valdez poked his finger in the air, this time in agreement with the broker. "Precisely. Such thieves seek to transform themselves into greater thieves by leaving behind for the victim only empty *bodegas* and much grief, with actions that lead to more riches for themselves alone, never riches for the good of the broader family that gives them protection."

Vanessa covered her mouth to hide the giggle set off by what seemed a caricature of the Spaniard himself. Surrounded by an obscenely luxurious setting, which rivaled the grandeur she had known as Mrs. Ewen Leetboer, she felt suddenly embarrassed by the richness of it and her voice lowered into a soft Irish farm brogue. "In a way we've all become thieves, I think."

"How so?" asked Clay Redmond, intrigued by her remark as well as her lapse into an agrarian accent.

Señor Valdez, picking up on the spirit of Vanessa's comment, wagged his big heavy finger in a chastising manner at the broker. "Don't you see? You took the land pirate's woman!"

"But not against her will I trust."

Vanessa snuggled into Clay. "I have no will," she said, "not where you're concerned. You own me, you're responsible now. I was only hinting that some things are quite ludicrous if you stop and think about it. For instance, who is a thief and who isn't? The line is so vague sometimes."

Clay kissed her lightly on her bright, full lips. "I find it hard to think of you as a thief."

"But you will admit that I robbed the old boy of his dignity, won't you?"

"No more than I did. I stripped him of his sense of manhood in front of his wife. Not exactly a fun-friendly way to clean a fellow's clock, now is it? Castration might have been more charitable."

"Ewen does have an ego, I grant you that, and a fine collection of toupees, but for all practical purposes the man was born a eunuch. Will you, then, please not refer to me as his wife ever again? In my heart I'm *your* wife, darling."

"You always were even before we met."

"You're sweet. Ewen never was. Besides, he needed his clock cleaned! Would you believe the monster wanted to kill me in the airport?"

"Maybe you just felt threatened. Frankly I don't think he's the killer type, not at close range anyway, not face to face. He'll rear-end a guy to death, though, with legal attacks designed to relieve him of his good fortune. As for me, yes, I have already been up front with you. How many times have you heard me say I wanted to twist his head right off his snaky neck?" Then Clay, not expecting a reply, motioned toward Señor Valdez. "Enough of Ewen. What about our distinguished host? In what way is he guilty of criminal goings on?"

Vanessa gazed at the Spaniard for a time, assessing him with the eager face of a young girl playing one of those "who" games. Even his huge body, his hard, dark face and intense eyes staring from under thick gorilla-like brows did not alarm her. He had become a father figure now, a lovable Kong, and she no longer felt uneasy in his presence. Yet the sound of her own words shocked her when she answered Clay's question with the soft Celtic utterance, "Señor Valdez takes money from criminals and drug addicts."

The Spaniard's eyes swelled with anger, as they usually did when he perceived an insult. His stare intensified for a few seconds but then it softened to match her tone. There was an innocence about her that he admired, even when she criticized him. After a noisy grunt or two, he yelled out, *Bravo! Bravisimo!* You did not spare me your insights. Some have lost tongues for saying less. How can I take offence, though, when you are right? So, yes, we are all guilty, we all take things, some more than others."

Clay Redmond had noted the fire in Señor Valdez's eyes and stiffened inside, but then his own eyes lost their defensive glare just as quickly on seeing the Spaniard's fire subside. For obvious reasons he did not relish being forced into a dogfight with this big "Master Don," and on his home turf no less. Still, he knew he'd have to protect Vanessa—or die trying—from whatever danger she faced, even from a friend's misguided assault. Clearly their joint purpose would be better served if they continued to concentrate on Ewen Leetboer, yet the placid, relieved expression that had just come back to the broker's face soon gave way to one bordering on gloom.

"Something is troubling you?" asked the Spaniard.

"No, nothing important."

413

"Is it the land pirate? Forget him. Did I not say I no longer hold you responsible for his execution?"

"It's not that."

"What then?"

"I can't let go."

"Perhaps you honor commitments too literally. I ask you again to forget him. You owe me nothing. Coto says you are a defender of life, not a taker. Does he not speak the truth?"

"Look, I'm a trained killer," Clay intoned after Señor Valdez prodded him further, referring with a kind of lethargic candor to his military experience. "It's not you. A part of me still wants to hurt him for all the misery, the loss, the unnecessary shit and trouble he dumped on my doorstep."

Señor Valdez nodded. His huge brutish face had lost all signs of its brief flare-up earlier. "It is a natural reaction," he said, "a heritage from our wild ancestors which we cannot escape."

"But we can manage it, don't you think?"

"Some of us can. Sometimes. We are still animals though, with instincts and fears."

"Maybe only a part of oneself can. Somewhere along the line the greater part of me decided against taking revenge on that old booty snatcher. Whatever I lost to his thievery—which was pretty damn big by my standards—now seems like raw peanuts compared to what I've since gained from this woman here."

"A very wise comparison," the Spaniard said.

43

Vanessa seemed undisturbed by the heated exchanges between the two men, though she did wince at times as she quietly listened, knowing they were talking about her husband, or *former* husband as she had begun to think of him. No doubt about it, the Dutchman's wife mused, they quite certainly had the old boy in their crosshairs. She chuckled inwardly over the term, one she'd heard Clay use more than once. But it didn't matter anymore. Ewen Leetboer's sins had simply caught up with him and the time had come to "pay for his mistakes," as others were made to do who fell into one of Stanley B. Conover's default traps. At that moment her attention was riveted on Clay Redmond. His loving remarks, sandwiched in between murderous language, caused the warm glow in her eyes to embellish an already gorgeous face the more she gazed at him, then when he moved closer and put his arm around her as he was giving Señor Valdez reasons for his own change of heart, words rushed out of her mouth in a passionate murmur, *"I love you!"* It was barely audible but a serious burst of emotion nonetheless that would no longer be quieted.

"And I love you!" Clay answered somewhat louder but in a similar gushing spirit. "You can lay that line on me anytime you like, sweetie pie. You know how I cherish those three little words when they come to me from you."

"Yes, and I'm immensely glad. How wonderful that my words can thrill you so!"

"They do! I can't even begin to tell you how much, but I can tell you the thrill doesn't stop there. It doubles when I say them back because then I can watch how that peewee alliance of letters puts giant twinkles in those pretty green eyes of yours and pulls a sugar-coated smile out of the sweetest, most kissable lips this old boy has ever had the pleasure of tasting. All of a sudden your whole body seems to hail reception of this amazing little string. You don't have to say a word; you just sit there looking like a woman in love while I sit here looking back and thinking how beautiful even silence can be with you in the picture and me feeling doggone good about how much we belong to each other."

"Wow! I won't dare try to answer, darling, except to say how bonny marvelous finding it all out in time truly *is*."

Señor Valdez seemed amused, even grateful for their openness around him. "You are obviously this man's treasure," he said to Vanessa. The big fellow rose from the couch and stepped over toward them, stopping with a soldier's abruptness in front of Clay Redmond, as if he'd been commanded to halt there. His deeply set, dark eyes peered down into the broker's. "Yes?"

"Hey—I agree!" Clay shouted, seeing that affirmation was expected.

"Thank you." The Spaniard laid his heavy hand on the broker's shoulder. "We are friends, no?"

"Of course, friends. Good friends."

"Good friends—*sí!* I like your expression. Perhaps, because you are a man of land and partnerships, you can help me. I need someone to manage affairs at Mara Paradiso, someone I can trust. This charming woman has already shown that I can trust her to speak the truth. Even at great risk she speaks it."

"Sorry. She's taken. Too bad we can't trust her husband—I mean, uh, her pending *ex* to speak it."

"Why do you even care about him?"

"I don't really. Just that he's already familiar with Mara Paradiso. The man's busting a gut to get started, too, and he's got plenty of money in case you run short again."

Señor Valdez walked over to the window and stared into the distance for a time, saying nothing. Moments later martial abruptness sent him into another quick move, a whirling about-face, and he gazed back at Clay with dark, sullen eyes. "I will not run short again," he said, scowling. "Neither will I allow *him* there—with or without trust!" A surliness clung to his face for a while, which did not fade until he turned to Vanessa. "Forgive me, Vanessa, for sounding cruel. May I call you Vanessa?"

"Please do."

"*Gracias.* I must be blunt, because, as each of us has agreed several times these past few days, the man to whom you are presently married is a thief of the lowest, most shameless class. Mara Paradiso must not come into existence with such a stain on its charter. It would mock the purity of my dear wife's heart and dishonor her dying request."

"I don't feel 'presently married' to him," Vanessa responded, her emerald eyes showing a little flare of their own.

"It is a matter of record that you are. Is this not true?"

"Yes, that part is true but it won't be for long. Once I get back to Miami I plan to file for divorce."

Señor Valdez stroked his mustache. His head, then bent toward the floor, struck a thoughtful pose. "Do not be hasty," he said. "Such an action may not be required."

Vanessa's lips parted and slowly spread into a smile steeped in curiosity. "What do you mean?"

The Spaniard returned to his spot on the couch, plopped down, crossed his legs and stared at her with darting eyes before speaking. "They tell me you are a rich woman, Vanessa."

"Oh no I'm not. Ask Ewen."

"Do you know where then is Ewen, the man you plan to divorce?"

"No, I don't. What have you done with him?"

"You see? It has been three days since we left Santo Domingo and you have not asked."

"Like Clay said, I don't really care. I was just happy that you didn't allow him to travel in the plane with us."

"Why should I? He has his own jet. Or did have before I added it to *Campo Bello's* receivership inventories. The fate of that plane will be determined later."

"Receivership? Out here? Can you do that, legally I mean?"

"What is legal in the jungle?"

Vanessa paused and chewed on her lip, thinking. "Staying alive I suppose. Otherwise it doesn't matter. I can't imagine Ewen without his *Air Clockwork,* though. Deprive him of that little toy and he'd be lost."

Señor Valdez chuckled. "He already is lost according to reports from my guards up there in the mountains where you have been this week looking with so much fascination."

Vanessa and Clay peered at the towering landscape again, their eyes searching as though they might spot the Dutchman standing on one of the many precipices visible in the distance."

"Okay," Clay Redmond finally said, "I'll bite. Where is he?"

Señor Valdez sighed, pleased that the broker was smiling and did not appear offended by his harsh manner earlier. He'd also been waiting for one of them to inquire. "Ah, yes. The land pirate, where he is you ask. Well, believe me or not, he is with Pepe doing what he loves most."

Clay laughed. "With Pepe? What on earth would that be? Forming another partnership to gut?"

"Very close. To use your words, the land pirate is gutting the earth with a shovel."

"Ewen with a shovel? I can't picture it."

"Then try to picture him digging some graves for the undead."

"Sounds creepy," Vanessa said, frowning.

Clay agreed with a nod. "Unreal," he added.

Grinning exuberantly, Señor Valdez leaned back, unfolded his legs and extended his arms along the top of the couch. "To him it is very real and very much hard work," he said. "Let me explain. We have a camp farther up in the mountains. Indians live there. They think they own the land since they have used it for centuries without complaints. Now the guerillas have come. They discovered great wealth in the leaves of those little bushes that grow so admirably in the cool altitudes. The land pirate's assignment, after his grave-digging labors improve his outlook a little more, is indeed to form a partnership, as you say. Two of them, in fact—one partnership with the Indians and another with the guerillas. He must gain their confidence as he did with you, Clay Redmond, before he gobbled up your retirement reserves like a fox in the henhouse—and you as well, Vanessa, by convincing you to marry him for worse only. Can you guess what his next duty will be? Wait—I tell you! To avoid more grave digging, the land pirate must steal the wealth the Indians create each year using their ancient knowledge of agriculture. Can you imagine what euphoria the successful completion of this assignment will bring him? The next duty will bring even greater euphoria, for the land pirate must steal again this treasure from the guerillas after they have applied modern processes to the leaves. We have excellent lawyers to guide him, lawyers equally as cunning as the one he killed off the coast of Cuba."

Clay and Vanessa both gaped at the Spaniard. "What's this? *Killed?* Killed who? You don't mean Conover—?"

"Indeed I do. My deal-making friend, you amused me earlier when you said Ewen Leetboer was not the killer type. It grieves me that we must disagree on the matter but I'm afraid he very much is. This Conover attorney was his latest victim. There may be others."

Clay's eyes rolled for a moment, then, "Actually I'm not surprised. I wondered a little about it but nothing made sense. How did *you* find out?"

"I have a friend in the Cuban Coast Guard. At my request he relayed the details to Pepe."

"Oh, yeah, the *El Capitan* guy. He was very helpful."

"To us as well. He was also impressed that you survived such inspired treacheries. It seems that the Dutchman, as you call him, did not trust the attorney. Blackmail became a big worry after he commissioned your death. He feared, knowing the attorney had no spine, that after a short torture the Cuban police would encounter little resistence in convincing him to talk freely. As you might suspect, this murder cannot be called a noble one. It lacked courage and imagination, with luck playing the crucial role."

Vanessa grimaced and clinched her eyes as if in pain, causing Señor Valdez to pause and wait for her to speak. She finally did, though she seemed so distraught at the news the Spaniard was relating that she could only whisper, "And to think I've been living with that blighter all these years! If his luck kept me a prisoner then, yes, Ewen Leetboer is lucky indeed."

"Ha! But not always, dear Vanessa. In this case the land pirate gambled foolishly." Pointing at Clay Redmond, he continued, saying, "Consider yourself blessed. Estranged husbands can be dangerous as well as foolish. This one with whom you hold valuable claims through marriage expected your lover's death sentence to be carried out by the attorney as they had plotted in Cuba. On the chance that the yacht's navigator might see too much, might witness the crime then become frightened for his own safety and try to escape in the lifeboat and later betray him, the land pirate hedged his bet by storing a bottle of rum in the boat's well, the bottle of course spiked with some drops of arsenic. A similar mixture was placed in a cooler by the helm for the survivor's convenient use."

"According to plan that would've been Arturo. Are you making this up? Sounds stranger than Venus's flytrap."

"Trust me, Clay Redmond. What I tell you now has been confirmed in the autopsy report which you can read for yourself. It is on the table in my library."

"Thanks. I'll check it out."

"I would be disappointed if you did not."

"Apparently somebody got to Arturo."

"The Portuguese—ah yes. Ewen Leetboer was correct in fearing the navigator's testimony, for the poor man saw everything. He told us how you were drugged in Varadero, how the attorney tried to force you to jump into a raging sea, how you tricked and overpowered him, tied him to the mast and turned the yacht away from its course to Miami and back toward Varadero to rescue Vanessa. Unfortunately for Attorney Conover, while he managed to free himself before you awoke from sleeping off the effects of the drugs, he elected to set himself adrift in the lifeboat and trust to the currents rather than face you again. To make matters even worse, the fool took with him the deadly cooler and, it seems, a considerable thirst for the rum inside."

"Yeah, he also took my gun."

"Ah, so. I was coming to this matter. My coast guard friend found the very pistola you speak of now."

Clay laughed. "I'm not surprised. What does surprise me is how the hell did it wind up in Leetboer's hands? That son of a bitch tried to shoot me with it."

"Only mystery can explain such a transfer," the Spaniard replied, feeling somewhat grieved that he could offer no ready answer. "It is possible," he went on, "the Dutchman convinced an official the property belonged to him, not to the dead man in the boat who merely worked for him."

"Or the crook bribed someone."

"Perhaps that as well. Bribery in Cuba makes claims of ownership easy to believe."

"Whatever," Clay grunted. "I'm just glad to have it back."

"Of course. So far your weapon has not killed anyone. It may have, however, if events had turned differently. As for the rum, well, rum you know is a very popular drink in the Caribbean whether one is native or tourist. Like Conover himself, not a drop survived the journey. The bottle was found without a cork, empty, rolling on the floor of the boat. Perhaps he drank it all or perhaps some spilled after he could no longer hold the bottle in his dying hand. This scenario you will find presented in the autopsy report. The Cuban Coast Guard also reported that the second bottle stored in the boat's well had not been touched. Apparently the attorney perished before his thirst for rum overwhelmed him again."

"Alas," Vanessa mumbled. A thin twisting smile was seemingly etched into her face.

"No, no!" shouted Señor Valdez. *"Adios serpiente* is better. We took Arturo's statement as well as the captain's. You will find both beside the autopsy report."

Clay had slumped forward, holding his head in his hands as he listened, his face full of frowns, which imparted an aspect of someone who wanted to believe yet found it equally exhausting not to believe what he was hearing. He remained silent for a time after the Spaniard settled into a watchful pause, then he slowly straightened up and glanced around at Vanessa with raised eyebrows, as if to say, "What do you think?"

She read his puzzled look instantly. "I'm appalled, I'm shocked, I don't know what to think other than both of us are bloody lucky we're still breathing."

"Blessed," Señor Valdez said.

Clay appeared moved by both views. He touched Vanessa gently on the cheek then turned and spoke to the Spaniard in a voice stronger and more decisive than she might have expected, judging by the frumpy cast on his face. "Great story, my good friend. I'd say you have served up some gourmet food for thought at the prosecutorial level. Let us sleep on it awhile, though. Got to sort some things out. In the meantime please pardon me while I admire your networking skills. You must have one helluva spy pool, Guillermo. It wouldn't surprise me to learn that you've planted a mole or two in the White House."

Señor Valdez burst into a siege of deep, earsplitting laughter. "No, but I do have a few loyalists, shall we say, scattered along the streets of Miami and Havana, among other places. One of them has recommended you as the man I can trust to oversee my beloved Mara Paradiso. Can I rely on you to help her grow, and soon, into this beautiful memorial I now see only in my dreams?"

Clay's head drifted into a comic tilt as he reflected on the Spaniard's curiously phrased compliment, not to mention the sudden seizure of faith in a real estate broker. After a long, squinting gaze he tried to make light of it by grunting, *"No comprendo. No hablo español."*

"Sí. Comprendes todo. You understand everything. This person was emphatic in your favor."

Clay grunted again, louder. "Vicente Coto?"

"No, not this time, although I am sure if asked for a candidate this valiant *prisionero* from Castro's ignoble jails would nominate you immediately. You should feel honored that Pepe, the one I trust most, the one who wanted to pop you with his silencer not so long ago, recommended no others when I showed him a list of names with yours included."

"Darling . . . ?" Vanessa nudged with her voice when Clay sat motionless and made no effort to respond. "I think you've just been offered the chance of a lifetime. Can't you speak?"

"Sounds like it'll take a lifetime, too," the broker answered. He continued to stare at Señor Valdez, tweaking his nose and chuckling under his breath. "I guess you're not kidding, right?"

"Absolutely right."

"Are you sure? I mean about Mara Paradiso . . . ?"

"Plenty."

"What makes you think I can pull your project out of the ground? I'm not a developer."

"Mr. Redmond, *por favor!* How can you underestimate my research after just hearing so many details concerning your heroic actions on the yacht against Attorney Conover? This was but one heroic action. There are many others I now know of. Your friend Silvio graciously referred me to several of your associates and real estate clients. Each person I managed to contact spoke highly of you in all capacities. One of them, Marcus Cunningham—"

Clay slapped his forehead. "Marcus Cunningham! How did you find out about him?"

"Silvio of course."

"Well, well! I'm surprised. Did you meet Cunningham?"

"Indeed. A fortunate meeting too. He supplied me with excellent testimony regarding Shopping Mall Xanadu and how you 'kept him on track,' as he phrased it. The man spoke about you with the passion of a father."

Clay chuckled. "Thanks for the tip. I'll be sure to call him 'Dad' next time we meet."

"Shopping Mall Xanadu embodies great beauty and, I must say, rare integrity for a commercial enterprise. Mr. Cunningham swore that you made his development possible."

"Yeah, I sold him the land."

"Now you are being modest. I am not interested in ambitious flatterers who can produce magnificent resumes. I want results. Everything I have seen of you and heard about you tells me you are a man who knows how to get results, whether you are fighting in the jungles of Viet Nam or quietly eating *sopa de pollo* at the Versailles in Miami while you plot intrigues with the Alvarez brothers. In brief, you make things happen in the fashion you desire. Mara Paradiso needs this kind of person to take charge."

"Look what a masterpiece you've created here in the jungle for Christ sake! Why don't you take charge? It's your project."

"This is only *Campo Bello,* a small place. As for Mara Paradiso, I tried many times to take charge, my friend, but such a huge work can quickly overtax one's sensibilities. I have no patience with details and delays and deportations by crazy dictators. Besides, I have business here to complete, new alliances to form, old ones to terminate. Whatever the land pirate stole from you I will replace with a partnership worth much more. I now have resources to continue work on Mara Paradiso."

"Drug money?"

"No. That is a separate matter. Most of my businesses are legitimate now, thanks to my dear Mara's insistence. She comes from a wealthy Catalan family. After her untimely passing, the family joined with me to establish a foundation in her name dedicated entirely to the project in Varadero that she had envisioned years before. My Mara called it her happy dream, which it has become for me as well. I trust you will agree to guide our dream through this happiness."

Clay Redmond glanced at Vanessa. "Help me out, kiddo. I don't know quite what to make of this."

Her face pulsed with ambivalence. "It's what Ewen wanted to do so badly. Varadero isn't far from Miami. May I visit you on weekends?"

"Weekends, huh?" Clay chuckled and turned back to Señor Valdez. "I can't leave Vanessa. Will you also trust me to choose her as my equal partner? Together we'll finish Mara Paradiso. Otherwise, no deal."

The Spaniard howled. "You see? This first action proves my choice as well as yours. Of course Vanessa belongs in the partnership. Of course this lady *must* work alongside the man she loves. Believe me, I would have insisted if you had not made the request. Through the two of you my eyes will see my lovely Mara and myself again, as we were when we started to dream about a paradise in Cuba for wandering *conquistadores* to sail to and rest their spirits. Now they may come and share it with my Mara. For this gift you are bringing me I will be forever in your debt. The work will never be finished, though."

"Never finished? Sure it will. It'll sell better finished."

"How can I agree to finish such a monument? Or sell it? Mara Paradiso will be a living memorial! Finish it and it will die.

Let this happy dream remain a living memorial forever. Income from leases will also flow forever. As partners neither of you will live a day without a share flowing into your joint bank account."

"What about Castro?"

"Let him talk. Unlike Mara Paradiso he cannot live forever."

44

Miami's skyline could still elicit a thrill after all, even though it was just a collage of bricks and mortar held in place by asphalt ribbons, with no snowcapped mountains or magnificent rain forests to give it the sort of majesty that had so recently filled them with awe. What Miami did have under its gritty façade, though: *memories!* Memories and magic. Memories and the stuff they ate out of and slept on. Memories of love regained.

Pepe flew them back in Ewen Leetboer's jet. In his circumscribed mafioso mind Miami didn't register as a thrill trip but screwing the land pirate out of his plane did. Call it a savory triumph made even tastier by flying the stately aircraft between continents and feeling Heaven's approval even stronger the higher above the clouds he rose. Neither asked about Ewen or dared to raise questions until the plane was halfway across the Caribbean for fear Señor Valdez might change his mind about trying to reconstruct such a case-hardened ego and pack the Dutchman along as well. At times Vanessa felt a tinge of remorse for leaving him—her *husband* she reluctantly admitted—in that wild country to God knows what fate. She shared her remorse with Clay Redmond but the broker offered little comfort, not because he didn't try but because he himself had been overwhelmed by the same ironies that had put her in such a difficult mood. At least down there in the jungle, they rationalized, the old thief would have Ramón and Elena to talk to now and then, for the two Cubans had elected to stay a while longer and enjoy a little more of the good life in Señor Valdez's guest villa that reminded Elena so much of places in her own revered country. Ramón, a connoisseur of Cuban cocktails, was doubly impressed when Señor Valdez instructed his rum specialist to offer *mojitos* on the terrace when the couple dropped by. Even Chin Lee, the chef, had mastered the art of serving the famous Hemingway specialty, which quickly became a staple at Ramón's *Campo Bello* plate as it always was at The Versailles and, of course, the incomparable *Bodeguita del Medio.*

"El Cojonudo has other plans for the land pirate," Pepe explained to his passengers—several times!—while they were in flight, and with little variation, except his laughter grew in volume and duration following each inquiry.

The mafioso left Clay and Vanessa at the airport. "El Cojonudo expects to see you both in Varadero—and *soon!"* he said. The underlying threat in his tone was only partially veiled. "You will sail the yacht over, yes?"

"Uh-huh. We'll wait in Miami until you and, uh, *El Cojonudo* patch things up with Castro, okay?"

"One week." he said, frowning suspiciously, as if he thought the broker had somehow mocked him. "One week. Expect my phone call no later. The marina authorities will reserve a berth for—for—*Qué nombre? Qué nombre?* How must I register the yacht?"

"As *Noche Buena.* Use Vanessa's name."

"Only Vanessa's?" Pepe's head began to swivel. He looked away then back, five or six times, while a smile formed around his swarthy mouth. "Maybe I tell them Señor y Señora Redmond, okay?"

Clay and Vanessa joined Pepe in their own light-hearted smile before answering. "Not yet," Clay said. "We have a little legal work to take care of first. Just say Vanessa. If Cher can get away with one name, so can she."

Clay Redmond and Pepe were still shouting last minute instructions to each other as the plane taxied off the tarmac. Seeing Pepe leave in high spirits and showing a bit of cheer about the way things had gone in Santo Domingo, and later at *Campo Bello,* brought quick relief to the couple. That little Shangri-La, tucked so mysteriously into its edenic place somewhere on the slopes of the Andes, had opened to them the human side of both Señor Valdez and Pepe. Even crook killers, Clay figured, had a right to feel good inside sometimes.

They took a cab to Bella Mar and spent the night there. That evening they made love with all the passion of childhood sweethearts on a long-delayed honeymoon, which, with due respect to conventions, it truly was a honeymoon, for they were one now, joined at the heart, mind and soul. Later, while still lying in bed, Vanessa asked Clay about the waiting period, the statute of limitations. "I think seven years," he answered, "but who knows? The laws are so fickle these days."

"What should I do?"

"Wait. Tomorrow I'll introduce you to a good lawyer friend of mine."

"Do you think we'll ever see him again?"

"Probably not."

"Oh, Clay—!"

"Do you want to see him again?"

"No, but I don't wish him ill fortune."

"Neither do I. Oh, a little *less* fortune perhaps. At first I wanted to kill him, remember?"

"How could I forget? You frightened me, laddie. I had never heard anyone say he wanted to kill another human being, not in earnest. You meant it, didn't you?"

"Yes, then. Now I don't. I've already wasted too much energy on that shifty old swindler. Anyway, the matter has moved beyond our control. Let the Cuban police deal with him. After all, Ewen *did* kill Conover in their territorial waters."

Vanessa was shaking her head in a portrait of agitated pity as she listened. "Conover was such a drip. I'm not even sorry, especially since Señor Valdez said he tried to kill you. If that pompous little squirt had succeeded—Heaven forbid!—I would've killed him myself!"

Clay snuggled closer. She was still warm and inviting and he responded with tenderness. "Don't forget who set it up. Even if we persuaded our Spanish partner to release Ewen, he's still a fugitive. Looking at it from his side, he's probably better off where he is, even if it means digging a grave now and then. In the meantime you have an empire to run."

"Ha! Empire—funny, funny. Run it under whose authority? Ewen never put me in charge of the smallest matter pertaining to his business. Never made me a cosigner on anything either. This penthouse is all of his I can lay claim to—and only that much because of you. Everything else—who knows? Really, darling, I haven't the foggiest where his accounts are and, what's more, what's in them!"

"Well, I can refresh your memory about a couple of things, not counting the sting money. Did you know he owns nine percent of Xanadu Mall?"

"Not the percentage, no. What do you suppose it's worth?"

"He put fifteen million in it. Probably worth double that. He also owns my share of a valuable tract on the Dixie Highway. My retirement nest egg, if you please."

She laughed at the semi-sad expression on Clay's face, as if he were apologizing for having to mention his loss again. "That's a start I suppose."

"I'll phone Guillermo. Nothing would please him more than an excuse to furnish you, his surrogate Mara, with a copy of Ewen's latest financial statement."

"Oh don't bother. Ewen will laugh at him, say he doesn't have one, which he probably doesn't, not down there in the jungle anyway."

Clay kissed her hand like a dutiful suitor then teased her with a tickle under the chin. "I'd say you were right if I didn't know better. Have you ever seen him leave home without his briefcase?"

Vanessa thought for a minute then tickled him back. "Well . . . he doesn't take it to the beach when we go to watch the sunset . . . ."

"You're cute. Remind me to marry you later. But I'm talking trips, honey bun, business stuff. Ewen is like the little guy that follows the President around with a black suitcase full of buttons. You know—the kind you push. That starchy pale rider is always just a step away from the Commander-in-Chief in case of a nuclear attack. Kind of spooky when you think of all the power over life and death he's hauling around. Ewen's briefcase reminds me of that musketeer's button box. The Dutchman packs a lot of power in it, too. A financial statement, for instance. He always has one tucked inside, sealed in a manila envelope for his own emergency use in case he finds a hot buy and needs to impress a bank or a future partner he plans to skin."

"You know a lot about him, don't you?"

"I know Ewen Leetboer doesn't travel without that briefcase."

"Are you sure he took it to South America?"

"Yep. Didn't notice it at first, not until Pepe started punching him in the gut back in Santo Domingo. The briefcase quickly became his shield and after we landed at *Campo Bello* he still had a white-knuckle grip on the handle."

"You're so observant, darling. I never even looked at him."

"Come to think of it, Ewen was nursing the bloody thing in his arms like a baby when Pepe pushed him into that four-wheeler and drove away to some graveyard."

"Oh God! Stop saying it!" Vanessa grew squeamish all of a sudden. "How horrible—making Ewen dig graves. He's never done work like that. The poor man must be aching all over."

"I'm sure he thinks he's digging for buried treasure. I'm also sure that whatever he carried inside that briefcase is no secret anymore. The contents, including an unsealed financial statement, are probably there in the villa, lying on the library table alongside Conover's autopsy report."

"We'll go tomorrow to South Beach and check through his office. Perhaps all we need is right there."

"Good idea. It's your property now. Might as well get familiar with its secrets."

"I hate the thought of going back to Canada, though."

"May not be necessary, not right away. Having heard stories concerning the persuasive powers of Guillermo Valdez, I imagine Ewen will be as pleased as punch to furnish whatever his Spanish *host* asks for, including account numbers, safety boxes, access codes, keys, and so on."

Vanessa grimaced. "I know you're trying not to make it sound as awfully brutal as it is, Clay, but don't you think coercion is wrong, that whatever we wind up with can be viewed as illegally obtained?"

"Moot point, my darling, considering the parties. I'd rather think *stylishly* obtained covers the case better. Remember Ewen's motto 'business is business'? Guillermo will take care of business his way, not *Clockwork, Inc.'s* way. The end result will satisfy the goals of either party."

Clay's play on words evoked a giggle from Vanessa. "You mean it's like rape versus seduction?"

"Uh-huh. You get screwed no matter who's on top giving you the business."

Vanessa giggled again and threw her bare leg over Clay. "Be careful, darling, with your analogies. I'm only human you know."

"And a helluva human you are, my fairest of the fair."

After a brief period of goose play, she turned serious. "Will you phone him then?"

"First thing tomorrow. I got the distinct impression that the good señor maintains an international team of legal experts capable of arranging whatever authority Vanessa Leetboer needs to take control of her missing husband's assets. They'll evaluate your situation from top to bottom. Whatever they can't get off the Internet, they'll get with a phone call and timely deliveries via FedEx and DHL. You'll be flooded with documents of course—joint ownerships, powers of attorney, titles, deeds, certificates, et cetera, et cetera, whether you request them or not."

"Sounds rather impossible to me. Doesn't it at all to you?"

"More than that. I hear the shake, rattle and roll of justice heading our way. Shall we dance?"

"I wondered if you were ever going to ask." Vanessa's face all of a sudden seemed bursting with ecstasy. "Oh, darling, do you think Señor Valdez would mind if we build our sweet little cottage at Mara Paradiso? The place sounds so idyllic, so brimming with love, so perfectly right for it!"

The next day was a busy one for Clay Redmond. The broker even closed his office, something he had wanted to do for a long time but had been painfully thwarted by Ewen Leetboer's theft of his partnership interest. Although it had served him well in the beginning, the office had become an albatross, a seething complex of rules and regulations and complicated tax returns. All he needed of it now was his cell phone and laptop. Ironies mounted in his mind. "What goes around comes around," he said, repeating to himself the popular belief he remembered having once blurted to the Dutchman in court, remembered that moment of anger and the pithy line which popped out of his mouth in lieu of the karate chop that came within a cat's whisker of prevailing. Had he mellowed, he wondered, or did his guardian angel set him up with a new pair of eyes while he slept? The world surely looked different. He felt different, too, felt that he might yet live a thousand years, thanks to Love Almighty which, he figured, had put up most of the new road signs.

He didn't mention Ewen Leetboer's dilemma to Marcus Cunningham other than to announce that the Xanadu partner was registered with the Bureau of Missing Persons. The mall tycoon seemed somewhat pleased about it actually, for the mall's surly watch dog, Frank Creuthop, would doubtless sweeten his disposition now that the Dutchman's wife would be sitting in board meetings during his absence, which, by all accounts, had the appearance of becoming a lengthy one. Recently amended documents showed Vanessa Leetboer to be a joint partner, sharing his beneficial interest equally, with right of survivorship. Curiously, foul play was never suspected, at least not the sort of foul play that a dutiful wife would or could commit, certainly not a wife who had been deserted and left with only a few pieces of property and a mountain of debt. News of Stanley B. Conover's murder and, later, Cuba's release of wanted posters and subsequent demand for Ewen Leetboer's extradition led to the widely pervasive conclusion that the Dutchman was indeed on the lam and, since none could be found, had taken his cash with him.

Marcus Cunningham and Heather Ambrose showed more interest in Clay Redmond and the splendid opportunity in Cuba that had opened to him. "I've been looking for a place I can sneak off to every now and then," he told Clay in front of Heather, suggesting to Clay that she would sneak with him. "Set me up down there, pal. To hell with the embargo!"

Clay and Vanessa also disappeared for a while. Only Silvio Alvarez knew that they had gone to Cancún, knew because he went with them. Clay closed the accounts he had set up for the two brothers, then, with Vanessa's blessing, established a new joint account in their names, giving them equal authority to sign. They now were sole owners of the two million dollars Clay had promised, a true brother's gift and a godsend of support in their struggle to reclaim their homeland, all of which boded ill for Castro now that they had money to burn. Here was their torch at last. With it they meant to set fire to the dictator's beard and derevolutionize Cuba.

Mara Paradiso lay ahead for the couple. Like Señor Valdez claimed, it was Heaven-sent. Clay and Vanessa never imagined at first the extent of their good luck in accepting the Spaniard's challenge, for there in Varadero lay the defining challenge of their lives. They would meet it head-on together. The place embodied far more than architectural elegance. A happy dream it was, monumental in every detail, a memorial to love that Clay and Vanessa—the future Mrs. Redmond—would share in as fully as Señor Valdez and the spirit of his incomparable Mara.

About The Author

- Robert Willis was born in Bagdad, Florida, on June 29, 1927. He served in the Marine Corps during WWII and the Korean Conflict. In 1957 he and Carole Ann Smith were married in her hometown of Quincy, Florida. They have 3 children (2 boys "surrounded" by a girl). Since marriage, they've lived in diverse places doing diverse things.
- Known as "Bobby Neal" to his childhood friends and "Buddy" to kinfolks, Robert attended Florida Southern College, the University of Texas, Stanford University, and the Florida State University, graduating in 1962 from the latter with a PhD in Educational Research and Measurement.
- Robert and Carole reside alone now in Bagdad. No dogs, no cats. She fishes, he writes. Crossing Clayborn is his first (published) novel.

20462127R00258

Made in the USA
Lexington, KY
05 February 2013